D0992415

Being Cool

BEING COOL

THE WORK OF ELMORE LEONARD

The
JOHNS HOPKINS UNIVERSITY PRESS
Baltimore

CHARLES J. RZEPKA

Printed in the United States of America on acid-free paper
2 4 6 8 9 7 5 3 1

The Johns Hopkins University Press
2715 North Charles Street
Baltimore, Maryland 21218-4363
www.press.jhu.edu

Library of Congress Cataloging-in-Publication Data

Rzepka, Charles J.
Being cool: The work of Elmore Leonard / Charles J. Rzepka.
pages cm
ISBN-13: 978-1-4214-1015-9 (hardcover : acid-free paper)
ISBN-13: 978-1-4214-1016-6 (electronic)
ISBN-10: 1-4214-1015-X (hardcover : acid-free paper)
ISBN-10: 1-4214-1016-8 (electronic)
1. Leonard, Elmore, 1925—Authorship. 2. Leonard, Elmore, 1925—Criticism and interpretation. 3. Detective and mystery stories, American—History and criticism. I. Title.
PS3562.E55Z85 2013
813'54—dc23 2012047775

A catalog record for this book is available from the British Library.

Special discounts are available for bulk purchases of this book. For more information, please contact Special Sales at 410-516-6936 or specialsales@press.jhu.edu.

The Johns Hopkins University Press uses environmentally friendly book materials, including recycled text paper that is composed of at least 30 percent post-consumer waste, whenever possible.

CONTENTS

PREFACE

I first became interested in Elmore Leonard because I like to read crime fiction and I'm originally from Detroit. It wasn't until I was working as an English professor in Boston, married with family, that a friend told me to read *Swag*. From the first page, I regretted the delay.

What hooked me almost instantly was Leonard's sense of place. This was Detroit just as I had left it: crowded, dirty, parochial, demographically diverse, built up and boarded up, spread out and burned out—not for tourists. Like so many other readers from places other than the Motor City, however, I was also captivated by the Leonard sound, which means the sound of his characters: the curt backhands of their conversations, their compulsive storytelling, the trains of ragged thoughts muttering along in their heads. This was some writing. But decades had to pass and changes in my academic life had to happen before I had the opportunity to try explaining, in my own writing, what made Leonard's so good.

Several years ago I coedited an anthology of essays on crime fiction, to which I contributed a piece on Elmore Leonard (Rzepka, "Elmore Leonard, 1925–"). It crystallized for me a recurrent pattern in his work—the master-apprentice relationship—that invited closer attention. It also emboldened me to contact Leonard to ask questions about his early life, his education, and his work habits that seemed crucial to animating this scarecrow of an idea. The result was several interviews comprising some twelve hours of recorded conversation. They form the core of this book.

I wrote *Being Cool* for three reasons: first, to say something significant about an important writer largely neglected by the academy, even by those knowledgeable in popular genres like crime and detection; second, in doing so, to persuade my colleagues that this writer should be neglected no longer. Leonard has been the subject of three brief literary biographies (Challen's is best on the details of Leonard's book and movie deals, Devlin's and Geherin's on literary influences and textual analysis), along with about a dozen scholarly essays and scores of interviews, reviews, and magazine articles. *Being Cool* is the first book-length study to pursue a single theme throughout Leonard's work, and I hope it will inspire more. There is so much remaining to be done: on the character of the artist and the writer in his fiction; on his semi-autobiographical trilogy, *The Hot Kid, Comfort to the Enemy*, and *Up in Honey's Room*; on other outstanding novels treated cursorily here for lack of space, such as *Freaky Deaky*, one of Leonard's personal favorites, or *Get Shorty*, his first meta-fiction; on how specific technologies of movie production, marketing, and viewing and their histories have affected his writing style, as well as on their representation in his work; on his use of costume and role-playing. I could go on. The first four interviews I conducted with Leonard, currently posted on the *Crimeculture* website (www.crimeculture.com/?page_id=3435), run to nearly thirty-nine thousand words. *Being Cool* comes nowhere near mining their full potential.

Thirteen years ago, James Devlin felt obliged to defend Leonard's status as a "serious" writer (128–33). That debate is over. Admirers now include Martin Amis, Walker Percy, Ann Beattie, and former poet laureate Robert Pinsky. Saul Bellow was a fan (Amis 1), and Leonard has even been mentioned in the same breath as "experimental writers" like Pirandello, Calvino, Robbe-Grillet, Borges, and Nabokov (Grella 36). Both the topical reach of his work and the span of his career and canon are enormous: six decades, dozens of short stories, and forty-five novels, not to mention movies, screenplays, and televised versions of his writings. Space limitations forbid a close examination of the latter body of work here, but such artificial restrictions also offer certain advantages, allowing the contours of his stylistic experimentation and his evolving thematic concerns to emerge more clearly in the one medium over which he has exercised total control.

My third aim was to enhance the reading experience of the nonacademic Elmore Leonard fan. If I've failed in the attempt, please blame me, not the critics and theorists I cite. Similarly, I take sole responsibility for any errors, factual or otherwise. Hopefully, they will incite readers to write more books and essays about Leonard to set the record straight.

In my work on this book I have benefited from the generosity of many individuals. Gregg Sutter, Leonard's long-time researcher and assistant, spent hours fact-checking, provided helpful feedback, and laboriously scanned and uploaded images. He also compiled, copied, and sent the unpublished stories, along with other vital material and information. The author's first wife, Beverly Dekker, and their children, Jane Jones, Christopher Leonard, Peter Leonard, Bill Leonard, and Katie Dudley, all consented to phone interviews, and Jane and Chris provided personal photos. David Geherin, a pioneering Leonard scholar, read the manuscript of *Being Cool* and offered advice and encouragement, as did my colleagues Jonathan Mulrooney of Holy Cross and Bill Carroll of Boston University (Renaissance man by day and Leonard fan by night). To all of them I offer my heartfelt thanks. I also thank Bob Scheffler, research editor at *Esquire* magazine; Kristine Baclawski and the staff of the Michigan State University Library Special Collections; Danielle Kaltz and Linda Culpepper of the *Detroit News*; and Nanette O'Connor and Veronique Tu of Campbell Ewald for providing images and information; and a special thanks to Joe and Cari Vaughn for Joe's wonderful photograph of Leonard relaxing in his backyard, as well as to Lee Horsley for posting the Elmore Leonard interviews cited here on her *Crimeculture* website. Finally, this project could never have been completed without the help of the Boston University Center for the Humanities, which granted funds for travel expenses and interview transcriptions and provided crucial leave time to complete a first draft of the book by awarding me a Jeffrey Henderson Senior Fellowship.

To all of these benefactors I am deeply beholden, but most of all to Elmore Leonard, for having me in his home, for never failing to pick up the phone when I called, for his patience and sense of humor throughout our time together. I hope he will find *Being Cool* at least a partial recompense for all his help.

A final word: saying anything worth saying about books almost inevitably requires giving away endings, so *caveat lector,* "Reader Beware"!

Being Cool

ONE

being cool
learning authenticity

No Wasted Motions: What Cool Is

If you've heard the name Elmore Leonard, chances are you've also heard him described as "the Dickens of Detroit." At one point in his career, this honorific appeared in the publicity pages of nearly every new paperback edition of an Elmore Leonard book and in the columns of nearly every fresh review. Anyone who's read Leonard can see why, even in its original, diminished form—"*A* Dickens *from* Detroit"—the epithet would have appealed to the *Time* editor who coined it in 1984 for the title of J. D. Reed's essay of appreciation. It certainly appealed to British novelist Martin Amis, who used it to introduce Leonard during an interview at the Writer's Guild Theater of Beverly Hills in January 1998. Amis said he considered Leonard "as close as anything you have here in America to a national novelist, a concept that almost seemed to die with Charles Dickens but has here been revived" (Amis 1).[1]

The title of Reed's article comes from his description of Leonard's colorful characters, "a crowded Dickensian canvas where social strata collide, and the gravedigger waits by the charnel house" (100). As a mirror of society, Leonard's world (whether we enter it through Detroit or Miami or Hollywood or Atlantic City or his birthplace, New Orleans) is indeed Dickensian, as is his eye for grotesques. It is populated by a well-trained ensemble of gangbangers, dope-dealers, bookies, and grifters and an intriguing assortment of psychopaths; by financial advisors, talent agents, shady attorneys, and their nouveau-riche clients; by female professionals ranging from hookers to singers to models to airline attendants to embassy personnel; by honest cops hampered by legal niceties and crooked cops on the take, Hollywood phonies and Delta mobsters, hanging judges and hit men, and dozens of eccentric blue-collar, beer-drinking extras. Academics, politicians, and old-money nabobs never wander into Leonard's fictional world, and with rare exceptions his novels unfold in a universe devoid of children. That said, the wide range of our nation's types and antitypes is well represented, as Reed and Amis suggest.

But if Leonard's reach from the top to the bottom of contemporary American society generally matches Dickens's with respect to Victorian England, the differences are more striking. For one thing, Dickens's universe is ruled by poetic justice: vice is punished, virtue rewarded, and repentant sinners saved. These are usually venial sinners, soft hypocrites like Pip or redeemable misers like Scrooge. The moral signposts in Dickens's London are clearly pointing up or down, and there are few characters about whose vertical direction we are ever in doubt.

In Leonard's work, by contrast, heroes and heroines rarely conform to standard patterns of virtue, and we can even be surprised by feelings of sympathy for the devil, often in his least appealing form. Unlike Pip or Scrooge, he has not seen the error of his ways or experienced remorse, although, like the Artful Dodger, he may have made us laugh despite ourselves. Typically, we sympathize because the devil suddenly finds he no longer enjoys what he's good at or he's no longer good at what he enjoys. It's not that he feels disgust, or revulsion, or an epiphanic commitment to self-improvement. It's just that, out of nowhere, he realizes he's not as attuned to what he does as he used to be. He has to think about it, he gets distracted, he's not "into" it. The innocence he has lost is not moral or ethical but kinetic or technical or procedural. It's the innocence of active oblivion, absorption in the task at hand. Here, for example, is Frank Renda from *Mr. Majestyk* (1974), a mob higher-up handling day-to-day business transactions, reflecting on his salad days as a professional killer:

> Five years ago it had been better, simpler. Get a name, do a study on the guy, learn his habits, walk up to him at the right time, and pull the trigger. It was done. [. . .] Now it was business all the time. The boring meetings, discussions, planning, all the fucking papers to sign and talking on the phone. He used to have one phone. It would ring, he'd say hello, and a voice would give him a name. That was it. He didn't even have to say good-bye. [. . .] He used to take a contract for five grand and had got as much as ten when it was tricky and the guy had a name.
>
> That's what he missed. The planning and then pulling the trigger, being very steady with no wasted motions. [. . .] He was good then. During the last few years he had caught himself wondering if he was still good. (121–22)

Renda has just taken on his first hit in five years, not because he needs the money—he's making more than $150,000 a year just "to talk on the phone and sign papers"—but because "he misse[s] the action" and wants to "experience the feeling again" (122). Unfortunately, he's found that getting back to where he once belonged is more difficult than he anticipated. He feels unfocused, out of place: "He asked himself, Where are you? What the fuck are you doing?" (121).

Perhaps "sympathy" is not exactly what we feel for Renda, except in the sense intended by Thomas De Quincey, a nineteenth-century essayist best known among general readers for his *Confessions of an English Opium-Eater* and among scholars of crime fiction for an essay entitled "On Murder Considered as One of the Fine Arts." In a brief squib on *Macbeth*, De Quincey praised Shakespeare's surprising ability to draw us into the mind of his murderous usurper. "Our sympathy must be with *him*," says De Quincey, adding parenthetically, "of course I mean a sympathy of comprehension, a sympathy by which we enter into his feelings, and are made to understand them—not a sympathy of pity or approbation" (83). Leonard seems to have in mind this meaning of *sympathy* in a passage from his early Western story, "The Captives" (1955), when young Pat Brennan reflects on his feelings toward Doretta Mims, the mousy wife of a blockheaded bookkeeper: "And for a reason he did not understand, though it had nothing to do with sympathy, he felt very close to her, as if he had known her for a long time [. . .]. He realized that it was sympathy, in a sense, but not the feeling-sorry kind" (341). Today we might use *empathy* instead of *sympathy* to describe what Brennan and De Quincey experience when they use their imaginations to comprehend someone without "pity or approbation." Renda's importance to Leonard as an object of "sympathy"—"but not the feeling-sorry kind"—is obvious: his self-examination takes up three pages (*Mr. Majestyk* 121–24).

If Shakespeare's "sympathy of comprehension," as the Opium-Eater puts it, resembles the kind of empathic identification with Renda that Leonard wants to encourage, there is also a crucial difference of emphasis here. De Quincey's Shakespeare wants to reveal the "hell within" his villains' souls. Leonard more often calls our attention to the hum of the body acting efficiently and the noise of distraction that portends breakdown: fear, inattention, boredom, fatigue, self-consciousness. "Where are you?" is a question we ask ourselves when we are most aware of not being ourselves, when we have lost the feeling of authenticity.

Contrast Renda's sense of dislocation from "the action" he misses as he comes to the end of his professional career (he'll be dead by the end of the book) with the sense of belonging, of being in the right place, that Jack Ryan experiences in *Unknown Man No. 89* (1977). The book opens with Ryan just beginning an unglamorous stint as a process server, after a life spent drifting from one job to another. He had wanted to play professional baseball, "but he couldn't hit a breaking ball if the guy hung it up there in front of him" (4). He's also been "into a little breaking and entering," but "it was more for fun than profit: see if he could get away with it" (3). And he did: "He had never served time" (3). While he doesn't like to "take any shit from anybody" (1), Ryan is, like most of Leonard's male protagonists, "always polite" (3). One day, fearing that at thirty-six he may have become "a misfit" (2), Ryan decides to "wak[e] up" and "get off his ass and make a run for it" (1), which is to say, get regular employment. At the suggestion of a friend in the Detroit PD, he tries his hand at "serving papers,"

> and it surprised him he liked it and was good at it. It surprised him that he was patient and had a knack for finding people. He wasn't afraid to walk up and hand someone a writ or a summons. As long as he didn't know anything about them personally it was all right. What they did, whatever trouble they were in, was their business, not his. He was polite, soft-spoken. He never hassled anybody. [. . .]
>
> The only problem he anticipated in his work was taking shit from people who didn't want to be served. [. . .] But he handled it in a way that surprised him. He just didn't let these people bother him. He realized they were frightened or reacting without thinking. [. . .] He realized they didn't mean it personally, so why get mad or upset? (3)

Ryan's feelings about his new job comprise the first seven pages of *Unknown Man No. 89*. As with Renda's reflections on the "better, simpler" days of contract killings, Leonard considers this topic—feeling comfortable with your job and enjoying it—important.

What Ryan has discovered is what Renda has lost: the feeling of being a natural at what he does. It's a feeling that can come as a complete surprise, as with an unlikely process server who discovers he not only enjoys his work but is also good at it. Or it can arrive as something you've prepared and trained for because you've known since childhood you *would* be good at it, like U.S. Marshal Carl Webster in *The Hot Kid* (2005). Or you could find that your training in one line serves you even better in another, like Joe LaBrava, a disillusioned former Secret Service agent who discovers that years of habitually scanning crowds for suspicious faces has equipped him for a successful career as a documentary photographer in *LaBrava* (1983). Feeling "natural" in what you do is what I call, drawing on the title of one of Leonard's late novels, "being cool." Leonard himself has defined "cool" as "without pretension of any kind [. . .] simply being yourself. And, of course, remaining reasonably calm," adding, "I think that it's more living in the now than anything else" (Challen 167). Leonard's characters are most authentically themselves, most "living in the now," when focused entirely on the task at hand. Whether we are talking about good guys like Ryan or bad guys like Renda, the question that intrigues their creator most is not the one that intrigued Charles Dickens, namely, whether or not people under pressure can still conform to standard notions of virtue, regardless of their flaws. Rather, it's whether or not they can stay "cool"—focused in pursuit of their goals—in the face of life's hassles, distractions, pressures, insults, abuse, betrayals, and other "shit."

Jack Ryan made his debut in Leonard's first crime novel, *The Big Bounce,* in 1969. Of him the author wrote, twenty years later, "All of my male leads [. . .] resemble Jack Ryan in that they have much the same basic attitude about their own existence, what's important and what isn't" ("Introduction," *Big* iii). Ryan's nonchalance, his self-control, his rarely tapped but ready reserves of violence—"Ryan learned early that in street fighting [. . .] you hit first and made it count and usually it was over" (*Unknown* 4)—and his refusal to "take shit from anybody," all counterbalanced by his new inclination to just get along—"Why should we fuck each other over and make life miserable?" (*Unknown* 5)—anticipate the salient features of several Leonard protagonists who would later make their author famous and (more) rich once they reached the cineplexes. John Travolta's Chili Palmer, a mob "shylock" trying to become a movie producer in MGM's *Get Shorty,* and George Clooney's Jack Foley, an escaped convict and professional bank robber in Universal Pictures' *Out of Sight,* are probably the best known to today's average moviegoer. They have evolved from a type that Leonard inherited from the classic American Western film, as epitomized by John Wayne in *Stagecoach,* Gary Cooper in *The Plainsman,* Henry Fonda in *My Darling Clementine,* and Gregory Peck in *The Gunfighter,* to name just a few.[2] These were the tight-lipped, self-reliant male protagonists he'd watched in darkened movie houses as a child, and the heroes he recalled as a young husband and father teaching himself to write professionally by trying his hand at Westerns. References and allusions to their star turns appear not only in his Western fiction but also in many of his better-known works in the crime genre, especially "eastern-westerns" (Grobel 275) like *City Primeval: High Noon in Detroit* (1980) and *Killshot* (1989).

What brands all of Leonard's central protagonists as his own, from cowpoke to ex-con, from process server to police detective, is that when pushed, challenged, or threatened, they somehow remain "cool." *Be Cool*, Leonard's 1999 novel about the pop music industry, represents a late reflection on the nature of "being cool," but the fundamentals remain the same. In the book's opening pages we learn that Chili Palmer, former loan shark enforcer and would-be film producer in Leonard's previous Hollywood novel, *Get Shorty* (1990), has made his movie, *Get Leo*, as well as a sequel, *Get Lost*, which flopped. Now he's thinking of getting into the music business. The word *cool* appears for the first time on page 8. Chili is sitting at a sidewalk café on Beverly Boulevard with record producer Tommy Athens, an old friend from Brooklyn. Tommy wants Chili to make a movie about his life. Chili expresses skepticism. Tommy makes his pitch.

> "The one thing you've always had going for you, Chil, you're the most confident guy I know. You have a cool way of making it sound like you know what you're talking about."
>
> "You saying I'm a bullshit artist?"
>
> "One of the best. It's the main reason, I think, in spite of your attitude, you can get this movie made." (*Be Cool* 8)

Whether or not we trust Tommy's cinema smarts, there is a grain of truth in what he says about Chili's "cool" confidence, even when bullshitting. However gifted at lies and flattery you may be, there's still an "art" involved, a technique honed by practice and experience. In any case, being cool is not about being honest or sincere, which, to the extent that they involve a self-conscious effort, can often interfere with feelings of authenticity. Being cool is less about "being yourself" than about letting yourself become whatever it is you are doing in any given situation, including smooth-talking someone with deep pockets into financing a dubious film project. That is, it's "cool" provided you enjoy doing it.

We get another glimpse of what it means to "be cool" forty pages later. Chili is leaving a restaurant with Linda Moon, a singer he wants to represent despite her binding contract with a "gangsta" band manager named Raji. At that moment, Raji and his massive Samoan bodyguard, Elliot, catch sight of them from across the street. Raji approaches and tries to rile Chili by directing insulting remarks at Linda, beginning with her performance that evening and ending with a few choice comments on her sex life. "That was for me," Chili tells Linda. "Stay right here, okay? Be cool" (48). Like Raji's insults, which are addressed to Linda though aimed at Chili, Chili's imperative seems directed as much at himself as at his companion—an impression that his subsequent behavior confirms by way of demonstration for Linda's benefit. A series of sly put-downs exchanged with Raji soon escalates to the critical point of Chili declaring himself to be Linda's new manager: "He had an idea what was coming and got ready." Raji calls on Elliot. What transpires, however, is not what a viewer of traditional Westerns or post-*Goodfellas* crime films would expect. In place of a head-busting, tooth-loosening free-for-all, Chili disarms Elliot with a flurry of "cool" grade-A bullshit.

> But now Chili, looking up at Elliot, started to grin. He said, "You're in pictures, aren't you? I'm pretty sure I saw you in something. The trouble is I see so many of the new releases, almost every day in the screening room . . . I'm sorry, I'm Chili Palmer, I did *Get Leo*?" (50)

After a bit more of this palaver, Chili invites Elliot to come by his office for a screen test and, from that point on, Elliot is eating out of his hand.

Two things about Chili's "cool" performance in this scene are noteworthy. First, he prefers to outwit rather than out-hit his opponent, exhausting all his verbal resources in an effort to forestall or avoid physical violence, of which he is not, in any case, fearful. (It's not as though he could "take" Elliot—just that in his former life, working for the mob, he learned what he could take.) Second, he is improvising, making it up as he goes along, seeing what works and getting a feeling about what won't. He's learned from Linda only a few moments ago that Elliot, who's growing tired of Raji's superior attitude and constant insults, "wants to be in the movies" (44). Now he's using that knowledge as a skateboarder might spread his shirttails to catch the breeze while weaving in and out of rush-hour traffic. When Linda tries to dissuade him from confronting Raji and Elliot, he replies, "We want to find out what happens next, don't we?" (45). In its purest, most highly developed form—especially as it emerges in Leonard's later work—"cool" avoids physical violence unless, like Chili's verbal technique, it also demands skill, intelligence, and improvisation. This is because naked, impulsive, brutal violence is an admission of defeat that often prevents us from seeing "what happens next"—that is, it prevents a story from taking its most interesting direction. Chili, who's thinking of writing a screenplay about his adventures in record production, here seems to be speaking on behalf of his creator, whose approach to plotting is to set characters in motion and "see what happens" (Lyczak 236). In art as in life, violence may be horrifying or comical or both at once, but it is uncool except as a last resort. Violence is for jerks.

Chili's version of "cool" does not correspond to what many of Leonard's most astute critics understand by the word. B. R. Myers, for instance, laments the turn toward violence for its own sake—or worse, for the sake of a laugh—that he thinks disfigures the versions of "cool" appearing in Leonard's crime-writing phase, as opposed to his earlier career of writing Westerns.

> In most of his novels the cool are to be chuckled with and rooted for, the less cool to be chuckled at and rooted against. Coolness itself is taken very seriously. For the crime-fiction Leonard, coolness is all about making things look easy, but readers may find themselves wishing he devoted more attention, as he did in his westerns, to just *what* is being made to look easy. True cool is the hero of *Hombre*, a white man raised by Apaches, leading whiny settlers through the desert without so much as a backward glance; it is *not* beating someone with a baseball bat, or throwing rocks through windows at a girl's bidding, as [Jack] Ryan does later on in *The Big Bounce*.

Myers's choice of examples reveals a category mistake. Jack Ryan's clobbering of a migrant crew boss and throwing rocks through windows in *The Big Bounce* is just the opposite of "cool," a fake version, and Leonard wants us to know that, as we'll see when we look at the novel more closely. The dramatic center of *The Big Bounce* is the male protagonist's gradually losing his cool under the influence of the thrill-seeking wastrel Nancy Hayes, until he finds it's too late to back out of the mess he's in, or to regain his composure. By the time he reappears in *Unknown Man No. 89*, Jack has grown up and learned to "be cool": focused, relaxed, at one with what he does. Regarding Leonard's characteristic sense of humor in the crime novels, Myers has this to add: "No writer can take violence seriously and joke about it at the same time, but it is significant that for the new Leonard the joke came first. At last he was in tune with the postmodern times." Leonard's "postmodern" sense of humor predates his turn to crime fiction, and writers from Homer to Kurt Vonnegut, one of Leonard's favorites (Grobel 256), have shown that taking violence seriously does not preclude joking about it—perhaps even putting the joke first. Moreover, "being cool" is not just about "making things *look* easy" but about making difficult things easy (or easier) *in reality*—that is, as we experience them. "Anything that's just good that works is cool," Leonard told me in an interview. "It's beyond cool." "If it works," I replied. "No wasted movement." "Yeah," he agreed. His present reputation as a cool writer, he added, was "not because I'm trying to be cool, it's just because I'm trying to be straight. I'm just trying to put it down the way it is, the way I see it, no affectation" (Rzepka, "Interviews 9").

Leonard's notion of "cool" resembles Ernest Hemingway's famous definition of courage or "guts," in a letter to F. Scott Fitzgerald of 20 April 1926, as "grace under pressure" (*Selected* 200; see also Parker 31), something that Robert Jordan, the hero of *For Whom the Bell Tolls,* epitomizes. It's easy to make this connection, for Leonard has cited *For Whom the Bell Tolls* as one of the earliest and most important influences on his writing, and Jordan himself, a young American explosives expert fighting Fascists in the Spanish Civil War, is an obvious source for "cool" protagonists like Chili Palmer. Chili wants to produce Linda Moon's debut album and he'll do whatever it takes, which is to say, whatever works, to make it happen. Jordan's only goal in a world filled with bungling officers, vacillating allies, ruthless Fascists, and inadequate materiel is to blow up his bridge. Like Chili and "bullshitting," blowing things up is what Robert Jordan is good at. As Leonard would say, "It's what he does," a signature phrase that also encapsulates the author's attitude toward his own writing: "Yeah, this is what I do" (Challen 91).

But Hemingway's "courage" and Leonard's "cool" differ in important ways. Both require self-control, determination, and prowess—all conventionally masculine virtues. They also involve improvisation, an ability to apply one's talents or skills to unexpected challenges. When Jordan's blasting caps are stolen, he jerry-rigs hand grenades to detonate his dynamite charges at the very moment the Fascist tanks open fire. "Courage," however, retains a moral dimension, despite Hemingway's well-known contempt for abstract moral imperatives, while "cool" is essentially amoral. "Courage" trails clouds of existential glory, making human actions meaningful in a world that death makes otherwise meaningless, while "cool" connotes a dispassionate disengagement from meaningfulness altogether. Hemingway's version of courage is ultimately hot, not cool—his "grace under pressure" is a form of self-control that stubbornly resists the tide of circumstances dragging the hero toward a choice between dishonor or death, and resistance creates friction, heat. Courage is thus highly self-conscious and principled and adheres to a recognizable "Hemingway Code" (Young 63).[3] Cool is different, a resistance that is, ideally, unwilled, because it is either natural to begin with or a second nature born of deliberate habituation, sometimes in situations ostensibly unrelated to the crisis at hand.

Above all, cool is "fun," or should be. At one point in *Be Cool,* Chili Palmer and a recording agency employee, Elaine, are confronted by Elliot, the Samoan bodyguard, in their office. Elliot has lost patience waiting for his screen test and has just taken a baseball bat to a television set to make his point. Chili remains calm and matter-of-fact. He gently scolds Elliot and, after giving him some lines to study before his "screen test," turns to Elaine and winks, "deadpan, looking serious but having fun." When Elaine tells him, "You're a cool guy, Chil. You know?" he simply shrugs—"this time serious," adds Leonard (208).

The struggle to make or keep things "fun" when circumstances conspire to make them "serious," or to make fun itself a serious rather than frivolous pursuit, is what takes the place of moral struggle in Leonard's fiction. Hemingway's "courage" is a grim affair by comparison. Nonetheless, Robert Jordan does recognize the importance of remaining "gay," not in its current sexualized meaning, but in the sense that Friedrich Nietzsche, prophet of modern existentialism, had in mind when he coined the term "The Gay Science" to describe the technical skill of the Provençal troubadours of the thirteenth century: "that unity of singer, knight, and free spirit which distinguishes the wonderful early culture of the Provençals from all equivocal cultures" (Nietzsche 294). Feeling "slightly overwhelmed" by the task in front of him, Jordan fends off his "gloomy" thoughts by thinking of his "gay" comrades.

> All the best ones, when you thought it over, were gay. It was much better to be gay and it was a sign of something too. It was like having immortality while you were still alive. That was a complicated one. There were not many of them left though. No, there were not many of the gay ones left. There were very damned few of them left. And if you keep on thinking like that, my boy, you won't be left either. Turn off the thinking now, old timer, old comrade. You're a bridge-blower now. Not a thinker. (*For Whom* 20)

This unthinking, "gay" feeling of unequivocal unity with the work at hand, despite its dangers, is what Leonard's coolest characters share, but its "complicated" and metaphysically ponderous entanglement with "immortality" is something else. One reason Leonard began to gravitate away from Hemingway in the 1950s, despite Papa's lean prose and realistic dialogue, and toward Richard Bissell, who wrote about the tragicomic lives of river pilots and bargemen on the upper Mississippi in the 1940s, was that writers like Bissell shared his sense of humor (Geherin 5).[4] The Leonardian hero, as he emerges in the writer's mature crime fiction, actively *enjoys* being cool, the simplicity and straightforwardness of it, its lack of "wasted motions," in short, its authenticity. He may be "surprised" that "he likes it and is good at it," but being good at it is what makes it "fun," and doing it for "fun"—which is why Jack Ryan once tried his hand at a little breaking and entering and why Renda misses his old job, despite its piecework wages—is what especially makes it "cool."

In this chapter and the two to follow, I'll be tracing the concept of being cool and several other related features of Leonard's writing from their origins in his earliest childhood to the end of his inaugural three decades as a professional author, first of Westerns and then, beginning in the late 1960s, of crime fiction.

Taking "being cool" as our highway through Leonard's life and works, we'll find plenty of byways to explore along the way. These include the relationship between Leonard's sense of identity as a writer and his style of writing; his attitudes toward art and artisanship; the reprising of male coming-of-age narratives in his fiction and their connection to scenes of mirroring, doubling, and other specular confrontations, as well as to themes of mentoring, apprenticeship, and technical prowess; the evolving role of women and minorities in these white male rehearsals of agency; his fascination with pop cultural and similarly mythic or mass-mediated influences on self-understanding and behavior in late twentieth-century America; and the psychology of violence. What crucially shapes the relationships between and among all these concerns is the notion of being cool.

Two ways of understanding "cool" as it emerges and evolves in Leonard's work will prove especially helpful for our purposes, one psychological and the other philosophical. As an experience, being cool resembles what the former University of Chicago psychologist Mihali Csikszentmihalyi describes as the mental state of "flow" that characterizes highly focused creative activity, an "order in consciousness" that occurs whenever a person "must concentrate attention on the task at hand and momentarily forget everything else" (6), including and especially oneself (33–34). "Flow" relieves the self of the "social controls" and instinctive desires of everyday life—love, food, sex, status—which are serial, diffuse, and distracting because one has little real control over their satisfaction. In *Flow: The Psychology of Optimal Experience,* Csikszentmihalyi writes that such desires create "psychic entropy" (39), or disorder, and ultimately feelings of anxiety or boredom because their aim is passive rather than active gratification, mere "pleasure" rather than the "joy" of accomplishment. Flow arises from "autotelic" experiences that have no goal other than their own achievement.

The "elements of enjoyment" that characterize flow include "a challenging activity that requires skills" (49), "the merging of action and awareness" (53), "concentration on the task at hand" (58), "the sense of exercising control in difficult situations" (i.e., a sense of mastery) (61), and especially "the loss of self-consciousness" (62)—not blacking out, but an unwavering focus of attention on what needs to be done rather than on the person doing it or the motives of the persons hindering it or the tools necessary to accomplish it, which seem, in any case, almost to move under their own power. Most of these elements also appear in Leonard's representations of "being cool."

Another approach, the philosophical, is in some ways more useful for our purposes, and I'll return to it when we get to Leonard's years at the University of

Detroit, where he majored in English and minored in philosophy. Csikszentmihalyi alludes to this approach when he begins his book with Aristotle's definition of "happiness," something that is sought for its own sake, while "every other goal—health, beauty, money, or power—is valued only because we expect that it will make us happy" (1). Csikszentmihalyi doesn't pursue this definition very far, because, for Aristotle, the only goal whose autotelic pursuit will make us happy is virtue, which the Greek philosopher identifies ultimately with service to the state or society. Virtue in this sense is a form of "social control" that, according to Csikszentmihalyi, necessarily interferes with "flow." He prefers instead to concentrate on how any activity undertaken for its own sake can become autotelic and, thus, a source of happiness or "enjoyment."

Leonard is particularly interested in a subset of Csikszentmihalyi's full range of autotelic pursuits, something closer to what Aristotle calls *techne*, or skill, which depends on innate talent, ideally enhanced by training, practice, and study. "Being cool" is above all performative. In its most basic form it is a "knowing how" rooted in the body and expressed in work[5]—for Leonard personally, the specific work of writing.[6] Although he avoids using the word to describe what he does because it sounds too much like drudgery (Rzepka, "Interviews 1"), *work* does apply both in the technical sense of whatever "works" and as routine labor (Leonard writes from 9:30 a.m. to 6:00 p.m. each weekday) using particular tools: notebooks, special pens—these days a Pilot #5 or #7[7]—unlined, buff-colored, 8½ by 11 sheets, and a typewriter (never a word processor) to revise. In sixty years of writing, this toolkit has remained essentially unchanged. Above all, the work of writing is a *manual* activity: Leonard still writes all of his first drafts in longhand before typing them.[8] And it results in a product, the "work of art," although a closer approximation might be the "work of the artisan."[9]

Csikszentmihalyi believes that "flow" can emerge from a wide range of activities, including mental and conversational, and manifest itself in varying degrees of self-absorption. In his crime-writing phase Leonard's sense of artisanship expanded to encompass something like this broader sense of "flow," perhaps more accurately termed "professionalism" or a sense of mastery—or merely confidence—in one's day-to-day job. In Devlin's words, Leonard displays "a Calvinistic respect for labor," and most often, "the guy who does his job [. . .] comes to a good end" (125). This type of professional attitude informed the tough-guy ethos of American crime fiction in the 1930s, when Leonard came of age. For hard-boiled detectives like Hammett's Sam Spade and Chandler's Philip Marlowe, notes John Irwin, "their work *is* their love" and, moreover, "their work is that special *doing* that constitutes their *being*" (273). Chili Palmer's skill as a bullshitting novice in movie and music production, a profession where that kind of verbal artisanship seems essential, exemplifies Irwin's "doing as being," but it's also something that Chili mastered in his former profession, where it proved more efficient than breaking legs when the "vig" came due: how can a deadbeat earn the money to pay you back when he can't walk? Whatever their differences, both Csikszentmihalyi and Leonard treat Aristotelian *techne* as though it were autotelic, something authentic, meaningful, and enjoyable in and of itself—Leonard would say, "fun"—simply because it can relieve the "technician" of one supreme distraction in particular: self-consciousness.

Invisible Man: Cool Narrative

Hemingway not only provided a more immediate and native source than Dickens for the leading traits of Leonard's "cool" heroes. He did much more than any other writer to shape Leonard's style, even if we allow for its evolution over six decades. Amis has described that style well. "Your prose makes Raymond Chandler look clumsy," he told Leonard in their 1998 interview: "Nothing sticks out, there are no 'elbows,' there are no stubbings of toe. [. . .] With you, it's all planed flat" (Amis 5). Leonard generally dislikes being compared to writers of detective fiction, but especially to writers like Chandler, and Amis's observation indicates one reason why. Chandler is famous for his PI persona, Philip Marlowe, whose incongruous similes and wisecracking sentimentality can stick an "elbow" into a reader's ribs and distract attention from what's going on. Dickens's authorial persona, likewise, is a mile thick compared with Leonard's, his sentences weighty, his diction powerful but ornate. Like Chandler, Dickens sometimes wrote in the first person, adopting the narrative persona of his male protagonist. Leonard almost never does. He hates calling attention to himself.

In his "Ten Rules of Writing," published originally in the *New York Times* as "Easy on the Adverbs" (2001), Leonard begins as follows:

> These are rules I've picked up along the way to help me remain invisible when I'm writing a book. [. . .] If you have a facility for language and imagery and the sound of your voice pleases you, invisibility is not what you are after, and you can skip the rules. Still, you might look them over.

To Leonard, the sheet of paper filling up before his eyes is like a pane of glass in which he can avoid seeing his own reflection only if he takes pains to remain outside the frame, elbows and all. He does so by keeping his readers focused on what lies beyond the glass, what his characters see and hear and think and say to each other, while speaking in his own voice as little as possible. It took a long time for Leonard to master, let alone formulate, the rules of his own writing, which might better go by the title "Ten Rules of Invisibility."

Leonard's mature style in the Westerns, achieved by the end of the 1950s, resembles Hemingway's in *For Whom the Bell Tolls*: direct and descriptive, with little authorial comment amid the flow of geographical, historical, and biographical narration, passages of dialogue, and representations of a character's thoughts in what sounds like his or her own words. At first, however, Leonard relied almost exclusively on an unanchored, omniscient, impersonal narrative voice to convey factual information, and while he would sometimes settle his narrative in a single character's point of view, it took him awhile to adopt a voice to match, something that Hemingway was very good at right out of the gate.

Consider, for instance, the opening paragraph of Leonard's first published story, "Trail of the Apache" (1951), which settles quickly into the point of view of its protagonist, the Indian agent Eric Travisin.

> Under the thatched roof ramada that ran the length of the agency office, Travisin slouched in a canvas-backed chair, his boots propped against one of the support posts. His gaze took in the sun-beaten, gray adobe buildings, all one-story structures, that rimmed the vacant quadrangle. It was a glaring, depressing scene of sun on rock, without a single shade tree or graceful feature to redeem the squat ugliness. There was not a living soul in sight. Earlier that morning, his White Mountain Apache charges had received their two-weeks' supply of beef and flour. By now they were milling about the cook fires in front of their wickiups, three miles farther up the Gila, where the flat, dry land began to buckle into rock-strewn hills. (1)

The paragraph goes on to describe the Apaches' campsites, then gives way to a third-person omniscient narrative of Travisin's solitary life, antisocial personality, and almost preternatural reputation as a scout among his fellow agents and cavalry officers. After five paragraphs of this, Leonard brings us back to Travisin sitting on the ramada: "He looked at the harsh, rugged surroundings and liked what he saw" (3). Except for this brief, concluding evaluation of the scene, there's practically no reason for Leonard's having adopted Travisin's point of view on the landscape, since nothing in the way he sees things has told us anything about him, and the voice doing the talking could belong to anyone—anyone fond of adjectives. If there is a point, it seems to be merely that showing us the landscape through Travisin's eyes helps keep Leonard out of sight. Even emotionally laden words like *depressing, graceful,* and *redeem* turn out to be generic: Travisin doesn't find the landscape depressing, nor does he think it's in need of redemption. He likes what he sees. Words like these are meant to reflect what we, as readers, would presumably feel were we to be sitting and gazing in the same spot as Travisin—which, in effect, we are.

In short, there's nothing distinctive about Travisin's "gaze" here because there's no one doing any thinking or feeling behind it. It serves as little more than a plate-glass window through which we are allowed to peer out at Leonard's version of the Arizona Territory, circa 1880—a version he's never hesitated to admit came straight from photographs he discovered in *Arizona Highways* magazine (Geherin 19). Making us see with Travisin's eyes helps keep his creator invisible, but does little else. Contrast this passage with the following from *For Whom the Bell Tolls*:

> They had come through the heavy timber to the cup-shaped upper end of the little valley and he saw where the camp must be under the rim-rock that rose ahead of them through the trees.
>
> That was the camp all right and it was a good camp. You did not see it at all until you were up to it and Robert Jordan knew it could not be spotted from the air. Nothing would show from above. It was as well hidden as a bear's den. But it seemed to be little better guarded. He looked at it carefully as they came up. (21)

As in Leonard's opening scene, we descend almost immediately from a floating, unanchored, objective description—"they had come . . ."—into a particular mind, a point of view initially pegged by "he saw" and fastened down by "Robert Jordan knew." But Hemingway creates a greater sense of intimacy with Robert Jordan in these 102 words than Leonard can create with Eric Travisin in six paragraphs. That intimacy is registered in the details that Jordan notices, the thoughts they provoke, and, above all, the voice in which both visual detail and thought come to our attention. That the rim-rock is where "the camp *must* be" is something inferred by Jordan, not by the author (who presumably knows whether it is the camp or not), and indicates that Jordan is used to camping unseen in the mountains. This hint is elaborated in what follows: "You did not see it at all until you were up to it" and "it could not be spotted from the air," where the young man knows the Fascist bombers make their daily or even hourly appearances. But the hidden camp seems to lack sentries, which makes Jordan examine it "carefully" as he and his companion approach. All of these details tell us that this former American college student is already an experienced guerilla fighter, and the simile comparing the hideout to "a bear's den" suggests that he may have become accustomed to living outdoors before joining the Popular Front: he knows what the hiding places of wild animals look like—perhaps he did some bear hunting as a boy.

One feature of this passage in particular, however, helps reinforce our sense of intimacy with the man noticing these details and making these judgments: the narrative diction and tone of voice. "That was the camp all right and it was a good camp": who is saying this, making this judgment? Strictly speaking, the author, but if that's the case, he seems to be ventriloquizing, speaking with the voice of his character. The *all right* and the conjunction *and* make the sentence colloquial, like something Jordan himself might say to his companion, Pablo, out loud. Had he done so, Hemingway would have used quotation marks and the present tense, not the past—"That is the camp all right and it is a good camp"—and he would have had to introduce the sentence with a question from Pablo or a debate between the two men: "Is that the camp?" "I don't know." Pause. "That is the camp all right. . . ." The *all right* indicates not only a tone of voice but the resolution of a doubt in the mind of the character through whose eyes we, too, are trying to discern a camp where he feels it "must be." The demonstrative pronoun *that* and the past tense, along with the absence of quotation marks, indicate that we have come under the spell of free indirect discourse, a literary technique so widespread in the modern novel that half the time we don't notice it working its magic on us.

The nuances and varieties of free indirect discourse (often abbreviated as FID and also known as "free indirect speech") are a subject of endless debate among rhetoricians, narratologists, and other scholars of fiction,[10] but for our purposes a few crude distinctions will do. First, unlike direct discourse, free indirect discourse appears without quotation marks. In a sentence like "He said, 'Nothing will show from above,'" everything after "He said" is direct discourse. In "He said nothing would show from above," the last five words are indirect discourse. *Free* indirect discourse is a variation of indirect discourse that creates an illusion of interiority, a sense that we, as readers, are listening in on a mind talking to itself: interpreting what it sees or hears, judging others, debating with itself, calling up memories, making plans. FID is devoid of speech indicators like "he said" and is always conveyed in the past tense, although it can unfold in the second person as well as the third: in Hemingway's "*You* did not see it at all until *you* were up to it," Jordan seems to be addressing himself, silently, as "you." The impression of immediacy in free indirect discourse is often reinforced by *deixis*, the use of words whose meanings depend on their immediate context, as if to place the reader "inside" the body of the thinking and perceiving character. Besides demonstrative pronouns like *that* and *this*, deictic markers include *here, there, now,* and *soon*. Interior monologue, which also dispenses with quotation marks, usually proceeds in the present rather than past tense and sometimes in sentence fragments, in which case we find ourselves reading "stream of consciousness" fiction like James Joyce's *Ulysses*.

It's important that we distinguish point of view from these three forms of discourse (direct, indirect, free indirect), as well as from the grammatical person (first, second, third) of the narrative voice. Point of view can be conveyed without the use of free indirect discourse, as we observed just now when examining Leonard's description of what Travisin saw through his impersonal "gaze." (The reverse, however, does not apply: FID always implies a point of view.) Note, too, that while Travisin's point of view in the opening paragraphs of "Trail of the Apache" is conveyed in the third person—"Travisin slouched"; "His gaze took in"—a story can also be narrated from a particular character's viewpoint in the second person, as in Robert Jordan's self-reflective "You did not see it at all [. . .]." And, of course, first-person narration using *I* implicitly conveys a point of view, although it also impedes the use of free indirect discourse because the speaking *I* cannot, like an omniscient narrator, "listen in" on what other characters are thinking, seeing, or feeling. To distinguish point of view more readily from "person" in this grammatical sense, narratologists sometimes use the term "focalization" (Genette 189–90).

Between a third-person omniscient point of view, in which events seem to be narrated from a position outside the fictive world in which they occur—a world the teller of the tale nevertheless knows everything about—and a third-person point of view focalized (with or without FID) through a single character within the story, there is a wide gray area that looks and sounds like third-person omniscient narration but in which all information is restricted to what only the participants in the scene can see and hear. This restricted multiple form gives an impression of reliable objectivity—whatever occurs has several witnesses—but lends itself more readily than third-person omniscient point of view to rapid shifts of focalization through the individual minds of characters in the scene, sometimes several shifts in a row.

Leonard deploys restricted multiple point of view so instinctively that it may be hard to detect, except when he makes a false move. Thus, in *The Hunted* (1977), at the beginning of chapter 24, Leonard has to cut away from the viewpoint and free indirect discourse of the dying fugitive, Al Rosen, which ended the previous chapter, to tell the reader, parenthetically, what's been happening beyond Rosen's horizon of awareness in the meantime: "(Two things were happening at the same time)" (247), "(The other thing that was happening . . .)" (247–48). Because the two events are occurring simultaneously unbeknownst to Rosen and within two other separate arenas of awareness—that of Leonard's hero, Marine Sergeant David Davis, and that of the three Detroit mobsters in pursuit of Rosen—Leonard can't use multiple restricted focalization and has to resort to an awkwardly parenthesized third-person omniscient point of view to handle the transitions. This is one of those rare moments in Leonard's writing where an authorial elbow is left sticking way out.

Leonard's use of restricted multiple point of view seems inherently cinematic, because the narrative camera never cuts away to provide extraneous information until a new scene begins, and there is no parenthetical "voice-over" narration, as there is in chapter 24 of *The Hunted*. "I feel much more confident writing in scenes—in dramatic scenes," says Leonard (LaMay 149). Given the enormous impact that movies had on his childhood, we should not be surprised to find that Leonard prefers to convey to us only those features of his fictional world that the characters in any particular scene can experience, whether singly or as a group.

Hemingway favored interior monologue—present-tense self-address—over free indirect discourse in *For Whom the Bell Tolls*, but can go on for pages revealing Robert Jordan's inner world in either mode. There is little of this kind of thing in "Trail of the Apache." More typically, Leonard will reveal what a character is feeling or thinking in direct discourse (whether as a single character's pronouncement or through dialogue) or simply have the narrator tell it to us outright: Travisin "liked what he saw"; "To Eric Travisin [. . .] it was bound to be amusing" (6); "Travisin felt his temper rise" (7); "De Both was surprised, and disturbed. He fidgeted in his chair, trying to feel official" (7). As a beginning writer, Leonard seldom shifts his register into FID to reflect a character's personality or (one of his favorite words) "attitude."

Interestingly, the few lines of free indirect discourse that Leonard does introduce in "Trail of the Apache" tend to focus on the mind of William de Both, a greenhorn West Point graduate assigned to help Travisin chase down the renegade Apaches and bring them back to the reservation. This should come as no surprise, once we observe how consistently Leonard highlights Travisin's fundamental unknowability, beginning with his uncanny survival instincts and intuitive understanding of Apache ways. Though white, he seems "more Apache than the Apaches themselves" (2), and his fellow scouts find him a fascinating cross-cultural mystery. De Both, by contrast, is the reader's stand-in as naive observer, and eventual pupil, of the gifted but impenetrable veteran Indian agent. De Both's innocence about life on the reservation is conveyed to us upon his first appearance, at the beginning of chapter 2. Approaching Travisin's office for the first time, de Both "had the distinct feeling that he was entering a hostile camp."

> As he drew nearer to the agency office, the figure in front of it appeared no friendlier. Good God, were they all Indians? (4)

Later, riding with Travisin and the other scouts through the roasting hills, de Both is made watchful by his companions' watchfulness, but has other things on his mind.

> The damned stifling heat and the dazzling glare were enough for a white man to worry about. [. . .] He could feel the Apache scouts laughing at him. How could they remain so damned cool-looking in this heat? (17)

In these two examples, the ejaculations and expletives—"Good God," "damned"—and the floating interrogatives—"were they all . . . ?" "How could they . . . ?"—along with the uninterrupted use of third-person past-tense narration, have the same colloquial impact as Renda's "all the fucking papers to sign and talking on the phone" or Ryan's "so why get mad or upset?" They indicate that we have slipped from an omniscient or multiple restricted description of events into the realm of interiority opened up by free indirect discourse. It's as though we were listening to de Both talking to himself in his head.

Despite passages like these, and despite Hemingway's example, Leonard was tentative in experimenting with, let alone trying to master, free indirect discourse at the very outset of his career. Since then his style has evolved radically, to the point where FID has become one of his primary expository devices.[11] This evolution began quite soon. One can find robust examples just two years after the publication of "Trail of the Apache," in "Blood Money" (1953), for instance, where bank robbers Rich Miller, "the boy," and Eugene Harlan, an ex-convict, have been cornered by a posse.

> Rich Miller watched Eugene move back to the table along the rear wall and pick up the whiskey bottle that was there. The boy passed his tongue over dry lips, watching Eugene drink. It would be good to have a drink, he thought. No, it wouldn't. It would be bad. You drank too much and that's why you're here. That's why you're going to get shot or hung. (269)

Like Hemingway, Leonard uses verbs of sensation and then thought or belief, not just to convey information about a character's inner life, but also to introduce passages of mental discourse, here including present-tense interior monologue as well as past-tense free indirect discourse.

By 1989, Leonard could dispense with most such markers of interiority, plunging us from the first line of *Killshot* directly into the self-deluding, alcoholic rationalizations of Armand "The Blackbird" Degas, a half-Ojibway hit man from Toronto and one of Leonard's most compelling, and strangely moving, portraits of homicidal psychopathy.

> The Blackbird told himself he was drinking too much because he lived in this hotel and the Silver Dollar was close by, right downstairs. Try to walk out the door past it. Try to come along Spadina Avenue, see that goddamn Silver Dollar sign, hundreds of light bulbs in your face, and not be drawn in there. Have a few drinks before coming up to this room with a ceiling that looked like a road map, all the cracks in it. (7)

It's not just Leonard's own experience as a recovering alcoholic or his express admiration for George V. Higgins's way with voices in *The Friends of Eddie Coyle* (1970) that accounts for the differences here. The voice in Armand's head belongs to him, unmistakably. Its rhythms and diction and defensive imperatives don't so much "reveal" as imply "a hell within" (to use De Quincey's words) that Degas himself seems unaware of, an abyss full of hidden demons that, ever since his parentless boyhood, have cut him off from any possibility of identifying with another person and, thereby, transforming silent, monologic rants like this into dialogues of understanding and, ultimately, of self-understanding.

While he may prefer writing in "scenes," Leonard says it's "always [. . .] from a character's point of view, so that the scene takes the sound of the character. Then even the narrative [. . .] has his sound" (LaMay 149). Leonard's sophisticated handling of free indirect discourse is part of what Amis means by his "planed smooth" style and what Reed calls Leonard's "Panasonic ear." "For the most part I'm copying a sound of speech," Leonard has said, "so that my 'sound' or style or attitude is the sound of the characters. You never hear *me*. You're never aware of words used by an author because I never use a word that my characters wouldn't or couldn't" (Skinner 41).[12] By now, Leonard's handling of the pace and arc of dialogue and the curtain-dropping one-liner seems instinctual. It is thus no surprise that, despite their spotty track record in the cinema, dozens of his books have been optioned by Hollywood and more than twenty, as of this writing, have made it to movie or TV screens. Portions of them can read like screenplays, and Leonard will sometimes strive to achieve that effect in order to attract the interest of the studios (Challen 136).

Most critics, accordingly, have swooned over Leonard's uncanny ear for dialogue. But Armand's demotic second-person soliloquy in *Killshot* reveals a mastery of free indirect discourse and interior monologue unsurpassed in our time, and among the surest of all time, even if we include Jane Austen, Gustave Flaubert, and Hemingway in the mix. It was a flowering hard to detect in the bud. When Leonard uses second-person narration in "Trail of the Apache," for instance, it emerges in the voice of a storytelling persona that, generally, he manages to keep out of sight. Here is his last paragraph:

> And along the Gila, the war drums are silent again. But on frontier station, you don't relax. For though they are less in number, they are still Apaches. (35)

The "you" here is clearly addressed to a presumed listener, and what the speaker offers is not a revelation of character but a generalized piece of frontier wisdom. Again, as Amis might say, an elbow is sticking out. A similar effect occurs at the beginning of a passage that goes on to describe de Both lying in ambush for an oncoming Apache: "Often when you haven't time to think, you're better off, your instinct takes over and your body follows through" (32). This might work as present-tense interior monologue if it introduced a train of vocalized reflections. Instead, Leonard simply describes de Both's sensations and "instinctive" reactions: "De Both pressed against the boulder in front of him feeling the coolness of it on his cheek"; "He heard the loose earth crumble"; "He heard the Indian's hand pat against the smooth surface"; "his heart hammered"; "the urge to run made his knees quiver." The effect is to isolate Leonard's generalization from what follows rather than integrate it. Oddly enough, it's a generalization about being cool.

To whom is it addressed? Ostensibly, as at the end of the story, to Leonard's readers. But just as Raji's put-downs of Linda Moon in *Be Cool* can seem bivalent—addressed to her, but aimed at Chili Palmer—so Leonard's obtrusive reflection on the hazards of self-consciousness can, if heard aslant, sound like advice he's giving himself while apparently speaking to us. It's something a new author might say under his breath while trying to master his craft, deliberately and self-consciously, step by step: laboriously studying mentors and models, gathering and checking facts and names, plotting, experimenting, starting over. In "A Conversation with Elmore Leonard," the introduction to a collection of his Western tales, Leonard tells Gregg Sutter, his researcher for the past three decades, how he reacted when his first Western was rejected.

> I decided I'd better do some research. I read *On the Border with Crook*, *The Truth about Geronimo*, *The Look of the West*, and *Western Words*, and I subscribed to

> *Arizona Highways*. It had stories about guns—I insisted on authentic guns in my stories—stagecoach lines, specific looks at different little facets of the West, plus all the four-color shots that I could use for my descriptions, things I could put in and sound like I knew what I was talking about. (xii)

Leonard kept all this information in a gray-green ledger book and drew upon it for his next tale. From then on, he kept this notebook, stuffed with facts and information, at his side while writing. In 1953 he began to devote the hours from five to seven each morning to his stories. Then he would leave for morning Mass (he was at that time a devout Catholic) and the Campbell Ewald advertising firm in Detroit, where he wrote ad copy to support himself and his growing family. The ledger book was crucial to Leonard's achieving a sense of legitimacy and authenticity as a writer of Westerns. But the oblique, second-person observation on thinking, instinct, and the body embedded in "Trail of the Apache" conveys a desire for authenticity fundamentally different from the mere possession of vast and accurate information, although it includes and incorporates that kind of knowledge. For a fledgling writer hoarding what little time he could from his day job and his family commitments and his religious duties, it might be the nearest he could come to an experience of grace under pressure: "sounding like I knew what I was talking about," but doing so without having to think too much about it. It would be as though his hand and pen were doing the writing on those unlined surfaces, "following through" instinctively, while the mind was focused on a voice—or voices—inside his head, "the sound of the characters."

To this day, Leonard retains a legendary obsession with the minutiae of gizmos, trades, and professions: not just law-enforcement protocols and gun specs, but the details of skills and fields as disparate as ironworking, record promoting, casino gambling, explosives, auto theft, distilling, and, in *Djibouti* (2010), LNG tanker technology, to name just a few. This version of authenticity, a documentary fidelity to fact and history, is clearly visible throughout his work and constitutes an essential feature of formulaic Western writing, according to Nathaniel Lewis. But even more important to Leonard was and is the authenticity of invisibility, losing himself in a task that he has finally gotten the hang of, his disciplined absorption in the work of writing: "I'm a serious writer," he says, "but I don't *take* it seriously, if that makes any sense. I don't stew over it, I try and relax and swing with it" (Grobel 281).

The affinities between jazz improvisation and compositional technique implicit in "swing with it" are more than just idiomatic for Leonard. "I listen to jazz and it inspires me to write," he told me in an interview at his home in Bloomfield Village, Michigan. "Some years ago we were watching Dizzy Gillespie outside and he was playing and having a good time, and I wanted to go home and write. I get into the mood of it, the beat of it" (Rzepka, "Interviews 4"). Leonard says that his "vibes are more closely associated with jazz" than with any other musical form, "a structured sound you do variations on, improvising, the artist's personality coming through" (Roberts). This is when the work of writing becomes "fun": "So once I get into it and I'm the character or both of the characters, or all of them, it's just a lot of fun and I get it going and try to entertain myself" (Rzepka, "Interviews 4"). Like a great jazz musician, Leonard wants to avoid self-consciousness at all costs by letting his "personality" come out as performance rather than persona, focusing always on what he wants to say with his instrument, not on how he wants to say it, and especially not on how it might sound to others.

Despite his desire for invisibility, Leonard's own voice would often give him away when he was just starting out. We can hear it surfacing in "Trail of the Apache," and not merely in the strident rhetoric of "the fury of it pounded in his head" (21) or Apaches "screaming like a band of vampires beating from a cavern" (33). It's also the voice that speaks through Travisin's mouth when he asks de Both how he'd feel if he were separated from his wife and family and forced to live a hundred miles away, like the Apaches confined on the reservation.

> And do you know why? For something you've been doing for the past three hundred years. For that simple but enigmatic something that makes you an Apache and not a Navajo. For that quirk of fate that makes you a tiger instead of a Persian cat. (8)

"Enigmatic something," "quirk of fate," tigers and Persian cats, and the stentorian anaphora—"For something . . . For [. . .] something . . . For that quirk": this is Travisin channeling his creator's indignation, not his creator speaking in Travisin's voice. Worse, the paragraph looks and sounds like writing, not speech, an unforgivable sin for any writer seeking invisibility. "My most important rule," says Leonard in "The Ten Rules of Writing," "sums up the [other] ten. If it sounds like writing, I rewrite it" ("Easy").

Within just a few years, Leonard will make his characters not only speak like themselves but also think like themselves. Eventually, during his great decade of experimentation in a new genre, the 1970s, he will learn how to make even his own narrative voice sound more like speech and how to create more opportunities for free indirect discourse by restricting point of view to a single character's mind for extended stretches of narrative, often comprising several consecutive chapters. Granting the voices inside him greater freedom of expression, he will lose himself in the work of writing, which in its purest form makes work into play. He will achieve authenticity by becoming invisible, above all to himself. He will learn to "swing with it" and "be cool."

Voices in Your Head: The Storyteller

The connection between invisibility in Leonard's work and letting the voices inside him have their say can be traced all the way back to his preschool years, when he made (in both senses of the word) an imaginary friend named "Boyee." Elmore forgot his invisible companion as he grew older, but his mother remembered. "I must have told her that Boyee and I went somewhere and did something," says Leonard. "I was always talking to Boyee, and talking about him" (Rzepka, "Interviews 1"). The Leonards—Elmore Sr., his wife, Flora (née Rivé), and their two children, Margaret and Elmore Jr. (figure 1)—were living in Oklahoma City at the time because that's where Mr. Leonard's job had taken them. He worked for General Motors, scouting new dealership locations in the south and southern plains. His son had been born on 11 October 1925 in New Orleans, his and Flora's home town, but the family soon began to move in step with his new assignments: first to Dallas and then, for the next two or three years, Oklahoma City. After a brief return to Dallas and a stay in Detroit for nine months, from late 1931 to mid-1932, the Leonards settled in Memphis for two years before moving back to Detroit permanently in 1934, when Elmore Sr. was offered a position in GM's middle management. His namesake was then eight years old and about to enter the fourth grade. Boyee had disappeared, from the boy's memory as well as his imagination, somewhere between Oklahoma City and the Motor City.

While the phenomenon is not as rare as once thought, having imaginary friends before the age of five or six is less common for boys than for girls (Carlson and Taylor 95). In all cases, children with imaginary friends tend to be advanced in verbal and social skills (Goodnow). "I had friends. I wasn't a loner," says Leonard (Rzepka, "Interviews 4"), and there's no reason to think otherwise, to judge from his close friendships and enthusiasm for team sports as a schoolchild. Constantly finding himself among new playmates would have offered young Elmore repeated opportunities to hone his innate verbal and social skills. But four moves in six years—from New Orleans to Dallas to Oklahoma City, back to Dallas and then to Detroit—can put a lot of strain on a gregarious preschooler, especially when he is just learning to "play together" rather than to "play apart." An invisible friend is there whenever you need him. You never have to leave him behind when your family moves on—when, in effect, you become "invisible" to the friends *you* are leaving behind. "We don't really know what happens down the road [with imaginary friends]," says Marjorie Taylor, a developmental psychologist, "but we suspect it's associated with later creativity" (quoted in Goodnow).

If Leonard's "sound" is, as he told Joel Lyczak in 1983, "the sound of [his] individual characters" (236), more often than not those sounds come echoing up from the cellars of memory: "I get dialogue from what I remember. From the years I was in the service as an enlisted man, from the construction summers I've worked when I was in my early twenties, from growing up with kids from blue-collar families" (Grobel 247). Over the years, Leonard has made "an effort to listen, not so much to specific words but to patterns of speech and cadence of speech" (Skinner 41). Asked what was more important when he watched movies based on his novels, the sound or the look, Leonard replied, "For me, the sound" (Grobel 270).

Not only can the sound of his characters haunt the narrative voice of Leonard's fiction, but these imaginary friends can also take over the plot, something with which their creator is "never that concerned" anyway (Rzepka, "Interviews 2"; Grobel 259). His style in fact "requires that the characters move the story," he says, "and I keep my nose out of it."

> I begin with characters [. . .]. Add a few more characters, inside and outside the law, throw in a few things I know [. . .] and see what happens. I don't know myself what's going to happen until I'm well into the story and I see how the characters interact" (Lyczak 236).

Someone "not planned as an important character," says Leonard, might "assume his way into a position of prominence" (Skinner 42; see also Grobel 282). Typically, the takeover begins when that someone finds a voice: "They sort of audition like that. Certain characters audition and if they play their role well, they could go on. [. . .] And that's the best kind of character to have. One who, on his own, elbows his way into the plot" (Skinner 42). When Taylor and her colleagues asked adult writers about their relationship to their own fictional characters, nearly all said that it was common for these shadows to come alive at some point and begin to make decisions for themselves, like imaginary friends. Leonard's characters usually achieve independent agency only when they've been assigned the right name. Franklin de Dios, who "came out of nowhere" to change the direction of *Bandits* (1987), was just a Miskito Indian from Nicaragua, lurking in the background until "I gave him a name," says Leonard. "Maybe he was just talking before, he was by his car in front of a restaurant talking to somebody else and [. . .] at the end of that scene, you say, 'And his name was Franklin de Dios,' which means, 'Remember this guy'" (Rzepka, "Interviews 2").

Although he turns against his boss eventually, de Dios starts out as a bad man working for an even badder man who cons gullible right-wing Americans into contributing funds to support the Contras in Nicaragua while planning to pocket the cash himself. As a monster of cold-blooded mayhem, Franklin stands two heads shorter than most of his fellow inmates in the holding cells of Leonard's imagination, characters like Curt Lazair in *The Bounty Hunters* (1953), Robbie Daniels in *Split Images* (1981), Teddy Magyk in *Glitz* (1985), Richie Nix in *Killshot*, or James Russell, aka Jama Raisuli, in *Djibouti*. Magyk, for instance, likes to rape and murder old ladies, while Rus*sell* will kill you just for using his birth name, especially if you place the accent wrong. And yet, "I accept my characters, all of them," says Leonard. "I have an affection for them. Doesn't mean that I like them."

> Like the guy in *Glitz* [Teddy Magyk] who murdered women? He's a bad guy. Then you see him with his mother and you start to understand a little bit about the guy. (Grobel 282)

Like their "sound," Leonard's De Quincean "sympathy of comprehension" for his characters is rooted in childhood. Glenn Most has noted the absence of families with children from Leonard's crime fiction (104), but it turns out children are everywhere. They're just hidden in the bodies of grownups: "I picture most of my characters as children," says Leonard. "I see them as they were at a certain age."

> Teddy Magyk in *Glitz* was kind of a loner and never got along with anybody. Kids picked on him. [He] probably picked his nose and ate it and everybody said, "Oh God, Teddy, Jesus!" He was just a weird kid. And as they grow up, they're still children. Some are childish and some are childlike. (Grobel 282)

This sentiment is often expressed in Leonard's books: Mrs. Pierce in *Gunsights* (1979) thinks of her lover, Bren Early, as "a little boy" (406); Carolyn Wilder thinks the same about both Clement Mansell, the "Oklahoma Wildman," and his antagonist, Lieutenant Raymond Cruz, in *City Primeval* (164, 202). The honor game these men play resembles the code of the schoolyard, where young males must either bully or be bullied. Elsewhere, Leonard elaborates: "Childish is selfish and childlike is open and honest, and wanting to learn" (Rzepka, "Interviews 1"). The struggle between these two kinds of adult "children" dominates his novels and is particularly intense for his male characters.

Despite its roots in his boyhood friendships and experiences, Leonard's fiction proves curiously resistant to prolonged biographical interpretation in one major respect. Unlike the tense and violent milieus of his books, Leonard's childhood was placid, even idyllic: no bullies, no abusive relatives, no fights, no guns (except of the toy variety), no vandalism or petty crime (except for the time he shoplifted a mitt for the catcher on his baseball team). Just school, sports, and lots of free time to hang out, go to the movies, and play the games of make-believe typical of boys the world over.[13] And perhaps get into a little mischief here and there.

The Leonards were, by and large, a happy family. During their years of exodus, Elmore's father might be away from home for up to "a week or two" at a time (Rzepka, "Interviews 6"). But he and his wife were openly affectionate with each other and toward their children, and Mr. Leonard, who was "easy going" by nature, would spend what time he could with his son, playing catch or going to the movies with the rest of the family or, once the Leonards had settled in Detroit, just listening to how young Elmore's day had gone (figure 2). "We got along very well," Leonard recalls ("Interviews 6"), although he never felt close to his father until after the war: "My dad was traveling a lot and he didn't read much. That is, he [. . .] didn't read what I was interested in" ("Interviews 4"). Before Elmore could read on his own, his sister Margaret, six years older, would read to him at bedtime, mostly from *My Book House*—Leonard calls it "The Book House"—a multivolume collection of nursery rhymes, folk tales, and abbreviated literary classics for children ("Interviews 6"). He attended Catholic schools, and at Blessed Sacrament Elementary in Detroit he made close friends with working- and middle-class kids (one boy's father drove a bus, another's was a judge) ("Interviews 7").

For someone who has never written a book that didn't include a fight, a shooting, an explosion, or all three, Elmore Leonard seems to have lived an unusually sheltered existence. And yet he has always been imaginatively drawn to violence. He is probably the most knowledgeable crime writer in America when it comes to firearms, although he's never owned a gun and doesn't want to, and was fascinated as a child by the proletarian bank robbers of the early Depression era.

> Machine Gun Kelly and Pretty Boy Floyd, and Ma Barker and her guys, all of these [in the] South-Midwest, where all these desperadoes were robbing banks in the '30s, when I was a little kid, reading the paper and doing a lot of train travel [to visit southern relatives]. We lived [. . .] where all this was going on. I think that made a real impression on me." (LaMay 151)

There is a well-known photograph of Elmore Jr. as a boy, shooting his cap pistol at the camera while standing beside the family car, his left foot on the running board (figure 3). The pose, he recalls, was inspired by news of the deaths of Bonnie Parker and Clyde Barrow in May 1934, when he and his family were still living in Memphis. He was trying to imitate a photograph that had appeared in the newspapers, of Bonnie smoking a cigar and holding a gun, with her foot resting on a car's front bumper (figure 4).

Leonard vividly remembers the first time he saw a real gun. It was at about the time he posed for his father's camera, holding his cap pistol.

> I remember in a railroad station, it must have been Memphis, we were just standing, waiting, I was supposed to board. And a man pushed his coat back with his right hand and I saw a pistol holstered on his hip. And it made me nervous. *I was surprised it did.* [. . .] [To] see a real one out in life, maybe that was it. There really are guns around, I thought. [. . .] I probably assumed this was a bad guy. He was probably a railroad cop. (Rzepka, "Interviews 7," emphasis added)

The incident seems common enough: a child is surprised to find that his fantasy life doesn't match reality. But what interests the grown-up Leonard is not the surprise. It's the source of the surprise: not the pistol's reality, but his own nervousness at seeing a firearm up close and for real, and at the thought that "there really are guns around." At the age of eight, he certainly knew the difference between his bright, Technicolor fantasies and the events taking place in the common light of day. Up to this moment in a Memphis train station, however, he had thought that fantasizing about violence would prepare him emotionally for the real thing, that his feelings of courage in handling make-believe firearms and shooting at imaginary foes would carry over to the world of real guns and "bad guys." Now, contrary to expectations, he felt anxious. The fearless hero inside him vanished when exposed to the world outside. Somehow the idea had not occurred to him. This problem, of how to enable the person "inside" to reach the outside and thereby become real, or how to know which of several persons inside could survive being made real, would haunt his fiction. Writing would become its performative solution.

The legends of Bonnie and Clyde and other gangland antiheroes that infatuated Leonard as a boy unfolded in the newspapers, on the radio, and in the movie houses—not on his street or in his yard, never in his immediate experience. They occupied the same region of his imagination as heroes like Robin Hood, Beowulf, and Ulysses in the stories from Olive Beaupre Miller's *My Book House* that his big sister read to him at bedtime and that he eventually learned to read himself. Much later, in *The Hot Kid,* Leonard would depict the mass media to which he had been exposed while growing up during America's interwar years as a myth machine, a spinner of legends, rather than as a mirror of reality. By the time his family moved permanently to Detroit, just months after the killings of Bonnie and Clyde and his first encounter with a real gun, Elmore Jr. had learned the importance of stories, whether fairy tales, legends, or the daily news, in constructing a heroic fantasy life, and the vulnerability of his fantasy life to the fact of violence, or its real threat. He was about to learn the further value of stories as things he could make himself: devices for gaining paternal attention, making and keeping friends, and constructing a sense of himself in the world.

The move to Detroit in 1934 was not immediately a move up, at least in living circumstances. The Leonards occupied a cramped apartment in the heart of the city, where young Elmore slept in a pull-down Murphy bed in the living room. When the family moved up to a home of their own in the residential Northlawn neighborhood a few miles away, near Highland Park, he would still share a bedroom with Margaret. With the Depression lingering, Elmore Sr. was lucky to have a regular job, although Leonard doesn't recall hard times making much of an impact on his family, or on his friends' families. Its effects were more visible back in Memphis, where hobos from a nearby rail yard would come to the back door looking for a handout.[14]

The New Deal and the Public Works Administration had begun to lower the unemployment rate by late 1934, but one or two positive consequences of the move to Detroit may have played a more important role in burnishing Leonard's memories of that time. For one thing, his father was now home every evening, and this is when the "telling times" began. "My dad was dry, funny," Leonard recalls.[15] "When I was very young we had telling time. He would sit down and then I'd come in and sit next to him or on his lap or somewhere and I'd tell him what I did that day" (Rzepka, "Interviews 4"). Flora had started things off: "I can just see her saying, 'Why don't you go tell your dad what you've been doing all day?' And then I began to refer to it as telling time" ("Interviews 6"). Leonard cannot remember his father ever sharing information during telling time. It was a ritualized storytelling event, but unlike his sister's bedtime recitations, here the storyteller with the captive audience was Elmore himself. This was his opportunity to tell the story of a day in his life to the most important audience he would ever have, the man whose love and acceptance of the young protagonist of that story would prove crucial to letting the person "inside" him come out, eventually, as a man and a writer.

The senior Leonard had not been without artistic ambitions of his own. By the age of eleven he was painting accomplished landscapes (one, a scene on Lake Pontchartrain, hangs in Leonard's home in Bloomfield Village). Several years later, while he was still in high school, Elmore Sr.'s own father, William Leonard, died in a sugar mill accident, and he was forced to leave school to support his mother and siblings, abandoning any dreams of becoming a professional artist. To his son's best recollection, Mr. Leonard never expressed any frustration at giving up a promising artistic career, nor did he continue to paint or sketch, even as a hobby. The sacrifice of his artistic dreams to support his family was both absolute and a choice he took for granted, as did his son at a crucial point in his own life just before becoming a writer.

It was Flora who nursed creative ambitions. She wanted to write professionally, and it was she who read the books that interested Elmore Jr. She was also the disciplinarian of the family. When young Elmore's "easy going" father came home, "now he's home and everything is fine," Leonard recalls. "My mother always got into the day to day stuff." Counterbalancing that, "she was always kissing me," he says, and was "a terrific cook," a skill she learned while growing up in New Orleans (Rzepka, "Interviews 6"). Mrs. Leonard subscribed to *My Book House* for her children's benefit, and joined the Book of the Month Club and the Delphian Society, "which is what it sounds like," says Leonard. "Culture. [. . .] All these ladies sitting around, and they would discuss books, and art and different things" ("Interviews 6"). It was through his mother's subscription to the Book of the Month Club that Leonard, as a high school student, first encountered serious adult authors like Hemingway, as opposed to the adolescent adventure and mystery writers of his early teens, like Rafael Sabatini, Jules Verne, Arthur Conan Doyle, and John W. Duffield, whose "Don Sturdy" tales sent the teenage protagonist to exotic locales with his uncles. Despite her ambitions, Flora "didn't write enough," says Leonard, and "her stories were so old fashioned they had no chance." As her son became famous, her professional longings found an outlet in his career. She created "a little shrine in the living room" of her home in Little Rock for him, "with the books, just the books on display. Everything but the rope, the [velvet] covered rope area roped off" ("Interviews 4").

Leonard's amused dismissal of the Delphian Society and, by extension, the feminized, middle-brow "Culture" of literature and the arts that it and the Book of the Month Club epitomized,[16] may seem inconsistent with his own choice of a literary career, but it helps explain his preference for popular masculinized genres and his attitude toward writing in general as work or *techne* rather than as "art" or, worse, "hoopdedoodle" ("Easy"). It also helps explain the long delay in his decision to become a writer at twenty-five. A young boy with imaginative and verbal gifts would naturally be drawn to literary expression, particularly when exposed to so much of it from an early age. But being a boy, especially in Depression-era America, he would just as naturally flee from anything "girlish" or domestic as he approached puberty, seeking to assert his gender identity by embracing more conventionally male pursuits, such as sports, which he enjoyed in any case. In the Leonard household, writing and imaginative storytelling were the province of the women, of Elmore's older sister and his mother, the would-be writer, who was also the disciplinarian of the family. It was Flora, after all, who had urged her son to start "telling" his father about his day. While Leonard has remained an avid reader throughout his life, it apparently took him awhile to realize that writing could be as conventionally masculine a pursuit as baseball or football: in subject matter, in style, in work habits, in its breadwinning potential. Here, too, Hemingway—a "man's writer," both in life and on the page—was probably formative, and it is somewhat ironic that Leonard should have been introduced to the writings of "Papa," his literary stepfather, through his mother's Book of the Month Club subscription.

Flora was fortunate to live long enough to witness her son's success. Leonard's father was not so lucky. He died in 1948, three years before Leonard published his first story in *Argosy*, two years before he graduated from the University of Detroit, and just one year before his marriage to classmate Beverly Cline. Elmore Jr.'s first and most important audience of one never guessed his son would grow up to become a writer.

Leonard cannot remember any specific events or feelings that he shared with his father during "telling time." He does recall beginning to keep a diary about then. It was an idea he got from reading a book about a boy keeping a diary. In his own diary, he "would refer to how many boys got licked in school," but these were imaginary beatings, inspired by the beatings in the fictional diary kept by the fictional boy (Rzepka, "Interviews 6"). As with his gangster fantasies in Memphis, the violent classroom reveries he recorded contrasted starkly with the placidity of his real life, both in school and out. Three other things are noteworthy about this activity. First, soon after the move to Detroit, young Elmore is vicariously identifying with a boy trying to cope with the reality of adult violence, just as he had, at one remove, when he caught sight of a real gun on a train platform in Memphis. Second, he is doing this not just in his imagination but also by physically acting out the boy's method of coping with the violence he witnesses: he is writing about it in his own fictional diary, pretending to be a character *in* the story who just happens to be the writer *of* the story. Third, the setting of the fictional violence is a school.

At the same time that he began telling the day-to-day tale of his own adventures to his father and keeping his make-believe journal, Leonard was rapidly making permanent friends at his new school, Blessed Sacrament. A big part of his popularity derived from his ability to tell stories, particularly summaries of movies he had just seen. Two of his favorites, *Captain Blood* and *Lives of a Bengal Lancer,* were released in 1935, just a year after the Leonards' arrival in Detroit. "At an early age," writes David Geherin, "he was thus displaying the kind of cinematic imagination he would later put to such good use in his fiction" (2). It's just as significant that Leonard was displaying that imagination through vivid, compelling narration. It wasn't enough for the boy to see a film; he had to put it into words for an audience of his peers, using enough skill to keep them interested and asking for more. That same year Leonard entered the fifth grade, where one of the two most often reported events of his early life occurred: inspired by seeing the movie and then reading part of a serialization of the novel in the *Detroit Times,* he staged a battle scene in his classroom based on Erich Maria Remarque's *All Quiet on the Western Front.*

Most critics describing Leonard's development as an author fasten upon this event as a formative, if not exactly pivotal, moment, perhaps because there is so little else in his boyhood that would point to an early passion for writing. Geherin, author of the first book-length study of his work, calls it Leonard's "first writing experience" (2), and Paul Challen includes it in a paragraph on the boy's early "passion for books" (21).[17] Only James Devlin seems to have recognized how little this dramatic debut contributed to Leonard's development as a writer, prefacing his two sentences on the incident by stating, "Although he was a bookish and imaginative schoolboy, nothing in those days foretells a literary career" (5).

Nor would anything else in the next thirteen years. While he would remain a reader and storyteller, Leonard evinced almost no interest in writing, either as a pastime or as a profession, until halfway through college. He says that he was "always interested in writing even in grade school," but he admits that this amounted to little more than the pleasure he took in his spelling and writing assignments (Rzepka, "Interviews 8"). It's not as though he wasn't encouraged. At the Jesuit-run University of Detroit High School, one of his teachers, Father Skeffington, told him that he could have a future in writing, to judge from the papers he was handing in, and in his senior year, Leonard wrote his only composition to see the light of print before "Trail of the Apache" in 1951. But "Dickey" was more of a two-paragraph joke than a story. In it, an old couple leaving a gravesite mourn the passing of Dickey, who turns out to be a canary. It was published in the school literary magazine, *The Cub*, in January 1943, just a few months before Leonard graduated and joined the Navy. He wrote nothing more for the next six years.

While it's natural to look to his fifth-grade play, based as it was, in part, on Lewis Milestone's 1930 film, for signs of the mature Elmore Leonard's "cinematic imagination" or precocious ear for dialogue, the performance may have represented less a first step toward becoming a writer than the last step on the boy's journey toward transforming the lurid fantasy world inside his mind into something fully realized but, crucially, under his control outside it. The play began as a recurring daydream: "In grade school in Detroit I fantasized story situations looking out the classroom window," he told Lyczak in 1983, "the school besieged by some oppressive army, and it was up to me to slip out through their lines and bring help" (235).[18] What may have been the precipitating factor in his endeavoring to persuade his fifth-grade teacher, the grim Sister Estelle, into letting him transform her classroom into a battle zone was the prospect of getting his new friends to help him make real what he had only, to that point, daydreamed while staring out the window. The mini-drama he conceived, cast, and directed enlisted them to act out his heroic fantasies in a world that was outside of and yet malleable to the dictates of his imagination.

One of the most important themes in Remarque's bitter antiwar novel is the shattering of schoolboy fantasies of the glory of war in the face of its terrifying and tedious reality. Narrated by Paul Baumer, a young German recruit, the story follows the exploits, sufferings, and bitter disillusionment of a group of schoolmates encouraged by their schoolteacher to enlist for the glory of the Kaiser.[19] At the age of ten, Leonard was unlikely to have absorbed much of the book's antiwar message, but his play shows he responded strongly to Remarque's and Milestone's prominent theme of schoolboy participation and comradery in acts of war. The action involves a wounded soldier snagged on barbed wire in the middle of No Man's Land and coming under enemy fire, who is rescued by "the coward of the outfit," Leonard recalls. The coward "redeems himself by going out and bringing the hero back" (Lyczak 235). Zenon La Joie played the coward. "[E]verybody made fun of him," says Leonard. "He always had ink around his mouth. He was always doing something with ink. That was one reason why I chose him, because everybody made fun of him" (Rzepka, "Interviews 4"). Leonard's best friend, Gerard Boisineau, played Captain Hayes, and Jack Griffin, another good friend and athlete, was "the star," "the hero" ("Interviews 7").[20]

Leonard's terminology is suggestive. For a writer who professes indifference to, if not contempt for, "redemption" as a theme,[21] the concept still resonates in his memories of this classroom dramatization. Did the ten-year-old Leonard identify at all with Zenon La Joie? His tagging the rescued "star" Jack Griffin as "the hero" of the piece suggests not. Jack, with his talent at sports, would have embodied a typical fifth-grade boy's ego ideal of male prowess and courage. But Leonard's focusing the action of the play on the "redemption" of the "coward," his attributing agency to the misfit and casting for the part a boy ridiculed for his odd behavior, especially with ink, points us toward a different kind of empathy at work here. Did Zenon call to Leonard's mind, on some level, an oddity of his own? "It's interesting that Zenon was eating what you were writing with [. . .] and got ink on his mouth," I observed after hearing Leonard himself tell the story of his playwriting debut. "Yes, isn't it?" he replied, adding, "Well, it makes sense" ("Interviews 4").

Significantly, although he did say a few introductory words, young Elmore assigned himself no part in his classroom drama. As in the stories he regularly told his dad before dinner or his pals after an afternoon at the movies, as well as in his fictional diary-keeping, he was discovering a way to let the world inside him, shaped by boys' adventure tales and the daily newspapers and the movies, take the form of something he could *make happen* outside, either in the imaginations of his listeners or in his own real act of writing fictional diaries or in his friends' dictated performances, without himself having to participate in it—in effect, while remaining invisible. He had outgrown the need for imaginary friends like Boyee, as well as for acting out the violent fantasies inside him by pretending to be a gangster or a bank robber in a world full of real criminals—or a war hero or a redeemable scapegoat, for that matter. The self-expressive action he now preferred, whether in the form of telling, writing, or playwriting, was aimed at creating in the real world an accepted place for himself as the maker of pretend worlds that others could inhabit, whether imaginatively or in act, while he stood in the wings.

These developments all indicate that at the age of ten, Leonard had the instincts of a writer. He did not, however, possess the inclination. Instead of consolidating the desire to write, leading to a phase of intense juvenile composition, the staging of his play drew upon his budding authorial talents mainly as a way of forwarding his socialization with his male peers. For this was, if nothing else, a *team effort*, a coordinated group activity in which he could play a dominant role. To this extent, the scripted scene functioned as a point of transition between an earlier period of serial friendships that never quite coalesced before the time came for him to move on and a new era of playmates with whom he could expect to build long-lasting and intimate relationships,[22] a group of peers among whom he had a distinct identity: gregarious, imaginative, adventuresome, and in the realm of make-believe, a leader. Thus, instead of helping him to complete the transition into an adolescent phase of writing juvenilia—a solitary pursuit of technical mastery in the art of prose—the socialization of Elmore Jr.'s budding literary interests led him in the direction of a more routinized and conventionally masculine group activity: team sports. He continued to devour fiction, he never stopped loving to read, and he could still tell a good story, but the nascent writer in him went into hibernation. He would have to learn the lessons of *techne*—discovering what you're good at, getting to know your tools, reading up on your craft, practicing relentlessly, finding good models—in a venue other than writing and with the help of other mentors.

Becoming "Dutch": The Team Player

Leonard became interested in baseball as early as his Oklahoma City years (figure 1), but it wasn't until after he moved to Detroit as a youngster that he began to play the game regularly, encouraged by his new friends.[23] A close-knit group he remembers vividly to this day (figure 5), they played pick-up games in vacant lots, where Leonard improved his technique until, at thirteen, he was good enough to join his eighth-grade team in the Class D division of the Detroit Sandlot League.

There were plenty of other activities to fill up this period of his life. In addition to watching movies and playing "war" and "hot cooloo" up and down Woodward Avenue,[24] Leonard and his friends became more adventuresome as they grew older. A typical sixth-grade odyssey involved riding the Woodward Avenue streetcar to the riverfront, catching the ferry to Windsor, and stopping off on their way home for a free ginger ale at the Vernor's plant. As the conductor called out the streets, young Elmore recited them in unison (Rubin).[25] During the summer following seventh or eighth grade, Elmore and four of his friends—Maurice Murray, Gerard and Jackie Boisineau, and Phil Kozinski—hitchhiked up to the Thumb area of Michigan to earn spending money picking strawberries with the migrant workers around Bad Axe. Twenty years later, Leonard would vacation with his family at a coastal town nearby, which he was to choose as the setting for his first crime novel, *The Big Bounce.*

Among this close group of playmates, Maurice Murray stood out. "He was not a leader," recalls Leonard, but he had "a very confident way about him, and he was a year older than the rest of us. A year older at that time [. . .] it's significant" (Rzepka, "Interviews 1"). Maurice was also slightly bigger, and kind of quiet. One day, at the Boisineau brothers' apartment house, Elmore and his friends were sitting on the roof with their legs hanging over the eaves when Maurice turned to place his hands on the edge of the rain gutter and swung himself off, dangling three stories above the alleyway below. Before the boys could react, Maurice pulled himself up and back onto the roof. This stunt was to resurface in Leonard's memory at a crucial moment in his development as a writer.

After leaving Blessed Sacrament and his eighth-grade Class D team, Leonard played baseball as a freshman at Catholic Central High School, which made it to the city championship on the strength of its pitching. On transferring to University of Detroit High School the following year, Leonard continued to play baseball and added football as a junior, first at center and then quarterback. It was sports, not writing, that inspired the second most often reported event of Leonard's childhood—his being nicknamed.

Leaving for high school meant leaving most of his grade school friends behind and making new ones. In his first year at U of D High, he received the nickname "Dutch" from a classmate, who said he needed one. "And boy, he was right," says Leonard, "because I did. 'Elmore' was a lot to handle back then" (Challen 2). His classmate had in mind another baseball player named Leonard, Emil "Dutch" Leonard, a knuckleball pitcher who just the year before, in 1939, had made the sixth-place Senators above-the-fold news by pitching twenty wins and eight losses. George Will observes some interesting similarities between knuckleball pitching and Leonard's writing style (quoted in Challen 22–23), but perhaps the first thing to note regarding Elmore Jr.'s nickname is that he received it upon entering a new high school. The switch from Catholic Central was motivated by the Leonard family's move to a better neighborhood of Detroit, within a block of U of D High (figure 6). Once again, forces beyond his control had placed Leonard in an unfamiliar social environment.

In *Killshot,* Armand "The Blackbird" Degas becomes infatuated with the new name his younger partner, Richie Nix, has conferred on him, seeing in it an overt sign of the self-transformation he's longed for since childhood: "The Bird. New name for the beginning of a new time in his life" (49). Names and naming are a recurrent theme in Leonard's novels, always in connection with a sense of new identities, new beginnings, new possibilities of self-expression or understanding, and the extinction of past selves. They are sometimes, as in Armand's case, false signs of the fresh start his characters desire, but Elmore Jr. embraced his new baseball moniker without hesitation, even calling himself "Dutch Leonard" in the story he wrote for *The Cub*. Later, in the Navy, he had the name tattooed on his arm, and he continues to use it with close friends at the age of eighty-six. All of which indicates that it might be worth lingering a bit over the role of sports in shaping this author's life and work.

Baseball and its history are recurring topics in Leonard's books. Baseball bats, like the one Elliot uses to intimidate Chili in *Be Cool*, are regularly featured as deadly weapons (Elliot and Raji even debate the head-bashing virtues of wood versus aluminum), and where no bat is handy, a substitute will do: "Foley [. . .] liked the way this piece of scrap wood was split and tapered to a thin end, like a baseball bat" (*Out of Sight* 15). Failed pros like Jack Ryan and ex-pros like "Chickasaw" Charlie Hoke in *Tishomingo Blues* (2002) become colorful, sometimes central characters in Leonard's fiction. Discussions of hall-of-famers regularly surface, along with their stats, and even porpoises play baseball (*Gold Coast* [1980]). You get the impression that Leonard is gently sending up America's love of its national pastime in these scenes, but also that baseball is an important principle of unity, tying together characters and events throughout his career and giving them a certain thematic coherence. What they all have in common is their creator's lifelong appreciation of the game as *techne*: its finer points, its complex but seamless expression of skill, talent, and self-possession, its adaptability, and the opportunities it offers for "being cool."

"Dutch" Leonard was good at baseball, and he was particularly good at first base. For one thing, he was ambidextrous, writing with his right hand but throwing with his left. Wearing his glove on his right hand facilitated throwing a fielded ball to other infielders and catching throws to pick off runners at first. Moreover, he was curious by nature and enjoyed learning new things. Coaching helped him master the skills he needed, but he also, characteristically, read a book to improve his footwork and even customized his equipment, taking the stuffing out of his glove and replacing it with mattress padding "so there wasn't a bulge around a pocket" (Rzepka, "Interviews 8"). Team sports like baseball and, later, football boosted Leonard's confidence and sense of belonging, providing a crucial bridge to his socialization as an adult. An only son and youngest child in a family quite small by Catholic standards, he now had a band of brothers united in a common cause, along with two surrogate fathers. His football coach, Bob Tiernan, played an especially important role in this respect.

In the summer following Leonard's junior year, Tiernan invited him and four other boys to spend a month at his cabin on Flathead Lake in Montana. He had done this on previous occasions with other members of the football team, to help build solidarity. Tiernan was trying to persuade Leonard to switch from center to quarterback and the trip apparently helped, since the young man accepted that leadership role for his senior season. During the same academic year, Tiernan took Leonard into his home while the boy's parents were living in Washington, DC. (Margaret, six years older, had already graduated from college and was living on her own.)

Elmore Sr. had been called to Washington, along with several other GM executives, to help coordinate the retooling of the nation's auto industries for the war effort. Leaving his namesake in the care of Tiernan solved three problems at once: "Dutch" could graduate with his class, his coach could keep the quarterback he had trained to lead his team, and the Leonards didn't have to vet a new school for their son in an unfamiliar city. Tiernan had two children of his own, a boy and an older girl, just like the Leonards, and young Elmore roomed with the son, who was much younger than he. The two "got along fine" (Rzepka, "Interviews 8"). Unlike Mr. Leonard, with his dry humor and easygoing sociability, however, Bob Tiernan "didn't talk much" and was "kind of gruff," recalls Leonard. "He was what I thought of as a typical coach. He didn't say many funny things. He was pretty much all business" ("Interviews 8"). Nevertheless, the two seemed to get along well enough to make the arrangement worthwhile.

Today, Leonard expresses no particular affection for Tiernan, or for his baseball coach either, but as we shall see, their "all business" approach to the *techne* of sport seems to have inspired an early and continuing fascination with "coaching" or, more broadly, mentoring relationships among his male characters. The late Western *Forty Lashes Less One* (1972) even seems to parody high school sports fiction in the efforts of the naive warden of Yuma prison, "Mr. Manly," to instill racial pride in two inmates of color by subjecting them to a rigorous training regimen of long-distance running and javelin throwing—with comically unintended consequences. In whatever way Leonard chose to represent them in his adult fiction, baseball and then football created, for the young "Dutch" just entering a new school environment, an extended family of male siblings with a literal, live-in father substitute in his football coach. Baseball, in particular, provided him with a nickname and a nominal sports genealogy for his new identity.

Several features of that new identity are worth noting here. First, it was based on a physical skill. Second, this skill came naturally, in part as a talent for coordinated movement, speed, and accuracy (although not visual acuity—Leonard soon discovered he needed glasses), and in the form of a physical anomaly, his ambidexterity, which fitted him well for a particular role on the team. Third, he learned that with focused effort and attention to detail, he could improve and perfect the skill that had come to define his new identity among his classmates, making it, in effect, a habituated, unselfconscious second nature. He could improve *techne* corporeally, in his footwork, his throwing, and his stance, as well as instrumentally, by physically altering his equipment, and intellectually, as he read up on technique and eventually mastered the rules of the game. All of these features—the possession of natural talent, the acquisition of information (including all the arcane statistical details that baseball fanatics cherish), training, and the perfection of skill or know-how through practice—would prove important not only to Leonard's later exploration and elaboration of the idea of "being cool," which represents the outcome of this process, but also to the work of writing itself.

Leonard graduated from U of D High in 1943 having written nothing aside from school assignments since his fifth-grade play, except for a two-paragraph joke published in the school's literary magazine. There is no evidence to suggest he found his voice while serving in the Navy for the next three years, where he helped maintain an airstrip, distributed beer, took out the garbage, lost his virginity, learned to drink hard, and experienced enemy fire once (figure 7). Nor did he take up the pen during his first two years stateside, after he matriculated at the University of Detroit in 1946. He did, however, read lots of books. "I wasn't writing because I was reading," Leonard says of those years, "and I was reading very closely—and deciding most people use way, way too many words" (Challen 27).

That Leonard was reading closely should come as no surprise: he was an English major, after all. But he was also a philosophy minor, and French existentialism—its focus and relevance sharpened by the Resistance—was in the air, literally. Jean-Paul Sartre had landed in New York in January 1945, just after the liberation of Paris, and had begun to preach his anti-gospel of the "Death of God" to the postwar American intelligentsia. Within a few years, his face would appear on the cover of *Life* magazine, which popularized his message for distribution to middle-class readers across America. His bleak, postwar vision of a world full of death camps facing atomic annihilation, a place where "existence precedes essence" and only the individual's absolute freedom to act makes life meaningful, or even bearable, began to find a place on the University of Detroit's course syllabi, in the company of Plato and Aristotle (Rzepka, "Interviews 2").[26]

Today, Leonard professes not to have understood existentialism completely but agrees that his heroes, like Hemingway's Robert Jordan, embody its central view of the world so fundamentally that neither they, nor he, have to think twice about it. He endorses the idea that existence precedes essence, that rather than adhering to a metaphysical doctrine or belief system and then conforming their behavior to the rules of that system, his protagonists tend to look at how they behave, how they exist in the world, and discover what they believe in how they act ("Interviews 2"). Often, the hero may be expected to conform to some principle embraced by a peer group or family or society or religion "outside" him that conflicts with the real person "inside." Typically, this separation between inside and outside, something Leonard felt from early childhood, can be overcome, and the two halves of the person can be fully integrated and made whole, in the self-immersive authenticity of "being cool."

As a philosophy minor in college, Leonard read classical as well as modern philosophers. While he was most attracted to Socrates for his noble suicide in the cause of truth and justice (a Christ-like sacrifice), not to mention his ironic dialectical ripostes (answering a question with another question, just like the Jesuits), he found Aristotle "to be the hero of the bunch, smarter than the rest" ("Interviews 5"). Leonard remembers little or nothing of Aristotle now—"I possibly did back in the late '40s" ("Interviews 1"), he says, when he started writing—but it's difficult to believe that an undergraduate philosophy minor at a Catholic university would not have been exposed, either directly or through osmosis, to the *Nicomachean Ethics,* which had a major influence on Thomas Aquinas, the intellectual progenitor of Catholic theology.[27] Given the spottiness of the author's memories of college at this distance in time, any direct influence Aristotle may have had on Elmore Leonard's writing career is a matter of speculation. Nevertheless, as I suggested earlier, some of the Stagirite's basic ideas can help fine-tune our understanding of Leonardian "cool."

One of the most important things Aristotle does in the *Nicomachean Ethics* is rank human activities according to whether the outcomes at which they aim are proximate or distant. "Now," he begins, "as there are many actions, arts, and sciences, their ends also are many."

> But where such arts fall under a single capacity—as bridle-making and the other arts concerned with the equipment of horses fall under the art of riding, and this and every military action under strategy, in the same way other arts fall under yet others—in all of these the ends of the master arts are to be preferred to all the subordinate ends; for it is for the sake of the former that the latter are pursued. (935)

As we have seen, the ultimate end, or *telos*, of all human activities, for Aristotle, is *eudaemonia*, or "happiness," often translated as "the good," and the ultimate good is political, which in his place and time can be understood to mean service to the *polis*, or state, and in ours, public service. For Aquinas, the equivalent "ultimate" would be salvation, attainable only in the afterlife through service to God in this life. *Techne*, or skill, is "know how," craft knowledge expressed in work whose immediate end, "making" (*poeisis*)—for example, making a product such as a vase or a shoe or a poem (a word derived from *poeisis*)—is far removed from these final ends. For this reason Aristotle considers *techne* inferior to *episteme*, or "scientific knowledge," and *arete*, or "virtue," whose ends are nearer to "the good." The example of *techne* that Aristotle gives—bridle-making—is clearly thought by him to be "subordinate" to the military art of riding that it supports, and this, in turn, to that of military strategy, a "master art" that is, by extrapolation, closer but still subordinate to the ultimate good: service to the state.

Leonard's instinctual understanding of *techne* is broader than that of Aristotle or his theological descendent Thomas Aquinas, since it includes immaterial results as well as material products: "making" the frontier safe, for instance, or "making" someone "disappear." For Leonard, the point of *techne* is to change the real world, to make something happen according to a set of (relatively simple) rules rather than abstract principles. Behavior according to principles is what Aristotle calls *praxis*, and conforming behavior to principles, which are often proposed by others, demands the continuous application of self-conscious reason and reflection. This is why Aquinas, like Aristotle, generally valued *praxis* above *techne*, because only acts that are self-conscious and based on deliberate judgment, or *phronesis*, can be virtuous.[28] Leonard, as we have seen, prefers *techne* to *praxis*, and especially *techne* perfected to the point of "being cool," a state of grace, similar to Csikszentmihalyi's "flow," uniting soul and body in a secular incarnation that diminishes or erases the impediments to harmonious action imposed by self-consciousness. In contrast, the self-conscious deliberation of *praxis* can lead to hesitation, shame, and the disintegration of identity—a Fall from unreflective innocence. Leonard's fiction—itself a form of literary *poeisis*—stages a recurrent struggle to maintain the balanced authenticity of *techne* in the face of two competing types of self-dispossession: on the one hand, phony role-playing that is either compelled by insecurity and need or deliberately chosen to conform to principle, and on the other, a loss of self-control through unreflective panic, rage, or reckless pride. This struggle is often intensified by threats of violence or dishonor. The temptation to play a false role or give in to impulse may add a moral dimension to Leonard's dramas of self-reintegration, but morality is rarely their focus of attention.

Outside the college classroom, the young Navy vet resumed socializing where he had left off in high school, taking his dates to jazz clubs, both black and "black and tan." In fact, his first surviving short story, the unpublished "One Horizontal," opens in one such club, a "joint on Beaubien" that is "semi-Black and Tan, more black than tan" (3). "My date was always reluctant," Leonard recalls, but "that's where the jazz was" (Rzepka, "Interviews 9"). In high school he and his friends would frequent segregated big band venues like Eastwood Gardens and the Paradise Theater to hear Count Basie (his favorite then as now), Earl "Fatha" Hines, Jimmie Lunceford, and Andy Kirk and his "Twelve Clouds of Joy." On his arrival in San Francisco from the Pacific in January 1946, Leonard says, "I headed straight for Oakland, where Stan Kenton was playing that night" (Roberts). Now, in addition to mainstreamers like Wild Bill Davison, a brash, hard-drinking cornet player (Rzepka, "Interviews 5"), he was drawn to new, virtuosic be-boppers like Dizzy Gillespie and the intellectual enigmas of melody and rhythm they posed. ("The hat check girl said it was 'Honeysuckle Rose,'" Leonard's protagonist tells us in "One Horizontal." "Quite a surprise" [4–5].) Eventually, the Modern Jazz Quartet, Dave Brubeck, and Ahmad Jamal would number among his favorite performers.

Leonard's attraction to African American bars and clubs, despite the pronounced aversion of his dates to late-night activities in black neighborhoods, reveals his early interest not only in the jazz idiom but also in minority or "outsider" culture. He enrolled at the University of Detroit little more than three years after the outbreak of the Detroit race riots in June 1943, the same month he had graduated from high school. Thirty-six people were killed, twenty-five of them black, and more than eighteen hundred, white and black, were arrested. Federal troops had to be called in to halt the violence. The racial Maginot Line of the disturbances was the long, sprawling playground of Leonard's youth, Woodward Avenue (Baulch and Zacharias). By the time he returned from the Pacific in 1946, tensions had begun to ease: rationing was over and postwar prosperity was on the rise. But the mutual suspicion between working-class, ethnic whites and the newly arrived southern blacks standing next to them on the assembly line had not abated. A white college kid hanging out at "colored" jazz clubs in Detroit in 1948 would seem to be making something of a statement—of defiance or manhood or solidarity, or all three. Whatever that statement said to the persons of color around him, it was also addressed to the young woman gripping his arm, and may even have conveyed something to himself about the kind of man he wanted to be.

It is worth considering whether Leonard's love of jazz as model or inspiration for his own compositional technique doesn't derive surplus energy from an instinctual understanding of its distanced critique of the dominant culture. Nothing was more "cool" than the postwar jazz revolution—the edgy, involuted challenges of bebop followed by the laid-back *ennui* of West Coast jazz. At the time Leonard began to graduate from the "trad" or "mainstream" big band performances of his high school years to the more intimate, esoteric, and extended improvisations of small-group soloists in what had to be, for a white boy from Northlawn, some pretty exotic club venues, the "birth of the cool" as a national, cross-racial idiom of nonconformism was already under way.

I take this phrase from the famous album *Birth of the Cool*, issued by Blue Note in 1959, a 33-rpm anthology of 78-rpm tunes recorded by black trumpeter Miles Davis and his nine-piece band from 1948 to 1949. A major inspiration for West Coast jazz—or, as its detractors called it, "cocktail jazz" or "wallpaper" (Marcus 18)—these early, minimalist recordings represented, according to Greil Marcus, the beginning of Davis's accommodations with white jazz culture and with white musicians like sax player Gerry Mulligan and arrangers like Gil Evans. This was not, says Marcus, necessarily a bad thing. "Cool" had emerged in black culture as a modernized version of the studied detachment and self-control adopted by the disempowered slave protecting his dignity as a man—while preserving his life—against white male violence and insult. The new, cooler jazz offered its performers, black and white, a similar opportunity within the dominant white culture to "take one step back" and interrogate it (Marcus 20),[29] much as Leonard's version of "being cool" has come to offer his predominantly white, male audience an interrogative, and ironic, perspective on their own culture's fundamental conformism.[30]

Whatever the case may be, Elmore Leonard was there at the inception, an habitué of the barroom incubators where "cool" emerged as cultural shorthand for "the ultimate revenge of the powerless" African American male (MacAdams

20), expressed in music that was historically black and beginning its spread, like a viral meme, along the disaffected white margins of Eisenhower-era complacency. Perhaps not surprisingly, the coolest boppers were drawn to the bleak worldview of the newly popularized Sartrean philosophy, expressing their solidarity in such fashion accessories as the berets, horn-rimmed glasses, and goatees of Gillespie and Thelonious Monk. These, says Lewis MacAdams, were the boppers' way of indicating the "merger of two potent stances—bebop and existentialism," the art and the theory, respectively, of postwar alienation (24).

While he was cutting his philosophical teeth on existentialism and Aristotle and hanging out in black jazz clubs, Leonard also began to establish a close relationship to his father, of whom he had seen little since his parents left for Washington at the beginning of his senior year of high school.[31] There had been talk, during that year, of his eventually attending Georgetown to study diplomacy, but once his parents were back in Detroit, his old high school campus had seemed more attractive. James Devlin suggests that the University of Detroit's more modern facilities may have made the difference (5), but the school's proximity to Leonard's father, if not decisive, was probably a consideration. On weekends, the Leonard men, Sr. and Jr., would golf together and have a few beers on the nineteenth hole or at a nearby bar, and "it was fun," recalls the author (Rzepka, "Interviews 4").

Around this time, Elmore Sr. began to focus his energies on acquiring a GM dealership in Las Cruces, New Mexico, a venture in which his son was to join him upon graduating from college in 1950. Returning veterans with young families were increasing consumer demand for new automobiles amidst a stunning rebound from wartime austerity. Mr. Leonard wouldn't be able to make a go of it alone (Challen 26), but with his son's help he might.[32] Mr. Leonard managed to acquire about a third of his dream in 1948, owing GM's financing operation, Motors Holding, for the remainder of the dealership's purchase price. With his son working beside him he expected to pay off the loan without much trouble. That same year, six months later, he died of a heart attack. He was fifty-six.

After negotiating with GM's loan officers, who denied him permission to take over the debt, Elmore Leonard, Jr., realized he would have to make a living in some way other than the one marked out for him by Elmore Leonard, Sr. He had tried to do the right thing, as his father had done when his own father died: put family first. He had agreed to join the dealership to please his dad and, after his father's death, to please his brother-in-law, who wanted to join him in the enterprise. And it was a step that would have benefited his future family as well. Leonard was set on marrying at this point and did so the next year, in 1949.

Now he would have to chart a different career course. It turned out to be a job in advertising with Campbell Ewald of Detroit, at an initial salary of $135 a month.[33] "I was their only married office boy," says Leonard (Challen 28).

It was at about the time of his father's death that Leonard, then a junior at the University of Detroit, wrote his first real short story. His English teacher, Mr. Gruwe, bribed him into entering a competition sponsored by the college writing club, The Manuscribblers, by promising him a B for the course if he did so. Leonard entered that year, when he placed in the top ten, and the next, taking second place (Rzepka, "Interviews 7"; Lyczak 235). Neither of his entries survives, but together they mark an important turning point in their author's life: trying it on what amounted to a bet, Leonard learned that he not only had a talent for writing but also enjoyed it.

Soon, he began to enter writing contests. The judge for one of these, a Detroit literary agent, invited him to join a writer's group, for which he composed the first-person crime narrative "One Horizontal" (later retitled "A Seven Letter Word for Corpse"), in the style of the hard-boiled pulp authors he was reading at the time, writers like Fredric Brown, James M. Cain, Erle Stanley Gardner, and Mickey Spillane (Geherin 4; Devlin 7). While he was not to return to crime writing for nearly two decades, Leonard made a calculated decision to try his hand at Westerns while keeping his day job at Campbell Ewald. In 1951, with the sale of "Trail of the Apache," he became a part-time professional writer.

Paul Challen considers the GM dealership in New Mexico "a close call that could have changed [Leonard's] life forever" (26) and denied the world a major author of crime fiction. It's an open question as to whether or not Leonard would eventually have become a writer if his father hadn't died.[34] Perhaps the Western scenery around Las Cruces would have inspired him, but when would he have found the time to write? In a family business, one's time is never really one's own, and with a huge loan to pay off and his parents' as well as his own family's financial health at stake, the demands on the young man's energy and attention would have been severe. There would be no getting away from selling cars.

That said, why Westerns? "One Horizontal" indicates that Leonard's first choice, ultimately vindicated by his later career move, had been modern crime fiction. He had already apprenticed himself to the likes of Gardner, Spillane, and Cain. Moreover, he had never been a fan of sagebrush sagas. "When I think of the nineteenth century, it has no appeal to me," he says. "I hadn't even read many westerns" (Grobel 255). However, Western movies had shaped his imagination since childhood, providing him with some basic templates and archetypes, and there were more pragmatic considerations. Western fiction sold well, so there was a real possibility of making enough money from it to achieve some financial independence from his advertising job, in time. And the demands of the Western looked pretty straightforward. The settings, the character types, their motivations, and the standard plots all seemed reducible to a few basic rules—it was a genre, in other words, with a highly specialized but simple *techne*. At the same time the rules were malleable, allowing for some creativity. In fact, their relative simplicity provided a zone of safety in which a greenhorn writer could experiment while minimizing the danger of shooting himself in his tender foot. Perhaps the deciding factor was that the competition wasn't very stiff. "When I picked up Zane Grey I couldn't believe it was so bad," says Leonard (Grobel 225). In all, as biographer David Geherin puts it, the Western "seemed a good place to learn" (4).

As we shall see, it was also a good place to work out some knotty problems regarding Leonard's relationship to the father whose long-ago decision to reject an artistic career Elmore Jr. would go on to remedy as a writer, applying the lessons in mastery and self-discipline he had learned from his paternal surrogates on the athletic field.

TWO

being other(s)

"making" imaginary friends

Up Looking Down: The Western Stories

The most prominent features of Leonard's Westerns reflect the patterns of relationship that shaped his childhood, adolescence, and young manhood. In summarizing that process, we might begin with an imaginative and sociable boy, responsive to the nuances of the human voice and the vicarious thrill of adventure books, Western films, and news accounts of legendary gangsters. This boy grew up in a loving household with a literarily ambitious mother and an older sister who read to him, but with a father indifferent to reading who was often absent for days or weeks at a time. He also faced the repeated task of constructing new circles of friends as his family moved from place to place. These patterns of relationship, both inside and outside the home, continued until the age of eight, when he, his sister, and his parents settled in Detroit and his father landed a nine-to-five job. The boy's natural storytelling abilities, modeled by his sister and informed by his mother's love of literature, then began to find an active outlet in "telling times" with his heretofore absent father as a captive auditor, in fictional "diaries," and in oral synopses of adventure films for his new, permanent circle of friends. This burst of narrative activity culminated in a staged reenactment of adult war fiction, enlisting his new companions as audience and participants. They recognized and appreciated his gifts, but as typical adolescent American males they valued other talents more, and the storyteller, the nascent writer in Elmore Jr. went dormant.

In most theories of child development in patriarchal societies, the father plays the dominant role in helping his children make the transition from understanding their place in the family to finding their place in the world outside, often with the help of adult surrogates who, if not always loved and admired, at least provide models to emulate or reject.[1] In this respect, Mr. Leonard's passive encouragement of his son's storytelling gifts, simply through patient and attentive listening, must have been formative, if short-lived. The crucial period of transition, however, is puberty and adolescence, and this is where one's choice of friends can make all the difference. No matter how loving and affirming one's family may be, at some point a child has to begin trying out an adult sense of himself in a place where parents cannot offer guidance or impose restrictions regarding the person he imagines growing up to be. To the extent that one's childhood friends create a safe space outside the family in which to embody that embryonic, imaginary adult, they provide an important arena for the child's construction and testing of possible roles that can achieve validation from others, including nonparental adults, and ultimately serve as blueprints for a mature sense of identity, of being-in-the-world.

While they may not have actively discouraged his writing talents, Leonard's friends at Blessed Sacrament and Catholic Central provided little room for them to grow, and the boy's natural gregariousness and skill at sports, coupled with a growing but vague awareness that writing was for females, led him in the direction of least resistance. As for his parents, neither seems to have encouraged the boy to write. They simply provided an admiring audience for his performances, whether with words or with a baseball glove. It wasn't until he was halfway through college that Leonard found himself in a position to live up to parental expectations regarding a career, since this was the first time in his life that either parent had expressed a preference for one. Not having decided on any particular course, he had nothing to lose by joining his dad in Las Cruces, and something to gain: here was an opportunity to reestablish an intimacy eroded by the paternal absences of early childhood and by separation from his parents during his senior year of high school. When Mr. Leonard died, however, it was as though a spell had broken, as if the grown-up writer frozen inside the obedient child had thawed and come to life. A year after graduating from college, Elmore Leonard, Jr., was a published author. He never looked back.

Among several recurrent features of Leonard's Western stories and novels, one in particular seems to reflect a surprising degree of self-assurance for a beginning writer, suggesting that, regardless of their specific contributions to his ultimate choice of career, Leonard's parents had at least instilled in him the confidence to pursue whatever path in life he chose. It's a feature that seems to reflect his approach to the writing process at this time. In at least a third of the short stories, as well as in *Last Stand at Saber River* (1959), Leonard opens with a point of view anchored in a character surveying the scene below him. In *Last Stand*, for instance, Paul Cable uses field glasses to examine, at a distance, the general store whose appearance means he's almost home. He also sees, for the first time, the man who will become his nemesis, Edward Janroe. The pair of eyes through which we envision Leonard's opening scenes need not belong to his protagonist, however, and can even be anonymous. "Red Hell Hits Canyon Diablo" (October 1952), written before "Trail of the Apache" but published later, begins in third-person, storyteller mode—"They called it Canyon Diablo"—but immediately places us next to a solitary Apache lookout, sighting down the barrel of his "fifty caliber buffalo rifle" at the "*blanco* horse soldiers" below (67).

It's easy to see the resemblances between this recurrent opening shot and the introductory scenes of countless movie Westerns, from *Stagecoach* to *Shane*, where credits fade in and out over cavalry, Conestoga wagons, or a lone plainsman riding across panoramas of butte, mesa, and sagebrush. But these cinematic surveys are impersonal; they "belong" to no one in particular, while Leonard takes care to lodge his opening perspectives in the consciousness of a single character. They take on added importance in the light of a recurring dream that also involved being up and looking down, which began when he "was starting out writing."

> I was always falling down these stairs. And they were steep and narrow and I'd fall down and you wait for yourself to hit the bottom and that never came. But it was that tightening up on the way down. Then I started to sell and I never had the dream again. (Rzepka, "Interviews 5")

This dream is reprised in *Djibouti*, when Leonard's highly successful female protagonist, documentary cinematographer Dara Barr, recalls "the stairway she would fall down in dreams until she'd won her first award" (277). In Dara's case as in Leonard's, the nightmares stop when success is achieved.

Aside from the film that she's making (also named *Djibouti*), we learn few details about Dara's *oeuvre*. We know a lot about Elmore Leonard's. In nearly every crime novel he wrote, a character falls to his or her death, or is threatened with death by falling, or imagines it, or is otherwise precariously hanging in space. Being-up-looking-down represents a threat, usually a fatal threat, whenever it appears in work from the second half of Leonard's career, and we'll be considering possible reasons why in a moment. But in the Westerns, whose very appearance in print confirmed his ability to "sell," being-up-looking-down is already a position of control, command, and foresight. To the extent that Leonard seems to be inhabiting the mind of the focused, reflective character he places in that opening position, it would also seem to represent his approach to writing when he first began, with everything carefully surveyed, planned, and plotted out beforehand. "In doing the westerns you had to think of an idea, a plot," Leonard says, in sharp contrast to his current freewheeling style, where he begins with a scene, a character, or even the sound of a voice, and then waits to "see what happens" (Lyczak 236).

Leonard's deliberate approach to writing in his early career was reflected in both his dogged historical research and his demanding writing schedule. Of those regimented, predawn hours devoted to writing before he left for work, Leonard recalls, "I made a rule that I had to get something down on paper before I could put the water on for the coffee. *Know where you're going and then put the water on.* That seemed to work because I did it for most of the fifties" (Sutter, "Conversation" xii). "Know where you're going": to the extent that improvisation entered at all into Leonard's writing during his first decade, it must have taken the shape of inspired planning rather than execution. Approaching the work of writing deliberately and carefully, with self-imposed rules and physical tools like his gray-green notebook full of facts and figures, he would reach a vantage point where he could get the lay of the land before taking aim at it with his ballpoint pen. His grasp of the *techne* of writing was, at this point, studied and premeditated.

Leonard's general preoccupation with *techne* is evident in his first two unpublished attempts at Westerns, "Charlie Martz" and "Siesta in Paloverde," the second a revision of the first. In each, the plot turns on the workmanship of a German gunsmith. In "Charlie Martz," Adolph Schmidt is voluble on the topic of his craft: "Most of my life I worked as a gunsmith . . . in the east . . . now I have a few cattle. [. . .] But my first love is still guns. It is a pleasant pastime, and I take great pleasure in my work. Just ask anyone if my work is not the best" (35). Leonard's own love of guns as a boy shines through Schmidt's words, as does his admiration of technical prowess in general. In "Siesta in Paloverde," that boyishness resurfaces in Sheriff Charlie Martz's appreciation of the new "external ornamentation" on his "old iron" (51), the handiwork of gunsmith Count Rudolph von Bock: "Charlie was a little boy with a new toy. He wasn't very subtle about it either" (52).

The problem with these early efforts has only partly to do with Leonard's general lack of familiarity with the historical facts of life out west, which makes the time he spends on the finicky details of gunsmithing look studied and disproportionate. It's more that he makes the plot of both stories hinge on accidents external to the actions of the hero, beginning with the *techne* of the gunsmith, who hasn't finished his repairs on the sheriff's firearm before the villain walks through the door, looking for revenge on the lawman who put him away. The gun looks great but can't yet fire. In each story, moreover, it's the villain who decides to switch guns with the protagonist, unaware that the beguiling workmanship on the outside of his weapon of choice belies its inutility.

In "Charlie Martz," the eponymous protagonist wins the conventional shootout, since he has the gun that works. In "Siesta in Paloverde," Leonard seems to have realized that this wouldn't do: the hero would never kill a man he knows to be unarmed. Instead, in a moment of inspired—and humorous—improvisation, Charlie whacks Reb Spadea upside the head with the working gun and knocks him senseless. Leonard has learned that the creative agency driving his plot should always be vested in the hero, not his antagonist. In both stories, however, an accident of *techne* anchors the plot and provides the essential condition of its possibility: no one's choices can matter to the story unless the gunsmith has been halted in the middle of his job. An interruption in the care and attentiveness of authentic workmanship is, quite literally and ironically, what makes Leonard's workmanship possible in these two practice pieces at the very beginning of his career.

Despite his limited time and methodical approach, Leonard was astonishingly prolific out of the gate, especially for someone holding down a forty-hour-a-week day job. Of the two-and-a-half dozen Western short stories he wrote during his career, more than half appeared in his first twenty-two months of writing, from December 1951 to October 1953, and all but three were in print by 1956. The dominant features, themes, and character relationships in the stories from these first five years reveal an almost obsessive concern with questions of identity and coming of age, and with the authenticity and self-integration of technical mastery. They are filled with scenes of apprenticeship, mentoring, and testing, and explore early versions of "being cool" as a way of defending against self-dispossession by anger or panic. Leonard was determined to be a writer, but he was also clearly working something out. Was it how to please his dead father, whose plans for him he had eluded by sheer happenstance? If so, his solution was fundamentally redemptive, drawing on the lessons in *techne* he had learned from his paternal surrogates on the athletic field in order to perfect the kind of creative skills that Leonard Sr. had been forced to set aside when his own father died. Moreover, he was doing so in the specific form that Flora Rivé Leonard had tried all her life to master, without success—which is to say, in the work of writing. To achieve his own mastery, however, Leonard turned to literary fathers like Hemingway and Bissell.

The most telling evidence for his father's ghostly role in overseeing the first few years of Leonard's career is that by far the most important relationship shaping his early stories is that between mentors and apprentices, where an experienced and skilled tracker, scout, Indian agent, hunter, soldier, or even outlaw will show the neophyte "how it's done." In "Trail of the Apache," Indian agent Eric Travisin takes West Point cadet William de Both in hand and teaches him the fundamentals of tracking and fighting renegade Apaches. De Both is aware of Travisin's reputation and wants to "serve under the best" (4), but the older man's informality confuses him. "To Travisin it wasn't a new story. He'd had younger officers serve under him before, and it always started the same way, [. . .] the old campaigner teaching the recruit what it was all about" (6). Travisin, in turn, learned his craft from a more experienced scout, Barney Fry, and this pattern is repeated in Leonard's first novel, *The Bounty Hunters* (1953), where his hero, Dave Flynn, trains R. D. Bowers—like de Both, a West Point cadet—after having been taught by Joe Madora, who is a generation older than Flynn. In "Red Hell Hits Canyon Diablo," Matt Cline, a civilian scout wearing a sweat-stained union suit and chewing a wad of tobacco, has to tread lightly as he schools the new lieutenant, Gordon Towner, in the ways of the Chiricahua Apache. Towner is "willing to learn but wishing he could have picked his own instructor" (70), especially when Cline corrects him in front of his men.

Scout Simon Street and Lieutenant Phil Langmade in "The Colonel's Lady"; Sheriff John Danaher and his deputy, Kirby Frye, in *The Law at Randado* (1954); Sheriff John Benedict and his deputy, Jimmy Robles, in "The Hard Way"; Marshal Ed Bohannon and Lyall Quinlan in "Saint with a Six-Gun"; hardened outlaw Frank Usher and his young sidekick, Chink, in "The Captives"; ex-con Ed Moak and his "son" Albie in "The Longest Day of His Life"—all repeat the mentor-mentee pattern. Similar relationships appear in "The Big Hunt" between the boy Will Gordon and buffalo hunter Will Cleary, who raised the child after his father was killed, and between reckless young Jack Ryan (Leonard liked the name so much he used it again in his crime fiction) and his older brother, Emmett, in "The Rustlers."

The earliest stories of the mentor-mentee type convey what's at stake in these situations. After proving himself under fire in "Trail of the Apache" and suffering a knife wound to the back, de Both feels "nothing. No hate. No pity," as he returns with his men, just "indifference, and he moved his stained hat to a cockier angle. [. . .] He knew he was a man" (34). Under Eric Travisin's tutelage, the green West Pointer from Boston has learned to subordinate his emotions—including his naive racial prejudices and foolish thirst for glory—to the business at hand: chasing down renegade Apaches and bringing them back to the reservation, preferably alive. The stereotype of the strong, silent Western hero is evident here, but it's been incorporated into a coming-of-age scenario centered on achieving a proud but "indifferent" mastery of the work one is paid to do. That "indifference" will turn out to be important in Leonard's later fiction. Taking things personally tends to get in the way of doing your job.

The father-son relationship underlying such testing or "coaching" situations is clearly registered in a story like "Law of the Hunted Ones." Here, outlaw Lew De Sana tells Virgil Patman, "You better have a talk with your boy [. . .] tell him the facts of life" (113), when the impatient teenager Dave Fallis tries to intervene between the brutal De Sana and his woman. Patman later tells De Sana he's giving Fallis "a little fatherly hand" by keeping De Sana covered while Fallis is out "courting" his "girlfriend" (127). In *The Law at Randado*, Sheriff Danaher thinks of his deputy, Kirby Frye, as his son (369), and there are several traces of Leonard's own early life story embedded in Frye's (379–81).

Like Mr. Leonard scouting dealerships for GM, Frye's father was often away from home prospecting while his family stayed in Randado, where Frye grew up. Taking the profits he made panning for gold, Frye's dad started a freight line, just as Mr. Leonard used his savings to buy a car dealership. Kirby Frye started out working for his father, as Leonard was about to do when Mr. Leonard died, but Kirby grew tired of driving a wagon and keeping the books—Leonard's view, perhaps, of the future he barely escaped. Young Frye left to work for a man supplying cavalry remounts until he could go into the same business for himself. Leonard was writing copy for Campbell Ewald while working on *The Law at Randado* and hoping, eventually, to succeed as a writer on his own. Frye takes after his mother, who, like Leonard's, is associated with literacy: she taught him to read and write (380). Perhaps most important, Sheriff Danaher decides to hire Kirby Frye as his deputy mainly because he *can* write. Finding a penciled message Frye left behind while on the track of Apache horse thieves, Danaher is persuaded: "The note clinched it in Danaher's mind. He carries a pencil! Maybe he couldn't spell Chiricahua, but by God 'Cherry-cow' was close enough and all the rest of the words were right" (378).

Elsewhere in these early stories, paternal example, influence, or advice helps sons in their first professional trials as apprentices and mentees. In "Red Hell Hits Canyon Diablo" (Leonard's publisher changed the title from "Tizwin"), "young Gordon Towner" (82) wins the "tizwin" (corn beer) drinking match that decides the outcome of the tale, leaving Apache renegade Lacayuelo and his men passed out, because, Towner says, "a long time ago my father taught me to drink like a gentleman," which is to say, how to hold his liquor and not succumb to inebriation (83). Much as Towner's dad helped him prevail in his first encounter with Apaches in "Red Hell," so Bowers's memory of his father's description of the Culp's Hill charge at Gettysburg helps him outsmart his enemies at the end of *The Bounty Hunters* (170), which also ends in a drinking match. In that book, both Flynn's and Bowers's fathers helped to secure their sons' first commissions as cavalry officers, and even Lieutenant Lamas Duro of the Soyopa *rurales* owes his position to his father, Don Agostino Duro, who was a personal friend of the head of the Mexican army.

Variations on this theme are not hard to find. In "The Big Hunt" and "The Boy Who Smiled," sons take charge of avenging their fathers' deaths in the face of adult diffidence, while in "Moment of Vengeance," "father" and "son" confront each other as in-laws and enemies who eventually reconcile. In "The Last Shot," an older man helps a younger man see his way clearly through the illusory demands of honor, and similar paternal-filial negotiations appear on the periphery of tales that have their focus elsewhere. By the end of Leonard's prolific first five years, however, this vertical master-apprentice axis of relationship loses urgency, and a horizontal axis of self-testing begins to emerge between the hero and a clearly designated antagonist, often a violent peer conforming to a familiar schoolyard type, the bully.

Far more than his everyman protagonists, Leonard's bullies stick in the memory. Fans of his crime fiction will readily call them to mind: men like Dual Meaders in *The Moonshine War* (1969), Clement Mansell in *City Primeval*, Richard Nobles in *LaBrava*, Richie Nix in *Killshot*, and Arlen Novis in *Tishomingo Blues*. Until they are taught better, Leonard's bullies don't know how clueless, and thus helpless, they really are. But meanwhile, they are dangerous—physically, but also psychologically. They know how to get under the hero's skin; they know how to make it personal. In "The Longest Day of His Life," outlaw-in-training Albie makes the young stage surveyor, Steve Brady, strip off his new suit at gunpoint before sending him ahead on foot to greet the stationmaster's daughter at Glennan in his underwear.

Leonard's crime-fiction bullyboys reach back to Western prototypes like Albie, to smart-ass loudmouths like Billy Guay in "You Never See Apaches" and Gosh Hall in "The Rustlers," or to more calculating, cold-blooded monsters like Curt Lazair of *The Bounty Hunters* and the scheming, spoiled rancher's son, Phil Sundeen, of *The Law at Randado*. Particularly infuriating are men like R. L. Davis in "Only Good Ones," who operate with impunity under the protection of a powerful boss like Frank Tanner. Leonard's classic bullies are anticipated in his earliest unpublished Westerns, in characters like Billy Bushway of "Charlie Martz" and Reb Spadea of "Siesta in Paloverde." Punks like these are not satisfied with defeating you; they want to shame you. Bushway and Spadea want to kill the sheriff who sent them to jail, but they insist on doing it with his own gun so they can add their notch to it.

The theories of French psychologist Jacques Lacan can help us understand what's at stake in these depictions of bullies, beginning with what Leonard has said about his "childlike" as opposed to "childish" characters: the former grow up to be open-minded, tolerant adults, while the latter somehow fail in the attempt. In Leonard's work, "growing up" is a matter not of accumulating years but of successfully negotiating what Lacanian psychologists would call "the mirror stage," that point in an infant's or an adolescent's development (the latter a more mature recapitulation of the former) when he or she first "assumes an image," becoming preoccupied by the self as it appears in the eyes of others who inhabit and understand a world with which the child is unfamiliar (Lacan 2). For the infant, this world is bounded by the family, and authoritative confirmation of the self comes to be lodged in the parents; for the adolescent, this world comprises the wider society of strangers outside the family, where it is often difficult to fix the site of authoritative self-confirmation in any single individual. In both cases, successful self-integration or "deflection of the specular I into the social I" (Lacan 5)—which is to say, "growing up"—depends on the child's having interiorized a parent's or parent figure's authoritative gaze to the point of dispensing, more or less, with overt mediations of self-awareness in the eyes of peers.

The primary emotions governing those who fail the task of interiorization are shame and rage, the signature affects of the bully's projected self-doubt ("*You're* the one who's got a problem, pal!") and externalized self-construction ("You lookin' at *me*?"). Leonard's scariest and most compelling psychopaths typically succumb to these two childish reactions. His heroes succeed in, and by, overcoming them. It's precisely because the bully knows how to shame the Leonardian hero so well that you begin to suspect there must be something of the hero's personality, his own weak points, in the bully, and vice versa. Both fear the same thing, the loss of face through public humiliation, but the bully handles his insecurities through overcompensation. He actively seeks opportunities to exhibit power through naked aggression and to express pleasure by inflicting pain in an attempt to deny rather than recognize and control his fear. Where he can't find those occasions, he will provoke or fabricate them. Leonard's heroes tend to overcome their fear of humiliation by immersing themselves in the task at hand, in the authenticating *techne* of "cool."

As the importance of the vertical relationship between master and apprentice fades over the course of Leonard's first decade of writing Westerns, his attention to horizontal, or peer group, antagonists shifts from renegade Apaches and the impersonal tests of apprenticeship they pose, to the *mano a mano* challenges of bullies and their protectors, and, finally, to more mature opponents like Frank Renda (not the hit man of *Mr. Majestyk* but the identically named boss of the prison camp in *Escape from Five Shadows* [1956]), or the embittered Rebel hold-out Edward Janroe in *Last Stand*, or powerful figures with social or political authority, such as Frank Tanner in *Valdez Is Coming* (1970). These older antagonists may employ bullies, like apprentices, to do their dirty work, but the main focus is on them, not their flunkies. By the effective conclusion of Leonard's Western period, with the publication of *Hombre* in 1961, the coming-of-age scenario featuring laconic mentors and abrasive bullies has lost its urgency, having given way to a more settled analysis of the dynamics of authenticity, *techne*, and self-integration that, when working in harmony, comprise "being cool." In *Hombre*, for instance, John Russell is neither an apprentice frontiersman nor assigned the task of training one, and while he has to overcome the opposition and intolerance of his fellow stagecoach passengers, as well as the ruthlessness and intelligence of the robbers pursuing them all, he's never confronted by the likes of a Phil Sundeen or R. L. Davis.

Anatomies of "Cool": The Western Novels

As Leonard's interest in the authenticity of *techne* evolved, he began to shift his focus from its emergence in "coaching" relationships to its application in new, challenging situations.

Eric Travisin, of "Trail of the Apache," displays all the elements that will eventually add up to Leonard's mature version of authentic self-integration through *techne*. He relies, first and foremost, on his "pure natural instinct" (2), a "strange instinct" that he does not understand himself (6). But he also recognizes that, as a tracker and a scout, he has to master "the steps necessary to survival in an enemy element. They weren't included in Cook's 'Cavalry Tactics': you learned them the hard way, and your being alive testified that you had learned them well" (2). Travisin brings natural talent to his profession and hones it with the technical knowledge and training he receives under the tutelage of Barney Fry, the older, part-Apache scout who is, in effect, Travisin's mentor (2). Travisin practices what he's learned even when relaxing. The game he plays with Sergeant Gatito of the Apache scouts, who tries to sneak up and catch

Travisin napping, is not just a way to pass the time: it produces "an officer whose senses were razor-sharp. Travisin even practiced staying alive" (3).

Leonard's reference to Cook's *Cavalry Tactics* accentuates the distinction between the habitual know-how of *techne*, acquired by practice, and Aristotelian *episteme*, or intellectual understanding. Travisin even gives the priggish de Both an introductory lecture pointing up the difference: "You can keep up the spit and polish if you want, but I'd advise you to relax and play the game without keeping the rule book open all the time" (7). The word *game* not only recalls Travisin's mock survival "game" with Gatito: it invokes the kind of bodily self-integration required to play a sport like football or baseball, where a first baseman can't start looking up the infield fly rule when the batter hits a pop-up to second with the bases loaded. Rules and the decisions based on them must be internalized step by step, deliberately and self-consciously at first, until they can be expressed and implemented in a split second that leaves no room for reflection.

As we have seen, the goal of *techne* is not necessarily virtuous: its transformation of rules into habit is not a form of what Aristotle calls *praxis*, or behavior according to principles, whether moral, ethical, or political, although nearly all of Leonard's frontier heroes are as virtuous as they can be, under the circumstances. From a moral point of view, Eric Travisin can appear "cold-blooded, sometimes cruel" in his official "role," but there's "another side" of him that understands how unfairly the Indians under his jurisdiction have been treated. This is the point of his lecturing de Both on how whites have abused the Apache nation and on the predictable result of their policies (8–9). Entrusted with their care as official Indian agent, Travisin takes the Indians' "health and welfare" seriously and is "completely honest" with them (2). As a result, he has "transformed nomadic hostiles into peaceful agriculturalists" in just three years (2). But Travisin is aware of the moral contradictions of his position: "Mister," he tells de Both, "I'm here to kill Indians and keep Indians alive. It's a paradox—no question about that—but I gave up rationalizing a long time ago" (9). The nearest thing to an ethical principle governing his behavior is a primitive reciprocity, something not susceptible to rational analysis: "I have to be fair—when they are fair to me" (9).

It would be a mistake to reduce Travisin's—or Leonard's—sense of fairness to a standard version of the "Code of the West" that typically governs this formulaic genre, or for that matter, the golden rule of doing unto others. It is that, but it is also more. In Leonard's Westerns, the feeling of fairness that transcends rationalization is as much a sign of arrival as a code of behavior. It measures the protagonist's mastery of the only *techne* that has a bearing on what it means for a writer, particularly, to achieve a sense of authenticity and wholeness: a complete understanding of what it is like to be someone else. Under Barney Fry's tutelage, Travisin learned that "it took an Apache to catch an Apache. So, for all practical purposes, *he became one*" (2, emphasis added). If the ultimate aim of *techne* is to achieve self-integration, to immerse the mind in what it has trained the body to do, then the only *techne* that really counts for Leonard as a man writing is the one that results, finally, in what we have come to know as empathy without sympathy, becoming one with another person, especially someone of an entirely different personality, culture, or (eventually) gender—and perhaps even with an enemy. The difficulty of that challenge is one of the greatest a writer can face, and its achievement is a hallmark of the work of writing in its purest, most "invisible" form.

If, at the start of Leonard's career, "Trail of the Apache" introduces us to the three basic elements of technical authenticity—natural ability, training under a mentor, and practice—that will eventuate in the fully self-integrated "being cool" of his later work, then *Escape from Five Shadows* and *Last Stand at Saber River* introduce us to its anatomy. Together with *Hombre* and *Valdez Is Coming,* they feature protagonists who, in a former stage of their lives, learned a skill (dynamiting, combat, wilderness survival) that they must call upon in order to prevail in their current circumstances. In *Escape from Five Shadows,* for instance, the unjustly imprisoned Corey Bowen must use the know-how that he acquired in his first three months at Yuma Prison, where he was assigned to a work detail using dynamite, to contrive a method of escape from the Five Shadows work camp for himself, his former partner, and another prisoner. Bowen has been transferred to Five Shadows because his expertise with explosives will prove useful in building a new road through a nearby canyon. But his partner and fellow prisoner Earl Manring also conspires to keep him there by tipping off the camp authorities when Bowen makes his first escape attempt, because Manring wants to use Bowen's expertise in his own escape plans.

Handling dynamite demands strict obedience to a set of rules. "That's another rule," Bowen informs Frank Renda, when the camp boss betrays his nervousness by telling Bowen to "Just hurry it up": "You don't hurry" (108). Bowen's familiarity with blasting gives him an authority over Renda that he enjoys brandishing. Again, rules, not principles, govern *techne*: "*I made a rule* that I had to get something down on paper before I could put the water on for the coffee." Leonard spends a great deal of time explaining to us, through Bowen, how to measure the burning rates of fuses, test the blasting power of dynamite sticks, fit and crimp detonators, set charges, and otherwise carry on the ordinary work of dynamiting a roadway, all with the ultimate goal of sealing the escapees off from possible pursuers as they head for the hills.

Bowen's handling of dynamite represents an interesting variation on self-immersion or absorption in *techne*, a variation in some ways closer to Leonard's approach to writing at this time, about midway through his Western phase. For one thing, Bowen's focusing of attention is spread out over several days of laying and detonating charges—in the planning and preparation, not in the final execution of his scheme. Thus, habit is not so much incorporated into skilled behavior as banished altogether by an enforced slowing of the pace of activity. Self-absorption takes the form of a rigidly undivided attention, rather than an acquired second nature. The skill involved here requires nerves of steel and an ability to ignore the real possibility that a wayward fuse might burn too fast or that an unstable charge might suddenly explode as Bowen gently tamps the sand in around it. To the extent that such distractions can be put out of mind, along with those posed by his two fellow conspirators, who seem to have plans of their own, Bowen achieves the authenticity of *techne* that is one hallmark of "being cool." If all goes right—and despite some unexpected developments requiring rapid improvisation, it mostly does—the complicated exploding machine that Bowen constructs out of dynamite charges, timed to go off in a particular sequence at particular intervals and in particular locations, should result in his freedom, but it cannot think for itself while doing so. Here, the mind of the craftsman has become completely absorbed and expressed in the mindless mechanism he has created, just as the mind of an author can become, in the end, completely absorbed and embodied in the inanimate material product of his pen or typewriter. The book is, in this sense, a machine for reading, over which the author, once he has completed it, must relinquish control. Like a series of dynamite charges, it is "set off" by the fuse of the reader's attention.

In *Last Stand at Saber River*, near the end of the Western period, we watch Paul Cable as he goes through the basic stages of "cool" behavior shaped by its ultimate goal, the desire to think like someone else, to achieve "sympathy of comprehension," first, with the wily Confederate general under whom he served, Nathan Bedford Forrest, and second, with his antagonists, the men working for Vern and Duane Kidston. Cable has already honed his physical and strategic skills in combat and, like Travisin, acquired "the habit of surviving" (*Last Stand* 2) while doing so, learning to "use patience and weigh alternatives and to be sure of a situation before he acted" (2). But you can also "think too much," Cable tells himself after being menaced by the Kidstons' men. "You could picture too many possibilities of failure and in the end you could lose your nerve and run for it. Sometimes it was better to just let things happen, to be ready and try to do the right thing, but just not think too much about it" (75). Reflection and preparation are required for proper execution, but overplanning can impede one's ability to react to contingencies. Warned by Edward Janroe of the odds against him, Cable twice replies, "We'll see what happens" (16, 20), confident that his own "habit of surviving" has prepared him to meet the unforeseen exigencies of this new, threatening situation.

That confidence is shaken when two of the Kidstons' men ambush Cable in his barn, take him back to his house to watch them threaten his wife and children, and then beat him almost senseless before their eyes. Thrown out into the night with a revolver holding a single bullet that he's told to put into his own brain, Cable knows his chances of overcoming his attackers with just one shot, especially with his family held hostage, are slim to none. That's when he asks himself, "What would Forrest do?" (84). With the help of "God's smile and Forrest's bag of tricks" (85), Cable improvises a counter-ambush exploiting his attackers' weaknesses, drawing them out into the darkness to their deaths.

Cable's thought process is clearly delineated in this extended scene through free indirect discourse and interior monologue: "you think it out and do it and maybe it will work. Whatever it is" (85). Thinking it out requires focusing on the task at hand: "When too many things crowded into Cable's mind, he would stop thinking. He would calm himself, then tell himself to think very slowly and carefully. A little anger was good, but not rage; that hindered thinking" (85). He especially wants to avoid thinking about his wife and children, but even when he does he keeps himself calm (86). Self-control, ignoring distractions from what needs doing, not taking it personally, these are central features of *techne* as unselfconscious, skilled execution, here as in *Escape from Five Shadows*. The "thinking" that Cable needs to do is not self-conscious but self-absorbing; "thinking" of his wife and children, by contrast, reminds him of what they mean to him, what his responsibilities are toward them, and stirs up emotions of fear and rage that get in the way of what he has to do now, at this moment.

At some point, however, the time for thinking ends and execution—"doing it"—begins: "Just get them out, he thought. Stop thinking and get them out" (86). Here, too, authentic *techne* requires the ability to see through another's eyes, even those of an enemy. Crouching in the darkness after firing his lone shot to make the men inside think he has killed himself, Cable pictures them "standing still in the room. Wonder about it, Cable thought. Then decide. Come on, decide right now. Somebody has to come out and make sure. You don't believe it, but you'd like to believe it, so you have to come see" (87). And indeed, just as he has imagined it, the two men appear at the door. When one of them comes out into the darkness to look for Cable's body, Cable kills him with a rock, takes his gun, and shoots the man waiting on the porch.

The question Cable asks himself, "What would Forrest do?" can only be answered by putting himself in Forrest's place, or rather, imagining Nathan Bedford Forrest in *his* place, with a single bullet facing two armed men holding his family hostage. But Nathan Bedford Forrest is not a stranger to Paul Cable, as the men in the cabin are, or as Apaches are to William de Both or R. D. Bowers. He is a mentor distinguished for his own ability to think like the enemy and whose example has been interiorized, like that of an admired parent, during the protagonist's previous experiences on the battlefield, his "coming of age" under fire, to the point where the older man's wisdom and example are now accessible through the younger man's subsequent acts of imagination. Leonard makes this clear when Cable reflects on the difference between his behavior now, waiting and scheming patiently in the darkness, and when he was a raw Confederate recruit: "Two and a half years ago, he thought, you wouldn't be lying here. You'd be dead. You'd have done something foolish and you'd be dead" (86). Cable has achieved a new level of adult self-integration under the tutelage of his commanding general. Now, with Forrest thoroughly "in mind," he can apply what he has learned from him—his acquired skills, his *techne* of war—to the new situation at hand and think like his opponents.

Cultural, class, and gender differences pose the greatest challenge to attempts at empathy, with or without sympathy, and to authentic mastery of *techne*, for both Leonard's protagonists and Leonard himself. A fascination with Apaches dominates his earliest tales, especially the first five Western short stories, where the Native American's cultural otherness is used to interrogate and contextualize the presumably universal legitimacy of Enlightenment rationalism and morality in general, and of doing things "by the book" in particular. Few of Leonard's Apaches are "noble" in the Rousseauian sense: in fact, most are conniving, treacherous, gullible, superstitious, and violent, especially when they've drunk too much tizwin. But nearly all of them are nothing but themselves, and that seems to earn them Leonard's respect throughout his Western phase. Like Eric Travisin, Leonard's "savages" nearly all know exactly how to behave in any given situation—whether tracking buffalo or roasting a kidnapped settler alive over an open fire—and they commit themselves single-mindedly to doing what's required, and doing it right. Whatever the limitations and dangers that arise when members of a dominant race try to represent the life-worlds of other cultures, Leonard never condescends to his Native American characters with attempts to excuse or sentimentalize their behavior. As in his portrait of Travisin himself, what most interests him is not a comparative evaluation of ethical principles but the routines of *techne*, enculturated or acquired, that subtend differences of *praxis*.

Leonard has a special fondness for his Hispanic characters, whether Mexican, Mexican American, or *mestizo* (mixed race Native American and Hispanic). As with his Apaches, Mexican Americans in his fiction run the gamut from truly admirable to truly despicable, although none of the most despicable becomes a primary antagonist. In general, the Mexican and *mestizo* nations seem to represent the possibilities of a mutual Euro–Native American accommodation of cultural and racial practices that avoids assimilation of one race by another, but that most of Leonard's white settlers, cowpokes, and cavalry officers, along with the "respectable" wives and mothers of frontier society, find impossible to endorse, let alone tolerate. The exceptions, as James Devlin dryly observes, "tend to show an understanding of other cultures quite unusual in the Arizona of the time period" (34). There is, in short, a risk of presentism as well as cultural appropriation in Leonard's imaginative forays into seeing the world through others' eyes, a risk that all the technical details culled from historical accounts and eyewitness encounters cannot entirely abolish.[2] Broadly speaking, the Westerns reflect the spreading awareness of racial injustice and budding multiculturalism of 1950s America. Those forces were to become even more evident in Leonard's work by the early 1970s—for example, in his interest in recovering the cultural history of nonwhite races in *Forty Lashes Less One* (1972) and the unjust treatment of migrant workers in *Mr. Majestyk* (1974). Devlin notes that Leonard's ability to see through the eyes of people of color has matured in his later fiction to the point where he has even been mistaken for a black writer by black readers (34–35).

Understandably, the imaginative challenges of class consciousness, which tends to emerge under the pressures of industrialization, capitalism, and modernity, appear more on the periphery than at the center of Leonard's Western stories, but they become increasingly important during his crime-writing career. In the Westerns, they shape his depictions of female more than male characters, perhaps because in the classic frontier tale going back to James Fenimore Cooper, women as a group represent the middle-class forces of civilization and socialized self-restraint for which the culturally liminal hero, white by blood but aboriginal by inclination and training, is making the frontier safe. Class differences are at play, for instance, in the antagonism between Lorraine

Kidston and her father and uncle, Vern and Duane, in *Last Stand.* Lorraine has been raised by her mother, back east, since Mrs. Kidston's estrangement from Vern, and finishing schools have ill-prepared her for the crudeness and tedium of life in the Arizona Territory when she returns to live with her father. It's all she can do to restrain herself from overt sarcasm when confronted by the pompous stupidity of her uncle, and her only recourse against crushing boredom is to get some kicks by throwing kerosene on the emotional brushfire raging between the Kidstons and Cable, or by attempting to seduce Cable in order to make his wife, Martha, jealous. As Devlin points out (13), Lorraine is the prototype for thrill-seeking Nancy Hayes, the bad girl of Leonard's first crime novel, *The Big Bounce,* whose class differences with the hero, Jack Ryan, are even more pronounced. In contrast to Nancy, however, Lorraine Kidston does not seem to engage Leonard's imagination.

In the course of his career, gender may have proven the most resistant barrier to Leonard's gifts of empathy, as he would be the first to admit. Westerns, after all, are a man's genre, and it was apparently under pressure from his first agent, Marguerite Harper, with her eye on eventually selling Leonard to more family-oriented "slicks" like the *Saturday Evening Post,* that he began to introduce female characters and the occasional romantic subplot into his masculinized universe. Not until the late 1970s, when his second wife, Joan Shepard, took him to task for his limited understanding of what a woman wants—particularly in a new age of women's liberation—did Leonard begin to invest more independence and agency in his female characters. Mickey Dawson, of *The Switch* (1978), reveals what Shepard taught him, as we'll see shortly.

Even if we acknowledge these limitations, however, Glenn Most is certainly overstating the case when she writes that women appear in Leonard's fiction "almost always as victims. If they become the object of lust, that is only another form of the attempted exercise of power" (104). Granted, of the first two women—both Apaches—to enter Leonard's Western androcosm in "You Never See Apaches" (1952), one is murdered and the other is molested by the young horse's ass Billy Guay, before the Mimbre chief, Victorio, takes revenge. But the first woman to play any substantive role is Amelia Darck, wife of local commander Colonel Darck in "The Colonel's Lady," published later the same year. Kidnapped by an Apache bandit, she stoically welcomes him into her arms as he tries to rape her, and then plunges the knife he has put aside into his back as she embraces him. Mrs. Darck has had plenty of frontier experience since leaving finishing school, so she knows how to keep her head: "I've lived out here most of my life," she tells Simon Street when the grizzled scout finally arrives to rescue her, only to find her waiting patiently with her captor lying dead nearby. "I heard Apache war drums long before I attended my first cotillion, but I have hardly reached the point where I have to take an Apache for a lover" (102).

When Leonard is not using his female characters to provide a perfunctory romantic interest, as with the mostly decorative and two-dimensional Milmary Steadman of *The Law at Randado* or boyish Karla Demery of *Escape from Five Shadows*, he tends to bestow on them the kind of agency that typifies his masculine protagonists. Like Mrs. Darck, they are admired for *not* giving in to panic and fear, to the hysteria presumably typical of their sex, and that's what makes them worthy of attention. Or their agency is represented as derivative and supportive of the male's. Martha Cable, Paul Cable's wife in *Last Stand at Saber River*, fits this type to some extent, but also represents something of an early breakthrough in Leonard's attempts to imagine seeing the world through a woman's eyes.

Martha is, as we would expect, a loving mother and spouse, but also experienced with firearms. Standing at the window of their home with a shotgun trained on Vern Kidston, she gives her husband an edge in his outnumbered situation. "You'd bring your wife into it?" asks Vern. "Risk her life for a piece of land?" "My wife killed a Chiricahua Apache ten feet from where you're standing," Cable replies. "They came like you've come and she killed to defend our home. Maybe you understand that. If you don't, I'll say only this. My wife will kill again if she has to, and so will I" (71–72). And yet, when Cable is pushed to the edge of doing something that will get him killed because "it's a question of proving myself to me," as he puts it, Martha's is the voice of reason that holds him back and holds up for interrogation the very idea of having to "prove" anything, least of all one's identity as a man: "It isn't a matter of principle, a question of whether or not you're a man. This is something that affects the whole family. We want to go home and live in peace. [. . .] [W]e want what is rightfully ours, but we don't want it without you." When Cable insists that "this will be settled with guns" sooner or later, Martha disagrees.

> "It doesn't have to be that way," Martha said urgently. "If we wait, if we can put it off—Cabe, something could happen that would solve everything!"
>
> "Like what?"
>
> She hesitated. "I'm not sure." (169)

As it turns out, Martha is right. Circumstances conspire to put Cable and his antagonist Vern Kidston on the same side in their final showdown with Edward Janroe.

Despite advances like the character of Martha Cable, Leonard's early female characters generally become a part of the action only as the male protagonist's ally or foe—or love interest. Even Martha Cable is a far cry from the women of Leonard's mature fiction, like Mickey Dawson in *The Switch,* Carmen Colson in *Killshot,* Linda Moon in *Be Cool,* Karen Sisco in *Out of Sight* (1996), or Dara Barr in *Djibouti,* who are empowered, or find empowerment, largely under their own steam and initiative.

Generically, David Geherin sees Leonard breaking no new ground during his Western phase, but rather experimenting, "especially with point of view" (23), as he shifts his attention "to the man behind the gun rather than the actions of the gun itself" (21) and to other characters, their "complicated relationships" and "secret dealings and double-dealing" (27). This is an accurate description of Leonard's development in general, but Devlin suggests there is more originality in Leonard's apprentice Westerns than Geherin detects. For one thing, the stories generally stay away from stock figures like cowboys, campfires, and high plains drifters and very often conclude with an "unfamiliar twist" (Devlin 7), which of course goes all the way back to "Dickey" and in the Western tales can take the form of a similar kind of joke. The drinking contest in "Red Hell" and *The Bounty Hunters* that replaces the generically standard shoot-out is one example, and there are many other conclusions, some comical, others merely incongruous, that depend on thinking fast—and appropriately—rather than beating an opponent to the draw. Sudden inspiration is their hallmark.

In "Apache Medicine," for instance, the experienced scout Kleecan uses this kind of improvisatory wit to plant an incriminating fetish on one of the bandits who are forcing him at gunpoint to take them across the Mexican border, and then contrives to lead them straight into the arms of a band of hostile Mescaleros whose chief, Pondichay, will recognize the fetish as belonging to his dead son, Juan Pony, and exact an appropriate revenge. The idea comes to Kleecan in a flash, on hearing one of the bandits insist they will "ride all night" if necessary: "And it was then that the idea had been born. *Even if we ride all night.* He had but two hours to think it out clearly" (48). Even Amelia Darck's stabbing of the bandit Mata Lobo is something she cannot entirely prepare for, but must improvise on the spur of the moment as she sees him lay his knife down, and similar episodes are thickly scattered throughout the early work.

By the end of the Western period, Leonard's improvisations result increasingly in an anticlimactic denouement in which a final settlement by violence is avoided, often due to someone's facility with words. We find the pattern emerging in "The Rustlers," where Charlie, the first-person narrator, finally gets up the nerve to talk Emmett Ryan out of hanging his brother, Jack, and then persuades the local sheriff that Jack's cattle rustling was all a big joke. At the conclusion of "Moment of Vengeance" we encounter, ironically, not a moment of vengeance but the victimized protagonist and his hostile father-in-law talking out their differences. *Escape from Five Shadows* ends not with explosions but with a complicated scheme to get Frank Renda to admit he beat Willis Falvey's wife, Lizann, while Willis eavesdrops, so that Willis will testify against the sadistic camp boss in court. Renda is made to stand trial for his crimes—not a typical Western wrap-up in which the Code of the West trumps the rule of law. At the end of *Valdez Is Coming*, the mayhem that Roberto Valdez visits on Frank Tanner's minions comes to a head with Tanner himself having to choose whether to draw or capitulate to Valdez's reasonable demands for compensation to the widow whose husband Tanner had his men murder in cold blood: the word wins out over the weapon, and Tanner gives in.

The ability to speak persuasively at the moment of truth, just like Chili Palmer's power of "bullshitting" nearly four decades later, reflects that ideal state of control over his own voice that any writer, but especially a beginning writer, prizes above nearly anything else. In their facility at improvisation, in their way with words, in their faith that a solution will come when they least expect it, Leonard's Western heroes epitomize his own nascent attraction to "being cool" as a function of technical proficiency, authenticity, and verbal self-integration. Like Homer's Odysseus, whom Leonard first met in the pages of *My Book House* and to whom Devlin explicitly compares Paul Cable (42), they reflect their creator's ideal of *poeisis*: a cunning mastery of storytelling, of eloquence and facility of expression, and inspired invention.

By the time he wrote *Valdez Is Coming* in the late 1960s, Leonard had learned how to hang a plot on his hero's creativity, how to become invisible behind the ventriloquy of free indirect discourse, and how to tease and twist the conventions of the Western with gentle mockery to make the genre more his own, branding it with his signature style. Gradually he became, if not a great writer, then a competent and distinctive one. Rapidly outgrowing his occasional lapses into breathless, purple prose and hoary old "storyteller" personae, he soon settled into a balanced rhythm of exposition, backstory, and dialogue, relying less and less on a third-person omniscient voice as he dropped efficiently into one or another character's point of view to convey the facts of setting and situation from different perspectives. Heavily indebted to Hemingway's spare, focalized descriptions and dialogue, which he infused with the humor of Richard

Bissell's first-person river-tug philosophers, Leonard didn't yet seem to recognize—or if he did, hadn't yet figured out how to exploit—the full potential of the voices in his head. Only occasionally do they display themselves in their astonishing, childlike power.

In *The Bounty Hunters*, a thirteen-year-old Aravaipa Apache boy has the bad luck to accompany an American peddler into Soyopa, where Apaches are subject to summary execution and their scalps fetch a bounty of a hundred pesos each. Stood up against a wall to be shot, the boy looks about him "with little show of concern," and we are prepared for a conventional Western tale of the "red man's" stoicism and defiance. Instead, we find ourselves suddenly in the mind of a child distracted by wonders.

> His trousers were too large, bunched at the waist and tucked into moccasins rolled beneath his knees. His shirt was dirty, faded blue, and only his moccasins and headband indicated that he was Apache. The two rurales, in their dove-gray uniforms and crossed bandoleers, were a half-head taller than the boy who would move his chin from one shoulder to the other to look at them, studying the leather cartridge belts and the silver buttons on the soft gray jackets. And all about the courtyard were these men with their guns and so many bullets that they must have special belts to hang them over their shoulders. The boy was aware that he was going to die, but there were so many things of interest to see. He hoped they might delay it for a little while longer. (37–38)

I quote at length in order to convey something of the seamlessness with which Leonard can shift from a third-person description of the boy to an intimate understanding of what it means to *be* him, through free indirect discourse. The boy's stature—half a head shorter than his executioners—and his too-large trousers heighten our sense of the outrageousness of treating an innocent child like a guilty man: "Boys grow into men," says Lieutenant Lamas Duro, who insists the execution be carried out. "Let's call these bullets the ounces of prevention" (39). Leonard's shift to the boy's point of view is signaled by an objective description of his moving his head from shoulder to shoulder to "look at" the men about to kill him. Diction is key here. Before we watch the boy watching, what he and we both watch is described in the technical language of adults—"uniforms," "bandoleers"—but immediately afterward, the bandoleers and uniforms are "leather cartridge belts" and "soft gray jackets" with "silver buttons." In the very next sentence, the overreaching *all*, the demonstrative pronoun *these*, and the adverb *so* in the partial comparative construction *so many*, a phrase reaching for but unable to find completion ("so many" that . . . what?) tell us we have entered the mind of a child absorbed in wonder and too inexperienced, at least in the lives of white men, to measure it. We are listening to him speaking to himself in the language of someone too young not to be fascinated by "these" strange things he sees, here, now, in front of him—and in front of us. After the phrase "so many" Leonard's diction shifts even further in the direction of curiosity and estrangement: not fully cased cartridges but the simpler "bullets," and not even "cartridge belts," let alone, "bandoleers," but "special belts to hang them over their shoulders." The diction becomes simpler the further into this Apache adolescent's mind Leonard draws us. "He was aware he was going to die," but being a child, that awareness is shoved aside by a hope, fed by a child's curiosity, that "they might delay it for a little longer."

Leonard's use of free indirect discourse to elicit a "sympathy of comprehension" with this Apache boy will strike some readers as implausible, or culturally appropriative, but that may only be a function of their own limited imaginations. The question Leonard asks himself, characteristically, is not, "*Would* a child of thirteen, even an Apache child, be this indifferent to the prospect of his own death?" but rather, "*Could* he be, *conceivably*?" Leonard imagines the circumstances in which he could, by wondering not only what it would be like to be raised, as he had learned Apache boys were raised, to remain indifferent to death, but also what it would mean for such a boy to remain a child nevertheless.

> The two rurales moved away from the Apache boy. His eyes followed one of them as the dove-gray uniform moved off towards the house. The bullets go even all the way down the back! He heard a command in Spanish. One word. And there are so many of them; each man has two belts, and who knows, there might even be more stored in that great jacale. Another Spanish word broke the sudden stillness of the courtyard. Would it not be fine to have a belt with so many bullets. He heard the last command clearly . . . "Fire!" (40–41)

Jumping, Bouncing: The Unpublished Stories

Leonard may have had his own reasons for starting out with Westerns, but the 1950s Western also raised questions about the Cold War politics and social conformism of postwar America. According to Stephen McVeigh, the movies *The Gunfighter* (1950), *High Noon* (1952), and *Shane* (1952), in particular, reflected the apocalyptic impact of the atom bomb on Americans' experience of lived time, as well as the stultifying effects of the Soviet threat and the doctrine of

Mutual Assured Destruction on citizens' everyday existence (55–56, 77–87; see also Slotkin 383–400). All three films had an immediate and long-term effect on Leonard, and it isn't hard to apply McVeigh's analysis to his Western phase. The preoccupation with time running out in *The Gunfighter* and *High Noon* dominate the action in "Three-Ten to Yuma" (1953), and one memorable scene in *The Gunfighter*, where Jimmy Ringo (played by Gregory Peck) bluffs a punk into backing down by lying about a gun pointed at him under the table, resonates with Cold War anxieties over Russia's nuclear intentions and first-strike capabilities. This particular confrontation was to haunt Leonard's writing for decades, beginning with the first scene of his first novel, *The Bounty Hunters*.

None of this is to suggest that Leonard was writing Westerns with a political agenda in mind, only that his work, like that of any other writer, mirrored some of the prevailing concerns of his time and place. The generic Western's traditional glorification of individual self-reliance also accommodated, quite easily, the young Leonard's no less timely attraction to a cool, nonconformist point of view deeply in tune with postwar America's love-hate relationship with normalcy. Nowhere was that relationship more in evidence than at his day job (figure 8).

James Devlin sees Leonard's "tour of duty" with Campbell Ewald as reprising his war experiences, but in business terms and using words as weapons. Here "the battle was to sell cars," and Leonard could watch the firm "conducting its fierce campaign" up close: "Writing was power. The pen really was mightier than the sword. He had seen them both. Now he could even combine them" (6). This may be true, up to a point: there are obvious connections between advertising and fiction (they both thrive on make-believe), and the language of advertising—"campaigns," "attack ads"—often mimics that of war. But Leonard hated advertising and the general run of advertisers (Geherin 3–4). As he climbed the corporate ladder into "Creative," he found his most exciting ideas shelved—"the good stuff never got published" (Grobel 255)—and was soon reaching for a drink before each client consultation (Geherin 5).

Despite steady raises and profit-sharing options, Leonard saw Campbell Ewald more as a no-man's-land of wasted lives than as an exciting theater of corporate war. In its offices and corridors he witnessed firsthand the impact of what Norman Mailer was to call the "totalitarianization of the psyche" ("Superman") imposed by the Eisenhower years and evinced by David Reisman's "other-directed" personality (21) and William H. White's "organization man." Leonard's writing became a way to interrogate this kind of conventional behavior by contrasting its groupthink and conformism with the behavior of independent-minded characters forced to act under extreme duress. Repeatedly, in the Westerns, we are confronted with the infuriating mindlessness and downright idiocy of bureaucrats, administrators, and their underlings, civil as well as military, and often with their easy slide into corruption. Colonel Deneen, the incompetent and cowardly departmental adjutant in *The Bounty Hunters*; F. W. Sellers, the embezzling Indian agent in "Trouble at Rindo's Station," and his counterpart in *Hombre*, Alexander Favor; Willard Mims, the corporate bookkeeper who betrays his wife to save himself in "The Captives"; and the egregiously misnamed Everett Manly, pious former preacher made temporary warden of Yuma Prison in *Forty Lashes Less One*—these are among the portraits hanging in Leonard's gallery of administrative fools and rogues.

Although his impression of Leonard's awed response to the white-collar belligerence of corporate advertising strikes me as mistaken, I think Devlin comes close to the truth when he notes Leonard's empathy for "the little guy, the 'office boy,' the swabbie handing out the beer," who must rise to the challenge of being kept down or threatened with violence by "the big shots" (7). A lot depends on what we mean by "the little guy," however. In general, Leonard's heroes are not "little guys" but size-regulars: ordinary, decent men trying to do their jobs or fulfill their obligations as fathers, sons, providers, and good citizens. Going about their business, they find themselves forced (by "big shots," two-bit thugs, or the bully down the street) to question, or discard entirely, their standard notions of decency. Unlike "little guys," they are seldom found among the anonymous stage extras, the office boys and swabbies, of everyday life. Polite, mild-mannered Constable Roberto Valdez, whom the "big shots" of Lanoria patronize or ridicule for trying to do his job in *Valdez Is Coming*, may be an exception, but "little" or not, Leonard's heroes are nearly always, like Valdez, underestimated because no one around them sees the real person "inside." Like as not, that inner person is a survivor from a heroic former life: Valdez was once a tough, smart cavalry scout under Major General George Crook. Other heroes might be Civil War veterans like Paul Cable, trying to make peace with civilian life. "The little guy," by contrast, is more often the butt of Leonard's humor, men like Bud Nagle in "Cavalry Boots," whose cowardice results, through a series of absurd accidents, in the Third Dragoons' surprise defeat of Cochise at Dos Cabezas, or Stan Cass, a naive and foolish young man, in "Jugged," whose "proud opinion of himself" (386) plays into the hands of the cunning jailbird Obie Ward.

Leonard has never thought of himself as a "little guy," but as someone with a person "inside" who had an unrecognized gift and needed only an opportunity—a time and place free of distractions—to perfect it. The little guys

Leonard met at Campbell Ewald, harried businessmen living lives of quiet desperation, are typified by Harry Myrold, a middle manager stuck in rush-hour traffic on the commute to his suburban home, in the unpublished short story "Arma Virumque Cano" (1954). The story's title is translated from the opening words, "Of arms and the man I sing," of Virgil's epic poem, the *Aeneid,* part of Leonard's curriculum at U of D High. Its irony is obvious once we recognize that Myrold's newest "weapon" has not been forged by Vulcan for the armory of Aeneas but tailored by Rose Brothers for a clothes closet in Bloomfield, Michigan: it's a new suit at a good discount price, "only forty-three dollars" (107), lying in a box on the back seat of Myrold's two-tone Chevrolet. Myrold is proud of the low price he paid. His purchase, like a suit of armor, defends his fragile sense of self-importance and business savvy against the dreary banalities of his dull job, his domineering wife, his pointless classical education, and his empty materialism. Despite the suit, and his chivalrous intentions, Myrold's commute ends in humiliation when he is scammed by a hitch-hiking Circe, a high school teenager who, on exiting his car, throws a pair of panties into the back seat (they land on top of the suit box) and threatens to scream rape unless he hands over his wallet. Finding only six dollars, she flings it contemptuously back in his face. "God, you're some big shot!" she exclaims, and tells him to go back to school. Arriving home late, Myrold finds himself facing an angry wife who suspects him of having stopped off at a bar (again) on the way home. The only cure for his double humiliation is a stiff drink and, the next day, the purchase of a more expensive suit.

Leonard's unpublished stories in contemporary settings are of interest both as seed material for his later work in crime fiction and for what they can tell us about his attitudes and intentions toward the literary marketplace outside pulp Westerns in his first decade of writing. As we have seen, his agent Marguerite Harper had been prodding Leonard, almost from the beginning, to write something acceptable to the higher-priced "slick" magazines, lithographed weeklies that paid by the story, not "by the word" (Devlin 9). Harper wanted to wean him from the less remunerative "pulps," which were devoted to formula fiction like Westerns, romances, and crime stories. In 1956 Leonard succeeded, selling the unconventional Western "Moment of Vengeance" to the *Saturday Evening Post,* just as the market for Westerns began to vanish under the competitive pressures of the TV product. By the next year Harper was urging Leonard to leave the genre altogether, as soon as possible. In January 1960, the year after he finished what would become one of his most successful Western novels, *Hombre* (it went on to become a major motion picture starring Paul Newman and to be named one of the best Westerns of all time by the Western Writers of America), Leonard received a letter from Harper insisting, "You just must switch to some other medium for now" (Devlin 10). It would be another year before Ballantine bought *Hombre,* and another three before Twentieth Century Fox purchased the movie rights. Leonard decided to face reality, but knew it would take every minute of his time and every ounce of strength. Just a month after receiving Harper's letter, he quit his job with Campbell Ewald to devote himself full time to his first novel in a new genre, crime writing. He expected to complete the book in half a year.

Leonard's previous luck with stories other than Westerns certainly would not have favored his chances of succeeding in another genre. In February 1960 he was batting something like .875 in the Western short fiction league, having published twenty-eight of thirty-two Western stories completed up to that point (not including the four novels), with three more yet to appear. Those twenty-eight hits included his only sale to a "slick," "Moment of Vengeance," the equivalent, perhaps, of a solitary home run. Publishing non-Westerns, Leonard was batting .083 in twelve at-bats: his only hit came with "The Bull Ring at Blisston," which he published in a pulp, *Short Stories for Men Magazine,* in August 1959. Leonard's decision to switch genres in 1960 was the equivalent of a hugely successful right-handed hitter trying to reinvent himself, in midcareer, as a lefty.

Besides "Arma Virumque Cano," Leonard's attempts at contemporary fiction included a blue-collar domestic vignette ("The Italian Cut"), a humorous middle-class story of adulterous temptations and mistaken identity ("Evenings Away from Home"), an overseas colonial suspense tale ("Time of Terror"), a Civil War story ("Rebel on the Run"), and a portrait *à la* Hemingway of ugly Americans and Brits at a Spanish resort ("A Happy, Light-Hearted People"). He also wrote three tales that would eventually contribute to full-length crime novels: two that read like sketches for *Killshot* ("For Something to Do" and "The Trespassers") and a dry run at the plight of migrant workers in Michigan's Thumb region ("The Bull Ring at Blisston"), a topic to which he would return in *The Big Bounce* and *Mr. Majestyk.* Many of these tales, like his published work, feature protagonists who apply skill sets from a previous life to new challenges or opportunities, just as Leonard himself was about to do in turning from Westerns to crime fiction. In "Time of Terror," Police Lieutenant Barney Clad uses his skills as a former race car driver to elude a rebel ambush, and in "For Something to Do," a husband defends his rural home from two drunken attackers, much like Paul Cable in *Last Stand at Saber River,* drawing on his veterinarian savvy rather than experience in war.

"The Bull Ring at Blisston," appearing the same year as *Last Stand,* was Leonard's only published story from his Western period to take place in a contemporary setting. It reflects his anxieties as a writer about to be forced out of the profession he loved and facing the distinct possibility of having to write ad copy for the rest of his life, the authorial equivalent of migrant labor.[3] In the story, a young former bullfighter, Eladio Montoyo, who has left bullfighting after being gored in the hip, finds himself reduced to picking tomatoes for gentleman farmer Sherman David, a spoiled rich kid who inherited his father's tool-and-die business. Threatening to kick Montoyo's brother and his family off the farm if the ex-matador refuses to follow orders, the wealthy grower coerces him into fighting an untrained bull for a hundred dollars, using an old blanket for a cape, to entertain some important guests. Montoyo resists, not just because an untrained bull is unpredictable, but also because, as he tells David's sympathetic fiancée, Megan, he is terrified at the thought of getting back in the bullring. His former agent, Luis Fortuna, handled him badly, getting him bad bulls and bad contracts, and David reminds Montoyo of Fortuna: "Maybe all bosses come from the same tree" (51). Of course, Montoyo performs beautifully, but his subtle performance is not appreciated—is in fact ridiculed—by David and his ignorant business partners. When Montoyo asks for his money, David refuses to pay him for such a bad "show" and leaves with his guests for dinner at the mansion.

Megan, who has some knowledge of bullfighting, understands what's just happened better than Montoyo himself. "You fought the wrong bull," she tells him, and points to the retreating Sherman David.

> That one. That's the one you have to face. You do well with a bull—you're sure of that now. But you're mixed up with these Luis Fortunas and Sherman Davids. They make you feel that everything's against you. Too much for one man to fight. They make you lose confidence in yourself and because of it you think you have a fear of the bulls. (53)

Megan also knows why Montoyo succeeded this time: "Because I was watching. It's true, isn't it? I was for you and you could feel it" (53). Acting on Megan's insight that he fought "the wrong bull," Montoyo confronts his drunken employer in his own dining room, in front of his guests, and demands payment. When David lunges at the bullfighter with a steak knife, Montoyo, like an adroit matador or (and here Leonard is showing off his technical knowledge) *banderillero,* sidesteps David's threatening "horn" and sticks him in the neck with a pair of improvised *banderillas*—two forks—sending him sprawling into the dining table.

Behind the bullfighting symbolism of "The Bull Ring at Blisston" lies a deeper message, a cautionary tale regarding the work of writing, whose lesson is to trust in what you know and can do well and not invest too much of your self-respect in what your "agents" or "bosses" (editors?) say you have to do. Otherwise, you will find yourself "gored" because of their bad choices (of genres, of venues) and begin to lose confidence in what you know. And pay no attention to what ignorant readers (the guests David is paying Montoyo to "entertain") make of your performance, either. Always keep in mind the ideal reader who understands and appreciates how you are handling this dangerous but tractable beast called writing. Write for her. Bullfighting in "Blisston" is equivalent to dynamiting in *Escape from Five Shadows*: a *techne* capable of complex, intricate, and even graceful displays of controlled violence, of pyrotechnics and quiet brushes with disaster, but only in the hands of a skilled expert. Not surprisingly, after defeating the only "bull" that matters, Montoya returns to being a matador in Juarez, and Megan breaks off her engagement with Sherman David to join him.

Among the remaining non-Western tales, "The Only Good Syrian Footsoldier Is a Dead One" resembles "Arma Virumque Cano" in featuring an unmistakable "little guy," in this case, a literal spear carrier in a Hollywood toga epic being filmed on a desert location in Spain. Although it ends with the last thoughts of its dying protagonist, it is actually a tragicomedy, as its title, playing on the Old West cliché, "The only good Indian is a dead Indian," suggests. The "good Indian" in this story is the extra, Allen Garfield, a Michigan boy from Royal Oak who caught the acting bug in high school and left for Hollywood, only to find himself reduced to being killed repeatedly in movies like *The Centurion*, which stars the moronic narcissist Harry Keating. In the casting office, Garfield is considered "a good dier" (205), but he thinks he knows more about filmmaking than the director himself, and certainly more about acting than Keating. The story is told from his contemptuous point of view as he fantasizes the movie he would like to make, revealing the director, producer, and star as the greedy, unprofessional buffoons (he thinks) they are.

Leonard's adoption of Garfield's jaundiced viewpoint reads like an endorsement of it, and one might conclude, prematurely, that this is the story of a "little guy," to use Devlin's words, oppressed like the Native Americans of Old West mythography and about to show the "big shots" a thing or two. That scenario never materializes, however, and we should begin to suspect that it won't when Garfield, lying "dead" in the hot Spanish sun while the crew sip cool drinks and discuss camera angles, tells himself to "Get up. Walk off right in front of them and don't say a God damn word or look at anybody" (213)—and doesn't.

Instead, as the production wraps up for the day, Garfield is called aside by the casting assistant for a close-up scene with Keating. This, he thinks, is his big break. Garfield is to leap down from a rock ten feet high and come at Keating, at which point the wounded Roman hero will run him through with his sword. The ambush requires eight takes, because Keating keeps screwing up and blaming Garfield. Each time Garfield is commanded by the director to jump, he jumps, until Keating stumbles on the last take and accidentally stabs Garfield in the stomach—for real.

What talentless "little guys" like Allen Garfield need to learn is never to let anyone treat you like shit, even if you don't have the skills—as Eladio Montoyo does—to prove them wrong. If you can't "put up," if you can't overcome others' doubts by rising to the challenges of your chosen profession, you need to "shut up" and walk away, although it may mean walking "all the way to Madrid" (213). If you don't leave when you know you've had enough, you may start "jumping" on command, like a trained flea, and literally end your life in a meaningless job you hate—perhaps as a nameless "extra" at a big advertising firm. Like the first story Dutch Leonard wrote, in high school, "The Only Good Syrian Footsoldier" is a joke that turns on a double-meaning: in "Dickey," a nickname for both humans and pets; here, the idea of "dying" well—too well. But humorous as it may be, the story also touches upon some serious concerns Leonard was experiencing with regard to his own professional future at about the time he wrote it in the mid-1960s, when he was flown to Spain to revise a screenplay and spent time with the film crew on a desert location.

When Leonard quit his job early in 1960, he expected the $11,000 he received from Campbell Ewald's profit-sharing plan to buy him enough time to complete his first crime novel. But the money began to disappear rapidly under the pressures of an expanding family that led to the purchase of a new home. For immediate income he turned to writing freelance advertising copy and documentary screenplays for educational films produced by Encyclopedia Britannica. He had already had some success in selling to Hollywood, with screen versions of both "Three-Ten to Yuma" and "The Captives" (retitled *The Tall T*) released by Columbia in 1957. When Twentieth Century Fox bought the film rights to *Hombre* for $10,000 in 1965, Leonard discovered just how lucrative screenwriting could be, and for at least the next two decades he would continue to write with Hollywood in mind, often transforming his own books into screenplays, or vice versa, as in the case of *Mr. Majestyk*. But meanwhile, as Devlin puts it, "for a man who still thought of himself as a writer, it was distressing not to write" (12). In 1965, using the money from *Hombre* to buy himself some breathing room, he began "Mother, This Is Jack Ryan," the first draft of what was to become *The Big Bounce*. At just about the same moment in his career—perhaps the year before—Leonard wrote "The Only Good Syrian Footsoldier," with its detailed description of Allen Garfield's jumping repeatedly on command. In his first attempt, the actor loses his balance and falls forward. In the second, "jumping out farther this time with his feet wider apart, he felt the shock but was moving forward [. . .] on his feet" (220).

Garfield's experience of jumping and regaining his balance after the shock of landing resembles Leonard's description of a dream that began to recur while he was working on *The Big Bounce*. In this dream, he says, "I had to jump off something and I'd think I don't want to do this but I'd do it and I'd hit and it hurt my feet for a moment, but I was never injured, never" (Rzepka, "Interviews 9"). The jumping dream appears to be a reworking of the falling-downstairs nightmares Leonard suffered at the very beginning of his career, before he started to sell. In this later dream, however, he is making a deliberate choice to jump when faced with a situation apparently offering no choice, and emerging unharmed. Moreover, he is avoiding ladders or stairs—the literal "step-by-step" routine of a young writer just learning his craft. Where Allen Garfield jumps on command, repeatedly, and ends up dead, Leonard jumps on his own initiative and at the time he chooses, and survives. In one of his jumping dreams, he is on a rooftop chasing someone who drops down to another rooftop, out of sight.[4] "And then I thought I've got to get off this roof quick," he says. The leap was about "three stories." "I jumped and I hit hard but I was okay" ("Interviews 9").

If space allowed, it might be worth exploring the significance of the word *stories* in Leonard's account or digging down into the archetypal substrata of falling or jumping dreams in general. Leonard is not interested in psychoanalyzing either his characters or himself, but he does recognize the significance of connections and patterns: when something "fits, it relates, yes" ("Interviews 9"). Here's something else that seems to fit. In *The Big Bounce,* Leonard's hero Jack Ryan drops off the roof of a vacation home that he and his partner are robbing, when returning guests force them to hide in an upstairs bedroom. Ryan tells Billy Ruiz to follow him out onto the roof outside the window.

> Ryan went down on his stomach at the edge of the roof and listened, not moving. After this he did not hesitate again; he rolled over the edge holding the gutter and dropped. (23)

Jack had taught himself a similar move, just for fun, as a boy of thirteen living in Detroit. After a trial run, just testing his grip, "he hung from the roof of their apartment building, four stories above the alley, to see if he could do it."

> It was a summer morning and he was alone on the roof, above the round tops of the elms and the peaks of the houses and the chimneys and television antennas. He could hear cars on Woodward Avenue a half block away [. . .]. When he was ready, he moved to the edge of the roof again and sat down with his legs hanging. He could do it and knew he could do it if he was careful and didn't let himself get scared or do anything dumb. But just knowing he could do it wasn't enough. (69–70)

The details of this scene—especially its proximity to Woodward Avenue—point to its source in Leonard's boyhood. It's Maurice Murray hanging from the rain gutter of the Boisineau brothers' rooftop, high above the alley below. That the scene should appear so prominently in an extended passage describing Ryan's childhood (one of the longest such passages of childhood backstory in Leonard's fiction) suggests that examining *The Big Bounce* for other autobiographical material would not be time wasted. That it should appear in a novel called *The Big Bounce,* Leonard's first attempt in the crime genre, and just at the time he is dreaming, repeatedly, of jumping from rooftops without getting hurt, is also significant.

Leonard says that he chose his final title after reading an *Esquire* article about young women looking for "kicks" or "the big bounce," women like his reckless, thrill-seeking *femme fatale* Nancy Hayes. He thought, wrongly, that the phrase would soon enter the pop lexicon. Like the names of his characters, however, it must also have resonated at a deeper level as an appropriate title for his first attempt at this new genre or he would not have kept it once it had become *passé,* as it did well before the book was published in 1969. *The Big Bounce* summarizes the hopes of an author at the "top" of his profession who has had to make the "jump" to another kind of writing but who doesn't know if he'll survive and is reluctant to let go of what he's good at.[5] Jack Ryan survives by hanging onto the roof of the house he is fleeing, before he drops to the ground and lands safely, as Leonard does in his new, recurring dream. As with dreams in general, however, the meaning of Jack's escape seems overdetermined: the house he is fleeing is not his. In fact, he is robbing it. The dream of jumping from the roof unharmed could thus represent Leonard's growing confidence that he would always find a "way out" of the new generic challenges he had posed for himself, and even make money while doing so, without risking a fall "down the stairs." In either case, Leonard wants more than to survive: he wants to "bounce back." Who is he chasing in that rooftop dream "three stories" above the ground, that man who drops so confidently and without hesitation onto a new rooftop, "out of sight"? Who if not himself, the writer he wants to be, leaping from roof to roof, bouncing from book to book, from genre to genre, without fear.

In the years of success that have followed Leonard's turn to crime fiction, the recurring scenario of death by falling seems to represent less a persistent fear of failure than an ongoing affirmation of having repeatedly faced and overcome that fear, and lived to write again. It also seems to represent Leonard's increasing desire to master the improvisatory technique for which he is now famous: just "let go," the dream seems to be saying, and trust in your ability to land safely, now that you've got the hang of it. *Tishomingo Blues*, featuring the high-dive artist Dennis Lenahan, crystallizes the meaning of this recurring *topos* in Leonard's mature writing, as well as in his dream life. Significantly, Lenahan's highest "dives" are all feet first, more like death-defying leaps than dives. Dope dealer Robert Taylor tries to persuade Lenahan to let him bankroll his professional dive show as a cover for laundering drug money, in effect prostituting his talent and depriving himself of any incentive to maintain his edge. However, Taylor is so impressed by Lenahan's cool, quiet self-possession on the diving platform that he changes his mind: selling one's soul and compromising one's talents for big bucks are not, after all, paths to success, he tells Lenahan. Take the great blues guitarist Robert Johnson, who played so well everyone thought he had sold his soul to the devil. They were wrong. "What he did," says Taylor, "was leave the Delta" and go "to the woodshed."

> "You know what's meant by woodsheddin'? It's getting off by yourself and finding your sound, your chops, what makes you special. [. . .] You understand what I'm saying?"
>
> "You want something," Dennis said, "work for it. If I want to run a diving show, get off my ass and make it happen." (379)

It's advice to which Leonard seemed particularly receptive as he began his new career in crime fiction.

Stumbling Forward: Jack Ryan's Trial Run

In the half-century arc of his writing life, Leonard's personal ontogeny has recapitulated the generic phylogeny of masculine pop fiction as described by Cynthia Hamilton, who has shown how modern crime genres came to separate themselves, early in the twentieth century, from the Western adventure tales with which they were originally packaged for working-class males in dime weeklies and yellowbacks. (See also Slotkin 217–28.) Thus, one might expect to find that writing crime fiction posed few challenges for Leonard. In fact, it took him about a decade to find his groove. For one thing, he experienced a profound change in his composition habits. Although he identifies *Valdez Is Coming,* a late Western (1970), as the first book in which he felt comfortable enough to let the plot unfold of its own accord, the event in Leonard's career that apparently tipped the balance between plotting in advance—the "up-looking-down" approach—and "letting go" like a good blues guitarist, to allow for more improvisation in his compositional routine, was rewriting the original manuscript for *The Big Bounce,* his first attempt in the crime genre. The book had been rejected eighty-four times by the end of 1966, as Leonard reported in a 1989 preface.[6] Ignoring the advice of the rejection letters, he set about revising with one goal in mind: "It needed a plot. It needed a promise that something was eventually going to happen" ("Introduction," *Big Bounce* i).

This exercise in rewriting for plot, rather than sticking to the one you started with, was to evolve into Leonard's mature approach to writing fiction: improvise and then revise. Make, then shape. This is why, spontaneous as they appear, the plots of Leonard's crime novels can often display surprising symmetries: in *Killshot,* for instance, Armand Degas gets the drop on Richie Nix in their first encounter because Armand just happened to leave his Browning automatic under the seat of his car, while in the climactic scene, Carmen Colson gets the drop on Armand because her husband just happened to leave his shotgun under their bed. "Well, evidently, I thought of that as I was writing," says Leonard. "But that's how you make the plot work. You take a little from here or you take from back here and put it up in the front so that you've got a setup now [for what comes later]" (Rzepka, "Interviews 2").

In *The Big Bounce,* this symmetry is most evident in the opening and closing scenes, which both feature a ballplayer "at bat." As the book opens, law enforcement officials are watching a movie clip about local migrant workers, taken by a documentary filmmaker. In it, Jack Ryan, a former minor league baseball player who had to quit after a freak back injury, swings a bat at the head of his crew foreman, Luis Camacho. The police are trying to see if Camacho is coming at Ryan with a knife—and he is, which means Ryan was acting in self-defense and should be released from jail. The parallel between this scene and the one in "The Bull Ring at Blisston," where migrant worker Eladio Montoya uses his former professional skills as a bullfighter to defend himself against the knife-wielding Sherman David, is reinforced once we learn that, after failing to make the majors, Jack has now, like Montoya, drifted into migrant farm work. As the book closes, Ryan is watching slugger Al Kaline of the Detroit Tigers batting against the Red Sox on TV—another visually mediated moment—while he and Nancy Hayes await the arrival of the police, whom Ryan has called to the scene. Hayes has just murdered a man, and Ryan, her accomplice in earlier acts of vandalism and unlawful entry, refuses to help her cover it up. Or does he? While he never agrees to support Nancy's outrageous fabrication of a break-in and attempted rape gone wrong, Ryan never says, in so many words, that he won't. He just remains silent as the police sirens begin to wail in the distance. Leonard leaves Jack Ryan's final decision, along with his fate and Nancy's, hanging like a curveball that won't break.

Baseball is one of a number of interests and concerns from Leonard's adolescent years that he incorporated in this text, including his memory of Maurice Murray's shocking, daredevil feat. Like Leonard, Jack Ryan grew up in the heart of Detroit and was the only boy in a Catholic family, but with a younger as well as an older sister. His family's home resembles the flat in which the Leonards lived right after their permanent move to Detroit: much like Elmore Jr., Jack "slept in the dining room on a studio couch" (49). Baseball is—or was—a central part of Jack's life, as it was of Leonard's during his teenage years, and (again like his creator) Jack played both baseball and football in high school. The scene of the story, in the Michigan Thumb area near Bay City, is where Leonard and his friends hitchhiked to pick produce when he was thirteen.

As Leonard's variation on Maurice Murray's roof-hanging stunt suggests, however, Jack Ryan's story is not so much Elmore Leonard's as a there-but-for-the-grace-of-God tale based on a composite portrait of his working-class childhood friends. Ryan's father, for instance, a morose, taciturn bus driver, is modeled after the father of a friend (Rzepka, "Interviews 5"). Mr. Ryan spends his off days drinking and playing solitaire, and he dies when Jack is thirteen. Not long afterward, Jack starts to get in trouble with the law, shoplifting and hot-wiring cars, and eventually breaking and entering homes and apartments that he and a black workmate, Leon Woody, scope out during their day jobs for a cleaning company. Jack "wondered if he would have started breaking into houses if his dad hadn't died. And then he would think: Why? What's that got to do with the price of anything? And he would think about something else" (101).

This is the kind of thing Elmore Leonard, Jr., might have pondered in 1966 regarding his own choice of profession, when looking back from the vantage point of a successful career that might never have opened up for him but for his father's death in 1948—pondered and, as Ryan's own rapid self-deflection indicates, refused to entertain. But whether or not Leonard ever wondered about the possibility, it does arise in *The Big Bounce* for a character whose history incorporates several features of Leonard's own. If we follow out the parallels between Ryan's successful rooftop escapes and Leonard's concurrent dreams of leaping safely from rooftops where he doesn't feel he belongs, we arrive, again, at an allegory *of* the work of writing that emerges *in* the work of writing, and just at the point of transition in his career when the writer in question is trying on another authorial identity. Like Hamlet's father's ghost, the image of the dead father—here associated, in the incongruous guise of bus driver, with Leonard's earliest childhood adventures beyond the family circle to the riverfront at the end of Woodward Avenue and beyond, literally to another country—arises unsummoned at the event of his son's second professional coming-of-age.

There is also a surrogate father in *The Big Bounce*, or at least, an older man who tries hard to get Jack Ryan to accept him in that role, and in this respect the book reinstates the pattern of paternal-filial surrogacy that dominated Leonard's early Westerns. Walter Majestyk, Geneva Beach's part-time justice of the peace and the full-time owner of a waterfront vacation inn, the Bay Vista, makes an effort to befriend Ryan after seeing the footage of his attack on Camacho (in the book's opening chapter). When asked by the assistant prosecutor for his reaction to the assault, Majestyk replies, tongue in cheek, "I think he's got a level swing, but maybe he pulls too much" (7). Here's another example of the comical, off-kilter tagline, dating back to "Dickey," for which Leonard will become famous. But it also represents what Majestyk, an avid baseball fan, sees in Ryan: the potential to "go straight" with a little fatherly coaching. Meeting him by chance in a bar after Ryan's release from jail, Majestyk says as much, after offering him work as a handyman and janitor at the Bay Vista: "You probably wonder why I want to hire you. Why you. Do you want me to tell you why?" he asks a sullen and indifferent Ryan. The answer is that he saw the film clip of Ryan's attack on Camacho.

> And I talked to the sheriff's cops about you and I said to myself, "That's a good kid. He stands up. Maybe he's had a rough life, bummed around, and had to work. No chance to go to college, no trade." [. . .] I think to myself, "What's he going to do? He's a good one. He's got something other guys don't have. The son of a bitch stands up." But listen, I know this. It isn't easy always to keep standing up. I mean, it's better if you got somebody to help you once in awhile. (57–58)

What Ryan's "got" at the moment is a huge chip on his shoulder. His sarcastic response to Majestyk's offer elicits perhaps the most accurate assessment of the young man's character in the book: "You can stand up, but Jesus Christ you're dumb, aren't you?" (58). Eventually, Ryan accepts Majestyk's offer, but only because it gives him a chance to stay in Geneva Beach near Nancy Hayes, the sexy nineteen-year-old mistress of Ray Richie, "Cucumber King" of southeast Michigan.

Majestyk's role as surrogate father is underlined by his paternal treatment of Ryan once the young man moves into the Bay Vista, where Majestyk assigns him his chores and sets ground rules for his daily routines, including mealtimes. Ryan, in short, is not just working for Majestyk but living with him like a stepson, just as Elmore "Dutch" Leonard lived with his football coach, Mr. Tiernan, in his senior year of high school. Like Tiernan, Majestyk is a former football player (45) who loves sports and comes across as "kind of gruff," although he's apparently more voluble than Leonard's coach ever was. Tiernan owned a hunting lodge in Montana; Majestyk is planning to buy a hunting lodge not far from Geneva Beach. Baseball soon becomes the most important bond between Majestyk and Ryan, while Nancy Hayes, whom Ray Richie has crowned "Cucumber Queen of Geneva Beach" to give their affair an official cover, poses the major stumbling block. At one point, seeing that Ryan has been driving Nancy's car, Majestyk tries to set him straight about her: she used the car to chase two innocent teenagers off the road, just for kicks, sending one to the hospital (116). Later, he again tries to warn Ryan to give Hayes a wide berth.

> "Listen," Mr. Majestyk said then. "That broad on the phone—"
>
> "Yeah?"
>
> Mr. Majestyk smiled, self-conscious, showing his white perfect teeth. He shrugged then. "Why should I say anything—right? You're old enough."
>
> "I was about to mention it," Ryan said. (179)

As if to underline Ryan's playing the rebellious adolescent in this scene of attempted instruction in the facts of life, Leonard next has him ask Majestyk if he can borrow his car after work (179).

Nancy is staying at Ray Richie's mansion, down the beach from Majestyk's motel, while Richie spends time in Detroit with his wife. And Nancy is bored. The life of a "Cucumber Queen" is not all it's cracked up to be. The plot of *The Big Bounce* hinges on Nancy's resentment of Richie's cavalier treatment of her. She plans to get revenge by persuading Ryan, who's experienced at breaking and entering, to rob Richie's monthly payroll, some fifty thousand dollars in cash that is regularly delivered to his nearby hunting lodge the day before his migrant workers get paid. This is apparently the plot that Leonard was searching for when he set about revising his original manuscript, "Mother, This Is Jack Ryan," whose title echoes the line Nancy imagines delivering when she brings Jack the Migrant Worker and Part-Time Burglar home to Miami to meet her wealthy but emotionally withdrawn mother—an occasion that never materializes.

The plot that Leonard settled on was taken from his earliest readings in the *noir* fiction of James M. Cain, which helped to inspire "One Horizontal." Specifically, Jack Ryan is a younger version of Frank Chambers, the petty grifter and road bum who narrates Cain's first novel, *The Postman Always Rings Twice.* Chambers is easily seduced into helping Cora Papadakis murder her husband for the insurance money, using what he's learned from years of run-ins with the law to hatch an elaborate scheme that will let them both get away with it. The grift goes haywire, Cora dies in a car crash, and Frank, the driver, ends up on death row. Like Chambers, who agrees to work for Cora's husband merely to pursue an affair with her, Ryan agrees to work at Majestyk's beachfront inn merely to be near Nancy Hayes, and Nancy, like Cora, threatens to turn her helpmate over to the law when he becomes hard to handle.

There are, of course, some major differences between Cain's protagonists and Leonard's. Cain's characters are truly sinister, compelling, complex, and brilliantly innovative in trying to get what they want, or think they deserve. Jack Ryan is a surly jerk who keeps making mistakes that he regrets—the biggest being Hayes—and Nancy Hayes is a cock-teasing airhead whose idea of "bounce" is sexually entrapping the fathers of kids she babysits and throwing rocks through, or shooting out, strangers' windows to prove something to her unloving mother and absent father—neither of whom could care less, even supposing they ever found out. As for the plot, what Alfred Hitchcock would call its "MacGuffin"[7]—the $50,000 payroll stash in Richie's hunting lodge that eventually gets the machinery of the book to creak forward—becomes irrelevant once Ryan is caught casing the lodge by Richie's foreman, Bob Rogers. Ryan's backing out of the robbery is what inspires Nancy to go for the "biggest bounce of all" (173): she plans to lure Jack to Richie's beachfront house late at night, shoot him when he arrives, and tell the police she thought he was an intruder. Unfortunately for her, but fortunately for Jack, he is delayed at the Bay Vista motel, watching baseball with Walter Majestyk, while fellow migrant worker Frank Pizarro shows up at Richie's home instead.

To use Leonard's own terminology, Jack and Nancy remain "childish" throughout *The Big Bounce,* unable or unwilling to mature into "childlike" adults.

Their impulses, desires, and even their vocabulary are adolescent. When Majestyk calls Jack "dumb," we can see that he's right on target. But when Jack uses the word (and he uses it often and indiscriminately) he's usually being defensive. Here's his reaction, rendered in free indirect discourse, when Billy Ruiz, who accompanied him into the vacation home they robbed with Pizarro, dares to hint that he should get the same cut of the loot as Ryan himself:

> The dumb bastard; the dumb cucumber picker. Ruiz wouldn't have gone near the house alone. He wouldn't have walked *past* it. Dumb skinny blank-eyed little weasel, [. . .] with his pants too long and sagging in the seat, too dumb to know how dumb he looks, how skinny ugly baggy-assed dumb. (25)

This is the kind of talk we might expect from an inarticulate high school student who wants to sound tough. *Dumb* is also one of Nancy's favorite words. Here she is, alone with her thoughts in Richie's riverside apartment in Detroit while Richie is in Chicago on business:

> She sat quietly while Ray and his group whipped off to Chicago to attend the dumb meeting or look at the dumb plant and make big important decisions about their dumb business. Wow. And she sat here waiting for him. (38)

If Jack Ryan is indeed, as Leonard has stated, prototypical of "all of [his] male leads" in his "basic attitude about [his] own existence" ("Introduction," *Big Bounce* iv), then it must be the grown-up version of this immature loser, the guy we encounter several years later in *Unknown Man No. 89*, that Leonard has in mind.

Like Leonard himself, apparently, Mr. Majestyk sees the potential in Jack, and his faith pays off, at least in part. Jack refuses to follow through with the payroll heist and, it seems, will refuse to help Nancy cover up her mistaken murder of Pizarro once the police arrive, even though he hates the man. Moreover, by doing so, he risks going to jail himself, since Nancy says she will turn Ryan in for robbing the vacation house with Ruiz and Pizarro if he doesn't go along with the cover-up. (She acquired the incriminating evidence from Pizarro.) Jack's decision not to protect Nancy from arrest is all we know about his change of heart before the book ends, which is as far as we can go in determining the success of Walter Majestyk's efforts to help him grow up.

Like a good coach, Majestyk sees sports as both a metaphor and a model for life, full of lessons for troubled young men like Jack Ryan. Those lessons center on resisting distractions from the task at hand and doing your job—in short, staying cool. As he and Jack watch the Tigers–Red Sox game that will end up saving Jack's life by keeping him riveted to a TV screen at the Bay Vista, well past his appointment with death in Ray Richie's living room, the two begin to discuss the Tigers' announcer, George Kell, a baseball legend. Not surprisingly, Jack's first thought is that being famous and successful makes you a target for criminals and kooks. Someone who "knows you're away playing ball, nobody home, he goes in and takes anything he wants. Or you're in a slump and some nut fan throws rocks at your windows," as he and Nancy have been doing to their neighbors' windows up and down Geneva Beach (185). Majestyk concedes the possibilities. "But when a guy is good, like Kell, you got to be able to take a lot of crap and not let it bother you."

> "Listen, you hit three thirty, three forty like Kell, the pitchers are throwing crap and junk at you all the time and it's worse than any rocks because it's your living, it's what you *do*. You stand in there, that's all. When they come in with a good one, you belt it." (185)

Majestyk tells Jack that if he'd stayed in baseball, stood in there, maybe "they'd be putting a sign up for you one of these days. [. . .] I mean if you didn't have the bad back." Jack's reply suggests that he may be ready to stop making excuses and blaming others for the course of his life: "Even if I didn't have it, I never could hit a goddamn curve ball" (185).

The Big Bounce may be many things, but one thing it's not is *noir.* Wading in the shallow end of the pool, far from the lower depths, it's really a coming-of-age tale. Once we begin to see the book this way, many of its otherwise anomalous features begin to make sense.

For instance, Leonard spends a good deal of time letting Majestyk reminisce about his experiences in World War II—experiences that are almost identical to those of Elmore Leonard on his tour of duty as a Seabee in the South Pacific, right down to the island, Los Negros, on which he served. Among other things, Majestyk describes how the Seabees would cut roads through the jungle, using their bulldozer blades to deflect enemy fire. Ryan is impressed, despite himself. Rejected by his draft board because of his bad back, he's in the habit of fantasizing Viet Cong combat scenarios. Even clearing rubbish from the empty beach frontage adjoining the Bay Vista offers him an opportunity to "fool around," "picking up cans and tossing them into the brush where the V.C.'s were dug in. He'd have to get [Majestyk's] bulldozer to clear the heavy stuff. [. . .] Come across the beach with the blade held high, as a shield against the V.C. automatic weapons. Imagine doing that" (74–75). That night, alone on the beach, Ryan pictures the "dark shapes" of the houses back in the trees as "the huts of a village. The boats lying on the beach could be sampans used by the V.C. The word was they had brought in a load of mortars and automatic weapons" (79). Ryan's thoughts are those of a kid playing war in a vacant lot.

> What some guys did in the war. Underwater Demolition or the Special Forces guys, moving through the jungle at night with an M-16 and their faces black, one false step and you've got a *pungi* spike up your behind. (79)

Ryan's fantasies are drawn, presumably, from talking to or corresponding with a buddy who was drafted into Special Forces (72) and from reading men's magazines like *True* (79), but also, as the bulldozer scenario indicates, from listening to the recollections of Walter Majestyk, his surrogate father.

Ryan likes being alone (79), especially in the dark, because it gives his imagination room to expand without encountering the waking reality of what others see him to be. He doesn't understand people being afraid of the dark: "some people would be afraid to be out here," he thinks (79). Not him. "You got used to it, that was all. You made up your mind you were going to be good at it and not panic." These are the words of a man—or rather, a boy—who has never faced combat, let alone enemy combatants in a dark jungle. His reflections lead him to a consideration of "coolness," "something you developed," he tells himself: "No, cooler than cool. Christ, everybody thought they were cool. It was a coldness you had to develop. The pro with icewater in his veins. Like Cary Grant" (80). Ryan's train of reveries leads him, a bit pathetically, from wishful fantasies of staying "cool" in combat to memories of watching Cary Grant in Alfred Hitchcock's 1955 hit, *To Catch a Thief.* In that film, Grant, the cinematic epitome of cool, plays John Robie, a reformed cat burglar out to capture a former confederate who is framing him by imitating his style of breaking and entering. Adopting a false identity as an American industrialist, Robie ensnares the affections of heiress Frances Stevens, played by Grace Kelly, whom he takes to be his copycat's next victim. "Pouring champagne for the broad," Ryan thinks, "or up on the rooftop with the guy [Robie's arch enemy, Foussard] with a steel hook instead of a hand coming at him, he's the same Cary Grant. No sweat" (80).

Ryan, like Leonard, understands that real "cool" is a matter of self-integration, self-possession, being the same person in all circumstances, even the most challenging and nerve-wracking, whether you're fighting for your life on the rooftop of a five-story building (Leonard's rooftop dream scenario again reprised) or pretending to be someone you're not. It's all a matter of staying in control, and control is a matter of talent, training, and lots of practice. Cary Grant appeals to Ryan as a model of cool in large part because Grant—like all great movie actors—is always himself, "the same Cary Grant," no matter what character he plays. Moreover, the character he plays in *To Catch a Thief* just happens to be a highly experienced professional, the ultimate "pro with icewater in his veins," and Jack Ryan considers himself a "pro," at least compared with amateurs like Billy Ruiz and Frank Pizarro. He can show you how to walk into a home as though you belong there, what to take, where to find it, how to escape, and even how to walk away: "They walked, they didn't hurry; they walked because Ryan said that's the way it was done" (23).

But John Robie is a fantasy thief living a glamorous fantasy life: he steals jewels, not random cash, and lives in luxury on the Riviera, not in a migrant shack or a motel in Geneva Beach, Michigan. That's what makes him such an attractive "grown-up" role model for Ryan, whose only successes in life so far (since he hasn't been caught at it yet) have come through burglary. Robie is "cool" because he is always, really, the highly skilled, coached, and experienced actor Cary Grant pretending to be John Robie, even when John Robie is pretending to be someone else. Cary Grant is the person "inside" Robie who, like Chili Palmer, is always coming out and asserting himself in "what he does," whatever part he plays. Similarly, Ryan is never more himself than when he's pretending to be someone who "belongs" in a home he's robbing or about to rob: delivering what looks like beer (the cardboard case is for hauling away the victims' wallets), or just cleaning carpets, as he used to do in Detroit with his partner in crime, Leon Woody, while studying or rigging the premises for a possible break-in later.

Ryan's memories of his breaking-and-entering days with Leon (who will resurface in a later novel) often come to him when he finds himself unexpectedly involved in Nancy's risky, thrill-seeking antics: breaking windows and running away or, better, walking in the back door and pouring herself a drink while her victims peer out the broken picture window in front. She even gets Ryan to break into the vacation home he robbed earlier with Frank and Billy, without his even recognizing it, for no other reason than to tease him by asking him to make love to her before the owners come back. The difference between what Ryan did with Leon Woody when he was younger and what he's doing with Nancy now boils down to one thing: with Woody he robbed people for a living. He made money at it. In the words Walter Majestyk uses to describe George Kell's batting prowess, it's what Ryan *did.* And for that reason, he worked at it and became skilled at it.

This is something Ryan cannot impress upon Nancy, try as he might, not even after she suggests they take up armed robbery. He can imagine doing something like that with Woody because they would have "studied the place and timed it," although "it could take all the nerve they had ever used during all the B & E's put together and it still might not be enough to go in with a gun" (120). Nancy's attitude is completely devil-may-care; she is full of nerve—"What else is there? I mean, that you can count on," she says (121)—but she has no skills whatsoever and sees no need for them. Ryan "wished he could ruffle her, shake her up a little" (122), get her to understand the real risks involved and how to deal with them, if only to show her he's more than just "some stiff she was hiring to do the heavy work" (123), that he is, in fact, a skilled technician. But Nancy just doesn't get it. "What's so hard about sneaking into a house?" she asks (124).

The difference between committing crimes for kicks and committing crimes for a living determines the difference between what we might call real as opposed to fake "cool" in *The Big Bounce.* When Ryan and Woody were robbing homes, they would often compete to see who could be "cooler" by taking calculated risks. Woody might pour himself a drink and take a few moments to read the newspaper, like an invited guest, and next time Ryan would answer the door as if he were the homeowner and pay for a dry cleaning delivery (81). The point was to remain in control of the situation rather than controlled by it and, most importantly, always to allow enough time for a clean getaway. Above all, like Cary Grant playing John Robie playing an American industrialist, Ryan and Woody had to become expert actors—pretending to be the owner of the house when the dry cleaner showed up, or if you were black, pulling off a persuasive "dumb nigger act" for an unsuspecting mark (80), or getting the neighbors to think you'd been called to do some renovations and drilling out the lock on the door in broad daylight (81). Being cool was a way to confirm your skill as a thief, which also meant as a performer, while never forgetting who you really were: a "pro" at what you do.

By contrast, whether he's breaking windows or breaking in with Nancy Hayes, the "cool" that Ryan now feels is inauthentic, self-conscious: "aware of himself almost all the time, [. . .] seeing himself and hearing himself and most of the time he looked dumb" and "never for more than a moment felt in control" (131). The problem is trying so hard to *look* "cool" that you can't *be* cool.

> She was being cool and he was being cool, each trying to be cooler than the other until pretty soon, Ryan decided, you get so cool you can't even move because of the chance that anything at all you might do might turn out to be dumb. Anything. What good was being cool if you weren't you? Whoever you are, Ryan thought. (131–32)

The "coolness" that Ryan displays in the presence of Nancy, chilled to whatever degree Kelvin, is not the "cooler than cool" coldness of a pro. It's all pose and no prowess. Instead of freeing him up, making him less self-conscious and giving him pleasure in what he does, it freezes him into immobility. Ryan knows Nancy is bad for him, because she has no use for what he is, an experienced professional, and that identity is subsumed in what he does. He's not just "some stiff" hired for the "heavy work," like an unskilled laborer. Denied the use of the tools and know-how that define him as a thief, Ryan becomes Nancy's tool—or rather, toy—in her endless, vindictive pursuit of "bounce."

How did Ryan the pro get himself into this amateurish gig? He and Nancy actually have a lot in common. Even in his professional days, Ryan's attitude toward breaking and entering was much closer to Nancy's than he might care to admit. "It was hard [. . .] not to think of it as a game. A kick. He was breaking the law and knew he was breaking it, but he never thought of it that way. It was funny, he just didn't" (113). "A game" is exactly how he puts it to Leon Woody when the more experienced burglar first catches him preparing a client's home for a later break-in. "I wasn't going to take anything," he tells Woody.

> Leon Woody looked at him. "Then, why do you want to go in?"
>
> "I don't know." It sounded dumb. "Just to see if I can, I guess." It still sounded dumb.
>
> "Like, man, a game?"
>
> "Yeah, sort of." (112)

Ryan does it at first for the thrill, the risk, like Nancy Hayes, but he already knows that's "dumb." It's Woody who teaches him what makes taking risks meaningful: "a white Mercury convertible and fifteen suits and twelve pairs of shoes and I don't know how many chicks I can call anytime of the night. *Anytime*" (113). Woody teaches Jack that breaking and entering isn't just a game. It's a living, a career, so you better learn how to do it right.

At the end of *The Big Bounce* we don't know what will happen to Jack Ryan. We know only that he has grown up to the point of taking responsibility for his choices in life, including his "dumb" dalliance with Nancy Hayes. Whatever hopes Walter Majestyk may have for him, one thing seems clear: the only profession in which Jack is experienced and has had some success is breaking and entering. But if he is to make a go of professional burglary, he has to stop thinking of it as *just* a game, like a kid, and begin to approach it as a skill, too, a demanding *techne* by which he can make a living for himself, like Leon Woody, and still have "fun" acting up. It's what he did when he took the game of baseball and tried to make it a career. He failed at it, yes, but that didn't mean he had to fail at everything. In the final analysis, Nancy's poisonous influence boils down to this: she thinks of crime as a game requiring no skill, only risk, and encourages Ryan to think that way. This thought occurs to him just after he tells Nancy he won't be breaking into Richie's hunting lodge after all.

> It was a funny thing, he could see himself going into the place, but he didn't look right. He could see himself going into other places with Nancy, the great boy-girl burglary team, and that didn't look right, either. He looked dumb, doing it because she wanted to do it. A game and not real at all. She talked about real life. It wouldn't be anything like real life. It wouldn't be anything like going into places with Leon Woody. That had been real. (174)

Nancy keeps Jack at the unreal, make-believe level of childish behavior to which he is naturally inclined—she even calls him "Jackie"—and thereby impedes his maturation into the adult joys of a childlike delight in *techne*. That delight is compounded by advancing skills, and skills advance best under the pressure of doing something you enjoy for your daily bread. That's when *techne* becomes not just frivolous but serious "fun." That's when being cool and not just looking cool comes within your grasp.

When we next meet Jack Ryan in *Unknown Man No. 89*, a decade after *The Big Bounce*, we learn that he managed to elude imprisonment: "He had been arrested only once, for felonious assault—belting a migrant crew chief the summer he had picked cucumbers up in the Thumb—but the charges had been dismissed" (3). So, apparently, Jack went along with Nancy's story and saved his ass, or the police and the DA refused to believe anything Nancy said, including her accusations against Jack. The important thing is that, at thirty-six, Jack is now "starting to worry that maybe he [is] a misfit, a little out of touch with reality" (2). He did not become a professional burglar, but nor did he become anything else, having drifted through a series of trucking and assembly-line and sales jobs. And he now has a serious drinking problem, just like his creator, Elmore Leonard.

In those eight years since his literary debut, however, Jack Ryan's character has been evolving through the pages of Leonard's fiction, the details of his life story and personality coming loose and attaching themselves to other characters fitting his phenotype. Tracing the details of that evolution up to 1980, with the publication of *City Primeval: High Noon in Detroit*, is the purpose of the next chapter. As we shall see, Leonard's authorial *nostos*, his imaginative return to Detroit as he seeks to master the writing of crime fiction, will provide a crucial turning point in the emergence of a uniquely Leonardian protagonist by stirring up the history he shares with the city, a history that spans his own growing up as a man and a writer. Detroit will become the workbench on which Leonard will fashion his new, contemporary heroes of *techne* and begin to explore, more determinedly than ever before, the authenticity of "being cool."

THREE

plays well with others

take five

Woodsheddin': Begins with "M"

The first decade of Leonard's career as a writer of crime fiction was interrupted at several points by work that harkened back to his Western phase, such as *Valdez Is Coming* (1970), *Forty Lashes Less One* (1972), and *Gunsights* (1979), and by work on screenplays. The latter include some that sold—*The Moonshine War* (1970, based on the novel of 1969), *Picket Line* (1970), *American Flag* (1971), *Joe Kidd* (1972), and *Mr. Majestyk* (1974, the basis for the novel published the same year)—and some that did not, like *The Sun-King Man* and *Jesus Saves* (both 1970). Not all the screenplays that sold were made into movies, but as Geherin points out (43), the income from screenwriting and from selling the film rights to books like *Hombre* and *Valdez Is Coming* helped support Leonard and his family while he tried to get his bearings in the *terra incognita* of a new genre.

Of the eight crime novels that Leonard wrote immediately following *The Big Bounce* in 1969, five are set in Detroit. (*Touch* is set in Detroit but is not a crime novel.) The Motor City Five, as I call them, appeared almost yearly, from 1974 to 1980, and comprise *52 Pickup* (1974), *Swag* (1976), *Unknown Man No. 89* (1977), *The Switch* (1978), and *City Primeval: High Noon in Detroit* (1980). In the non-Detroit novels leading up to *52 Pickup*, we find Leonard experimenting with heroic prototypes, exploring contemporary variations on the Western settings he was used to, and looking for ways to help his Jack Ryan character mature into a hero of *techne* who has mastered "being cool" as prowess rather than pose. *The Moonshine War* (1969) and *Mr. Majestyk* (1974) are set in significant locations, temporally and geographically, and both protagonists' last names begin with "M," as in Walter Majestyk.

The Moonshine War takes place in 1931, near the end of Prohibition, and unfolds in the Appalachian hill country of fictional Marlett, Kentucky, a region close to that of *Justified,* Leonard's hit TV series on the FX Network. Leonard's hero Son Martin, who makes moonshine the way his father did, is backed by a colorful cast of 'stillers, small-town citizens, dyspeptic constables, and bootlegging gangsters straight out of the newspaper columns that filled Leonard's early years with lurid tales of Bonnie and Clyde and Ma Barker's Boys. The book's remote mountain setting in the days before the Tennessee Valley Authority, when electricity was home generated and Federal prohibition agents were looked upon as advance troops of an invading army, makes *The Moonshine War* an anachronistic version of the frontier Western, a genre that Leonard already knew inside and out.

The screenplay version of *Mr. Majestyk* is set in Colorado, but in the book based on it, Leonard returned to the Arizona Territory of his early Westerns, updated. The Arizona setting, whose rugged landscape was mapped out in Leonard's imagination early in his writing career, figures importantly in the final chapters of the book, and its Hispanic migrant workers, farmhands, and foremen, as well as the young woman who becomes the protagonist's love interest, all play roles similar to those assigned to the marginalized Mexicans and Mexican Americans of his Western stories.

In these two familiar but displaced chronotopes of the Old West, Leonard sought to remedy the less appealing features of his overgrown adolescent "rebel without a cause," Jack Ryan. He began by making his new "M" protagonists older and more experienced—Son Martin is thirty-five, Vincent Majestyk about thirty—and giving them each a traumatized familiarity with violence and a well-honed set of skills to handle it calmly, efficiently, and with improvisational dispatch. Each man is a combat veteran, Son Martin of the Great War, Vincent Majestyk of Laos and Cambodia, and each finds himself forced to use the arts of war to preserve or restore the arts of peace—namely, distilling whiskey and growing melons.

In fact, it might be more accurate to say that Leonard momentarily set aside rather than developed his Jack Ryan prototype in favor of exploring the heroic potential of Jack's otherwise unassuming mentor in *The Big Bounce,* World War II veteran Walter Majestyk, minus twenty years. While Jack merely fantasizes about taking on the Viet Cong, Walter's namesake, Vincent, captured members of the Pathet Lao after being captured himself and earned a Silver Star for his exploits. He also went on to train Rangers at Fort Benning after his return to the States. Son Martin left his father's farm and his new bride to fight "over there" and returned to find his wife and mother dead from the flu epidemic of 1918. Instead of trying to cope with the bitterness and desolation of civilian life, he re-upped as an army engineer and acquired expertise in the handling of explosives. He came back to Marlett in 1927 only two months before his father, John W., died in a mine accident, an angry old man furious at the psychological damage inflicted on his son by the U.S. Army and Wilson's War.

Leonard's paragraph-long, circumstantial description of Son's way with moonshine—"clean," "pure," "slow," double distilled, charcoal filtered, and "worth a wait" (235)—mimics, in its pace of writing, Son's own patience with the details of making corn whiskey. In fact, Leonard could be describing his own writing process. During his years in the army corps of engineers, Son, like Corey Bowen in *Escape from Five Shadows*, has also learned to handle dynamite, a skill even more demanding of patience, care, and undivided attention than distilling. The MacGuffin this time is 150 barrels of whiskey, eight years old and about to "come of age" (242) as the story opens, which Son's father left him as an inheritance in lieu of cash, investments, or Liberty Bonds from the hated U.S. government. At current black market prices under Prohibition, the whiskey has a retail value of $120,000, more or less (248). Rumors about the stash of whiskey and its hiding place have been making the rounds of the neighborhood for years, but it isn't until an old army buddy of Son's shows up as an official Federal law officer charged with hunting down and destroying illegal stills that the search begins in earnest, with fatal consequences.

Frank Long doesn't plan on destroying Son's cache of booze or turning it over to the government once he finds it. He's made a deal to sell it to bootlegger Dr. Emmett Taulbee (a former dentist convicted of sexually molesting female patients under sedation), whose factotum, Dual Meaders, is handed the lion's share of mindless violence in the book. Taulbee, of course, has no intention of sharing his profits with Long, and his heavy-handed attempts to pressure Son into revealing the whiskey's whereabouts eventually drive Long to ally himself with his former comrade in arms. The book ends with a standoff between Taulbee's men and Son, who is barricaded in his father's house along with Frank Long and Son's black hired hand, Aaron.

The whiskey turns out to be hidden within sight of the house, down an abandoned mine shaft disguised as the grave of John W. Martin himself, who is actually buried elsewhere. The grave is illuminated at night by an electric light attached to a "new-looking Delco Farm Electrification System" in the basement and controlled by a switch in the kitchen (292). However, what looks like a gesture of filial piety is in fact the triggering mechanism for 150 sticks of dynamite buried along with the whiskey—"a stick a barrel" (372). Needless to say, that dynamite, like Chekhov's gun,[1] will go off before Leonard's story is through, sending Son Martin's enemies and his daddy's moonshine to kingdom come. Son would rather destroy his inheritance than have to surrender it to his foe.

Son Martin's name is almost too obvious a pointer to Leonard's interest in the intergenerational dimensions of *techne* and profession, whether as nature (temperament, talent) or nurture (Son's reprising his daddy's distilling expertise in his own operation). In broad terms, however, *The Moonshine War* can be read as an allegory of Leonard's rejection of the career path his father intended for him, namely, to share in the wealth generated by the family business. Only by rejecting his inheritance, which has created nothing but trouble for his friends and neighbors at the hands of Taulbee's roughnecks, can Son assume a place of his own in the community from which the Great War alienated him, selling his own moonshine, not his father's, by perfecting his expertise to match, or even surpass, John W.'s.

Like scenes of falling or leaping from dangerous heights (repeated here when Meaders forces Aaron to leap from the hayloft of a barn), explosions don't become a recurrent feature in the novels until Leonard switches to crime fiction, beginning with *The Moonshine War.* In his next book, *Mr. Majestyk,* fatal falls and explosions achieve a gratifying symbiosis as Vincent Majestyk forces first one and then another car carrying Frank Renda's henchmen off the shoulder of a winding mountain road, to plunge to their deaths. The first car dives fifty feet, killing all occupants (191), and the second falls five hundred, exploding in flames (196). The *techne* to which Vincent Majestyk remains true, however, his prime motivation and the only thing that apparently gives his life any meaning, is harvesting his melons and getting them to market before the season ends. When union organizer Nancy Chavez shows up in the town of Edna with four fellow pickers looking for work, her preemptive belligerence elicits from Leonard's hero only the laconic reply, "I don't care if you're union or not, long as you know melons" (16). Majestyk does know melons, having "picked way more'n I've ever grown," as he tells Nancy (109). But Leonard won't let things rest there. In a later scene, Larry Mendoza, Majestyk's foreman, is forced to explain, in circumstantial detail, the finer points of melon picking to "an Anglo kid" with "muscular arms and shoulders" but no idea how to handle unripe melons, or even how to tell them from ripe ones. "Like it's easy," says Nancy, after watching Mendoza chew the kid out (88–89).

Having picked melons himself, Majestyk understands that a skilled worker will save the grower money in the long run, because there's more to picking melons than yanking them off the vine and hauling them to the truck. That's why Majestyk gets mad at Bobby Kopas and the cut-rate winos and street bums that he's hired to harvest Majestyk's fields (demanding in return a steep broker's fee), without the grower's permission and with several implied threats of strong-arm reprisals if he doesn't go along. Majestyk gets so mad that he ends up chasing Kopas off his property with the man's own shotgun, and that, in turn, is why Majestyk is arrested the next day on charges of assault and battery.

It's clear that the charges are bogus, but Majestyk has, we learn, a record—he was once arrested for hitting a man with a bottle in a bar fight and sent to Folsom prison for a year. Thus, the police are more inclined to believe Kopas's self-exonerating version of events than Majestyk's. The bar fight from his past brings to the surface of the narrative Majestyk's difficult adjustment to civilian life after his return from Vietnam and Laos and a three-year stretch as a Ranger instructor at Fort Benning. Like Son Martin, he became irritable and unsociable. He lost his job and his marriage broke up. Last year, he sank everything he had into trying to grow melons, and failed. He's got to succeed this year or go under. That's why what little money he has must go to his workers rather than a lawyer or a bail bondsman (32–33, 36). As a result, Majestyk remains locked up awaiting trial during the most critical week of the harvest season, while his melons begin to rot in the fields.

Leonard is careful to disabuse us of any notion that Majestyk is worried only about losing his investment. When Majestyk takes hit man Frank Renda on a forced march to his remote hunting lodge in the desert and handcuffs him to a bed, after hijacking the prison bus transporting both of them to their arraignments, the mobster offers him "broads," "booze," and twenty-five grand in exchange for his freedom—way more than any melon crop is worth. Majestyk, however, knows that a notorious criminal like Renda is a much bigger prize for law enforcement than some two-bit melon grower and intends to turn him over to the police in exchange for his own freedom. In refusing Renda's offer, Majestyk doesn't cite moral principles. "I want to get a melon crop in," he says. "I grow melons" (61). In other words, it's all about the melons, not the money, or as Aristotle might say, it's all about the *techne*, not the *telos*. Majestyk can get more cash by letting Renda go than he could probably make in a decade of melon farming. But as a fugitive from the law, he would be unable to harvest his crop. "I got to be there," he says.

As so often happened in Leonard's Westerns, and will happen many more times in the crime novels to come, it turns out there's "another person, inside" this otherwise unprepossessing hero, a product of natural talent, relentless training, and hard practice in skills that will, when called upon, defeat his sworn enemy, once Renda finally comes after him. Renda doesn't recognize this side of Majestyk until his second car full of hired guns is forced over the cliff.

> He realized now he didn't know anything about the man. It was like meeting him, out here, for the first time. He should have known there was someone else, another person, inside the farmer. The stunt the guy pulled with the bus and trying to take him in, make a deal [with the cops]. That wasn't a farmer. He had been too anxious to get the guy and had not taken time to think about him, study him and find out who he was inside. (198)

In short, Renda is about to be defeated because his empathic imagination, his ability to think like his opponent, has been clouded and impeded by his rage. And that failure, in turn, is a function of having made his feud with Majestyk personal instead of professional.

Ironically, Majestyk *is* a farmer, a professional farmer, which is the very reason he refused Renda's offer in the first place. But he's also, on the "inside," a professional fighter, and what the farmer and the fighter have in common is their uncommon devotion to performing their jobs with coolness, efficiency, and adherence to the rules imposed by the skills they have chosen to master: never pick an unripe melon, gently loosen it from the soil, and be sure not to turn it toward the sun; never fight an opponent on his own ground, but when pursued, gradually draw him onto yours, and when cornered, attack. Above all, *never make it personal*. That, ultimately, is Renda's downfall, as his sidekick, his lawyer, and his partners in crime keep trying to tell him. They fear that Renda's vendetta will draw unwanted attention from the law and interfere with business. He shouldn't be "worrying about a 160-acre melon grower," says the lawyer; he should be "attending to his commercial affairs. [. . .] That's where the money was to be made; not in shooting people" (117–18). Renda won't even settle for giving the job to a lower-level operative: "*I* want him," he says. "I want him to see it and know it's me" (77).

Put off his game by rage, Renda can't be patient, can't delegate, and ends up making mistakes. Instead of arranging to have the grower murdered in jail, he pressures Kopas to drop his assault charges so Majestyk can go free, putting him within reach but also arousing the suspicions of the police. (Majestyk's leverage with the law, when he offered to bring Renda back in exchange for his own freedom, disappeared when Renda walked on a serendipitous technicality.) The mobster tells his second-in-command to recruit some "guys who know what they're doing" (125) and to borrow a stake truck from Bobby Kopas to haul them to Majestyk's farm and lie in wait—not tomorrow, "tonight." It turns out, however, that these killers are as unskilled and incompetent as the winos and bums that Kopas usually carries around in his truck. Unwilling to follow the rules, to be patient, to depend only on workers he knows—as Majestyk does when he goes into Edna, in the opening chapter, to select his melon pickers himself—Renda becomes the "Bobby Kopas" of professional homicide. By the time Majestyk corners and shoots him, all seven of his associates are dead, six of them victims of the melon grower's cool, wily combat tactics and the seventh, Kopas, a victim of the final gambit that Majestyk has forced on Renda himself.

Making it personal interferes with empathy, the ability to imagine the person inside your opponent. Keeping it impersonal is good advice for pros in any profession: for melon growers, for combat advisors, for hit men, and, of course, for writers. Leonard simply can't dislike even his most despicable characters. He can't take what they do personally. That's one reason why, for all their menace and capacity for pure evil, few of Leonard's bad guys come across as melodramatic, one-dimensional villains. They may start out that way, but if they're allowed to hang around long enough, they often reveal a human trait they share with the hero who's about to put them away: a longing for the self-integrating consolations of *techne*. In Renda's case, as we've seen, that means reliving the good old days when killing was simple and straightforward, if you followed the rules: "He was good then" (122). The hit that sent Renda to jail to share a cell with Majestyk, early in the book, was exactly the opposite, sloppy and overdone, a job he had taken because "he missed the action" and then "hadn't blueprinted [. . .] the way he should have."

> Christ, an off-duty cop sitting there watching. Empty the gun like a fucking cowboy and not have any left for the cop. Or not looking around enough beforehand. Not noticing the cop. Like it was his first time. (122–23)

Renda is getting old, past his prime, losing a step or two. But he still knows, and welcomes, that exhilarating feeling of mastery when it comes. When Majestyk finally corners him in his mountain hideout and yells at him to come out and "finish it," "a thoughtful sort of pleased expression," "not really happy, but relaxed," comes over the mobster's face (205). He suddenly knows just what to do, and how to do it—and he almost succeeds. But by this time it's too late to get to know his opponent. Pinned down behind the open door of his car at the end of the siege, and seeing Majestyk watching him from the porch with a shotgun cradled in his arm, Renda "knew he could do it, hit the guy before he moved. Farmboy standing there not knowing it was over" (215). At the word "farmboy," we can see how this will end.

Venues and Ensembles: Eddie Coyle's Motor City Friends

The single literary event that had the biggest impact on Leonard's writing in the 1970s was his reading of George V. Higgins's *The Friends of Eddie Coyle* in 1972, two years after its initial publication to rave reviews (figure 9).

All three of Leonard's biographers consider Higgins's book a turning point in the writer's career, and Leonard himself can't stop praising it to this day.[2] Higgins taught him "how effective graphically realistic (and frequently obscene) dialogue could be," according to Geherin, and Higgins's use of extended subjective monologues "reminded Leonard that describing events from a character's point of view rather than his own could enhance the realism of the work" (44). Devlin sees *The Friends of Eddie Coyle* as Leonard's new "enchiridion" (16), the "handbook" he used at the start of his crime-writing career, just as he used *For Whom the Bell Tolls* to write his early Westerns. He even compares Higgins's influence to that of Ralph Waldo Emerson on Walt Whitman, "who said he had been simmering until Emerson brought him to a boil" (17).

While it certainly played a role in the inception and development of the Motor City Five, beginning with *52 Pickup, The Friends of Eddie Coyle* appears to have had little immediate or long-lasting effect on Leonard's style, per se. *Mr. Majestyk,* the first book Leonard wrote after reading Higgins, does show a freer use of obscenities, especially in Renda's speeches and free indirect discourse, and the amount of dialogue seems to have increased compared with *The Moonshine War*—but the book began as a screenplay, after all. Perhaps for the same reason, the pace at which Leonard shifts points of view among his characters seems faster in *Mr. Majestyk* than in his previous two books.

Higgins's narrative is almost entirely composed of long, rambling stories that his principal characters tell each other, usually punctuated with replies or retorts to make them sound conversational. They are full of colorful if occasionally (and intentionally) pointless digressions and the (presumably accurate) details of gun trafficking, copping pleas, and underworld rules of engagement drawn from Higgins's years as a public prosecutor. Higgins captured the voices of his robbers, gunrunners, jaded cops, and hit men with unerring pitch-perfection. The combination of digression, detail, and *patois* blew Leonard away, but its impact on his writing was, at first, more a matter of degree than of kind: Leonard felt encouraged to do more of what he was already good at rather than to transform his style in any radical way. He had never been a fan of the long monologue, shunning first-person narration generally, and he didn't want to become one after reading Higgins, who uses practically no free indirect discourse, a form at which Leonard was already adept. With the exception of three brief shifts to third-person narration from the viewpoints of bank managers forced to cooperate with the robbers, practically everything in *The Friends of Eddie Coyle* is told in the literal voice of one or another criminal.

Higgins's biggest impact on Leonard's crime writing was in showing, first, what could be done with a sense of place that is taken for granted, continuously implied but rarely named or described in much detail, and second, how to do it with a Jack Ryan rather than a Walter Majestyk kind of character. *Fifty-Two Pickup*, the first installment of the Motor City Five, shows Leonard beginning to apply the first lesson, and his next book, *Swag*, the second.

Boston and eastern Massachusetts are to *The Friends of Eddie Coyle* what Detroit would become to Leonard's crime books in general: a real-world milieu with a specific geographical *ethos*, or character, that emerges gradually rather than in lengthy, explicit passages of narrative description. Higgins manages this emergence with patient discretion. On his first page, where Eddie Coyle allows "his coffee to grow cold" as he negotiates a gun deal with young hotshot Jackie Brown, an early rush hour crowd hurries by and a "crippled man hawk[s] *Records*, annoying people by crying at them from his skate-wheeled dolly" (3). These sparse but vivid details tell us only that the scene is set in an urban—probably downtown—coffee shop in a large American city with a needy and obtrusive underclass. On the next page, Coyle refers to a customer of his who "went to M.C.I. Walpole for fifteen to twenty-five" (4)—that is, to those in the know, to the "Massachusetts Correctional Institution" in the Boston suburb of Walpole. On the same page, Coyle's story of being disciplined by his "nun" in Sunday school, coupled with his working-class diction and grammar, tells us we're in a Catholic working-class town, and even though Coyle is as yet unnamed, just "the stocky man" so far, the title of the book gives away his Irish ethnicity. It's not until chapter 2, when Higgins's characters drop a few more place names—"New Hampshire" (11), "Burlington," "Wrentham, Massachusetts," "Portland" (13)—that we can be fairly certain the book is set in the Boston area. But "Boston" doesn't appear for another twenty pages or so, and aside from the opening scene, none of the action has thus far taken place in Boston.

What's most striking about Higgins's technique for evoking a sense of place is its economy of resources, which enhances the naturalism of the voices telling

Figure 1. The young slugger in Oklahoma City, ca. 1930. Courtesy of Elmore Leonard

Figure 2. Elmore Jr., in knickers, with Elmore Sr. in a Detroit park, ca. 1938. Courtesy of Elmore Leonard

Figure 3. Memphis, 1933. Elmore with sister Margaret (*left*), mother Flora, and an unidentified woman. Elmore, age 8, assumes a bad guy pose, complete with toy gun, inspired by the Bonnie Parker photo below. Courtesy of Elmore Leonard

Figure 4. Bonnie Parker, 1933. © Bettmann/Corbis

Figure 5. Elmore's buddies get ready for a game, ca. 1937. Standing are Bob Brandon (*left*), Elmore, and Ted Schuette. Kneeling are Jack Schuette (*left*) and Dick Baumgartner. Courtesy of Elmore Leonard

Figure 6. The Leonard family in front of their new home in Northlawn near U of D High School, where he was a sophomore, ca. 1940. *Left to right,* Leonard's mother, Flora; his father, Elmore Sr.; his older sister, Margaret; and Elmore Jr. Courtesy of Elmore Leonard

Figure 7. Elmore Leonard, Jr., as a Seabee stationed in the Admiralty Islands, 1945. Leonard's wartime experiences contributed to the character of war veteran Walter Majestyk in his first crime novel, *The Big Bounce*, published in 1969. Courtesy of Elmore Leonard

"*. . . Now, from the other direction, came faintly screams and shouts and a few people were reaching the square. They were calling something. The sound of horses now and a half-dozen rurales were galloping into the square. Their cries were shrill, unintelligible with the sharp clatter of hoofs . . . Then one word was clear . . . and it was a shriek that hung hot in the air like a knife blade raised in the sunlight—* 'APACHES!' "

from "The Bounty Hunters," a novel by Elmore Leonard.

Meanwhile, back at the agency

. . . Elmore Leonard was sighting along his trusty Remington, drawing a bead on a particularly meaty word. For "Dutch" Leonard is a connoisseur of words. He likes to make one do the work of two. As a rising young writer of Western novels (three books published) this gives his prose a spare and muscular quality; his gunsights never become entangled in fancy verbal foliage; he builds character for his characters out of what they *do*, not out of 1000 words of steam-heated description.

This addiction to hard-fleshed words also makes Dutch a top hand in Campbell-Ewald's copy department. Because this agency is a lot more concerned with what words *do* . . . with how hard they hit and how well they sell . . . than it is with artful alliteration or the thunderous shouting that passes for "hard sell" but actually deafens the listener.

That doesn't mean we make a fetish out of short copy; on occasion we've popped up with the richest textured writing seen this century. Actually, it comes down to choosing the right ammunition—sometimes birdshot works better than a .45 slug—and picking sharpshooters who can center the crosshairs right on the customer's pocketbook. We're lucky; we've got a whole posse right up in the Wyatt Earp class.

CAMPBELL-EWALD *Advertising*

Detroit • New York • Chicago • Los Angeles
Hollywood • San Francisco • Washington • Denver
Atlanta • Dallas • Kansas City • Cincinnati

Figure 8. Elmore Leonard, the Western writer, ca. 1956. This was one of a series of ads produced by Campbell Ewald, the advertising agency Leonard worked for at the time, publicizing its writers. Courtesy of Campbell Ewald Company.

Figure 9. Elmore Leonard, crime writer, 1972, in front of a poster for *Joe Kidd*, starring Clint Eastwood, for which Leonard wrote the screenplay. Also in 1972, Leonard read George Higgins's *The Friends of Eddie Coyle*, a major influence on his Detroit novels of the 1970s, beginning with *Fifty-Two Pickup* in 1974. Photo by Harold Robinson, news photographer, courtesy of The Detroit News

Figure 10. Elmore and wife, Joan, look over the manuscript to *Bandits*. Joan Leonard passed away in 1993. Courtesy of Gregg Sutter

Figure 11. Elmore meets with researcher Gregg Sutter, ca. 1985. Sutter has been Leonard's researcher since 1981. Courtesy of Gregg Sutter

Figure 12. Elmore Leonard in the backyard of his home in Bloomfield Village, Michigan, in 2001, a year after the publication of *Pagan Babies*. Courtesy of Joe Vaughn. © Joe Vaughn

the story: native inhabitants take their habitat for granted. They don't need to provide information their listeners already know. Like priming a well, Higgins's sparse details encourage the reader to fill in the blanks with his or her own life experiences of, say, a coffee shop, an otherwise nondescript shopping center, a stop on a turnpike, a commuter train parking lot, a neighborhood bar, a decrepit stadium. For each reader, those experiences will be as different as the lives they have lived, but for all readers they will materialize and give personal relevance to a place that had, by 1970, acquired a distinct public personality. Higgins's Boston was already a down-and-out has-been, the former Birthplace of Freedom, Hub of the Universe, and City on a Hill that, like Humpty Dumpty, rolled off at some point early in the twentieth century and was still lying in shards. Its postwar image had been shaped by Edwin O'Connor's portrait of machine corruption in *The Last Hurrah* (1956); by the Standells' 1966 hit "Dirty Water" (referring to the polluted Charles River); and by lurid news accounts of the Boston Strangler and the Irish Mob wars of the 1960s. By the time, about thirty pages into *The Friends of Eddie Coyle*, that Higgins's reader understands that this nameless city is Boston, with all that the name itself represents in the popular imagination, he or she has been given the chance to make it conform to the contours of his or her *own* imagination. The power of Higgins's spare but powerful evocation is registered in the book's transformative influence on the writing of American crime fiction to the present day. Before *The Friends of Eddie Coyle* appeared, Boston was a backwater on the generic map of *noir* fiction. Since its publication, Beantown has become practically the capital of Crimeland, its Emerald City, on screen and in print.

In *52 Pickup* Leonard showed what he had learned from Higgins about creating a metropolitan *mise-en-scène* from scraps of information. The first chapter takes place entirely outside the urban center, at a generic townhouse kept by Harry Mitchell, a moderately wealthy, middle-aged factory owner whose mistress, Cini, has been living there for several months at his expense. The action is narrated in the third person from Harry's point of view, much in the way Higgins narrates portions of his book from the viewpoints of the three bank managers who are victimized by the robbers in *Eddie Coyle*. Harry arrives to find Cini gone, replaced by two men with stockings pulled over their heads, just like Higgins's gang members. They sit Mitchell down and show him movie footage of his trysts with Cini. They want $105,000 in exchange for the film, or they will send it to his wife, Barbara, and the local newspapers. The anonymous townhouse could be anywhere in suburban America, but a reference to Harry's residence in Bloomfield Hills and to the Dodge Main plant where he used to work on the assembly line ("Dodge" means "cars") help Leonard place it in the Detroit area.

The city itself, however, makes no appearance, either nominally or visually, until the beginning of the fourth chapter, when Harry begins his private investigation of how the blackmailers managed to use Cini in their shakedown scheme. Remembering that she once posed in the nude for a sleazy "modeling" studio that rented Polaroid cameras to men off the street, Harry finds himself standing outside what "had been a sporting goods store at one time—Mitchell remembered it because he had stolen a baseball glove from the place when he was in the seventh grade and his dad was working at the Ford Highland Park plant."

> It was on Woodward six miles from downtown in a block of dirty sixty year old storefronts. The showcase windows of the sporting goods store were painted black now and white-wash lettering four feet high read: NUDE MODELS. (26)

There's a whole history of Detroit's civic implosion after the 1967 riots—racially, economically, and morally—inscribed in those starkly color-coded black and white panes of glass. Leonard points directly at that history a few pages later, when ghetto pimp Bobby Shy, one of the blackmailers, hijacks a Gray Line sightseeing bus at gunpoint and tells the bus driver to take his customers on a tour of "the historic remains of the riot we had a few years ago" (34), while the passengers empty their valuables into a shopping bag held by his partner, Doreen. No need to explain which riot. Leonard expects his readers to recall the violent TV footage, headlines, and front-page news photos of seven years previously. Leonard's city of apocalyptic violence and decay was already a media-generated mythic site in their imaginations.

The scene outside the former sports shop also had a private meaning for Leonard, which marks *52 Pickup* as the occasion of his imaginative homecoming after more than two decades as a professional writer. This is the scene of his own first (and according to him, only) crime: shoplifting a catcher's mitt for his team, just as Jack Ryan did in *The Big Bounce* (111). Other details of Harry Mitchell's life align it more closely than that of any previous hero with the life of his creator, while his age continues Leonard's trending of his protagonists' years in the direction of the retired Walter Majestyk. Mitchell and his wife are in their forties, with a son in college and a married daughter living in Cleveland. Leonard was in his late forties, with five kids, ranging from high school age to grown-up, when he wrote *52 Pickup*. Mitchell—another "M" hero—is a World War II vet and a self-made man who, like Leonard and Vincent Majestyk, went from working for others to working for himself, from an assembly-line job (similar to writing advertising copy or picking someone else's melons) to being founder and owner of Ranco Manufacturing (writing one's own books, growing one's own melons). Harry and Barbara live in Bloomfield Hills, not far from where Elmore and his first wife, Beverly, were then living.

Significantly, Mitchell has achieved success by going to night school and acquiring engineering skills that he's applied innovatively to several patented devices made at his plant. These patents are the main reason for his firm's success, and the main motivation for his being targeted by the blackmailers, whose ringleader, Alan Raimy, zeroes in on Mitchell's patent income when calculating just how much he and his partners can expect to squeeze out of their victim. The patents are to Mitchell's gizmos what copyright is to Leonard's books: they prevent others from poaching on the source of income he derives from the original and creative application of the *techne* he has worked hard to acquire. They are, in short, more than a way to make money; they are a source of personal pride with which Leonard can closely identify. But Mitchell's final solution to the blackmailers' ever more desperate attempts to make him cough up what his creative genius has earned him (they murder Cini and try to frame Harry for it, then Raimy kidnaps and rapes Barbara) depends, like Son Martin's and Vincent Majestyk's, on a combination of natural talents, training, and practice that reapplies the skills of war to the defense of the productive skills of peacetime, whose profits are the blackmailers' target. It's his training as a fighter pilot that's helped Harry Mitchell perfect his natural cool into what Barbara wants to call a "cold-blooded" (88) but in any case "unpredictable" response to the unexpected: "Not vicious or mean," she adds. "Quiet and calculating. [. . .] Always mild-mannered—until someone steps over the line and challenges him" (89).

Like Son Martin and Vincent Majestyk, Mitchell becomes energized when cornered, tracking down Alan Raimy and his fellow blackmailers, Bobby Shy and Leo Frank, getting to know them, and sowing suspicion among them until they start bumping each other off. Also like the other two "M" protagonists, he uses his wits more than his fists to defeat the bad guys, and the technical solution to his problems comes to him in a moment of inspiration, a random connection between ideas that catches fire because *techne* has provided the train of skills and habits of thought that are lying there, like a trail of gunpowder, waiting to ignite. In the mind of Son Martin, trapped with no escape in his father's house, suddenly "one idea was leading to another, an idea that could end this" (*Moonshine War* 393), prompted by a casual observation from Frank Long. In response to a "crazy" suggestion from Nancy Chavez, Vincent Majestyk pauses: "I've got a half-assed idea that might be worth trying," he says (*Mr. Majestyk* 177). Watching his car go up in flames after the pushy and arrogant union rep, Ed Jazik, torches it, and holding a defective "switch actuator housing" in his hand, Mitchell "toss[es] the scrapped part in the air about a foot or so and catch[es] it, playing with it," like a kid (*52 Pickup* 162). The next thing we know, Mitchell is literally back to his old drawing board, using his engineering know-how and his innovative genius to design an exploding briefcase, with the discarded switch as a trigger. In each case, what Leonard would call a "childlike" openness of mind leads to a solution that a childish, personalized reaction—impulsive, panicked, enraged, reckless—would have foreclosed.

In *52 Pickup*, Leonard redeploys several character types and patterns of relationship common to his Westerns. While it is not pronounced, the mentor-mentee dynamic makes a distinct reappearance when assembly-line worker John Koliba becomes a kind of protégé to Mitchell, who encourages him to use the plant's equipment after hours to pursue his idea for an improved "handling rig" (185). Alan Raimy refers repeatedly to Bobby Shy as a "godammed gunslinger" (170) and a "fucking cowboy" (173), and Shy calls his Gray Line heist "robbing the stagecoach" (33). Shy is Leonard's brash Western bully painted black and transplanted to the urban ghetto. An audacious loudmouth in love with his own cowboy "style" (170) and able to back it up with deadly force when crossed, Shy is nonetheless capable of drawing a laugh through his outrageousness and sense of humor—something his Western predecessors rarely accomplished.

Not until his next Detroit tale, *Swag*, did Leonard show what else he had learned from Higgins besides creating a sense of place with dispatch—namely, just how far you could get by making bad guys your protagonists and, specifically, what could be done with the Jack Ryan kind of character. In this respect, Eddie Coyle himself was of little or no use. The eponymous antihero of Higgins's novel is a hen-pecked, middle-aged, small-time gangster who, through a series of mishaps and risky decisions, ends up dead. The book, as its title implies, really belongs to Coyle's "friends," and to two in particular. Dillon is a loquacious bartender, a human switchboard for gangland gossip, and part-time professional hit man who has no choice but to murder Coyle after he starts cozying up to the Feds. Dillon's charming and affable monologues, many with cops he likes to string along, probably take up more room than any other character's. But it's another name that starts things off: "Jackie Brown at twenty-six, with no expression on his face, said that he could get some guns. 'I can get your pieces probably by tomorrow night. I can get you, probably, six pieces. Tomorrow night' " (3). And the book is launched.

Jackie Brown is unmistakably "cool." He's in his mid-twenties, about Jack Ryan's age in *The Big Bounce*, shares Jack's first name, drives a souped-up Roadrunner, and has contacts inside an army base and a gun factory that can get him machine guns and brand-new handguns with fake, and thus untraceable, registration numbers. He never lets himself be put in a position of need, either with suppliers or with customers, and he is cautious to a fault—except for his one slip-up with Eddie Coyle, who accidentally catches a glimpse of machine guns in the trunk of Brown's car. Coyle trades on this information with his police contacts in order to draw a walk at his upcoming trial for driving a truck full of unlicensed booze across state lines. It's this betrayal of his friends that ultimately leads to Coyle's assassination by Dillon, who in "friendly" fashion treats the unsuspecting mark to a Bruins game and a night on the town before blowing him away.

The speech patterns of Jackie Brown's opening monologue—staccato, obscene, colloquial, fragmentary, and insistent—tell us he's a no-nonsense kind of guy, all business, and that he knows his business. When Coyle balks at Brown's asking price and says he can do better at a gun store, Brown replies, "I would sure like to be there when you tell the man you got some friends in the market for thirty pieces and you want a discount. I would like to see that," and adds, "I can tell you right now there isn't anybody for a hundred miles that can put up the goods like I can, and you know it. So no more of that shit" (7). Brown knows guns and he knows what they go for. And he's only twenty-six. Leonard must have stayed up reading all night.

Jackie Brown influenced Leonard's conception of not one, but two protagonists in *Swag* and lent his surname—and voice—to a third, whom we'll get to in a moment. Leonard bumped up the age of Brown's character to bring it more in line with that of his "M" heroes, and split it into a duo modeled on *The Odd Couple*, which had just ended its five-year TV run in 1975, the year before *Swag* was published. Ernest "Stick" Stickley, Jr., is, like Jackie Brown, a pro who knows his business—namely, grand theft auto—and like Jackie Brown makes a mistake by teaming up with an unreliable partner, Frank Ryan (no relation to Jack Ryan, although Jack is mentioned in the book by his old sidekick, Leon Woody [178]). If Stick inherits Jackie Brown's professionalism, Frank inherits Jackie Brown's personality: he likes the fast life with its fast broads and flashy cars (he buys a brand-new Thunderbird, reminiscent of Brown's Roadrunner, on his own initiative with his and Stick's loot) and is naturally gregarious and loquacious. Stick is more contemplative, closemouthed, and fastidious, a homebody who worries about domestic finances and nags his messy partner to pick up after himself, like Neil Simon's Felix Ungar. Frank—the Oscar Madison of the couple—even accuses Stick of sounding like "a broad, a wife" (55–56), with "a broad's mentality" (138), and Leonard underlines the campy, faintly homoerotic parallel with Simon's duo by having his two protagonists wake up together in their undershorts, sharing a bed in a seedy motel, after a drunken night of barhopping to celebrate their new partnership. "Where'd you sleep?" asks Frank. "Right there in bed with you," Stick replies, "but I swear I never touched you" (18).

Stick and Frank were born in places where Leonard's family lived before their final move to Detroit, and they are assigned criminal histories that draw on Jack Ryan's in *The Big Bounce*. Stick was born in Norman, Oklahoma, and Frank in Memphis, Tennessee, but both were raised in Detroit and each had a father who, like Harry Mitchell and the father of the Boisineau brothers, worked in an auto plant. Stick's criminal history of stealing cars draws on Jack Ryan's early years of joyriding; Frank's experience at breaking and entering parallels Jack Ryan's later career with Leon Woody. Frank even teamed up with "a black guy" who "went into numbers or something," just as Leon Woody later went into drug dealing. In response, Frank, like Jack, "quit before [he] got in too deep" (12).

There is, in short, a lot being worked out in *Swag* that has its roots in Higgins's book, in Leonard's childhood, and especially in the Jack Ryan character, and one of the most important of these is figuring out how to help the Jack Ryan character grow up. Both Frank and Stick arrive in Leonard's opening chapter with some degree of experience and skill in lower-level crime. Each has left that way of life to try living straight, with varying success. Stick married, fathered a daughter, worked for a cement company in Florida to support his family, and eventually got a divorce. Now Stick is back in Detroit doing what he did best all along. After Frank quit breaking and entering, he moved to California for three years before returning to Detroit. He's been married twice and is now selling autos for Red Bowers Chevrolet, where he first makes Stick's acquaintance as Stick is about to drive a hot-wired car out of Red Bowers's front lot. Frank is an excellent salesman who knows a business opportunity when he sees one. Rather than cooperate with the police in putting Stick in jail, he proposes that the two of them set their professional sights considerably higher than car theft or burglary and take on armed robbery, the crime that Jack Ryan almost tried before getting cold feet. Not banks, though—too much security—just supermarkets, liquor stores, and similar retail outlets with high cash flows.

Stick's and Frank's rap sheets represent two similar outcomes for the Jack Ryan character following the end of *The Big Bounce*, in each case as a professional or semi-professional criminal who eventually tries to go straight and decides it's just not worth it. Each, in short, has a specific criminal skill that hasn't taken him very far. In *Swag*, they hope to team up and "graduate," as it were, to a higher, more challenging, and far more lucrative trade, and they plan to do it by following the "rules" of a far more complex, and dangerous, *techne*—ten rules for armed robbery, to be exact, that Frank writes down on cocktail napkins as he and Stick make the rounds from bar to bar the night their new business partnership is "consummated."

Ryan's Rules was the alternative title of *Swag* in some editions, a reminder that, for Leonard, what counts most as a guide to "being cool" is *techne* and not *praxis*, rules rather than principles. The rules that Frank Ryan has been formulating for several years while studying cases of armed robbery include items like "Always be polite on the job" and "Dress well" (17). These can become sources of humor when, for instance, the team discovers they have to scare a store owner into handing over his money, or when they realize they might get typecast and "pretty soon the police would be writing a book on the two dudes who always wore business suits and said please and thank you" (53). "Writing a book" on these "dudes" is exactly what Leonard himself is up to, and it's not too difficult to find parallels to Frank Ryan's ten rules in Leonard's "Ten Rules of Writing," which he compiled several years later for an address to Bouchercon 2000, the World Mystery Convention held in Denver that year, and later published in the *New York Times*. Ryan's second rule, "Never say more than is necessary," for instance, corresponds roughly to Leonard's rule 10 for writing, "Try to leave out the part that readers tend to skip" ("Easy"), and like rule 10, it epitomizes Leonard's Ten Rules in general, nearly all of which, in one way or another, are directed at cutting out unnecessary words so as to make the writer's prose more efficient and, consequently, the writer himself less conspicuous.

Like rule 10, Leonard's writing rules 1 and 2 proscribing descriptions of weather and prologues in general, rule 4 against adverbs, and rules 8 and 9 prohibiting detailed descriptions all conform to Ryan's second rule for stick-ups: "Never say more than is necessary." Leonard's third, fifth, sixth, and seventh rules against verbs other than "said," exclamation points, clichés, and regional dialect are directed at keeping the writer from "sticking his nose in" too "obtrusively," to use the language of rule 3. In fact, Leonard's deep desire for authorial invisibility is what motivates all of his rules for writing. Using an adverb with "said," for instance (prohibited by rule 4) is not only writing more than is necessary but also calling attention to the writer himself, who "is now exposing himself in earnest, using a word that distracts." If we return to Ryan's Rules, we soon see that nearly all of them are similarly intended to avoid calling attention to Frank and Stick, to make them "invisible," which is to say, unidentifiable personally while in the act, or untraceable after the fact: "Never call your partner by name," "Never use your own car," "Never count the take in the car," "Never flash money in a bar with women," "Never tell anyone your business" (17). In short, keep your head down.

As neophytes at armed robbery, Stick and Frank are "invisible" to law enforcement as long as they remain "businesslike" (16) and follow the rules set down by Frank, the ostensible brains of the partnership. In three months they make $25,000, which Frank spends on new clothes, his new T-bird, booze, parties, and an ultramodern apartment in a building they share with several young, sexy career women. Frank doesn't hesitate to start bed-hopping his way from floor to floor, but Stick merely becomes morose and withdrawn. Remaining something of a farm boy from Oklahoma, he thinks their cream-colored and chrome apartment looks "like a beauty parlor" (41), and he misses his daughter. He wants a meaningful relationship with someone, not just a sex playmate. After three months of sharing Frank's empty, glitzy, and self-indulgent lifestyle, he asks himself, "What do you want to do with your *life*?" (45). Hearing no answer, he settles for the pointlessness of the life he shares with Frank.

Although Devlin feels that Leonard "deliberately made nothing of the names" Frank and Ernest (55), Frank himself considers them almost an omen. At the police lineup after the Red Bowers incident, it's Stick's real name, "Ernest," that gives Frank the idea that this might just be the "business" partner he's been looking for: "I started thinking about the old saying about being frank and earnest. [. . .] It seemed to fit" (10). It would be odd for Leonard, who appreciates the power of names, to leave such rich onomastic possibilities untapped. In fact, the partners' nicknames reflect their personalities: Frank is outgoing, gregarious, and if not sincere and honest, at least very good at pretending to be. Explaining to the swinging singles lounging around the pool how he and Stick earn a living as "sales motivators" for car dealerships, Frank says, "I demonstrate what we call the *frank* approach, how to appear open and sincere with customers, sympathetic to their needs" (71). By contrast, Ernest is . . . well, earnest: tongue-tied, serious, searching for meaning and what Csikszentmihalyi would call "joy," not just in his relationships, but also professionally. This difference in their personalities is what, in the end, causes their falling out and gets the two of them in trouble. Frank, the loud-mouthed poser, begins to fall in love with his gangster pose and becomes overconfident to the point of breaking his own rules, with disastrous consequences.

"They were pros, that's why it was easy," thinks Frank after the team's first successful three months. "They knew exactly what they were doing" (41). In short order, Frank starts cutting corners, taking unnecessary risks, and thinking too big. He gets back in touch with his old breaking-and-entering buddy, Sportree, the black gun dealer who originally supplied the duo with their weapons, to concoct the ultimate heist: the payroll office at Hudson's Department Store in downtown Detroit. Sportree knows a secretary who works there, Marlys, and a violent drug dealer, Leon Woody, who will be able to help out, and before Stick knows what's going on, Frank has broken at least three rules: he's gone back to an old hangout, Sportree's bar; he's told a stranger, Marlys, their business; and he's associating with known criminals. Respect for the rules is what makes Ernest Stickley, Jr.'s nickname resonate in a book originally entitled *Ryan's Rules*: he wants to "stick" to the rules, and we eventually see that he was right. The Hudson's caper comes off nearly without a hitch, but Sportree and Woody, with Marlys's connivance, manage to double-cross their "ofay" partners. It's Stick, of course, who comes up with a scheme to turn the tables on Sportree and Woody, and if it weren't for his "earnest" desire for a meaningful relationship with Arlene Downey, one of the young women in their apartment building, he and Frank would have gotten away with the money, too, instead of going to jail.

In *Swag*, Leonard dispenses with the mentor-mentee relationship as he explores the difficulty of achieving the "cool" of *techne* through self-instruction alone, and the consequent dangers of mistaking a counterfeit "cool" for the real article. "There weren't any textbooks on armed robbery," the partners soon realize. "The only way to learn was through experience" (52). At least, that's their only option: having no one to train under, they must train themselves. But experience will take you only so far without a trusty guide, and for someone like Frank, even a little experience can lead to a swelled head, making you think you *are* a pro when you're still just a journeyman. In the Hudson's robbery, Frank and Ernest are taken to school by the real experts at violent crime. It's Sportree who's the pro, says Stick. "He's into, Christ, probably everything you can think of. He has people *killed*" (198). Stick's opinion of Sportree has evolved since the Hudson's job, which to him looked like "amateur night" (146), not planned sufficiently, and not carried out according to plan. In fact, he comes to realize, it was all designed to ensure that Frank and Stick got stuck with three bags of uncashable checks while the pros got away with the greenbacks.

Despite all his talk of being "businesslike," Frank's fundamental motivation for becoming an armed robber is the lifestyle, the glamour and the thrills that an unlimited flow of illicit cash can provide. Specifically, as he tells Stick at the outset when asked what he is, besides a used car salesman and a "sport" who drinks ouzo at Greek bars, "It's not so much what I am, as what I want to be" (11). Frank wants to become somebody else, like so many of Leonard's characters, but there's no person "inside" Frank waiting to get out: the outside—the clothes, the cars, the dirty jokes, the fake sincerity—that's all there is to Frank. True, he's smart: he's studied the angles, the statistics, the logistics of armed robbery, and his rules really work. But Frank has no personal affinity with the *techne* of armed robbery. He's good at it, but it soon bores him and, like Nancy Hayes in *The Big Bounce,* he starts trying to manufacture artificial thrills—not just overreaching in the Great Hudson's Heist, but doing stupid things like intentionally dawdling during an ordinary getaway until, before he and Stick know it, the cops are pulling into the parking lot with sirens and flashing lights. "Frank said, 'Let's get out of here.' Not quite as cool as before" (96).

As it turns out, Stick is the one who has being cool down to an art, if not, like Frank, a science. When it comes time to get the drop on Sportree and Woody in the motel room that the two pros have set up as an ambush, Stick doesn't hesitate: he shoots Leon Woody in the face as he emerges, gun in hand, from the bathroom and then plugs Sportree "twice in the body, dead center" before he can react (214). Unlike Frank, who hasn't the temperament for it, Stick *knows how* to learn *know-how*: he's done it before, following the rules as a car thief and an armed robber, and he can now apply the lessons he's learned to acquiring any new skill, such as killing people, and do it thoroughly, to the extent that control of his tools—a car, a gun—and self-control are merged in one, smooth, efficient action. Practice does help, however: earlier in the book, cornered, spooked, Stick had shot and killed two would-be muggers in the parking lot of a shopping mall. He was surprised to find himself capable of pulling it off.

The difference between being cool and just pretending, between making *techne* part of you and wearing it like Frank's new safari suit, emerges in the scene where Stick has to calm Frank down as they try to figure out how to get their money back from Sportree and Woody. Frank is furious and wants to go into Sportree's apartment with guns blazing, but Stick says, "Don't do anything dumb. [. . .] As your old buddy [Woody] would say, be cool."

> "I'm going to cool him," Frank said, "the son of a bitch, sitting back, all that time blowing smoke at us."
>
> "Sitting back ready. [. . .] I'm saying you got to be careful and do it right. Put yourself in his place. If he's smart enough to pull this deal, he's not going to let you walk in and take it away from him." (198)

As we learned in *Mr. Majestyk,* being cool means not taking it personally. It means putting aside your childish pride and rage so you can "do it right" and "put yourself" in your opponent's place. But there is another sense in which taking the situation personally can be beneficial, and that is when you can see it as a rivalry rather than as a matter of reciprocal humiliation and vengeance. That's when fighting back begins to appear, in a child*like* way, as a game with a worthy opponent, a problem your enemy poses that makes you think about a solution rather than your hurt pride. Later that night, as Stick is lying in bed, awake, he thinks, "It was a terrible mess, but it was also kind of interesting, exciting" (199).

> The funny thing was, he still kind of liked the guy, Sportree. [. . .] He admired him, the way he pulled it, and really didn't blame him. Why not? Sportree didn't give a shit about them one way or the other. (*Swag* 200)

While Stick understands Frank's rage and humiliation, his particular way of keeping it "personal" frees him from the distraction of hating his opponents.

> Keep it personal. He liked both of them. Leon Woody, too. [. . .]
>
> He respected them.
>
> But he also wanted them to respect him. And that was the whole thing. His only option. (201)

Not revenge, but earning his opponent's respect as a worthy adversary in the *techne* of crime is the motivation that allows Stick to think clearly. By 4:30 in the morning, he has formulated a plan "that might work" (201).

Unfortunately, the plan requires the cooperation of Arlene Downey, a pinup girl for an auto-supply company who lives in the same building and has, accidentally, witnessed one of Frank and Stick's impromptu holdups in a crowded bar. Stick is "stuck" on Arlene to the point where he believes that her love for him will motivate her to smuggle the Hudson's "swag" to Florida after he and Frank take it from Sportree's apartment, and that she will give up her low-riding modeling career to live big with Stick in the Sunshine State. All goes well until the last moment, when Arlene, who is supposed to meet Frank and Stick in

Miami with the money, impulsively changes her mind and buys a ticket to Los Angeles in order to compete in her favorite "silver costume" (220) for the honor of being chosen official pinup girl at the National Hot Rod Association Grand Nationals. Her chances are good: she won it the year before (58). She leaves the swag behind in a locker at Detroit Metro Airport and the key in an envelope at the ticket counter for Frank and Stick. As it happens, the moment they find the key is also the moment police detective Cal Brown and his men swoop in for their arrest. Arlene's key leads to the locker full of money, and prison sentences for Stick and Frank. What becomes of Arlene at the Grand Nationals is left to the reader's imagination.

Something about Arlene's spur-of-the-moment decision at Detroit Metro is worth noting here. Leonard's wry but gentle humor is fully on display in the scene where Arlene is packing her bags and has trouble parting with the silver costume and photograph albums and other memorabilia of her short stint as a model for Hi-Performance Shifters at local drag races (220–21). But her attachment turns out to be more than just whimsical. Of all the characters in the book, including her fellow "career ladies" in Frank and Stick's apartment building, Arlene alone appears to have the best chance to advance professionally and get out of the rut she's in. Quitting a dependable but dead-end job in Detroit, she refuses an equally dead-end love affair with Stick to head out to LA and try to make her life professionally meaningful by doing what she enjoys, and what she's good at. In the end, Frank and Stick are defeated, not by the criminal "pros," but by an ambitious apprentice—and a woman at that—who is seeking mastery of another *techne* entirely. Unlike Nancy Hayes, a kept woman for whom "Cucumber Queen of Geneva County" is merely a cover for her affair with Ray Richie, Arlene Downey rejects being kept for keeping her cool. Posing at drag races in her skimpy silver costume is "a pain in the ass"—"the dust and grease and all. The noise, God" (59). But it's what she *does*.

There's one more character worth mentioning from *Swag* who is gifted at his craft, although it's easy to overlook his importance since he doesn't appear until two-thirds of the way into the book. He's Cal Brown, the police detective who solves the Hudson's case and whom Leonard gave Jackie Brown's surname, apparently for his attitude, but also for his voice. Here's a sample from a long discussion Cal Brown has with Emory Parks, the "young little fat black assistant from the prosecutor's office" who is handling Stick's arraignment and trial after the Hudson's job. The "numbers" are firearm serial numbers, the window washer was an innocent bystander in the Hudson's stick-up, and the Northland shopping center is where Stick shot and killed his two would-be muggers:

> Murder? We got two murders. We got all fucking kinds of numbers going. That's why we're talking. Listen—the gun used on the window washer? Same one killed the two guys out at Northland. In the parking lot. (167)

Cal's speech rhythms and diction—the repetition, fragmentation, colloquialism, and obscenity—are those of Jackie Brown.

If Arlene Downey's devotion to her modeling career is the proximate reason for Stick's and Frank's defeat, Brown's expert police work is the final cause. He's the cop who discovers a tiny but crucial clue in Hudson's toy department, leading to Stick's arrest. He's the one who recognizes Arlene Downing's name on the list of witnesses to Frank and Stick's spontaneous bar hold-up and tracks her down. He's the one who traces the guns used in the Hudson's job to Frank and Stick. And he's the one who cannily begins to sow distrust among the four thieves—beginning with Stick himself.

Cal Brown is Leonard's first attempt at a serious police detective character. He plays the "cowboy" role in *Swag* the way Bobby Shy did in *52 Pickup*—but lightly, with no overt posing or explicit references to the Old West. It's Stick, the Oklahoman, who makes the connection for us. On first seeing Cal (a country-western name), he is reminded of a bull rider he once saw in Yankton, South Dakota, "a skinny guy [. . .] spitting over his hip and saying, 'If I cain't ride 'im, I'll eat 'im' " (164). Cal Brown is still another "grown-up" avatar of the original Jack Ryan: like Son Martin, the two Majestyks, and Harry Mitchell, he's a war veteran, a former infantry officer in Vietnam, but still a "young guy." Like Jack himself, he tried out for professional sports, but had to give it up when he injured himself before his first season.

Having put some tried and true performers into new ensembles in *52 Pickup*, Leonard adds new personnel and new arrangements to play in *Swag*, without abandoning his primary thematic concerns with *techne*, self-integration, authenticity, and being cool. Like a jazz musician experimenting with chord changes on an old standard or learning a new instrument in order to play long-familiar tunes in a different register, Leonard begins to "swing" in his new genre by drawing on George Higgins's songbook. Cal Brown, for all the brevity of his moments on stage, provides as good an example of what Leonard is learning as any character in *Swag*.

Leonard will work the Cal Brown character into the web of his protagonist's primary relationships in his third installment of the Motor City Five, *Unknown Man No. 89*, as Jack Ryan's Detroit police detective friend, Dick Speed, another failed pro sports wannabe. But neither Brown nor Speed will ever have a chance to open up to us through the magic of free indirect discourse. Not until *City Primeval,* the last installment of the Motor City Five and the first novel in which Leonard makes a police detective his central protagonist, does the author open a window into the soul of a contemporary law enforcement officer. Before getting there, though, Leonard writes two Detroit crime novels that reflect and comment on important changes beginning to take place in his life as he was working on *Swag*: first, his joining AA in 1974, a consequence of his struggle to give up drinking after being hospitalized with gastritis, and second, his separation from his wife Beverly that same year and his subsequent relationship with Joan Shepard, whom he would marry in 1979, two years after his divorce (figure 10).

Playing the Changes: New Takes on the Cool Songbook

In *Unknown Man No. 89* (1977), Jack Ryan, now a recovering alcoholic, finally decides to grow up: he joins AA and remains dry for three years, during which he manages to hold down, and even excel at, a regular job as a process server. In *The Switch* (1978), Mickey Dawson reprises the betrayed-wife role played by Barbara Mitchell in *52 Pickup,* but instead of standing by her man, an abusive drunk named Frank, she stands him up and leaves their marriage to set free the "new Mickey" she has discovered inside her. These two books, together with *The Hunted* (1977) and *Touch* (completed 1977, published 1987), which we'll examine more closely at the end of the next chapter, introduce a new theme in Leonard's work that was to become more prominent after 1980: the need or the desire to change one's life entirely, from the ground up, and the challenges and vicissitudes of trying to "be cool"—natural, self-integrated, in control—while doing so. *Unknown Man No. 89* and *The Switch* also show Leonard settling into an increasingly confident handling of free indirect discourse. He comes to rely less on straight description or dialogue tenuously anchored to one or another character's distinct point of view and begins to focalize the narrative through his major character for much longer periods of time, maintaining his authorial invisibility throughout.

Leonard had already discovered, when writing *52 Pickup* (Geherin 10), that he could go much further than previously in describing things from one or another character's point of view by using that character's discursive style of interiorized speech. In fact, Leonard seems to be deliberately apportioning point of view and free indirect discourse from the very start of the book. Chapter 1 belongs to the adulterous hero, Harry Mitchell, and what happens to him at the townhouse love nest he is renting for Cini; chapter 2 is dominated by Barbara Mitchell's reflections on her marriage and Harry's odd recent behavior; chapter 3 begins as a dialogue between Mitchell and his lawyer, O'Boyle, but then narrows to Mitchell's point of view exclusively when he breaks off the conversation in his office to deal with the obnoxious union rep, Jazik, and then takes a phone call from the blackmailers at the end of the chapter. With chapter 4, which opens outside the former sporting-goods shop, we settle firmly into Harry's point of view and free indirect discourse, which predominate for the rest of the book, interrupted by distinct strategic shifts of focalization through the minds of Alan Raimy, Barbara Mitchell, Bobby Shy, and Leo Frank.

In *Swag*, the confidence Leonard began to display in *52 Pickup* is more pronounced. We sense that he is in control now at every step. Chapter 1 turns out to be Frank's, chapter 2 predominantly Stick's. And the alternations continue almost imperceptibly throughout as Leonard, like a practiced stock-car driver working one of the Hurst Shifters he once helped advertise, downshifts from touring-speed description in third-person omniscient or multiple restricted point of view to passages of indirect discourse (reported conversation without quotation marks), then to the immediacy of quoted dialogue, and at last to the lowest gears that provide the most emotional torque and traction—not just his two protagonists' thoughts relayed in free indirect discourse, but also those of other characters, like Arlene Downey packing for the airport.

Unknown Man No. 89 and *The Switch* show what Leonard learned from his experiments with voicing and point of view in *Swag*. Each novel begins by tightly focalizing the narrative of events through the perceptions, thoughts, and memories of the protagonist—Jack Ryan in *Unknown Man*, Mickey Dawson in *The Switch*—and then maintains this point of view on the action, almost without interruption, for dozens of pages while sliding repeatedly, and effortlessly, into and out of that character's thoughts through free indirect discourse.

In *Unknown Man No. 89*, for instance, where Jack Ryan returns from his long hiatus after *The Big Bounce*, Leonard begins with what sounds like narration in omniscient third person.

> A friend of Ryan's said to him one time, "Yeah, but at least you don't take any shit from anybody."
>
> Ryan said to his friend, "I don't know, the way things've been going, maybe it's about time I started taking some."
>
> This had been a few years ago. Ryan remembered it as finally waking up, deciding to get off his ass and make some kind of run. (2)

With "remembered," Leonard places us inside the mind of Jack Ryan and retroactively draws the exchange of words preceding it into the framework of Ryan's point of view, as something he is recalling. Ryan's free indirect discourse is registered in the coarse and colloquial "get off his ass" and "some kind of run." Except for two isolated, single-page excursions into other characters' points of view (48, 67), Leonard doesn't depart from this frame until the beginning of chapter 7, seventy-four pages later.

Like *Swag, Unknown Man No. 89* largely dispenses with the mentor-mentee theme and pits an autodidactic neophyte—a process server behaving like a private eye in training—against a couple of criminal pros. Unlike *Swag*, however, the neophyte gets away with the girl and the money, and also unlike *Swag*, he does it almost entirely by pure luck. Jack Ryan never graduates, as Stick does, to the higher degree of proficiency in swindling and murder attained by his nemeses, Mr. Francis Xavier Perez and Perez's homicidal goon, Raymond Gidre. Perez and Gidre make money by tracking down unwitting stockholders in big corporations and offering to go halves with them in exchange for revealing the details of what stock they own. If their clients show any reluctance, Perez and Gidre resort to more violent methods. Nor is Ryan in the same class as professional hit man Virgil Royal, who thinks he deserves a piece of Mr. Perez's action, too. Ryan comes out on top even though he is outmaneuvered by Perez (twice), outwitted by Royal, makes himself vulnerable to arrest as an accessory to fraud and then for stealing police evidence, and is so inept with a firearm that he can empty a .38 at Gidre from less than a hundred feet away to no effect (282). Even after firing a gun, Jack doesn't recognize the sound of gunshots when he hears them (310). Finally, it's only because his pal Dick Speed violates police regulations (against his better judgment) to let Jack photocopy crucial papers from a confiscated suitcase that our hero ends up with the money and the girl. Feeling a bit out of his depth despite his victory may be one reason why, at the end of the book, Ryan walks away from Perez's invitation to join his little "business" enterprise. Although his hesitation before responding shows he's tempted, Jack is not about to push his luck.

The book opens, as we've seen, with the old Jack Ryan turning over a new leaf and "waking up," determined to take some shit for a change, as Walter Majestyk in *The Big Bounce* had advised (185), in order to "make a go" of living a normal life after a decade of serial unemployment, fistfights, and one wrecked marriage. At Dick Speed's suggestion, he buys a bullet-riddled Oldsmobile at a police auction and tries his hand at process serving. He's "surprised" to find he's good at it and even likes it (*Unknown* 3). He's also "surprised" at how patient he is and at his knack for finding deadbeats and alimony fugitives (3), at how he "handles" "taking shit from people" so calmly (4), at how "organized" (6) and "conscientious" (29) he can be. It's not until chapter 6 that we learn the reason for Ryan's almost perpetual astonishment: he's a recovering alcoholic who, with the help of AA, has managed to stay sober for three years. In that time the real Jack Ryan "inside" the clueless jerk we met in *The Big Bounce* has emerged, with just the array of talents and personality traits to suit him for the *techne* of process serving: patience, politeness, organization, conscientiousness, and the ability to remain dispassionate—that is, strictly professional—in the face of belligerence and insult. In practically no time, Jack has surpassed the only other member of his profession who could qualify as a possible mentor, the sadistic Jay Walt, to become the most reliable and skillful process server at the Frank Murphy Hall of Justice, even something of a legend. By the time Walt hires him to track down Robert Leary, aka "Bobby Lear," Ryan has his own private practice, Search and Serve Associates, just like a hard-boiled private investigator (15).

Ryan's problems with alcohol don't become apparent until he locates Denise "Lee" Leary, wife of the criminally insane Bobby Lear. He finds her drunk in a bar at two in the afternoon, aggressively so: "Ryan had to be patient. He knew he had no choice; he was talking to a drunk. He could resign himself to it, sip his Tab, or get up and leave" (42). If drinking Tab in a bar doesn't clue us in, we have to suspect that Jack's familiarity with drunks comes from personal experience when he hands Denise his business card in case she decides to quit and needs help. Later that night she calls him, and their shared struggle to get and stay sober comprises a good portion of the remainder of the book, including several long scenes of mutual self-revelation. Predictably, Jack and Denise fall in love, and Ryan, who was working for Perez while remaining unaware of his client's more sinister intentions regarding the stock Denise will inherit from her deceased husband, turns the tables on Perez and secures her entire bequest, worth $150,000.

While Jack is finding out what his "inner" person is good at, Denise Leeann Leary rediscovers her former skills as an artist. "I don't want to be inside me, but I can't get out," she tells Jack during her initial phone call (73). The fresh, clean, caring, and sober "Denise" that wants to bust out of the haggard, dirty, hostile, and drunken "Lee" she feels trapped in is a graduate of Detroit Arts and Crafts, where she studied graphic design and devoted herself to sculpting, carving, painting, and drawing whales. The "Left Bank atmosphere" (177) along the Cass Corridor near Wayne State University drew Denise into a Bohemian scene of grass, booze, easy sex, and "cool" black dudes like Bobby Lear. Now, as she gets sober and learns she can "be [her]self" and not "have to play a role, put up a front, pretend to be something [she's] not" (158), Denise resumes her painting: her living room becomes "dominated" by a "drawing board," "tubes of paint and brushes," and oil paintings of killer and sperm whales, and on the wall she writes in bold, Japanese calligraphy, "No More Bullshit" (174). At an AA meeting she expresses "surprise" (that word again!) at how positive the program is, based not simply on abstention from alcohol but on "substituting something positive for it, a totally different way of life" (159). For Denise, that "substitute" for drinking is her work—which includes, as the *sumi* lettering on her wall indicates—the work of writing.

Lacking such a positive work substitute from his former life, the new Jack Ryan has had to find or create one. The day after she calls him at 2:00 a.m. for help, Denise drops out of sight for three weeks as she struggles to get sober, and at the end of that time, having failed to locate her, Jack starts drinking again. Before he goes too far, he seeks out the nearest AA meeting, where he runs into Denise. Jack confesses to the group that he got drunk because he's been away from meetings too long and started relying on himself instead of the program. "I forgot," he says, "that when you give up one way of life, drinking, you have to substitute something else for it. Otherwise, [. . .] you're sober but you're miserable [. . .] a dry drunk" (157).

Leonard knows the truth of this statement, having lapsed repeatedly for three years before taking his last drink in January 1977.[3] But it's not the whole truth, at least for Jack. Leaving the program may have made him vulnerable to temptation, but it's his failure to locate Denise that has pushed him over the edge. His immediate attachment to her as a fellow alcoholic is part of the book's romantic subplot, and his losing track of her is a bitter disappointment. But Jack's failure to find Denise is also a failure of *techne*: he's now a legendary pro at finding missing persons. His deeply gratifying and self-absorbing work as a process server has become the professional "substitute" for drinking that he needs to stay sober, now that he's abandoned his AA meetings. Were it otherwise, he would have fallen off the wagon long before now. When he fails to find Denise he fails not just at love, but at the very thing that has come to sustain what Denise calls the "totally different way of life" offered by sobriety to the chronic drunk. For Jack, as for Denise, *techne* is what defines the new "person" he is. It is his salvation.

The lessons that Jack Ryan learns as a recovering alcoholic are the lessons his creator learned after he joined AA. But during this same span of years, 1974–77, Leonard was also going through a separation leading to divorce from his first wife, Beverly, and some of what he learned about himself as an alcoholic spouse seems to have been incorporated in his portrayal of Frank Dawson, Margaret "Mickey" Dawson's husband in *The Switch* (1978). Frank's more belligerent characteristics, however, were taken from Leonard's experiences with similar country club boozers,[4] and his clueless aggression is clearly a defensive reaction to his unacknowledged drinking problem. Like Jack Ryan when he falls off the wagon in *Unknown Man No. 89*, Frank can put away a prodigious amount of alcohol while under the impression that he's completely sober.

The Switch differs from the rest of the Motor City Five in a number of significant ways. To begin with, it showcases, for the first time in Leonard's writing career, a female protagonist. Second, Leonard's heroine is not confronted with a crisis of *techne*—in fact, Mickey has trouble deciding what she wants to do with her new life. The emphasis throughout the book is on liberation, on Mickey's finding the guts to be honest with herself and with Frank and, finally, to walk away from her marriage. The question of what to do when she's free is barely addressed. Third, no one is killed in *The Switch*, with the exception of the fat, bumbling psychopath Richard Monk, whose death in a shoot-out with the police is more farcical than frightening. And finally, there is no sexual consummation between the protagonist and her romantic partner, unlike the situation with Stick and Arlene Downey, Jack Ryan and Denise Leary, and Harry and Barbara Mitchell after they reconcile. The budding relationship between Mickey Dawson and her reluctant kidnapper, Louis Gara, remains chaste to the end of the book, although there remains a potential for further developments, if only because Mickey ends up part of the kidnapping gang—which includes Louis—that originally held her for ransom.

Her route there was a circuitous one. Her three kidnappers knew that Frank was sitting on a pile of money he'd raked in from fencing stolen goods and laundering the proceeds through his real estate empire. What neither they nor Mickey knew, at the moment they snatched her, was that Frank was about to divorce her for his blonde and busty mistress, the conniving Melanie, who will not only persuade Frank to call the kidnappers' bluff by not paying the ransom (why pay to get back a woman he doesn't want?) but also try to cash in on the failed caper. Richard Monk's ludicrous incompetence and Louis's quick thinking save Mickey's life, allowing her to pull a "switch" on Frank and Melanie by persuading the remaining two kidnappers, Ordell Robbie and Louis Gara, that what Frank wouldn't pay for his old wife, he will certainly pay for his new mistress. As the book ends, an unsuspecting Melanie enters the living room of Ordell's apartment to find her two recent partners and Mickey wearing Richard

"Tricky Dick" Nixon masks—their playful way of signaling that they're about to turn the tables on her. Mickey can't wait to "go home and watch Frank get his phone call" (216).

As is well known among Leonard's fans, it was Joan Shepard, his recently divorced lover who would soon become his second wife, who encouraged the author to move beyond the supportive partners, bratty bad girls, and motherly widows and divorcées comprising the female cohort of his previous fiction. The break-up of Mickey Dawson's marriage is based in part on Shepard's experiences, and Mickey herself is very much a product of 1970s' feminism. Taken for granted by her family when she's not being emotionally abused, confined to an unfulfilling role as housewife and mother, out of touch with her anger, half-enlightened but not yet empowered, she epitomizes the target readership for the new *Ms.* magazine and for second wave feminist writers like Germaine Greer, Gloria Steinem, and Susan Brownmiller, whose 1975 book about rape, *Against Our Will,* is referenced at the moment Richard Monk tries, with grotesque ineptitude, to rape Mickey before killing her (149).[5] Accordingly, *techne* takes a back seat to liberation of a conventionally feminist cast: self-integration for Mickey Dawson means getting in touch with her anger and making the decision to leave her husband in order to find out who she "really" is. If anything, *techne* is an object of parody in *The Switch,* reduced to the array of high-tech firearms and gadgets of surveillance collected by Richard, the Nazi-loving cop-wannabe who can't even hold onto his job as a security guard. Neither Louis nor Ordell has much use for this arsenal of overkill. They just need Richard's mother's house for a hideout, and their clueless partner is easy to manipulate.

Since there is no master of *techne* "inside" Mickey struggling to find a proper arena for her talents, temperament, and skills, as there is with Denise Leary, her degree of self-alienation is expressed through a different spatial metaphor, namely, looking down on herself from above—the recurring experience of the severely traumatized. The self as spectator is the "real" Mickey (149), and the object of her attention, the false, everyday self in its role as "Tennis Mom" (10) to her teenaged son, or as one of the country club "ladies" (30) chattering poolside, or as supportive spousal ornament to her bullying drunk of a husband, is the "Nice" or "Little Mickey" (25, 149). Sitting with her friends at the club, for instance, "was a strange thing." "She would be perched somewhere watching the group, herself in it—the same way she saw herself with Frank when they were arguing. Never completely involved" (30). The replacement of the "nice" Mickey by the "real" Mickey, the straight-talking, take-charge "new Mickey" (192), is completed only near the end of the book, as the result of a forty-eight-hour conversation, covering two chapters, that she has with Louis Gara in Ordell's apartment after their flight from Richard Monk. By the time she leaves the apartment, Leonard's protagonist has become "Mickey the ballbuster" (174), the "new Mickey": "free" if still not "used to the idea" (191). Eventually, she and Louis—who has, in effect, served as her therapist—will become partners in crime, with Melanie as their first kidnapping victim. To this extent, perhaps, we can say that Mickey has taken an initial step, if a comically perverse one, toward finding something "meaningful" to do with her life (195), a step she was not interested in taking earlier in the book. Beginning with Leonard's next novel, *City Primeval: High Noon in Detroit,* a younger generation of sisters will carry the struggle for liberation and self-determination forward into the white-collar professional and artistic arenas, taking on the challenges of mastering *techne* and being cool that were heretofore reserved for Leonard's male protagonists.

The first four installments of the Motor City Five offer what amount to serial portraits of being cool in different circumstances and using different subjects, as Leonard plays variations on old material and begins to move in new directions. In *52 Pickup,* which reprises the situations of combat veterans Vincent Majestyk and Son Martin, Leonard creates a hero more closely modeled on himself than ever before. Harry Mitchell retrieves the *techne* of his earlier careers in the military and in engineering to defeat the bad guys who seek to destroy his honor, his business, and his marriage, which is, like his creator's at this point, less than ideal. In *Swag,* Leonard makes bad guys his protagonists for the first time, as Stick and Frank try to move up from a lower to a higher level of criminal prowess under their own tutelage. In *Unknown Man No. 89,* our old friend Jack Ryan finally removes the gigantic chip on his shoulder, overcomes his drinking problem, and discovers the *techne* he's naturally suited for, achieving a sense of self-integration and purpose in his new, sober life as a process server. In *The Switch,* Leonard first tries his hand at creating a female protagonist. Fashioned in response to the promptings of his second wife and the influences of 1970s' feminism, Mickey Dawson makes the first move toward finding out who she "really" is, short of acquiring a profession or skill, by shedding her old life and beginning to stretch her new wings as an apprentice kidnapper.

Over the course of his first four Detroit-based crime novels, Leonard is also experimenting with evocations of place, with new variations on former character types, and with an ever-increasing range of "voices," inspired by the example of George Higgins's *The Friends of Eddie Coyle.* In particular, he is investing more of himself in the work of writing free indirect discourse and perfecting, in this new genre, the arts of invisibility that had become, for him, the hallmark of "cool" writing.

Swingin' with It: Double Time

City Primeval: High Noon in Detroit represents both the culmination of Leonard's decade of experimentation in his new genre and an inaugural work with respect to the characters, themes, and concerns that would come to dominate his writing for the rest of his career. In it, Detroit's geography becomes so explicit that a reader can follow every car chase, stakeout, and trip to the convenience store street by street, as if on a map. The book is almost a laboratory for testing different tonalities and styles of vocalization, including those of Leonard's independent narrative voice, and, as its subtitle indicates, it brings to fruition his interest in hybridizing genres and chronotopes through the insertion of premodern (mainly Western or "cowboy") tropes and character types into contemporary urban settings. The professionalization of women, an emerging interest in his previous books, here becomes a major theme, especially in the relationship between defense lawyer Carolyn Wilder and detective Raymond Cruz. The role of popular culture and the mass media in shaping personality and behavior, a recurrent focus of attention in Leonard's subsequent work, is introduced as a central influence on the male protagonist. *City Primeval* is Leonard's first police procedural; his first full-bore "eastern-western"; his first crime novel to feature an ethnic minority hero (thoroughly assimilated); and the next to last book he researched on his own. After *Gold Coast* (1980) he would begin his long and fruitful relationship with his hired researcher, Gregg Sutter, which has continued from *Split Images* (1981) to the present day (figure 11).

One would think, from a glance at the crime novels for which Leonard is now best known, that his resort to extended passages of free indirect discourse in *Unknown Man No. 89* and *The Switch* would have continued in *City Primeval,* if not become more pronounced. While the book does contain a great deal of mental vocalization, it also displays a variety of other narrative styles and devices. Leonard begins with a four-page prologue in the form of an investigative report by the "Judicial Tenure Commission" looking into "the matter of Alvin B. Guy, Judge of Recorder's Court" (7). Adopting the formal, impersonal tone, diction, and syntax of an appointed official reviewing Guy's high-handed mistreatment of prisoners, court officers, lawyers, and police, the prologue introduces us to most of the main characters appearing in the story to follow, each with a reason to want the judge dead. Guy will be murdered at the end of a high-speed car chase in chapter 1, which opens with the indirectly discursive, third-person testimony of a parking attendant at Hazel Park Racecourse who saw Guy leaving the track after colliding with another car. Unlike the style of the "Judicial Tenure Commission" report, Everett Livingstone's voice is distinctly colloquial, but by keeping it indirectly discursive and not using quotation marks, Leonard makes it sound as though Livingstone is being deposed by a police detective investigating Guy's murder. On the next page, after a line space, Leonard uses *free* indirect discourse to place us immediately at the scene of the crime and inside the head of one of his most compelling sociopaths, Clement Mansell, the "Oklahoma Wildman," as Mansell begins to tangle with Guy's Lincoln Mark VI in the racetrack's parking lot. The effect of these successive transitions along a line of increasing discursive proximity—from dry bureaucratese to indirect colloquial testimony to the real-time intimacy of free indirect discourse—is like the pull of a massive but distant sun's gravitational field: inescapable, inexorable, and continually accelerating toward violent impact.

Elsewhere in *City Primeval,* Leonard adopts a storytelling voice that sounds uncharacteristically deadpan and informative, as at the beginning of chapter 7:

> Technically, Squad Seven of the Detroit Police Homicide Section specialized in the investigation of "homicides committed during the commission of a felony," most often an armed robbery, a rape, sometimes a breaking and entering, as opposed to barroom shootings and Saturday night mom and pop murders that were emotionally stimulated and not considered who-done-its. (57)

Leonard has already learned how to assign the task of providing information like this to a character, couched in an appropriately colloquial tone of voice. Here, by contrast, he seems to be reprising the style of an article on the real Squad Seven, the homicide unit of the Detroit Police, which he was asked to write for the *Detroit News Sunday Magazine* in November 1978. Researching "Impressions of Murder" gave him unprecedented access to the procedures, strategies, rituals, crime lore, and above all, voices and personalities of police work that would contribute to the gritty realism of *City Primeval,* filling its margins and those of the book that followed it, *Split Images,* with real-life cases. The prose style of the newspaper essay seeps into passages like this one, where Leonard describes Squad Seven's office space, as well as its bureau assignment, using not only the same voice as in his *Detroit News* article, but also precisely the same details, down to the Norelco coffeemaker and the sign on the wall that says, "Do something—either lead, follow, or get the hell out of the way!" ("Impressions" 18).

City Primeval was not the first book in which Leonard's third-person objective narrative voice occasionally displayed a distinct personal or professional tonality. The same thing occurs, for instance, at the very beginning of *Swag*, which is worth quoting at length to convey the full effect:

> There was a photograph of Frank in an ad that ran in the *Detroit Free Press* and showed all the friendly salesmen at Red Bowers Chevrolet. Under his photo it said *Frank J. Ryan*. He had on a nice smile, a styled moustache, and a summer-weight suit made out of that material that's shiny and looks like it has snags in it.
>
> There was a photograph of Stick on file at 1300 Beaubien, Detroit Police Headquarters. Under the photo it said *Ernest Stickley, Jr.*, 89037. He had on a sport shirt that had sailboats and palm trees on it. He'd bought it in Pompano Beach, Florida. (1)

This is written from no character's point of view and yet it comes across as informal speech, despite the parallel structure of its two paragraphs. We might say it has a kind of laconic, indifferent "attitude," to use Leonard's word for it. The initiatory "There was [. . .]," the colloquial "it said," and the vague substitutions of "had on" for "wore" and "that material that's shiny and looks like it has snags in it" for a specific fabric name—something an omniscient author should know—convey the marking-time and circumlocution of impromptu, lower-class speech, George Higgins's métier. In addition, other "voices" move about beneath the colloquial working-class surface: the ironized language of advertising and promotion in "all the friendly salesmen at," and the voice of the cynical smart-ass who includes Frank's smile among other items of personal grooming and dress he "had on."

If Leonard is obsessed with remaining "invisible," adopting so distinct a storytelling persona at the outset of *Swag* doesn't seem the way to do it. But I think it makes more sense to see this colloquial, brass-rail pose as vocalic camouflage for the *writer* who has constructed it. The writer of *Swag* makes himself invisible, not by trying to adopt, as in earlier works like *The Big Bounce* or *The Moonshine Wars*, a neutral middlebrow style, the refuge of college-educated authors the world over, but by making his writing invisible the way George Higgins did, disguising it as speech. In his "Ten Rules of Writing" essay, we may recall, Leonard says his "most important rule"—an unofficial eleventh—summarizes the rest: "If it sounds like writing, I rewrite it. [. . .] I can't allow what we learned in English composition to disrupt the sound and rhythm of the narrative. It's my attempt to remain invisible, not distract the reader from the story with obvious writing" ("Easy").

This tone of voice, distinct but unattached to focalized, free indirect discourse, emerges elsewhere in *Swag*—never for long, just as a kind of reminder of the anonymous narrator's wise-guy presence: "What it was: a sheet of Ace Tablet paper [. . .]" (31); "They liked supermarkets. Get a polite manager who was scared shitless [. . .]" (46); "The way it started, Frank went out for a couple of hours [. . .]" (115). These sound bites belong in passages of Stick's or Frank's free indirect discourse, but they seem to have strayed outside the frame of any particular point of view. Sometimes Leonard shifts to a precise, unostentatiously neutral style to carry the narrative: "In the late afternoon and early evening Sportree's offered semidarkness and a sophisticated cocktail piano [. . .]" (22). This is writing, not speech, but writing that is about as invisible as it can be and still do the straight-ahead, descriptive work of writing, and it occurs rarely. In *Swag* Leonard was beginning to experiment directly with Higgins's impressive vocal stylizations, not only in the free indirect discourse of a character like Cal Brown, but also at the narrative level, getting the hang of them in order to add them, eventually, to the repertory of voices already in his head, new cloaks of invisibility to be hung up with the old standbys in his stylistic wardrobe.

The tonal variations at the beginning of *City Primeval*, published four years later, differ from those in *Swag* in one important respect: they are all variations on types of writing, not speech, and writing that does not strive for invisibility as such. Bureaucratic officialese, a transcription of eyewitness testimony, and journalistic prose join the colloquial voices of free indirect discourse that Leonard has by now thoroughly mastered to produce the greatest stylistic range to appear in any of his books. The important thing about all these styles and tonalities is that, whether they come across as speech or as "obvious writing," none of them can be identified as belonging to "Elmore Leonard" the novelist. Together they create a kind of textual mosaic of voices and texts behind which the author who constructed it can still remain hidden.

In *City Primeval*, the detective figure sketched out in the characters of Cal Brown and Dick Speed comes fully to life in Lieutenant Raymond Cruz, who is based, like several of his colleagues, on one of the real-life homicide investigators Leonard met in Room 527,[6] Squad Seven's office at 1300 Beaubien, Detroit Police Headquarters at the time. Despite his almost total assimilation into white, middle-class culture, Cruz's ethnicity aligns him with Hispanic characters from

Leonard's Western phase, like the similarly quiet and unassuming Robert Valdez, the underestimated constable of *Valdez Is Coming*. Unlike Valdez, however, Raymond Cruz is anything but underestimated—except, perhaps, by himself. Despite his intuitive gift for detection, his years of training, and a recent promotion in recognition of his accomplishments, his insecurity about having taken on new duties as temporary lieutenant in charge of the squad appears in his preoccupation with his image: he deliberately attempts to make himself look like Gregory Peck's gun-slinging character Jimmy Ringo, from Henry King's popular 1950 Western film *The Gunfighter.*

This cowboy infatuation is noted early in the book by Sylvia Marcus, a belligerently feminist, self-righteous young reporter for the *Detroit News*, who is interviewing Cruz for an article on male cops and their difficulty with intimate relationships. In response to Marcus's accusation that the recently divorced Cruz seems to be "playing the role" of a John Wayne or Clint Eastwood and that his facetious rejoinders and "smart-ass attitude" in general are "*machismo* bullshit" meant to keep him from examining his emotional "center" (24), Cruz says that what influenced him most, coming onto the force, was the example of "the old pros" (25). It's not long before we find him sizing them up, in his mind, as ego ideals: "He *was* a police officer," he tells himself. "But what kind?"

> He could be dry-serious like Norbert Bryl, he could be dry-cool like Wendell Robinson, he could be crude and a little crazy like Jerry Hunter . . . or he could appear quietly unaffected, stand with hands in the pockets of his dark suit, expression solemn beneath the gunfighter mustache . . . and the girl from the *News* would see it as his Dodge City pose: the daguerreotype peace officer. (35)

By confining us to Cruz's point of view throughout the interview and repeatedly resorting to free indirect discourse, Leonard makes it easy for us, as readers, to share his protagonist's irritation with Marcus—"The girl from the *News* kept punching at him" (25)—and her glib psychobabble about "contact[ing] your center" and "transference" further lowers her in our estimation. But the newspaper reporter is not as dumb as she sounds, as Cruz's supervisor, Inspector Herzog, later observes with respect to her work on Guy's murder: "Sylvia's a very bright girl," he tells Cruz, who responds with skepticism: "You think so?" "Well," replies Herzog, "she asks good questions" (153). Indeed she does. The transparent access Leonard grants us to his heroes' minds can convey the impression that they are transparent to themselves. Often that's an illusion. Early in *Unknown Man No. 89*, Leonard makes this point explicit with respect to Jack Ryan, who thinks Jay Walt is so stingy "he must still have his bar mitzvah money. Ryan didn't know he was being a smart-ass when he thought this; he believed he was being funny" (11). Here's a rare elbow—maybe just a pinkie—sticking out from the otherwise planed-smooth surface of Leonard's prose. Even this late in his career, Leonard didn't always trust himself enough to let the blind spot in a character's self-awareness appear in what others think and say about him, or through verbal or behavioral inconsistencies. If Ryan himself doesn't know when he's being a smart-ass and no one tells him, Leonard seems to think the only way we can find out is by telling us himself.

The blind spot in Raymond Cruz's self-awareness appears in his repeatedly thinking of Marcus, dismissively, as "the girl writer" (21) or just "the girl"—"I have a name," she reminds him when he conspicuously fails to use it (22)—and in his preoccupation with his image, not to mention his fussy taxonomy of the "kinds" of police detective types that are currently available. Cruz is eager to individuate himself—"quietly unaffected [. . .] with hands in the pockets of his dark suit, expression solemn"—among the "old pros" who have already "established [their] image[s]" and thereby staked out the available territory of "police officer" identities. But, in fact, he is only falling unwittingly into mythic typicality: his "gunfighter moustache" betrays the Gregory Peck role he denies playing. "Why would she tell him he was posing? Playing a role, she said. You had to know you were doing it before you could be accused of posing" (35). But "knowing you are doing it" is a mark of maturity, Leonard's ironic sign of self-integration, because it involves some degree of free choice and childlike play. Knowing what you're doing is not the same as watching yourself doing it. You know who you are when you *choose* to be somebody, not when the mirror of celebrity or myth *tells* you who you are.

With the introduction of the topic of "old pros" in this, his first attempt at an eastern-western, Leonard begins to reprise the mentor-mentee schema of male relationships that dominated his early Western fiction. But Cruz's appropriation by, rather than of, Peck's *Gunfighter* archetype makes him vulnerable along the horizontal axis that transects the vertical relationship between pros and apprentices in Leonard's Westerns: the axis of mirroring antagonists. In *City Primeval*, Cruz's nemesis, Clement Mansell, exploits the lieutenant's weakness for sagebrush heroics by repeatedly inviting him into the personal honor "game" that distinguishes the traditional genre of the Old West from the modern police procedural. Clement is Cruz's dark double, his secret sharer: "Everybody [. . .] has to have somebody to tell secrets to," Cruz informs Carolyn Wilder, unaware that his most knowledgeable and appropriate confessor is her client. In fact, Cruz feels "a strange rapport" (77) with Clement, who recognizes that the lieutenant is mirroring him as early as his initial interrogation: "Me and you," he tells Cruz, "we're sitting here looking at each other, sizing each other up, aren't we?" (91). Alluding to Cruz's failure to put him away three years previously due to a legal technicality, the "Oklahoma Wildman" says, "See, now it *does* get personal. Right?"

> "Well, I have to admit there's some truth to what you say."
>
> "I knew it," Clement said. "You've got no higher motive 'n I do [. . .]. You don't set out to uphold the law any more'n I set out to break it. What happens, we get in a situation like this and then me and you start playing a game." (88)

Cruz's reply gives nothing away: "Some other time—I mean a long time ago—we might have settled this between us. I mean if we each took the situation personally." He could be rejecting Clement's understanding of their relationship because it is anachronistic, but he could also be admitting its legitimacy by citing restraints that, upon reflection, seem arbitrary rather than axiomatic. Significantly, it's not the laws that Cruz is sworn to uphold—in effect, the "rules" governing what is and is not allowed in his profession—that, in his mind, prevent the two of them from playing Mansell's *mano a mano* game. It's their being born in the wrong place and time, as well as (Cruz implies) any lack of personal motivation, at least on his part. But when your self-understanding has been mediated by Hollywood Westerns, historical constraints soon weaken, and making others "take it personally" is something that Leonard's bad boys are very good at.

Despite his quiet demeanor, Cruz is holding back a lot of anger in his "center." One reason he broke up with his wife was that he couldn't tell her about his job. The day-to-day details were too ugly, too brutal and horrifying. When he tries to illustrate the problem by "sharing" one of his cases with Sylvia Marcus, she is so revolted she terminates their interview, as Cruz knew she would. Apparently, Cruz can take a punch and give it back. The boxing metaphor that comes so easily to his mind when talking with Marcus resurfaces in a later conversation with Carolyn Wilder (95), who has given him reason to believe he can share with her the secrets he could never share with his ex-wife: "Raymond stepped quickly, quietly, inside her guard" (95). On the next page the metaphor becomes literalized as a real urge "to punch Carolyn Wilder" for refusing to "quit being the lawyer" and respond frankly to his concern for her health and safety in response to the looming threat posed by the man she is defending. The urge reminds Cruz of times when he wanted to punch judges like Alvin Guy, who interfered with what he saw as the course of justice or maintaining public safety. Cruz's repression of the violence he cannot talk about makes it easy for a "Wildman" like Clement Mansell to push all the right buttons and get him to take things personally. What Cruz loses as a result is not his life but his authenticity.

As the novel unfolds and Clement, protected by legal technicalities, gets away with ever more outrageous behavior—including a sniping attack on Cruz himself and a vicious beating of Wilder, who has by now become Cruz's lover—the police find themselves unable to establish a connection between Mansell and Judge Guy's murder weapon that will stand up in court, despite their best efforts. Sandy Stanton, Clement's girlfriend, has vanished, taking the gun with her. Finally, Cruz and his partners, with Wilder's tacit consent, decide they have no choice but to make the Wildman disappear by sealing him up alive in a hidden vault beneath the apartment of Skendar Lulgjaraj, his last victim. "It's done, Raymond thought. Walk away" (210). But Cruz knows that this solution is neither legal nor, more importantly, honorable according to the rules of Clement's game. Later that night he returns to the vault alone, opens the door, walks out before Clement sees him, and waits in the outlaw's apartment, where he has arranged to settle things face to face by placing two guns within arm's reach on the dining room table and daring his opponent to draw.

Things don't go as planned, however. Clement, suspicious now, refuses to go for his weapon, checkmating Cruz in his attempt to kill Clement outside the law, but with honor, like a Hollywood gunfighter. Instead, Clement heads into the kitchen for some drinks and returns with a bottle of beer for Cruz. When Clement reaches into his pants to get an opener, the detective shoots him three times, thinking he's going for a hidden gun.

> Clement said, "I don't believe it . . . what did you kill me for?"
>
> Raymond didn't answer. Maybe tomorrow he'd think of something he might have said. After a little while Raymond picked up the opener from the desk and began paring the nail of his right index finger with the sharply pointed hooked edge. (222)

Cruz's final gesture mimics the conclusion of the scene from *The Gunfighter* that most impressed him (and apparently Leonard himself) as a boy: when a local braggart finds Gregory Peck, the reluctant gunslinger, sitting quietly at a barroom table and challenges him to draw, Peck, who is weaponless, bluffs him into backing down by suggesting he might have a gun under the table, already pointing directly at the young man. In fact, Peck turns out to be paring his nails.

As often happens with Leonard's pop cultural allusions, *City Primeval* turns the meaning of this scene upside down and inside out. In *The Gunfighter* the good guy (the gunslinger trying to go straight) bluffed the bad guy (the bully) into backing down, and two lives were saved. In *City Primeval* the good guy is drastically mistaken in his reading of the bad guy's intentions and ends up killing an unarmed man, under an illusion fostered by his obsession with Hollywood stereotypes. Thus the good guy ends up playing the trigger-happy bad guy, and the bad guy the unarmed victim, with fatal results. Far from "being cool," shooting a man for pulling a bottle opener out of his pants shows Cruz has lost his cool, badly. When he pares his nails after killing Clement in cold blood, his imitative behavior seems as much a suppression of personal awareness and responsibility as a sign of bravado, an aping of cinema self-possession belied by his inability to come up with an answer to Clement's question. Maybe tomorrow *will* bring the answer, but probably not, because Hollywood has no answers to provide. While we come away from *City Primeval* relieved that Clement is dead, we are also left wondering about the state of Raymond Cruz's soul, a site now haunted by a "Gregory Peck" who never existed except as an image on the silver screen. Sylvia Marcus turns out to have been right: Cruz's cowboy pose is what helps him stay detached from what makes him fully human. More importantly, for an Elmore Leonard hero, it has interfered with "what he *does*" professionally, which is to say, with being rather than just looking "cool."

Did Cruz have any other choice? Yes, to keep working at it until he got it right, and that was still a real option: the gun Cruz placed on the dining room table for Clement to grab was the original murder weapon, which Sandy had decided to turn in to police headquarters before leaving town. How hard would it have been to place that gun in Clement's apartment, where he'd always kept it, and return with police backup a minute after the Wildman arrived home? Killing Clement Mansell outside the law may have been satisfying, but it was also a professional failure, a lapse in Cruz's mastery of the *techne* of law enforcement. Taking things personally has led to a personal vindication, but at the expense of authenticity.

Split Images offers a kind of make-up test for Cruz's failure of professionalism. Its status as a "sequel" to *City Primeval* (Sutter, "Getting" 8) may not be apparent at first glance, but the police detective protagonist of *Split Images*, Bryan Hurd, was originally Raymond Cruz—he even sports Cruz's *Gunfighter* mustache (38) and, like his predecessor, wraps the grip of his service revolver with rubber bands (70).[7] Leonard had to change the name of his hero when he learned that United Artists, the studio that had bought the film rights to *City*

Primeval, had also paid for exclusive rights to the character of Raymond Cruz. *Split Images* is itself split geographically, with half the action occurring in Palm Beach, where the book begins, and the other half in Bryan Hurd's police jurisdiction of Detroit, where it ends. Hurd, like Cruz, faces a maddeningly clever psychopath, Robbie Daniels, who enjoys murdering with impunity and especially gets off on being videotaped in the act. Whereas Cruz's girlfriend, Carolyn Wilder, is badly beaten by Clement Mansell, Leonard ratchets up Hurd's motive for vengeance by having his lover, Angela Nolan, murdered by Daniels—a shocking event that Leonard depicts, with graphic power and efficiency, through the viewfinder of a video camera.

As the book nears its conclusion, Daniels remains untouchable and the scene is set for a repeat of *City Primeval*'s extralegal showdown, or even Hurd's outright assassination of Daniels. "I'm trying to keep from killing people" (260), Hurd tells his fellow officers. His superior, Eljay Ayers, can see the pressure his lieutenant is under and warns him against taking matters into his own hands. Instead of threatening him with an internal affairs investigation, however, Ayers appeals to his professionalism: "the best homicide dick I know doesn't fuck up" (266–67). Ayers has in mind disgraced ex-cop Walter Kouza, Robbie Daniels's current chauffeur, bodyguard, and videographer, who made a habit, when in uniform, of planting weapons on suspects he shot to justify the use of deadly force. Hurd takes Ayers's words to heart and uses his detective smarts to outwit Daniels, nailing him, not for the murder of Angela Nolan, which Daniels has prepared for, but for the wrongful death of Kouza, whom Daniels killed, and promptly forgot about, when Kouza tried to blackmail him.

Split Images, as its title suggests, foregrounds Leonard's growing interest in the mediated alienation of identity through mirroring and "echoing" technologies like film, television, photography, videography, and, eventually, sound reproduction—an interest that dates from as early as the opening chapter of *The Big Bounce,* with its documentary footage of Jack Ryan's assault on Luis Camacho. These technologies are all, in effect, narcissistic machines for self-fashioning, prostheses of selfhood. As Cruz himself demonstrates, *knowing* you are posing indicates a childlike playfulness, but *watching* yourself do so indicates an unhealthy, childish investment in the pose itself. Robbie Daniels can achieve confidence in his identity only by watching himself in the act of performing the person he thinks he is, namely, an international vigilante who knows "who the bad guys are" (164). For this reason he feels compelled not only to assassinate a frivolous, recreational drug dealer like Chichi Fuentes (the first step in what he imagines as a long career of covert operations against evil) but also to stage the hit as a Rambo-like combat mission, complete with military weaponry and camouflage outfit, for the video camera he's paying Kouza to operate. Angela Nolan, appearing unexpectedly on the scene, ends up as collateral damage. Daniels's obsession with watching himself perform his fantasy role is just one step beyond Raymond Cruz's preoccupation with the *Gunfighter* cop-image he wants to project in *City Primeval*, an image that is also technologically mirrored for him through the mass medium of the Western film.

This is not a topic confined to Leonard's crime fiction. His last Western novel, *Gunsights*, published the year before *City Primeval*, takes the mass mediation of identity and of historical reality as one of its central themes. The book is set in 1893, the year that historian Frederick Jackson Turner declared the American frontier to be, for all intents and purposes, "closed," which is to say tamed—surveyed, sold, civilized. From the start, we are reminded that the struggle between the squatters of Rincon Mountain, who are fighting to defend their homes and families, and the mining companies, which are paying goons and railroad cops to push them out, has incited a competition among East Coast newspaper reporters vying to turn the conflict into hot copy by packaging it as an epic myth of the vanishing Old West. Essential to their efforts are two frontier legends and former partners, Dana Moon and Bren Early, who have ended up on opposite sides of the struggle but will, before the dust has settled, become allies. "The Rincon Mountain War" and the lurid hype with which the reporters have surrounded it reach a simultaneous climax when the owner and star of a professional Wild West show, with photographers standing by, interrupts the final standoff to offer Moon and Early contracts to join his outfit, at which point Phil Sundeen, the bullyboy leader of the bad guys, challenges Dana Moon to go for his gun and is perfunctorily shot dead by Moon's wife, Kate, who has been standing behind a wall with her "big Henry rifle at her shoulder" the whole time (500). Then everybody goes home.

Kate Moon, whose last name Leonard will reassign to ambitious female performers in *Glitz* and *Be Cool*, is a younger, "cooler" version of women like Martha Cable, Paul Cable's level-headed wife in *Last Stand at Saber River*, and hotel owner Kay Lyons, Son Martin's mistress in *The Moonshine War*—patient but skeptical women whose men labor under the spell of extralegal codes of honor and vengeance. They love their "little boys" but can also recognize macho baloney when they hear it and, like Janet Pierson, Bren Early's mistress in *Gunsights*, they are likely to seek a grown-up lover if things don't change. What Kate Moon has that her older sisters don't is *techne*. Martha Cable can shoot a gun if she has to, and has even killed a man to protect her family, but Kate can ride like an Apache, shoot like Annie Oakley, and take the initiative when necessary (she doesn't seek Dana's permission to plug Sundeen). She's not about to let her man lose his life in what amounts to a game of cowboys and Indians, with real guns, for something as silly as what Bren Early calls "a question of honor" (490). When Kate pulls the trigger it's not to defend anyone's honor but to keep her husband from being killed in Bren's honor game. And unlike Raymond Cruz, who adheres to the Code of the West even in the modern "City Primeval" of Detroit, Michigan, she's not about to play to her opponent's strengths by giving him a fighting chance: she shoots him before he knows what hit him.

Carolyn Wilder, Clement Mansell's defense attorney (known respectfully among her colleagues at the Frank Murphy Hall of Justice as the "Iron Cunt" for her cold, relentless courtroom technique), has the "cool" of a Kate Moon: she has mastered a complex *techne*, the practice of law, and even when she falls in love with Raymond Cruz and his "little boy" ways, she sees no reason, initially, to give up "what she does" just because it rubs Cruz the wrong way. However, after she is violently beaten by her Teflon-coated client, she acknowledges the superiority of the lieutenant's frontier wisdom, abandoning both the skills and the ethics of her profession by tacitly agreeing to let Clement be locked away in Skendar's underground vault. If we finish *City Primeval* with a feeling of disappointment at Wilder's capitulation to Cruz's demands that she put aside the "lady lawyer" for the traditional Old West role of damsel in distress, we can take heart, not only from her counterpart in the last Western novel Leonard ever wrote, but also from Detective Maureen Downey, Raymond Cruz's quiet, unflappable, and superbly competent colleague, who will reappear in *Split Images* under the name Annie Maguire and whose later death to uterine cancer will leave her husband, detective Frank Delsa, adrift and emotionally vulnerable in *Mr. Paradise* (2004). It's gun-toting Kate Moon, not Carolyn Wilder, who will become the template for a new breed of "cool" female professionals in Leonard's fiction—a line running from Sylvia Marcus and Maureen Downey, on through Kate's ambitious namesakes in *Glitz* and *Be Cool*, past gun-toting U.S. Marshal Karen Sisco in *Out of Sight* (1996) and Dara Barr, fearless documentary cinematographer of Somali pirates in *Djibouti* (2010), to end (for now) with young poker expert Jackie Reno in *Raylan* (2012).

FOUR

choruses

after 1980

In jazz, a "chorus" is a single iteration of a basic song or tune, usually twelve to thirty-two measures long. A jazz performance can comprise dozens of choruses, starting with the first, or "head," which is typically played as written, followed by successive improvisations on the head's fundamental chord structure. The results can both surprise and delight, incorporating melodies that may bear little resemblance to the original tune aside from their conformity to the "changes" of its basic chord sequence. New chords may even be substituted in the sequence itself.

I've used the terminology of jazz in chapter 3 to designate the stages, styles, and elements, as well as the patterns of combination and recombination, that characterized Leonard's creative evolution over his most formative decade of writing. Like the jazz greats of midcentury, Leonard forged an individual style immediately recognizable on several levels, most notably in its "Panasonic" voicing of free indirect discourse and dialogue, its deft manipulation of point of view, the sure rhythms of its pacing and plot twists, and its responsiveness to the farcical elements lurking in even the most terrifying situations. Above all, like the musical performers he admires, Leonard found something to say and creative ways to vary how he said it each time he picked up his "instrument." The body of work he has produced over the second half of his career can be segmented by theme, character type, geographical locale, or any number of recurrent preoccupations, but what has remained constant throughout is his focus on "being cool" in the sense that emerged by the end of his first decade as a crime writer—namely, the achievement of self-possession (confidence, control over one's life) through the acquisition (ideally the mastering) of a skill, an expertise, a profession, a *techne,* some form of "know-how" or competence that can meet new and challenging situations through improvisation or adaptation. Feeling comfortable with "what you do" is less a *being*-in-the-world than a *doing*-in-the-world that resists the disintegrative pressures of fear, doubt, hesitation, second-guessing, guilt, shame, blame shifting—all the affects of self-dispossession that characterize an understanding of oneself mediated through others. By focusing attention on the task at hand rather than on the "I" performing it, "being cool" removes the disabling burden of self-consciousness. It informs every distinct feature of Elmore Leonard's signature style: his discursive ventriloquism, his immersion in his characters' points of view, his letting them decide "what happens next" in the construction of plot, his playful insistence on the "fun" of taking things seriously—in short, the self-absorbing joy he takes in the work of writing.

If the question of how to "be cool" is what Leonard sets out not only to render moot by the act of writing but also to address in the stories he writes, his many answers to that question—in the form of some forty-five novels to date—constitute a series of improvisatory "choruses" on a handful of interrelated melodies or "heads," three of which I'll be examining in this chapter: alienation, alterity, and agency. Each of these reveals an important facet of Leonard's lifelong preoccupation with being cool and poses an ancillary question that began to emerge at about the time he stopped drinking, became divorced, and ceased going to Mass in the mid-1970s. It's a question we've seen him raise as early as *Unknown Man No. 89* and *The Switch,* namely, "How do I change my life?"

Doing It with Mirrors: Alienation

> Now you see me, now you don't.
>
> —*Teddy Magyk,* Glitz

After 1980, Leonard's work continued to dramatize the vicissitudes of acquiring, defending, losing, improving, betraying, adapting, misapplying, rejecting, faking and failing at, deploying and desiring, and tiring of *techne* in the quest for self-integration. Over the course of more than three decades, the scope of this interest has broadened to include nearly any activity or skill, even the most mundane, and degrees of mastery that may fall considerably short of self-oblivion and yet resist alienation. Handwriting analysis, housecleaning, insurance adjusting, magic tricks (in the aptly named *Out of Sight*), writing bail bonds, reading auras, pole dancing, eating and drinking underwater, growing pecans, killing an alligator, smuggling cash, selling homes and invading them—even miracles can be performed well or ill. It's not enough to have a gift—you've got to work at it. As Dawn Navarro, the scamming (or is she?) clairvoyant of *Riding the Rap* (1995), tells bookie Harry Arno, "You can get better at it, but you have to be born with some degree of paranormal abilities" (42). Ambition is often an asset. "What's wrong with wanting to do better?" Dawn asks U.S. Marshal Raylan Givens when he accuses her of being a publicity hound. "I *have* the gift" (208). Even if she's faking it, the important thing is that Dawn knows how to fake it well. Sometimes even a skeptical U.S. marshal can find himself stumped. "Each time she took [Raylan] by surprise like that, he'd try to keep from asking how she knew" (209).

Dawn's downfall, despite her natural talent and ambition, stems from treating her gift as a means to an end—that is, getting rich—rather than as an autotelic end in itself. For Dawn, "doing better" means making more money: hence her desire for publicity. But what if your attempts at publicity fail and your ministry (Dawn calls herself "The Reverend") is about to go under? Extortion is one answer but, as it turns out, not the right one. Agreeing to help slacker Chip Ganz, his houseman Louis Lewis, and the volatile Bobby Deogracias in their scheme to kidnap Arno, Dawn places the gullible bookie in a state of past-life "regression" in order to get him to reveal, under hypnosis, where his money is stashed and to render him helpless against ambush. It's not long, however, before Dawn finds herself out of her depth, and Raylan has little trouble reading *her* mind as she watches the kidnappers turn on each other—and on her.

It's important to remember that, for Leonard, there's nothing wrong with making money, as long as you are good at it and enjoy making it more than having it. Whether you are a financial whiz kid, like Barry Stam in *Stick* (1983), or an elite bank robber, like Jack Foley in *Out of Sight*, if getting money, by whatever means, is "what you do," and you work at it and above all enjoy it, you will (or in any case, you deserve to) succeed in Elmore Leonard's universe. Dawn's problem is that she is not good at making money by *any* means. Resurfacing in *Road Dogs* (2009) with a spiritualist come-on featuring Jack Foley as a fake medium, she ends up having to match wits with Jack and his former cellmate, Cundo Rey (like Dawn, they are characters from previous books), and almost succeeds. What finally defeats her is her incompetence in the art of blowing people away, something she doesn't recognize, first, because she's in love with a menacing image of herself rather than with the demanding craft of killing, and second, because she makes her fight with Cundo and Jack personal—which, as we've learned, is nearly always a big mistake.

Dawn's self-infatuation is registered in two mirror scenes in *Road Dogs*. In the first, she is trying to figure out how to cope with the "guy thing" that keeps Jack and Cundo loyal to each other and teamed up against her. Dawn's mental dissociation is evident in her attribution of agency to her mirror image as she reflects upon her problem: "Cundo would make a remark and look at Foley to get his approval. He doesn't ever look at you. The one in the mirror said, 'The prick' " (173). The solution seems to arrive with Dawn's physical transformation of the image in the mirror: she outlines her eyes with kohl paste to make herself look like the female pharaoh Hatshepsut, one of her "past lives," who cross-dressed "as a male ruler" to "[hold] off the guys with their Upper and Lower Nile guy-thing and the threat of revolt."

> "That was you," the Dawns said to each other, and thought, If you were pharaoh and a couple of hieroglyph rock chiselers were giving you a hard time . . . What would you do? (174)

Dawn's channeling of her "past life" does help her get the better of Cundo, who's lost his prison smarts "on the outside." Drawing on traditionally feminine skills as old as Hatshepsut, allied with good cooking, Dawn gets the drop on Cundo at dinner by pulling a gun out from under a dish cover and shooting him three times point blank: "No blood to clean up," remarks her lover, Tico, looking at the back of Cundo's chair.

> "But there's some on the tablecloth," replied Dawn. "Take it off and soak it in cold water with a little vinegar."
>
> Tico grinned. "You know the secrets of a good housewife and how to shoot somebody." (210)

The traditionally female *techne* of good housekeeping will not work, however, against the street smarts of Jack Foley, and in taking him on, Dawn overestimates her skill set, or rather, that of the wily Hatshepsut inside her. To prepare herself for murdering Jack, Dawn again consults her mirror image with its kohl-blackened eyes, "seeing herself as Hatshepsut" and, like her Nile pre-incarnation, cross-dressing as a male. Wearing Cundo's black raincoat and hiding a gun in the right pocket, she notices, "It didn't fit, part of her hand would be out of the pocket. It was all right with Dawn" (250). "It didn't fit," along with Dawn's indifference to this fact, is the first clue that all will not go well when she makes her two attempts on Jack's life. The second clue is her rehearsing what she will say while gauging its effect in the mirror: "Hi, Jack, I was in the neighborhood and thought I'd drop in."

> She said [to her image], "You're kidding, right? You thought you'd drop *in*? Just take out the fucking gun and shoot him."
>
> The gun was ready?
>
> She checked it. Loaded, cocked, ready to fire.
>
> She brought it out. The hammer caught for a couple of seconds on the hem of the pocket. She released the hammer and drew the Walther again. Good—it came right out. She'd fire without cocking it. Unless she might have a few things to say first. (251)

And she does. The clumsy practicing in the mirror, the rehearsing of lines, the prolonged effort of "trying to think" (251) about every detail of the scene in which she will star, all tell us that Dawn is outmatched. And the fundamental reason is clear: she is obsessed with being the image in the mirror instead of inhabiting her own body, which is to say, losing herself in "doing" Jack. In the end, she lacks mastery of the habitual routines and physical moves for killing a person, while the skills she has supposedly mastered, fortune-telling and mind-reading, conspicuously fail her when she needs them most. Jack appears unexpectedly as she is on her way to kill him, throwing off her timing, and when she gets a second chance she can't tell that Jack has removed the bullets from the gun she turns on him.

Dawn's betrayal of, and by, her paranormal powers contrasts markedly with Leanne Gibbs's enthusiastic channeling of her "spirit guide," the twelve-year-old slave girl "Wanda Grace," in *Maximum Bob* (1991). When Judge Robert "Maximum Bob" Gibbs (so dubbed by the media for his harsh sentences) first meets her, Leanne is barely older than jailbait, working as a mermaid at Weeki Wachee Springs and already certain she is clairvoyant: "Oh, my Lord," she exclaims upon meeting the lecherous old Gibbs. "I may have been your mother in a previous life" (24). Be that as it may, after a near-death experience involving an alligator that has strayed into her underwater performance area, Leanne finds herself channeling Wanda Grace instead. Unfortunately for Judge Gibbs, the consequences of Leanne's "Experience" emerge only after the two of them are married. In one short passage conveyed from Bob's point of view, Leonard tells us all we need to know about the Gibbses' life together since that day, couched in the colloquial syntax of free indirect discourse.

> Now Leanne claimed she could be present while the other person spoke, the other person occupying only her invisible etheric body, her spiritual self. See, while she remained in her actual body.
>
> The one putting on weight. (27)

Channeling is not a bad metaphor for a writer's ability to ventriloquize the voices inside his characters' heads by releasing the voices inside his own, and the layering of voices here, while funny, is also structurally significant. Bob's discursive memory of Leanne's psychobabble mimics Leanne's psychic channeling of Wanda Grace, "the other person" inside her, which, in turn, mimics Leonard's own vocalic legerdemain. As the anagrammatic similarity of their names suggests, there is more of *Lean*ne in *Leona*rd himself, and vice versa, than we might guess.

Leanne is eager not only to improve her new spiritual powers but to share them as well. She begins attending "psychic workshops and seminars in Florida, Georgia, and as far north as Ohio" (30), and eventually starts organizing her own. She finds she can assess a person's spiritual health from his or her "aura," and Bob's, an angry red, tells her he is badly in need of crystal healing, which she is willing to supply. Leanne is crazy, but acute. Bob Gibbs does have difficulty managing his anger, often letting it get the better of him in court and expressing it in sarcasm and facetiousness. He clearly enjoys showing off this side of his personality, and Leonard wants us to enjoy watching him do so. That said, the scenes in which Wanda Grace takes over Leanne's "etheric body" and speaks through her "actual" mouth, while hilarious, are anything but beside the point. Communing with Wanda Grace empowers Leanne to confront Bob—and us—with the long shadows cast by his impromptu stand-up comedy. When Gibbs dares to make a joke at Wanda Grace's expense—"Maybe you can get her to dust and do the windows"—we laugh, but Leanne's reaction is meant to be more than just funny: "Your idea of fun is cruel. Sending people to prison, degrading those less fortunate. Wanda Grace was a *slave*. All her people died of the fever except she" (34).

Leanne trusts her new powers, and her new spiritual guide, and commits herself to them unreservedly. Going professional and making a career out of them in workshops and seminars is her mission, not her grift, and it would be an understatement to say that Leanne's self is merely immersed in "what she does." It is, in fact, replaced. In sharp contrast to Dawn Navarro's cynical misuse of her paranormal powers, Leanne's sincere commitment pays off. At the end of the book, when Elvin Crowe arrives at the Gibbses' home to put a bullet in the judge who sent him to prison for "the maximum," it's Wanda Grace who tells an unsuspecting Leanne to grab her husband's Walther .38 from the bedroom nightstand and head for the backyard, where she takes over Leanne's "actual body," raises the gun, and fires, saving Gibbs's life.

As Dawn Navarro's conversations with Hatshepsut suggest, mirror scenes in Leonard's work register moments of self-doubt that can easily slip into specular entrapment. But they may also indicate opportunities for growth. When Mickey Dawson, in *The Switch*, sees herself in the mirror after realizing that being kidnapped means "she didn't have to worry about a nice mom image" anymore, that "she could be herself," she asks her reflection, "Who are you?" and discovers that she "like[s] the feeling, being excited, and calm at the same time" (91). Mickey's self-interrogation means she's ready to change, and her mixed feelings of excitement and calm—similar to those of "being cool"—show that, whatever the answer to her question, she can now handle it. This openness to unexpected answers marks the difference, as we have seen, between the childlike and the childish. Those who become entrapped by their mirror images, the childish, have already decided on the answers they seek. They are, like Dawn Navarro, posing before the mirror to confirm something that the very resort to a mirror shows they doubt or to frame out something about themselves they fear is true—something others might see in them that they want to believe can't be seen. Teddy Magyk's experiences in *Glitz* conform to this pattern.

Teddy's surname alludes to his uncanny ability to remain "invisible" as he goes about murdering three people in the weeks following his release from prison, all while looking for an opportunity to kill Lieutenant Vincent Moro for sending him to jail. Once the lieutenant learns what Teddy is up to, he tries to rattle him into a confession by confronting him with Modesto Manosduros, a purported psychic and the wife of Magyk's first victim, a cab driver. Modesto has no trouble using her "powers" to identify Magyk as her husband's murderer, but she cannot place him with either of his other victims. "Is hard to see him," she says. "Now you see me, now you don't," Teddy replies. "Mr. Magic," says Modesto. "No police can catch him" (229).

Teddy's vanishing act is empowering, but also expresses his deepest fear: being seen by Moro at all. "How would you like it?" he asks his mother's parrot, Buddy, referring to the day of his arrest. "Guy thinks he knows more about you than you do? Like he can look in your head and see things that make him want to blow your head right off." Buddy, who repeats Teddy's surname whenever he appears, also "parrots" Magyk's ocular fears and desires: "Would you like to peck my eyes out so I can't look at you no more?" Teddy asks. "Would you? 'Ey, then you know what it feels like" (100). After three weeks of invisibly tailing Moro from Miami to San Juan to Atlantic City and back to San Juan, including one week of long-distance photo surveillance, Magyk has yet to act on his resolve. His procrastination is becoming "an expensive proposition. The gun, air fare to Puerto Rico, the hotel, the car . . ." (100). Teddy can't make his move until, like Dawn Navarro, he discusses it with his image in the mirror.

"Haven't I seen you someplace before?"
"Now you do, now you don't."
"Wait."
He stared at himself in silence, not grinning now.
"When you gonna do it?"
"What?"
"You know what."
He stared at himself in silence.
"Tomorrow. Didn't I tell you?" (241)

Vanishing at will may be an advantage when you're trying to assassinate someone, but the need to keep out of sight can also reduce your opportunities, especially when, like Frank Renda stalking Vincent Majestyk, you need your victim to know who's murdering him: "I want to be looking in your eyes as I pull the trigger" (247), Teddy tells Moro when he finally corners him. Teddy's contradictory desire to remain unseen resurfaces, however, when he demands that the lieutenant acknowledge not his identity but his opacity: "You don't know anything about me or what I feel," he says. "You *think* you do." Unarmed, with a gun trained on him, Moro has no choice but to agree—"No, I'd be the first to admit that" (247)—thus mirroring back to Teddy his "magic" image of himself: an illusory surface with no accessible interior.

Mirrors in Leonard's crime fiction are only the most concrete example of a wide range and variety of mediating devices that can seem like powerful tools of self-definition and then turn around to threaten autonomy: video recording and surveillance, movies and photography, audio recordings and, as we saw in *Gunsights*, their printed counterpart, newspapers, whether fictional, factual, or somewhere in between. *LaBrava*, published in 1983, provides an outstanding example of mediation as two-handed engine. Like nearly all the rest of Leonard's later work, it dramatizes the struggle to "be cool"—in control of the situation and of oneself, at one with the task at hand, true to one's talent and *techne*—under the impetus of the desire to change one's life and the pressure of specular forces that threaten to throw one off balance at precisely the most vulnerable moment of transition. For Joe LaBrava, these forces are concentrated in two particular technologies of visual mediation, photography and cinema.

We first hear about LaBrava, a neophyte photographer, as a topic of conversation between old pro Maurice Zola and Evelyn Emerson, owner of a photo gallery in Miami's Coconut Grove neighborhood. Zola made his reputation as a documentary photographer during the Great Depression by taking snapshots of turpentine camps, road gangs, and natural disasters for the Farm Security Administration. Playing the role of mentor to LaBrava, he is trying to persuade Evelyn to display his mentee's work: "He's got the eye, Evelyn. He's got an instinct for it, and he's not afraid to walk up and get the shot" (2). "The shot" here echoes its first iteration by Maurice on page 1—"Come on, Evelyn, the shot"—and it resounds four more times in this opening chapter: "He shoots people" (3); "It was LaBrava took the shot" (5); "he got off two shots" (5); "the one shot" (5). These hints of gun violence are clarified when we learn, at the end of the chapter, that Joe LaBrava was formerly a Secret Service agent. "[Y]ou watch him," says Zola. "Joe walks down the street he knows everything that's going on. He picks faces out of the crowd, faces that interest him. It's a habit, he can't quit doing it" (6). LaBrava also has "more natural ability than I had in sixty years of taking pictures," Zola admits (2). In short, Joe LaBrava's experience in the Secret Service, where he was trained to identify potential assassins and "shoot" to kill in a heartbeat, has perfected his inborn talents into a habituated way of seeing and behaving in the world, a *techne* that is perfectly suited for his new career.

Ironically, LaBrava has never had to shoot anyone with a gun. In fact, the reason he quit the Secret Service and took up photography is that he became bored with his last assignment, guarding the house of Harry S. Truman's widow, Bess. "He'll tell you he was in the wrong business," Zola says of LaBrava. "Now he spots an undesirable, a suspicious looking character, all he wants to do is take the guy's picture" (7). LaBrava discovered the right business while on undercover assignment, surveilling counterfeiters with a Nikon.

> Loved it. Snapping undercover agents making deals with wholesalers, passers unloading their funny money. Off duty he continued snapping away. [. . .] He felt himself attracted to street life. It was a strange feeling, he was at home, knew the people; saw more outcast faces and attitudes than he would ever be able to record, people who showed him their essence behind all kinds of poses—did Maurice understand this?—and trapped them in his camera for all time. (19)

His attraction to "street life," to the point of feeling "at home" among "outcast faces and attitudes," suggests that LaBrava, too, is an "outcast"—if not actually destitute, then at least psychologically distanced from ordinary life—and that he, too, has an "essence" not immediately apparent to others. Photography is for him another form of *secret* service, revealing the "secret" persons behind others' outcast poses and giving expression to the "secret" photographer hidden inside Agent Joseph LaBrava. His black and white photos are, like every mimetic art, a mirror of life, but a magic one, conveying the truth beneath and behind surfaces, even his own, to everyone who looks into them.

LaBrava is full of "secrets." Maurice Zola has "a secret " (9), namely, that he doesn't just manage the hotel where he lives; he owns it, and used to own the one next to it. This means he's richer than he lets on, a fact later confirmed when LaBrava hears "the old guy who loved the neighborhood and would never leave" discussing real estate values "like a man who had money, a lot of it" (167). Jean Shaw, the faded queen of *noir* cinema who has become a target of Richard Nobles's extortion threats, once achieved on-screen fame for her "cool expressions, knowing something, never smiling except with dark secrets" (69). Nowadays she uses "some kind of secret cream, placenta tissue extract" (135), to preserve her looks, says Franny Kaufmann, who should know. She's a professional artist who earns money for her canvas and pigments by selling cosmetics, a debased form of painting as *techne* that depends on knowing (or appearing to know) the secret to keeping age a secret. Later, Franny asks LaBrava to tell her some "secrets" about his former life, and the scene concludes with LaBrava thinking that "the secret of a happy life, if anybody wanted to know a secret," was to "be serious and still have fun" (219)—that is, to be cool. Like most of Leonard's heroes, LaBrava enjoys doing what he takes most seriously, but he also enjoys the secrecy of it. He doesn't just "shoot" people from a distance—"peeking into their lives as he picked them off one at a time"—he also savors being "alone with them again" in the "amber darkroom light" (204), like a taxidermist with his specimens.

"Shooting" a camera and "shooting" a gun, "peeking" at and "picking them off," bear an obvious relationship to each other in this book: both require a good eye and a steady hand, both aim at arresting life, and both can be, for LaBrava, acts of aggression. In his first confrontation with Nobles at a local crisis clinic where the bullyboy came looking for Shaw, LaBrava blinds his antagonist with the flashbulb on his camera in order to throw him down, hold him still, and put a gun in his mouth. When Nobles later learns that the photographer has been taking pictures of him at a distance—that "LaBrava shot him" (185)—he panics and wants to curl up "into an almost fetal position" in his car so as not to be seen (199). Leonard suggests there is an atavistic violence to the secret way LaBrava approaches his art, as though in capturing a subject's image he has removed the soul from its body and placed it in photographic formaldehyde.

In the cozy solitude of his darkroom, LaBrava tries to probe and unpack the interiors of his subjects, wanting "to ask them questions about where they'd been and what they'd seen" (204), much like the cop he used to be, interrogating suspects. This very quest for interiority will confound LaBrava's dedication to his new craft and imperil the change of life that hinges on it, when an image floats up from his developing tray that he recognizes, with a shock, as the face of Jean Shaw, "the movie star he had fallen in love with the first time he had ever fallen in love in his life" (54). Suddenly, LaBrava finds himself regressing to the age of twelve as his gift for probing the minds and hearts of his subjects encounters a unique challenge. The "dark secrets" of Jean Shaw's "knowing" smile, revealed at the end of every B movie she ever starred in, will defy LaBrava's sharp eye for interiority and sap his interrogative willpower in real life, compelling him, instead, to illuminate their opaque recesses with his resurgent adolescent fantasies.

The face LaBrava expected to see in the darkroom tray was that of Jeanie Breen, an old friend of Maurice's who'd apparently been hitting the bottle hard enough to get taken to a crisis clinic. That's where LaBrava first laid eyes on her, passed out on a daybed, when Maurice sent him inside to snap some pictures meant to shame her into drying out after she came to. Maurice had said "Jeanie" used to be a movie star, but LaBrava hadn't recognized her as Jean Shaw until this moment in the darkroom, because, since childhood, "he had seen her only in the dark. Had watched her, how many times, in the black and white dark of movie theaters, up on the screen" (53).

As we watch LaBrava watching the print of Jean Shaw float into visibility for the first time, it is hard to resist the conclusion that his darkroom is a magnified version of his mind, an analogy whose pedigree goes back some three centuries to English philosopher John Locke's *Essay Concerning Human Understanding.* Locke famously compared the mind to a *camera obscura,* a "dark room" into which images of the world enter through the five senses to be displayed on the *tabula rasa,* or "blank screen," of consciousness.[1] "A still picture is more powerful than a motion picture, more memorable," LaBrava reads in an issue of *Aperture,* and he agrees. "Because the film pictures of Jean Shaw in his mind all seemed to be stills. Jean Shaw in black and white giving [. . .] the look" (196). Even "feelings," thinks LaBrava at one point, can be "save[d]" and "looked at later" (146).

Leonard's transformation of Locke's metaphor into LaBrava's workspace is crucial to understanding the photographer's peculiar vulnerability to Jean Shaw's seductive machinations. In the "dark room" of every mind are drawers filled with movie stills of our past experiences, and every print has a corresponding celluloid negative through which we project onto the world our dreams and fantasies, using the light of our imaginations. Turning the *camera obscura* of memory inside out into a projector of his adolescent libido, LaBrava finds himself inhabiting a world that miraculously unfolds like one of the *noir* films he viewed as a boy, unaware that its screenwriter, director, casting coach, and frame-by-frame projectionist is none other than the *femme fatale* herself. As LaBrava—and Leonard's readers—learn a bit too late, Jean Shaw has plans for her boy-toy. Meanwhile, the starstruck photographer wanders about in an almost perpetual state of astonishment at the realization of his dearest pubescent fantasy, suspecting it to be fabricated but unwilling to pinch himself awake. The first time LaBrava is formally introduced to Shaw, he is overcome by memories of his first sight of her profile "as she stood at the window" (65) in a film called *Deadfall,* and begins projecting the movie in his head.

LaBrava's inability to see Jean Shaw as anything other than the tantalizing "spider woman" (73) or seductive "Woman as Destroyer" (74) he remembers as a child is perfectly matched by her apparent inability to stop behaving like her screen persona, right down to repeating lines and gestures from her best-known roles, as well as those of actresses even more famous. The next evening, in Maurice's living room, LaBrava sees a "familiar look from long ago, the calm dark eyes. A screen gesture . . . Or was it real?" (100). Shaw quotes a line of Ida Lupino's from *High Sierra* (104) and later, at the door to her room in Maurice's hotel, gives LaBrava a kiss on the cheek to thank him for helping to rescue her at the clinic. "Was that familiar?" he wonders. "Seeing her eyes and then the door closing, filling the screen. He wasn't sure" (106). Later, after they go to bed together, Shaw's posing becomes more overt. Looking back on it from a postcoital perspective, LaBrava tries to reassure himself that the "movie star was a regular person. Underneath it all, she was." But he has to admit "that she was never a regular person for long."

> She said, "You're good for me, Joe. Do you know that?"
>
> Familiar. But he didn't know the next line, what he was supposed to say, and the words that came to mind were dumb. [. . .]
>
> She said, "I have a feeling you're the best thing that could happen to me, Joe."
>
> Another one, so familiar. He sipped his Scotch. He looked at the ceiling and a scene from *Deadfall,* early in the picture, began to play in his mind. (146)

Much of the fun of reading *LaBrava* comes from watching Leonard devise composite simulacra of generic *noir* chestnuts, imaginary dark gardens with real-life reptiles in them. Robert Mitchum, Elisha Cook, Victor Mature, Gig Young, and Henry Silva strut and fret their ninety minutes upon the screen opposite Jean Shaw in late-night TV fodder with made-up titles like *Deadfall, Obituary, Nightshade,* and *Let It Ride.* Joe LaBrava soon finds himself sounding like one of these patsies as the lines that eluded him start popping automatically out of his mouth: "If she wanted to play, what was wrong with that?" he wonders. "Play" (168). Of course, nothing's wrong with that, as long as you know what you're playing at. And it can be hard to stop playing. When LaBrava, catching wind of Richard Nobles's extortion scheme, warns Jean to be careful, he's surprised to find it's in the language of *noir*: "I have a feeling you might be in danger" (169).

> She said, "You're serious, aren't you?"
>
> *Yes*, he was serious. He was trying to be. But now even his own words were beginning to sound like lines from a movie. (169)

The next time Jean's lines seem familiar, they don't "sound so good," and again LaBrava has to reassure himself "that playing was okay, they were just having some fun" (188). He knows his relationship with Jean is a dream they conspire to maintain together, and he can't bear to wake them both up. But he suspects that at least one "player" is being played.

In *LaBrava* it is almost but not quite true that, as Glenn Most observes with a flourish of postmodernist bravura, "reality is imitating art and we can no longer confidently draw the line between what is fiction and what is truth" (109). However difficult it may be, we can and must be able to draw that line for the protagonist's choices to make any sense. The day after LaBrava first tells Jean that she "might be in danger," he realizes why it "didn't sound right": "people who were into danger on an everyday basis," as he had been at one time, "didn't talk like that, they didn't use the word" *danger* (171). They remained cool, detached. People like LaBrava himself, but also like Jill Wilkinson, who runs the crisis clinic where Shaw was taken after she threw her drink at a police car. Later, after being beaten and almost raped at her apartment by Richard Nobles, in an attempt to get information about LaBrava, Jill describes the ordeal from her hospital bed in a voice as calm as when she warned Nobles that if he made her go down on him she'd "bite it off, I swear to God" (118). Never once does she use the word "danger," or anything nearly as grim.

LaBrava met Jill at the clinic where Nobles, a bodybuilding redneck from the Florida Everglades and twice Jill's size, first came looking for Shaw. LaBrava "liked her confidence. [. . .] A good-looking girl who knew what she was doing" (35). Jill knows her "consumers" (clients), her staff, her job, and how to handle arrogant "assholes" (187) like Richard Nobles. Seeing Jill in action at the clinic, "LaBrava was falling in love with her" (38). Wilkinson is "cool" personified: experienced, direct, confident in the *techne* of administration, never panicky, and "out of character as victim," thinks LaBrava on seeing her at the hospital (117). After Richard left her apartment, Jill didn't call the police, she tells LaBrava, because he "didn't *do* anything. I mean you have to consider the kind of creepy stuff I run into every day, at work" (120). She also wants to take the vacation she has coming in Key West, and signing a complaint would tie her up in court.

One cannot help but think that Jill would have made a perfect match for steady, patient, quiet, competent, cool Joe LaBrava, if Jean Shaw hadn't appeared in his darkroom tray. Franny Kaufman seems an even better fit: unpretentious, outspoken, inner-directed, confident in her choice of life and career, and a visual artist, like our hero himself. From the moment they meet, LaBrava feels they are "old friends" (107), "old pals" (158). Franny can even crack jokes about Jean's obvious cosmetic surgery without making him "feel protective or take offense." It isn't long, however, before the jokes begin to grate, and not just because Jean Shaw is probably old enough to be LaBrava's mother—a topic to which we'll return. Trying to decide whether to have sex with Franny, LaBrava has to tell himself that he wouldn't be "cheating" on Jean—"How could it be cheating? He hardly knew the movie star" (216). After their lovemaking, Franny expresses the same attitude: "it was just for fun and not serious" with the movie star. This time, however, hearing it out loud, LaBrava becomes "mad" (237) and starts "pouting" (238), especially when Franny speculates that sex with Jean Shaw "wasn't the big thrill you thought it was gonna be. [. . .] she's too much into herself for that" (237); "she's always on stage" (238).

Franny's comments hit a nerve. In fact, making love to "the movie star" wasn't "the thrill" LaBrava thought it would be—it was a different kind of thrill altogether, the kind you get from "thinking about how great it's going to be, how unbelievable," and from watching yourself "do it" instead of from actually "doing it" (145). It was the thrill of a twelve-year-old, not a man of thirty-eight, as Leonard conveys from inside LaBrava's head in free indirect discourse.

> Look at him. He was making love to Jean Shaw, he was honest-to-God making love to Jean Shaw in real life. He didn't want to be watching, he wanted to be overwhelmed by it, [. . .] he wanted the overwhelming feeling of it to take hold and carry them away. [. . .] He had to stop thinking if he was going to be overwhelmed. He had to *let* himself be overwhelmed. (143–44)

Despite his best efforts to let go, however, LaBrava has to acknowledge that the "idea of it, the anticipation, the realization, was more overwhelming than the doing of it. Although he could not say that would be true of all movie stars" (144). When making love to movie stars, as in every other test of competence, it's talent, experience, and practice that count in achieving the desideratum of total self-immersion, of being "overwhelmed" by what you are doing—in this case, paradoxically, of being cool while getting hot.

Throughout his work, Leonard shows a heightened sensitivity to the difference between good and bad sex, a sensitivity shaped, no doubt, by his Catholic education, but at the same time deeply personal and, it seems, appealing to his predominantly male readership. This is surprising in light of America's popular cultural stereotype of "real" men as sex machines. I can think of very few male, or even female, writers of crime fiction who take conventional romantic love as seriously as Leonard, or who portray sex without love as seriously inadequate. Much of that seriousness, as we might expect, arises from his focus on getting lost in "what you do." Lovemaking, however, is distinguished from every other form of *techne* in Leonard's books by the fact that its ideal goal—*mutual* pleasure or, as Csikszentmihalyi calls it, "joy"—cannot be achieved single-handedly (so to speak). Loss of self-consciousness in pursuit of this goal must therefore be reciprocal: the self "doing it" must be absorbed in the task of giving pleasure to the partner whose cooperation in the "doing" of it is crucial to its achievement. Anything else is just mutual masturbation.

With Franny, his "old pal," LaBrava can "be serious and still have fun" (219). She is playful but not always playing a part, unlike Jean, who has "played so many parts she doesn't know who she is anymore" (238). Franny knows when she's posing, and because she makes sure LaBrava knows it too, it's not a constant source of anxiety as it is with Jean. Franny is good for him. With her electric, frizzy red hair, she is all about energy, color, sunlight, and composition. She loves painting the deteriorating facades of South Beach hotels, because the people who designed them "had imagination, knew about color [. . .] and crazy lines booming" (49). She appreciates the beauty of surfaces, the genius of art as an autotelic pursuit, not as the pursuit of personal secrets. She doesn't spend half her life in a dark room poring over black and white faces; she takes color Polaroids (159). LaBrava wants to "act as natural as this girl" but knows "she ha[s] a lead on him" (216). We hope that LaBrava will follow Franny's lead, but our hope fades as he gets pulled further and further into the spider woman's net.

Jean Shaw's scheme comes straight from the *noir* film vault. She intends to swindle Maurice Zola out of $600,000 by pretending that Richard Nobles is extorting that much from her through physical threats. Once she's made herself look like a potential victim, she and Nobles (whom she's promised to cut in on the deal) type up and send threatening notes to her apartment. Soon the police are involved, aided by former special agent Joe LaBrava, and Jean talks them into adopting her plan to entrap Nobles (whose authorship of the notes they cannot prove), along with his unknown accomplice, Cundo Rey, who later resurfaces in *Road Dogs*. The sting, however, requires fronting $600,000 in real cash, which the police cannot secure from officials on the flimsy evidence they have. Maurice gallantly volunteers to pony it up (as Jean knew he would) on the understanding that the money will be returned once the trap is sprung. Needless to say, things don't go as anyone but Jean Shaw expects. Pulling all the strings in her hidden web, she manages to bamboozle the police, the FBI, Nobles, Rey, LaBrava, and her putative best friend, Maurice Zola. Even though the authorities strongly suspect they've been had, they have no way to prove it.

The most mysterious feature of Shaw's scheme is that she doesn't need to steal money from Maurice: he has said repeatedly that she can have all the money she wants—she only has to ask for it. Jean, however, doesn't want to be beholden to Maurice, or to any man. She would rather steal the money than accept it "like an allowance" (212). This motivation, already somewhat weak on the face of it, becomes even flimsier when we consider the extremes to which Jean Shaw is willing to go to have her way—not just swindling her oldest and, it seems, only real friend but murdering her unsuspecting accomplice, Nobles, to keep all the loot for herself. The only way it makes sense is if we assume that Jean is a psychopath, just like the spider women she played in the movies. But she's not grim or sinister or edgy enough to be convincing in the part when she's not on screen. Moreover, if Jean is literally a *femme fatale*, then her agreeing to marry Maurice in the last chapter should disturb LaBrava, and us, more than it does.

The reason it doesn't, I think, is that the true master—or mistress—of *techne* in *LaBrava* is not the title character. It's Jean Shaw. That means Leonard is rooting for her, and his enthusiasm is infectious.

Like many of her predecessors in Leonard's fiction, and like LaBrava himself, Jean Shaw has mastered an art in her former life that she is trying to apply in her present circumstances. We know that Jean is devoted to her craft the moment LaBrava tries to commiserate with her for never ending up "with the star" (73): "I played Woman as Destroyer, and that gave me the lines. I'd rather have the lines any day" (74). Unlike LaBrava, Shaw maintains a cool, disinterested relationship to her art. She never takes it personally or uses it to scratch some private itch. She is, in short, a pro. Moreover, like Frank Ryan and Ernest Stickley in *Swag*, she's attempting to "move up" to a higher, more challenging arena in which to exercise her talents. No longer content to read the lines others write for her, Jean has decided to write her own and get others to do what she says. Her scheme, in fact, is based on a screenplay she once pitched to producer Harry Cohn at Columbia Studios, about a young woman who is offered anything she wants by a rich playboy. The girl refuses, because getting it that way "is unsatisfying, too easy." She then cheats the young man out of a pile of money "and is happy because *she* did it, she earned it herself" (321). Cohn told Jean "the idea stunk" (321). Now, some thirty years later, she is playing the lead in her own screenplay—and making it work.

Cohn's rejection of Shaw's script tells us that Hollywood producers know nothing about autotelic joy, only about the bottom line: why would anyone turn down free money? Perhaps because it offers no creative opportunities, no challenge to the skills that define a true artist, and thus, no chance to be cool. And Jean Shaw is nothing if not cool. In her manipulation of Nobles—getting him to write the extortion notes himself but dictating the words he is to write, priming him by showing him the film, *Obituary*, that will provide the blueprint for their scam, seducing him and then plugging him full of lead when he's outlived his usefulness—we are watching a Renaissance woman at work: writer, director, and actor all in one. As for Cundo Rey, he's left holding the bag—a garbage bag of old newspaper. True, Shaw makes a mistake or two along the way. She should have known better, for instance, than to trust Nobles to dispose of the incriminating typewriter, which somehow ends up in Rey's blackmailing mitts. Fearing that her number's up, Jean utters the monosyllabic line of the defeated *femme fatale* in *Obituary*, who is on her way to jail and "out of the picture" (283) as the credits begin to roll: "Swell." But as far as LaBrava is concerned, "It's not over yet" (377).

"This isn't the movies," LaBrava warns Shaw when he discovers what she's up to (367). He should know: he was a cop. Instead of behaving like a real cop and turning her in, however, LaBrava offers to help cover the whole thing up and retrieve the typewriter if Jean will just return the money to Maurice. At this point we may begin to think, "He *was* a cop. But what is he now?"

The answer is, the chump detective in *Obituary* played by Victor Mature (354), the actor whose very name casts an ironic light on Joe LaBrava's role as a detective in his dealings with Jean Shaw: anything but mature and far from the victor. It's a part for which Shaw has worked hard to cast LaBrava from the first moment he asked her about Nobles, who was at the clinic looking for her on the night he and Maurice went to pick her up. Only moments after he poses the question, Shaw gives LaBrava the first of many "familiar look[s]"—"A screen gesture . . . Or was it real?" (100)—and the game is on. Shaw is wary of LaBrava, especially when she discovers his background in law enforcement. The way to his heart, it turns out, is not only through his cinematic memories but also through his *techne*, photography.

Despite his natural talent, LaBrava is still a little insecure in his new profession. We can tell because when Franny, on first meeting him, asks, "You're the photographer, aren't you?" his first thought is "Recognition" as he "lean[s] on the cool marble-top counter" and adopts a self-captioned pose, "artist relaxed, an unguarded moment" (49). As concerned with his image as he may be, however, he's still not adept at maintaining it. A running joke throughout the book is LaBrava's idea of what a real Miami Beach photographer should wear. Since he has no color sense, his choice in shirts runs to "bananas, pineapples and oranges" (13) or huge red hibiscus blooms that make him look, in Maurice's and Franny's estimation, like "Murf the Surf" (13). The first thing the exquisitely tasteful Jean Shaw says when she learns LaBrava ran into Richard Nobles is, "You know, that's a lovely shirt. [. . .] I love hibiscus" (136–37). The next thing we know she's using the oldest come-on in Hollywood cinema—"Come up and see my etchings"—but turning it around to suit the occasion: "I want to see more of your work, I think it's stunning. Will you show me?" (137). Then, moving in closer for the kill, she adds, "You think you're hidden, but I can see you in there, Mr. LaBrava. Show me your pictures" (140).

Sitting next to Shaw in his apartment, his photos lying in front of them, LaBrava tries to come across as a plain and uncomplicated kind of guy, like his pictures, by disparaging the comments he overheard the art crowd making about his work at Evelyn's gallery: "a frontal attack against the assumptions of a technological society," or "a compendium of humanity's defeat at the hands of venture capital," or "the aesthetic subtext of his work is the systematic exposure of artistic pretension" (141)—the last a comment that a critic for the *Village Voice* once used to describe Leonard's books (Challen 108). "I thought I was just taking pictures," says LaBrava, adding that the only remark he heard that made any sense was "he takes pictures to make a buck" (*LaBrava* 141). Before we decide that LaBrava is simply echoing the apparent reverse snobbery of his creator, we should note that when Jean asks him what he sees when he shoots, his answer is couched in language every bit as challenging as what the gallery goers had to say, and more to the point: "I see 'images whose meanings exceed the local circumstances that provide their occasion'" (142)—a quote from Walker Evans. LaBrava is not as naive and unsophisticated as he likes to pretend. Also to his credit, he can tell when Shaw's making up gnomic comments to persuade him she understands his artistic sensibility. "Simplicity. It is what it is. [. . .] And what it isn't, too," she says. "He didn't want her to try so hard" (141).

And she doesn't have to. Despite his respect for the demands of his craft and reverence for the masters that preceded him, LaBrava's adolescent need for Shaw's approval and admiration undoes him. Shaw's clinching line is one we should have anticipated: "What do you see when you look at me?" Goodbye Walker Evans; hello Woman as Destroyer.

When Jean Shaw says she sees the real Joe LaBrava hidden inside the thirty-eight-year-old man in the hibiscus shirt, and asks to see his pictures, who does she see and what pictures is she looking for? Does she see Joseph LaBrava the former Secret Service agent and surveillance expert, or Joe LaBrava the photographer, or Joey LaBrava the twelve-year-old watching *Deadfall* in a Detroit movie theater? Is she asking to see the photographer's pictures, up in his room, or the photographic memories stashed away in the *camera obscura* of LaBrava's mind? The answers are, all three and both. If the true self that's hidden "inside" can only be incarnated impersonally, in *techne*, then the true photographer "inside" LaBrava can only emerge as he pursues the autotelic joy of mastering his art. The photographer who emerges instead, in response to Jean Shaw's seductive praise, is the cop-photographer who once used his Nikon to "shoot" drug pushers and counterfeiters at a distance, long before finding out he loved it (18), and that cop fills his assigned role in Jean Shaw's *noir* scenario the minute LaBrava begins to investigate Richard Nobles's background and tail him around the city with a telephoto camera. As a Secret Service agent, LaBrava also tracked down letter writers who threatened presidents with violence, examining "postmarks, broken typewriter keys, different clues" (18). Now he is using the same techniques to trace the person who is typing threatening notes to Shaw.

To the extent that the *techne* of photography has been instrumentalized by LaBrava as just one more technique placed in the "secret" service of protecting Jean Shaw, it can no longer provide autotelic satisfaction. Even worse, the "cop" using it for this purpose can't seem to remember he is no longer a real cop, as Buck Torres, LaBrava's detective friend, tells him when he hears that Joe has lost his cool with Nobles and broken his arm with a baseball bat while interrogating him: "You don't carry a gun anymore, Joe, you're a civilian now. You and I can talk, I appreciate it; but you got to stay out of it. [. . .] It's not anything personal, it's the way it is" (314).

The cop "inside" Joe LaBrava who comes out as he closes in on Nobles does take things "personal," however. He's the cop LaBrava saw in the movies as a kid, a cop like Victor Mature in *Obituary*, who lets his emotions get tangled up in his work instead of doing his job dispassionately. Nobles can push all LaBrava's buttons because, as we might have expected, he is LaBrava's dark double. Nobles was once a "Federal snitch" who turned in drug-running friends and relatives to save his own hide (173); LaBrava also worked undercover at times and grew to hate it because, in effect, he would have to "snitch" against men who had come to consider him their "new buddy" (17). Nobles is a former security cop; LaBrava is a former Federal cop. In the scene where LaBrava breaks Nobles's arm, pins him to the ground, and puts a gun in his mouth (reprising their first encounter at the crisis clinic), he "felt he could kill Nobles; in this moment he could. Pull the trigger." "Something was happening to him. The cop in him coming out. After all that waiting. Nine years or more of official waiting, hanging back steely-eyed and looking smart" (307). But LaBrava knows he is "losing it" when Nobles, the shadow self who knows him so well, calls his bluff and refuses to give anything away: "It was hard to keep it up," thinks LaBrava, "unless you were honestly detached enough to go all the way and break the guy's jaw looking into his eyes. [. . .] He couldn't do it" (310).

The "cop" coming out in LaBrava as he sits astride Nobles is not the cop he was, but a cop he never was, a black and white ghost lurking in his childhood memories. During his years in the Secret Service, he had never pulled or even reached for his weapon, let alone shot a suspect with it, or for that matter punched anyone. His entire uneventful career as a Federal officer was spent "waiting" for an opportunity like this, but when it arrives, LaBrava can't follow through. And it's a good thing, too. A real cop—a professional like Buck Torres—would never use a baseball bat on an unarmed man and then threaten to kill him, or even break his jaw, except in the line of duty, and only if the suspect presented a clear and present danger. LaBrava was never cut out to be a cop in the first place. That's the lesson of his switch to photography. Under the spell of Jean Shaw, the cop that Joe LaBrava has now cut himself out to be is nothing more than a *noir* caricature of police anarchy, a twelve-year-old boy's fantasy of law enforcement as personal vendetta.

To his credit, LaBrava pulls back at the last minute from committing himself fully to the cinematic detective persona that Jean Shaw has managed to draw out of him. He remains, however, putty in her hands. The full recognition that he was never meant to be a cop, real or celluloid, comes to LaBrava only later, when he realizes that, in putting down his gun and handing Cundo Rey a garbage bag full of cash for the return of Jean Shaw's typewriter, he has also handed over the "small bluesteel automatic" that Jean had hidden inside it.

> He had looked in the bag himself in Jean's apartment when he picked it up and had brought out a handful of bills, but it hadn't occurred to him to ask what she did with the gun. He could pretend to think like a cop and he could put on a cop look with a gun in his hand, but he couldn't take it all the way. (393)

LaBrava will live to "shoot" another day and so, by some meta-fictional miracle, will Cundo Rey, in *Road Dogs*, even with three bullets "up the center groove of his rib cage" (*LaBrava* 395). But it won't be because either has demonstrated any particular mastery of the *techne* of violence.

Returning home, LaBrava finds he can't stand any of his photographs, "all that same old stuff" (397). He is tired of "trying to be a character" but cannot go back to being himself—until Franny appears at his door. "He smiled because it didn't matter what kind of mood he was in. When he saw her he smiled and knew he would not have to bother choosing an attitude" (397). Franny lets him be himself. After she leaves, LaBrava puts on his banana shirt and looks in the mirror.

> He liked that banana shirt. He looked at his photos again and began to like some of them again, the honest and dishonest faces, enough of them so that he could say to himself, You got promise kid.
>
> Who was it said that?
>
> Who cares? (398)

LaBrava still lacks color sense, but at least he's comfortable with the familiar portrait of the artist he sees in the mirror, the one who doesn't care how he looks or what others say. Goodbye Victor Mature; hello Murf the Surf.

Still wearing the banana shirt, LaBrava goes down the hallway to deliver Jean's typewriter to her. He finds her with Maurice and learns, to his shock and dismay, that they intend to get married. This revelation accentuates the autotelic motive for Jean's plot, but also renders pointless every effort LaBrava has made on Jean's behalf and brings into clear relief the Oedipal drama lurking beneath the surface of the narrative throughout, with LaBrava playing the incestuous son to Shaw's *mère fatale* and Zola's "old man" (9), whose position the neophyte had tried to usurp, not as mentee and according to the rules of his craft, but as Mommy's bedmate. On hearing the news, LaBrava "didn't say anything because he didn't want to say anything he didn't mean [. . .] or cover up whatever it was he felt" (402). LaBrava wants no more secrets, but he still can't resist waiting for the right line to occur to him. Eventually he finds it. Completely "out of the picture," infantilized and discarded, duped every which way by the murderess that he dodged the law and risked his own life to protect, "What he finally said was, 'Swell'" (402).

Divas and Dancing Partners, Sidemen and Manimals: Alterity

Go play with your gun.

—*Joyce Patton,* Riding the Rap

The character of Jean Shaw was not unprecedented in Elmore Leonard's fiction. In *Gold Coast, femme fatale* Karen DiCilia, *née* Karen Hill, wriggled her way out of her mob husband's cold, dead hands by studying the moves of Bugsy Siegel's girlfriend, Virginia Hill. Frank DiCilia thought he could keep Karen from remarrying after his death by making her inheritance conditional on her eternal chastity. Instead, Karen ends up independently wealthy. She gets what she wants from her men, and what she needs, while making patsies of petty crook Cal Maguire and freelance enforcer Roland Crowe.

Since the publication of *City Primeval,* Leonard has become as skilled at handling the alterity of gender as he has of race: that sense of "otherness" that helps to distinguish, by contrast or reciprocity, the defining features of his white male protagonists. Like Leonard's heroes, his heroines can be distributed along two perpendicular axes of differentiation: one of them, tracking conventional morality, extends from "Bad Girls" to "Good Girls," and the other, tracking independence from men as opposed to cooperation with them, extends from what I'll call "Divas" to "Dancing Partners." Whether good or bad, divas or dancing partners, the women in Leonard's fiction tend to succeed, like the men, by mastering the skills appropriate to getting what they want while staying cool in crucial situations challenging that mastery.

The divas are in the game largely for themselves. Like their counterparts in the world of jazz and popular music—Billie Holiday starting out with tenor sax player Kenneth Hollan, for instance, or Tina Turner in the "Ike and Tina Turner Review"—their initial alliances with men are doomed to fail, although success in subsequent relationships may depend on how well they've handled the men their first time around. The breakup might come because they're greedy and self-absorbed, like Rene Cherry, Max Cherry's ex-wife, in *Rum Punch* (1992); or their natural talent forces them to leave their partners to get ahead, like Linda Moon in *Be Cool* (1999); or their men abuse or scare them, like Mary DeBoya in

Cat Chaser (1982); or, seeing that the guys are about to drive over a cliff, they decide to jump out of the passenger seat at the last moment, like Arlene Downey in *Swag*.

The Bad Girl Divas derive from Lorraine Kidston of *Last Stand at Saber River* and her crime-fiction successor, Nancy Hayes; the Bad Girl Dancing Partners, from desperate housewives like Lizann Falvey in *Escape from Five Shadows* and conniving prostitutes like Norma Davis in *Forty Lashes Less One*. Nancy Hayes types, like Dawn Navarro in *Road Dogs* and Robin Abbott in *Freaky Deaky* (1988), are female versions of Leonard's male bullies: they like to needle their male accomplices and victims alike, question their manhood, see them squirm. Bad Girl Dancing Partners like Jean Shaw and Karen DiCilia tend to be older, more cunning, and typically more successful. They are often divorced, or divorced and remarried, or, like Ginger Mahmoud in "When the Women Come out to Dance" (2003), looking for a way out of marriage that will let them keep the money they married for. Unlike Shaw and DiCilia, however, Ginger ends up worse off than when she began—the exception that proves the rule of Bad Girl cool.

The title of Leonard's short story comes from Book of Judges 21, describing how the tribe of Benjamin chose wives from among the "daughters of Shiloh" when the women came out to dance for the Lord during a feast day. Ginger, a redheaded hustler from the wrong side of the tracks, has used her skills as a stripper and lap dancer to seduce a rich Pakistani doctor into marrying her, and now discovers that she is utterly "bored with her life" (48). Unfortunately, the discovery came after she signed a prenuptial agreement leaving her nothing in case of divorce. "What do I do?" she asks her new Colombian housemaid, Lourdes (pronounced, in Spanish, "*Lour*-des"). "I exist. I have no life" (49).

The only time Ginger seems happy is when she's doing her aerobics, dancing in her underwear to the music that used to accompany her strip act. Despite her original desire to abandon it, there's a real note of pride in the account of her former life as Ginger tells it to Lourdes.

> I started out in a dump on Federal Highway, got discovered and jumped to Miami Gold on Biscayne, valet parking. I was one of the very first [. . .] to do Southern hip-hop, and I mean Dirty South raw and uncut, while the other girls are doing Limp Bizkit, even some old Bob Seeger and Bad Company. [. . .] But in the meantime I'm making more doing laptops and private gigs than any girl at the Gold and I'm twenty-seven at the time, older than any of them. (45)

As a stripper, Ginger was moving up—valet parking!—and working at the cutting edge of her performance art, way ahead of the game even having to compete with younger girls. When she gave Wasim Mahmoud "the million dollar hand job and became Mrs. Mahmoud" (46), however, she betrayed her talent and career for a life of "hang[ing] out" with nothing to do but shop and catch some rays next to the pool. None of her old friends—"friends who also danced naked, or maybe even guys," Lourdes imagines (47)—are allowed to visit her.

Lourdes, by contrast, knows exactly what she's good at and she intends to keep doing it. She used to make bathtub stains disappear. Now she does the same with unwanted husbands. Lourdes was hired because Ginger had heard that her Colombian friends knew how to arrange accidents for inconvenient spouses, men like Lourdes's own abusive husband, Mr. Zimmer, who vanished for days before police discovered his body in a pile of hardened concrete. As we watch her in operation, we get the idea that Lourdes has arranged this kind of thing before and that her *techne* lies less in servicing contracts than in handling clients and closing sales. She knows, for instance, how to wait days, even weeks, for Ginger to get to the point—"How much does a load of concrete cost these days?" (52)—all the while listening patiently to her sob stories and rationalizations. Lourdes is not fooled for a moment when "the redheaded woman" says she fears her husband will set her on fire now that he has a new girlfriend, the way "towelhead[s]" (50) like him do in Pakistan when they want a new wife. "Giving herself a reason, an excuse," thinks Lourdes (52), who also knows just when and how to close the deal.

> Lourdes believed the woman was very close to telling what she was thinking about. Still, it was not something easy to talk about with another person, even for a woman who danced naked. Lourdes decided this evening to help her.
>
> She said, "How would you feel if a load of wet concrete fell on your husband?" (51)

Ginger gets Lourdes to lower her price, and two days later Wasim is found dead from an apparent carjacking. That evening Ginger goes out to celebrate. When she returns at 1:00 a.m., she finds Lourdes, wearing her employer's green bikini, dancing inside a "ring of burning candles" before two Colombian men, to the sounds of *cumbia*—"music for when you want to celebrate," says Lourdes. "We having a party for you, Ginger. The Colombian guys come to see you dance" (56). Are the Colombians there to collect the rest of their fee? Or, now that Ginger is about to inherit millions, have they set their sights higher? Extortion? Remarriage followed by . . . an unfortunate accident? And what's with the candles? "The candles are a part of it," says Lourdes. "*Cumbia*, you should always light candles." Out of the Pakistani frying pan, into the Colombian fire.

If you're going to dance with someone, stay true to your *techne* and choose your partner carefully. Otherwise, dance alone. Leonard's Good Girl Divas tend to follow the pattern of Arlene Downey of *Swag* and Denise Leary of *Unknown Man No. 89*. They comprise the largest group of female protagonists in Leonard's later fiction. These are the women who have mastered their respective professions or fields of expertise and actively enjoy "what they do," whether it's painting (Franny Kaufman in *LaBrava*), writing (Angela Nolan in *Split Images*), law enforcement (Karen Cisco in *Out of Sight*), investment advising (Kyle McLaren in *Stick*), flight attending (Jackie Burke in *Rum Punch*), singing (Linda Moon in *Be Cool*), tail gunning (Louly Webster in *Up in Honey's Room* [2007]), modeling (Kelly Barr and Chloe Robinette in *Mr. Paradise*), or filmmaking (Dara Barr in *Djibouti*), to name but a few. The older Good Girl Divas are usually seeking to change their lives by learning a new profession or moving up in their current one. When Adele Foley, Jack's ex-wife in *Out of Sight*, loses her job as a magician's assistant because she's too old, she decides to start her own act, be her own magician.

The desire to "dance" with the men, to establish and preserve relationships of reciprocity with them, is to many of Leonard's female characters what panic and fear are to their male counterparts: a major challenge to the authenticity of being cool. Whether to become or remain a dancing partner, which means running the risk of letting a male lead you around the floor like Fred Astaire leading Ginger Rogers, is often the most important question facing a female professional in Leonard's fiction. Generally, it's not a desirable, or even feasible, choice for a smart and talented woman who derives joy and satisfaction from her skill set. Why submerge or subordinate your talent when, as the 1970s' feminists said of Rogers, you can do everything the man can do, backward and in high heels?

Good Girl Dancing Partners include sympathetic wives like Frank Delsa's deceased spouse, Maureen, a former police detective herself, in *Mr. Paradise*, and conflicted girlfriends like Joyce Patton, a former topless dancer and initially Harry Arno's main squeeze, in *Pronto* (1993). Patton attaches herself to U.S. Marshal Raylan Givens because she admires his self-control and mastery of the situation in *Pronto*, which threatens her life and Harry's, but in the sequel, *Riding the Rap*, she returns to the dumpy, aging bookie, despite his egotism and alcohol problems, because Givens is too quick to rationalize the violence he's good at, too ready to seek it out, and too unreflective to ask himself why he does either. During a fortune-telling session with Dawn Navarro, Joyce is told to "follow your true feelings" (*Riding* 253). Dawn can see Joyce is "having trouble" with

Raylan's killing a mob hit man in an altercation the lawman himself provoked. Dawn can also tell that Joyce misses Harry, or rather, misses "taking care of him" (256). "He represents like stability, [. . .] security, karmically speaking" (256), Dawn says.

Afterward, Raylan asks Joyce how the session went.

> "I need to kick back," Joyce said, "karmically speaking. Sort of let it happen."
> "Let what happen?"
> "My life."
> "Isn't that all anybody has to do?"
> She said, "Why don't you go play with your gun." (257)

Letting life happen, for Raylan, means not thinking about it. For Joyce, it means getting in touch with your "true feelings" and letting them show you what you really want. Raylan admits that killing Tommy Bucks was "a personal matter," but isn't sure "how he felt" (37). Is Leonard telling us that the threat to being cool posed by making it "personal" can be contained by simply refusing to think about how you feel? Givens's success, along with that of Raymond Cruz and especially Carl Webster in *The Hot Kid*, whose "cool" borders on numbing moral frostbite, suggests the answer is yes.

But in setting up Tommy Bucks to be killed in a quick-draw match he knows he'll win, does Givens show any more professionalism than Raymond Cruz in his handling of Clement Mansell, or Joe LaBrava in his beach brawl with Richard Nobles? Givens's superiors don't think so. In *Riding the Rap* we learn he's been "exiled" to the Palm Beach County Sheriff's Office (36) until the fallout from Bucks's extralegal execution can be dustpanned and disposed of. If making it personal can be contained, the "cool" that's achieved is usually at the expense of a broader, more professional authenticity, which means that, to one degree or another, it's fake. Leonard's sympathetic depiction of Joyce Patton's struggle to learn what she's feeling about Raylan gives us the distance and perspective to see this, and Givens's Western affectations, especially the cowboy hat that seems glued to his head in both books, in the TV series *Justified* that they've inspired, and in Leonard's latest novel, *Raylan*, should tell us that despite (or because of?) his creator's obvious fondness for him, Givens is teetering precariously on the edge of cool caricature. "Man to man," says Joyce. "You have an image of yourself, the lawman." "It's what I am," Raylan replies (*Raylan* 37)—not "what I do."

In general, the emotional wisdom of Leonard's Good Girl Divas and Dancing Partners gives them a leg up on the men with whom they share the professional playing field, a field supposedly leveled by modern feminism. They are the childlike adepts at handling major transitions in life while still having "fun" with their sense of who they are, because they remain in touch with their emotions and, thus, know what they really want. The best of them can change roles like fashion accessories, while inhabiting each with complete authenticity. This is true in the bedroom as well as the boardroom.

The delicate dance between U.S. Marshal Karen Sisco and professional bank robber Jack Foley in *Out of Sight* is a case in point. When Foley breaks out of prison and almost immediately finds himself locked up with Sisco in the trunk of her car, he falls hopelessly in love with her. Even though he knows it could never work, especially when she's doing all she can to track him down and return him to the lockup, he can't stop wondering what a relationship between the two of them would be like. And neither can Karen. Their friends, family, and colleagues all worry that these feelings for each other are warping their better judgment. Karen's father, a former law officer, fears Karen might do something unprofessional that will let Jack disappear for good. Jack's partner in crime and in flight, Orren "Buddy" Bragg, watches with horror as Jack repeatedly jeopardizes their freedom just to be near Karen. Jack has told him that after three stretches in prison he would rather be killed resisting arrest than sent to jail again.

In Detroit, Jack and Karen agree to call a "time out": they have drinks at the top of the Renaissance Center and spend the night in Karen's hotel room, where they find, for a brief, miraculous moment, that they are perfect together. Afterward, Jack regrets having chosen a life of crime, not out of moral compunction, but because it means he can never share it with Karen Sisco. Of their night together he tells Buddy, "It wasn't about getting laid."

> "[. . .] it was too late, you know, to have a regular life. I knew that. I still wanted to know what might've happened if things were different."
>
> "You find out?"
>
> Foley said, "Yeah, I did," not sounding too happy about it. But what did that mean? He was disappointed by what he found? Or was sorry now he'd robbed all those banks? (275)

The answer is, both. Foley is dismayed by the discovery that if he hadn't robbed all those banks, he could have spent his life with Karen.

Karen's reaction to their night together is different. Awakening the next morning, she's tempted to keep her eyes closed and pretend Jack's still there, to maintain the romantic illusion, but then tells herself, "Oh, for Christ sake, grow up" (271): "She was thinking too much, wanting to know how it would end. She thought, Well now you know. And got out of bed" (272). Jack can't get over Karen, but that won't prevent him from continuing to rob banks. Karen has to get over Jack to keep doing "what she does," which defines her identity, namely, catching bank robbers like Jack.

As the book nears its foregone conclusion, Karen imagines being cross-examined by her father: What if Foley resists arrest? Tries to get away? Would you let him? If not, "you'd have to shoot him, wouldn't you?" Karen doesn't know. "He told you he's not going back [to jail]. [. . .] So whose choice is it, really, if you have to shoot him?" Karen made her choice when she joined the U.S. marshals, so now (she hears her father say) the possibility of having to shoot people "is a fact you have to abide by" (281). Inevitably, Foley is cornered and refuses to surrender. As Karen's backup team enters the room with guns drawn and Foley prepares to go down in a hail of bullets, Karen, "with almost a sigh" (339), shoots him in the leg. Later, when her dad tries to sympathize, she replies, "He knew what he was doing. Nobody forced him to rob banks." "My little girl," says Dad, "the tough babe" (340–41). Not so tough, however, that she doesn't remain in touch with her feelings: emotional self-control does not mean denial. Her last words to Jack, who is lying on the stairs with a bullet in his leg, are, "I'm sorry, Jack, I really am" (340). And she means it.

We've touched briefly on another category of alterity in Leonard's fiction besides gender: racial and ethnic identity. Minorities tend to be "sidemen" in the staging of the central character's struggle to become or stay cool, although even in that role, a minority character can assume disproportionate significance in the plot or the exploration of a theme. During his Western phase, Leonard was primarily interested in Native Americans and Mexicans or Mexican Americans. Since he began writing crime books set in major U.S. cities, African Americans have become the dominant nonwhite cohort and Hispanic ethnicity has been extended to include other Latino nationalities. Native Americans appear rarely in the crime fiction, with Franklin de Dios, in *Bandits*, a prominent exception, along with *mestizo* figures like Nestor Soto's father-in-law, Avilanosa, in *Stick*, or "The Hot Kid" himself, Carl(os) Webster. A variety of other ethnicities pop up as well, including Albanian, Polish, German, Ukrainian, Nigerian, Somali, and, of course, Italian (take your pick of mobsters).

Pronounced ethnicity tends to disqualify a character for the spotlight role of a Leonard protagonist, although thoroughly assimilated second- and third-generation ethnic Americans like Carl Webster can make the grade. Chris Mankowski of *Freaky Deaky*, for instance, is Polish in little more than surname.

Despite their marginal status, however, Leonard's minority sidemen can dominate the action for chapters at a time as *eirons* to Leonard's leads or choral onlookers to the principal *agon,* not only surviving their less cool counterparts among the walk-ons but even thriving as second bananas. Many are expert at playing the "wily servant," as ancient and durable as the comedies of Greece and Rome, and a role that often comes with benefits.

Ex-con Cornell Lewis, for instance, head of household for financial wizard Barry Stam in *Stick,* knows just how and when to put on the Stepin Fetchit routine for his employer, who likes to parade his staff of compliant parolees and hard cases in front of his guests and bask in their reputation for toughness—"rub against danger without getting any on him," as Cornell puts it, and "feel like the macho man" (98–99). But Cornell knows how to roll with it. "Grin and chuckle," he tells Stick. "Put on the clown suit and they don't see you. Then you can watch 'em. Learn something. . . ." What? asks Stick. "I don't know. *Something.* [. . .] There must be *some*thing you learn listening to all these rich folks" (101). And there is, as Stick discovers when he goes to work as Stam's chauffeur. Meanwhile, whenever Stam is away on business, Cornell plays Nubian sex slave to Mrs. Stam, giving her the "Freaky Deaky." In *Tishomingo Blues,* black drug dealer Robert Taylor does Cornell one better, not only sleeping with the wife of his Detroit mafia boss but also arranging to have him killed and usurping his place in Detroit's takeover of drug trafficking in the Mississippi Delta.

Alterity in Leonard's fiction also includes sentient nonhumans. Animals and animal symbolism appear in a surprising number of stories and books, going back to "The Nagual," a Western he wrote in 1956, and extending forward to the talking-animals storybook he wrote for his grandchildren in 2004, *A Coyote's in the House.* During the latter half of his career, animal symbolism has often been linked to themes of personal identity and transformation. Trained porpoises in *Gold Coast* provide a symbolic commentary on Karen DiCilia's marital situation. Lili, owner of Lili's Bar in *Split Images,* likes to serve drinks in a tiger dress. Teddy Magyk, in *Glitz,* confides in his mom's parrot, Buddy, and even brings his mom a parrot statuette from Puerto Rico. Cundo Rey, in *LaBrava,* works as a male stripper in a cat costume; he considers his partner, Richard Nobles, a "swamp creature" (60). Leanne Gibbs, wife of "Maximum Bob" Gibbs, starts out as a half-fish, half-woman mermaid at Weeki Wachee. Chino, in *Out of Sight,* wonders if the magician that Adele Foley used to work with ever turned her into a lion. Lions prominently flank the front steps of Woody Ricks's mansion in *Freaky Deaky,* and Greta Wyatt considers Woody himself a strange kind of animal—so strange his mind can't be imagined (205). Even animal minds are not beyond the imaginative powers of Elmore Leonard, however. In *Maximum Bob* he offers us a brief tour of the antediluvian brainpan of a twenty-foot female alligator trapped in a screened patio (61–62).

In no other Leonard novel do "manimal" themes play as prominent a role as in *Killshot*. Characters are asked what animal they'd like to be. Owl? Blackbird? Deer? Eagle? A hunter tells his partner to "read the deer, think like them, and you'll get your shot." "Pretend you're a buck," replies the partner (17). Men living in the wetlands of the St. Clair River look like "muskrats" (77, 135). A female character who wears "cat-lady glasses" (22) and looks like "some kind of bird" (50) also has a peacock bedspread (120) and collects stuffed animals (51). Another female character is named Lenore, after the dead beloved of Poe's "The Raven," and decorates her home with bird prints.

The inflexible alterity of nonhuman species in *Killshot* corresponds, often ironically, to personality and temperament, but it also provides a running commentary on characters' attempts to control their own self-transformations, a skill crucial to their survival. *Killshot*'s major antagonist, Armand "The Blackbird" Degas, goes by several names, each eliciting a different personality and self-image. The book's female protagonist, Carmen Colson, has undertaken at least three major transformations in her adult life and by the end of the book will have attempted a fourth, unimaginable to her and to the man she kills. She enjoys wondering what it would be like to be another person and gets to find out when she and her husband go into the Federal Witness Security Program. There she meets a deputy who introduces himself interrogatively: "Was it his accent [. . .] or wasn't he sure who he was?" (161). Her mother habitually answers the phone by asking, "Who *is* this?" (197), and when Carmen's blue-collar husband loses his temper she tells him, "You're a completely different person" (121). At one point, wearing a suit and tie, he's in fact mistaken for her boss, and plays along (56).

Interwoven throughout, the theme of *techne* is registered most prominently in the book's title. Murderer-for-hire Armand Degas acquired his nickname, "the Blackbird," from his two brothers, back before the three of them used to work hits together. The older brother, Gerard, is now in prison, and the younger one, Jackie, is dead, shot by a policeman while resisting arrest, all because Gerard violated a fundamental rule of the "killshot": leave no witnesses (81). The remaining list of rules governing Armand's *techne* is short: "the only time you take out your gun and aim at somebody is when you gonna kill them" (68); "Never talk to them before" (285); and "One shot, one kill" (69). The point of all the rules is summarized in the injunction, "don't think about it" (81).

In Armand Degas, a mixed-race Ojibway and French Canadian whose totemic nickname suggests a scavenger of carrion, Leonard has created a human killing machine that comes close in its blind efficiency to the cold, unconscionable mastery of Raylan Givens. There are crucial differences between the two, however, besides the fact (a trivial one for Leonard) that Givens is a lawman and Degas a hit man: differences in race, in age, in their level of alcohol dependency, and in their ability to understand women. Despite some shortcomings, Raylan is way ahead in the last department, although he has trouble understanding why women don't understand him. Armand has yet to reach the starting line. As his younger partner, Richie Nix, reminds him, "Shooting a woman and understanding a woman are two entirely different things" (90). Armand's inability to grasp the difference is his ultimate undoing, aided by the cumulative effects of the other three things that distinguish him from Givens: racial insecurity, advancing age, and an increasing resort to the bottle. Because he has trained himself to remain oblivious to his own feelings, Armand cannot tell what he wants to do with his life, leaving him adrift in the deep but inexorable currents of self-disesteem and alcoholism while he attempts, unsuccessfully, to transform himself into a person who can make others respect him for what he does, despite their contempt for who he is.

The book begins in a seedy room at the Waverly Hotel in Toronto, where the Blackbird receives a phone call from the Toronto mob, asking him if he wants to "do" their patriarch, "Papa," who is visiting Detroit for a ballgame between the Tigers and the Blue Jays. Armand accepts because he wants to visit his grandmother, a "medicine woman" (12) living on an Ojibway reserve upriver from Detroit where he and his brothers spent their boyhood summers. Arriving at Walpole Island after killing Papa, however, Armand learns that the old woman has died. He toys with the idea of fixing up her dilapidated house and settling down among his own people, but he is promptly discouraged by one of the inhabitants, who knows what he does for a living. Afterward, in the parking lot of a nearby restaurant, he meets Richie Nix, one of Leonard's most memorable wildmen, who's been working on an arson-extortion scheme targeting a local real estate firm and needs a partner to help him cash in.

In carrying out the extortion plan, Armand and Richie run afoul of the Colsons. Carmen, one of Leonard's Good Girl Dancing Partners, is a real estate agent at Nelson Davies Realty, and her ironworker husband, Wayne, is visiting her office for the afternoon to see if he might like to join her in selling homes—a professional move up in Carmen's eyes, but little more to her husband than "fool[ing] with papers" (55). Wayne, whom Leonard's criminal odd couple mistake for Nelson Davies himself, chases the thugs off with a big, heavy "sleeve bar" from his pickup truck, and the rest of the book becomes a cat-and-mouse game in which Degas and Nix stalk the Colsons while the police camp out in the couple's home. When Carmen has to drive Armand off her back porch at gunpoint and Richie shatters their front windows in a drive-by shooting, the Colsons agree to enter the Federal Witness Security Program. One week in Cape Girardeau, Missouri, where the deputy marshal on duty treats them like criminals who've turned state's evidence, sends Carmen back to Detroit on her own initiative, setting up Leonard's terrifying conclusion.

In an "eastern-western" like *Killshot,* which alludes to the Old West on nearly every page, we would expect Armand Degas's designated nemesis to be Wayne Colson, the white male ironworker whose parents named him after John Wayne and who is called "Cowboy" by his co-workers (36). Lean, strong, fearless, and quick-tempered, but otherwise affable, and first spotted wearing a blue jacket bearing the legend "Ironworkers Build America," Wayne lives with Carmen in a renovated farmhouse on the fringe of suburban Detroit, near open fields and a stand of trees where he can set out salt blocks to attract the deer he likes to hunt. Like Fenimore Cooper's Natty Bumppo roaming the frontier between civilization and an untamed wilderness, he'll often take along his Chingachgook, an Ojibway hunting guide and former ironworker named Lionel Adam, who lives on Walpole Island. The frontier references don't stop there, however. Wayne's job, riveting steel sixty floors up, recalls that of his lumberjacking ancestor, Matts Colson (160), who helped "build" America by topping trees in the primeval forests of the Great Lakes region, like Paul Bunyan.

As a contemporary version of the self-reliant frontiersman "building America" while the little woman tends the homestead (all the improvements to the farmhouse are initiated and undertaken by Carmen), Wayne seems destined to square off with Armand, the stoic, tizwin-drinking "Bad Injun" of the tale. Or if not Armand, then his trigger-happy partner, Richie Nix, who fancies himself a modern-day Billy the Kid and wears cowboy boots.[2] As it happens, Wayne Colson does neither. He's MIA as the book reaches its climax in the dining room of his modest farmhouse. There, an exasperated Armand plugs Richie in the head and in turn receives his own killshot from none other than Wayne's little woman, or "the wife," in the words of U.S. Marshal John McAllen (158), who likes to sprinkle his talk with cowboy riffs like "Whoa, now!" (140).

Homesteaders, hunters, lumberjacks, outlaws, Indians—Leonard's book is populated by the mythic avatars of America's Manifest Destiny, including the river pilots and runaways "lighting out for the territory" immortalized by Mark Twain in *Life on the Mississippi* and *Huck Finn*. And there are deities still walking the earth, like Elvis Presley, who for Donna Mulry, Richie's skanky, aging girlfriend, is the "Jesus Christ" of popular music, complete with twelve pop "apostles" and a bodily resurrection. In *Killshot*, white males may "build America," but it's America's legends of independence—of starting over, of self-invention, of defiant, countercultural self-assertion—that in turn "build" white male identities.

The fun-house mirrors of publicity, pseudo-history, and myth that figured prominently in *Gunsights* and much of Leonard's subsequent work resurface in *Killshot*, shaping the American Dream and the characters trying hard to live it today. Their script, or screenplay, has been written by the past—or at least, by America's fantasy versions of it. Figuring the "New World" as a magical place for changing who you are, for starting over in the "pursuit of happiness," Leonard begins with a story out of *Shane* or *The Plainsman* or *Stagecoach*, pitting white outlawry and Native American savagery against the lone, heroic, white male frontiersman, and ends up focusing on the two figures traditionally relegated to the shadows of the formula Western—one nonwhite, the other non-male—who are trying to build new identities for themselves outside the inherited paradigm. By the last chapter, *Killshot* has become Carmen's book. She alone seems to have retained agency and authenticity while mastering the art of self-transformation, while Leonard's three male protagonists remain trapped in frontier archetypes they feel compelled to act out: the unfeeling Red Man, the Homesteader pushed one step too far, the reckless and arrogant Outlaw.

For each of these male characters, authenticity of identity resides in mastering one skill in particular—contract killing, armed robbery, ironworking—and each is distracted in his attempts to find or maintain that mastery by an emotional challenge demanding self-transformation. Only Carmen, who is both nimble in acquiring new skills and most in touch with her feelings, as well as sensitive by nature to the feelings of others, succeeds in keeping her emotions under control when it counts the most, mastering the only skill that, in the end, can save her life and Wayne's: the "killshot" of the title. Her male counterparts, by contrast, including her husband, lose control of the skills by which they would define themselves, because they cannot handle their most basic impulses, needs, or dependencies. Instead of remaining at one with what they do when threatened by emotional derailment, Wayne Colson, Richie Nix, and Armand "The Blackbird" Degas embrace a self-alienating, specular relationship to their own identities, a relationship mediated by a pop-cultural understanding of their historical archetypes. To Armand Degas in particular, Richie Nix holds up a distorted mirror of archetypal self-misunderstanding.

A creature of impulse and a motormouth, Richie's goal in life is to rob more banks than Billy the Kid, to rob a bank that Jesse James robbed, to eat chicken every day like Red Sox third-baseman Wade Boggs, to shoot a woman, to shoot an Indian, to do it with a shotgun, to do it . . . well, with whatever comes to mind. With a sense of identity molded by America's legendary rebels, eccentrics, and outlaws, Richie is, as Devlin observes, a walking case of homicidal ADHD (100). His inability to make a plan or stick to another's, coupled with his need to feel mad at anyone he kills (unless he's trying to fill in a blank on his rap sheet resume), makes him untrainable in the *techne* of the killshot or, for that matter, in any skill that requires forethought and steadiness of heart and hand. While he has tons of nerve, like Nancy Hayes in *The Big Bounce*, it's unfortunately coupled with vastly less intelligence. When Richie tries to hijack Armand Degas's Cadillac from the parking lot of Henry's Restaurant by making the Toronto hit man drive it to a remote spot at gunpoint, he ends up with Armand's Browning .380 pointing at his own head (33). In fact, Armand's decision to partner with the feckless Richie is inexplicable, and implausible, unless we examine closely the multitude of clues that Leonard has planted by way of explanation, beginning with Armand's decision not to "do" Richie when he has the chance.

The way Richie lost control of the situation is characteristic. He was distracted. Laying his revolver aside to examine the bulging contents of Armand's wallet, Richie doesn't notice that his mark has reached under the driver's seat and retrieved a gun he left there (by mistake, it turns out) before he walked into Henry's for his meal. "The hell you do they pay you this kind of dough?" Richie asks.

> Armand felt himself changing back, no longer Armand Degas, dumb guy taken for a ride. He was the old pro again as he came up with the Browning auto and touched the muzzle to the side of the punk's head.
>
> "I shoot people," the Blackbird said. "Sometimes for money, sometimes for nothing."
>
> Without moving his head or even his eyes, staring at that wad of cash, Richie Nix said, "Can I tell you something?"
>
> "What?"
>
> "You're just the guy I'm looking for." (33)

What Richie sees in Armand is obvious: experience and expertise that he can put to immediate use. His enthusiasm, in turn, shows us what Armand sees in

Richie: "Telling him, 'No shit, I mean it. I'm glad this happened.' Telling him, 'Man you have to be somebody, drive a car like this, a piece under the seat.' Respect in his tone of voice" (50). Armand's need for the kind of respect that Richie can provide, the respect of a "punk" or "apprentice" (38) for an "old pro," will lead the Blackbird to mistake Richie's genuine nerve, which is nothing more than the fake cool of a man too stupid to be afraid, for a solid foundation on which to build *techne*. Soon, Richie is calling Armand simply "the Bird." "The funny thing was, Armand didn't mind it."

> The Bird. New name for the beginning of a new time in his life. Different, not so Indian-sounding as he played with it in his mind. Who are you? I'm the Bird. Not a blackbird or a seagull, but his own special kind. He liked the way Richie Nix said it, the guy sounding proud to know him, wanting to show him off. (49)

Armand's turning to Richie for affirmation of his new identity betrays a degree of self-uncertainty elsewhere hinted at by the Blackbird's alcohol dependency and multiple names. His French Canadian "white" name confirms his identity as a Canadian citizen and a "person of interest" to law enforcement. While it does not capture his current sense of who he is, he will fall back on it later in the book as he loses faith in the totemic power of his two animal nicknames. In contrast to "Armand Degas," the white "dumb guy taken for a ride" by Richie Nix, the Blackbird that Armand feels himself changing back into as he points his gun at Richie's head is "the old pro" at killing. Given him by his literal brothers in crime, Jackie and Gerard, "the Blackbird" is an "Indian sounding" name that aligns what Armand does with the legendary cold-bloodedness of his race—legendary, that is, in the eyes of white America—and it's the name by which, up to now, he has achieved a high degree of self-respect, if not the real respect of his white employers. When he's on a job, as he was when "doing" Papa earlier that day, the Blackbird pays attention to his appearance, wearing his good wool suit, despite the heat, with a white shirt and "green-blue tie that had little fish on it" (14). Tucking in his shirt after taking his gun out of his belt, he straightens his tie and buttons his coat again before going into Papa's bedroom—"He had to feel presentable. It was something he did for himself; no one else would think about how he looked. [. . .] The old man wouldn't care" (14).

The "made guys" of the Toronto mob refer to Armand, contemptuously, as "Chief," reducing him to a Native American caricature. When Armand asks to be paid for the Detroit job not with cash but with a year-old, sky-blue Cadillac owned by the son-in-law who is setting up the hit, he imagines this "punk" telling "his people, see, he's crazy. You can give him trading beads, a Mickey Mouse watch" (9). But that "was okay" with Armand. "The Blackbird knew what this guy and his people thought of him. Half-breed tough guy one time from Montreal, maybe a little crazy, they gave the dirty jobs to. If you took the jobs, you took the way they spoke to you." To "Chief," "It wasn't social, it was business" (8). That's what being a professional is all about: you can't take your business personally and survive—a fact that, as Armand will soon realize, Richie finds impossible to grasp. But even if you make a habit of not taking insults personally, they can still take away your person. "Don't think about it" could serve as the motto of Armand's life, as well as his profession. He remains unaware of the deep scars in his psyche left by white contempt, despite the evidence of his susceptibility to Richie's flattery, not to mention his pride in the absurd new nickname—"Bird"—that goes with it. The mob needs him for their "dirty jobs," but it needn't respect him for doing them well. Not only does this white man need him; he admires him, too.

Armand's unacknowledged need for white approval reflects the extent to which he has adopted the values of the white world along with its money, so much so that the Ojibways to whom he is related by blood have come to seem, in his eyes, contemptible. This contempt emerges when Armand visits Walpole Island after carrying out his contract hit on Papa. The summers Armand and his brothers had spent on Walpole Island were formative ones. It's where Jackie and Gerard gave him his nickname, and where the three of them earned their tough reputations, shooting the neighbors' dogs and cats with their .22 hunting rifles when they couldn't find muskrats. Their grandmother's notoriety as a "medicine woman" protected them from repercussions. She could change people into animals, or get seagulls to shit on their cars (13).

At Walpole Island, Armand learns that his grandmother is dead and finds her house in ruins. In a momentary fit of nostalgia, he imagines fixing up the house and moving in, perhaps working as a hunting guide, and asks Lionel Adam (who, we later learn, tracks for Wayne Colson) what he thinks. Armand "couldn't imagine staying here for more than a few weeks. Still, he wanted Lionel to say sure, that's a good idea, live here, become part of it" (19). Lionel has known the Degas brothers since childhood. "There's no life for you here. There's nothing for you," he says, to which Armand wants to reply, "Then tell me where there is." Instead he asks Lionel if he'd like a ride in his Cadillac. They can go to a bar off the reserve and get drunk (19).

Armand doesn't want to live on Walpole Island. As his offer to Lionel shows, he's become assimilated into the white world and to its lowest criminal class, for whom a Cadillac and a limitless bar tab are a mark of prestige. He suggests he could be a hunting guide, like Lionel, but he is contemptuous of Lionel's working for "those big-shot hunters" (19) and thinks the tracker's wilderness expertise is just "some goddamn Indian thing" (77). Armand mocks the reserve's ban on alcohol sales and its bingo games (19) and doesn't understand a word of Ojibway (13). Nevertheless, he *wants to be asked* to stay.

After Lionel's rejection, Armand starts throwing back "doubles, good ones" (27), of Canadian Club as he waits for his meal at Henry's.

> He asked himself, Why would you want to live here? Answered, I don't. Asked himself, Why do you want Lionel or anybody to want you to live here? That one, facing it, was harder. He took a drink and answered, I don't. I don't care or want to live here or ever come back. He knew that but had to hear it. No more Ojibway, no more the Blackbird. He knew that too. What was he losing? Nothing. You can't lose something you don't know you have. What would he get out of being Ojibway? (27–28)

The "harder" question that makes the inebriated Armand hesitate is why he wants to be wanted anywhere, but the hardest question, which remains unasked, is the one he didn't ask Lionel, If not here, where? Supposing Armand could stand to live on Walpole Island or, alternatively, be a "made guy" in the Toronto "family," "he wouldn't ever belong to them" (10)—in the first case, because he's a professional killer, and in the second, because he's an Indian. Like Lionel Adam, the Ojibways in the Silver Dollar bar in Toronto keep away from him, and the new white punks coming into the bar, "crazy ones who colored their hair pink and green," call him "Blackbird" in a way "he didn't like" (10). No one except Richie wants to be associated with Armand for what he does, which is the only thing that has ever defined who he is.

It's in this frame of mind, fleeing his old life in Toronto and alienated from his Ojibway heritage even to the point of insisting he's "French Canadien" (30) ("Don't you wish," replies Richie), that Armand first encounters Richie Nix and responds to the "[r]espect in his tone of voice." If Armand is *only* what he does, and it's always been as the Blackbird that he's done it, then his rejection of his Ojibway heritage moments before—"no more Ojibway, no more the Blackbird"—presents a problem, because he cannot kill Richie, or anyone else, apparently, without "changing back" into "the Blackbird" identity he rejected. But what if he could be another kind of "Bird," not so "Indian sounding," and still deliver the killshot?

Richie seems to offer Armand the chance to be "his own special kind" of "Bird," but it's really just Richie's kind, a "Blackbird" with the "Black" removed, leaving it white. What Richie wants is not a mentor but a useful tool, a "passenger," "along for the ride" on an ill-conceived trip that has practically no chance of arriving at its destination (95). Every effort Armand makes to teach this "punk" something, to act on what he takes to be Richie's respect for his authority as "the old pro," is either ignored or met with sarcasm, disdain, or honest incredulity. Even if Armand shows him "where to point" his gun (72) and Richie does as he's told, he can't do it efficiently, unemotionally, or with any degree of authenticity. When Armand orders him to "do" Lionel, for instance, Richie has to wait until he gets "pissed off" first, then takes three shots and uses two hands, "like in the movies" (79). Filmland is also where Richie learned to talk like a gangster: "blow a guy away," thinks Armand. "That was something he picked up at the movies, that blowing away" (71). It's not long before Armand decides he doesn't want to be called "Bird" anymore. It's "Armand" from now on. Richie initially agrees to use his partner's "faggy name" (90) but soon reverts to "Bird" for the remainder of the book, right up to the moment the Blackbird shoots him in the face at Carmen's dining room table. The explanation? "He called me Bird for the last time, that's what he did" (278).

Whether it's the drinking that's caught up with him, or just that he's "getting old" (282), or misses his two brothers, or feels "tired of being alone in hotel rooms" (281), something has begun to impair the Blackbird's mastery of the killshot well before his fateful meeting with Richie Nix. Leaving his gun under the driver's seat of his car instead of throwing it in the river as soon as he used it on Papa is something a punk would do, not a pro. He is also getting careless about his appearance. When he "does" Papa, his suit's not pressed, and it's too tight (14)—he's beginning to eat too much. Worst of all, Armand talks to Papa before killing him. If you talk to your victims, you make them human. You become aware of having feelings toward them. When he sees the old man "staring at him," the Blackbird feels compelled to ask, "Don't you know who I am?" and launches into a story he will repeat three more times, to three different listeners, in the course of the book.

The story is about how his grandmother, the "medicine woman," wanted to turn Armand into an owl. "I said to her, 'I don't want to be no owl, I want to be a blackbird,' and that's how I got this name, from my brothers, when we were boys and we visited there" (12–13). There's a gap in this story that will not be filled in until Armand tells it for the last time, at the end of the book: if his grandmother changed him into "the Blackbird," how did he get the name from his brothers? But Papa doesn't seem to be listening.

> "You remember us, the Degas brothers? One dead working for you, shot dead by the police. One in Kingston doing time for you. Papa, you listening to me? And I'm here." (13)

The poignancy of this moment reverberates throughout the rest of the story. Armand is addressing the man he is about to kill as "Papa," as though, in lieu of the biological father the Degas brothers never knew, this mob godfather had been the step-equivalent of their "great white father." Killing Papa is not just an oedipal gesture, though: it's putting paid to a long-standing debt the Toronto mob owes the Degas brothers for assigning them the "dirty jobs" all these years, then refusing to stand by them when things went bad, because they did not "belong." Once Armand has put his gun in Papa's mouth and pulled the trigger, he's cut himself loose from any meaningful ties he might still have as a professional stepson to his Toronto "family." When he discovers that his Ojibway grandmother is dead as well, there's nothing anchoring Armand to another living soul, making him a prime target for Richie's flattery.

It's important to Armand that Papa know "who I am," as he puts it, and that the old man listen—"you listening to me?" As the book proceeds, Armand will become increasingly insistent that people listen to him—Richie Nix in particular, who even with "ten stitches in his chin" can't shut up (72), and at the very end, Carmen Colson. Who needs to talk and who can keep silent when the urge to speak is most pressing determines who will succeed in *Killshot*. Unfortunately, Armand has reached the point in life where he needs to talk, and what Armand needs to talk about, apparently, is how he ended up becoming "the Blackbird." Perhaps what he is trying to figure out is how to become something else. Perhaps that's why he wanted to see his magical grandmother again in the first place. Staring out of the sixty-fourth-floor window of Papa's Renaissance Center suite, Armand sees a panorama of his entire life spread out before him, reaching to the horizon.

> Now he was looking at Canada from six hundred feet in the air; Windsor, Ontario, across the river, Toronto two hundred and fifty miles beyond. Not straight across but more east, that way [. . .]. Keep going and you come to Walpole Island. Staring in that direction he squinted into the distance. (11)

Armand's vantage point on his own life history has been constructed, literally, by ironworkers like Wayne Colson, one of a long line of white men who "built" the America in which the Blackbird has tried, since birth, to discover who he really is.

All of the male characters in *Killshot* need to talk, mainly about themselves, but only Armand has anything important to say. Wayne wants to talk about his various construction jobs—the Renaissance Center, Standard Federal, One-Fifty Jefferson—the way Richie wants to talk about his bank heists and murders. For Wayne, they are props to his identity, although, unlike Richie, he is no longer a "punk," or apprentice. Like Armand, his mastery of *techne* defines who he is. Early in his marriage to Carmen, when she was a stay-at-home mom raising their only son, Matthew, Wayne especially enjoyed "stopping off" at a bar with his co-workers before heading home. There he'd "unwind" from his "stressful" job (41) among talk of "spud wrenches" and "sleeve bars" and "bull pins" and "yo-yos" (37–38), and "settle any differences" that were too dangerous to discuss while "raising iron" (41). Stopping off meant lonely evenings and dinners at nine for Carmen, who was raising Matthew practically on her own. Making matters worse was a series of subsequent miscarriages leading to a hysterectomy that left Carmen depressed and listless for months. What eventually brought her "back to life" (40) was a determination to master new skills, first as an auto plant worker and then as a real estate agent.

Carmen had been trying for years to get Wayne to quit "stopping off," asking him why he couldn't "unwind at home" (41) with her, and then "sit down and have a beer and he could help Matthew with his homework for a change" (41). When reason doesn't work, she refuses to "pout, whine or nag" (41)—always, for Leonard, confessions of weakness. Instead, once Matthew is in junior high she goes to work on an assembly line, a move Wayne initially supports until Carmen starts coming home from work later than he does. Asked if she had car trouble, she retorts with a barrage of technical jargon worthy of a UAW wildcatter: "I work a whole shift with that air wrench, eight hours bolting on drag links and steering arms in all that noise, I need to unwind after" (41). To which Wayne replies, less in sympathy than in solidarity, "See? If you feel that way working on the line, imagine coming off a structure after ten hours" (41). Carmen's not about to be outmaneuvered so easily. "I like to be *with* you," she says. "Isn't there something we can do together? [. . .] some kind of work or business we could both get into [. . .] and be together more" (41). Thus is born Carmen's plan to transform Wayne from someone in whose life she is just "along for the ride," like Armand with Richie, into a real dancing partner—not just in their marriage, but also in their working lives. Eventually, she talks him into visiting Nelson Davies' real estate office.

Wayne's passive impersonation of Nelson Davies when Richie and Armand walk in the door, along with his sudden reversion to a proletarian tough guy wielding one of his trademark tools as a weapon, underlines Leonard's theme of identity transformation, in this case a failed one. But its very failure also fits a larger pattern of correspondences between the two dominant relationships in the book: Armand's with Richie and Carmen's with Wayne. Both Carmen and Armand are trying to figure out who they are and, in the process, undergoing a series of self-transformations that hinge on achieving (for Carmen) or retaining (for Armand) mastery of a professional or technical skill. To succeed, they need to transform their recalcitrant partners into compatible sidekicks and, especially, sidekicks *who can listen*. We've seen how well Armand is doing. Carmen is, at first, on track to do much better, partly because, as Leonard makes clear throughout the vicissitudes of their married life, the Colsons remain in love with and loyal to each other.[3] By the time Carmen has begun her career at Nelson Davies, she's managed to bring Wayne along to the point of listening to her own trade talk once in awhile. When she makes her first sale, he takes her out for dinner "and *listen[s]* to her tell how she'd closed the deal, Carmen glowing, excited, telling him what a wonderful feeling it was, like being your own boss" (43, emphasis added).

Getting an obtuse, self-absorbed sidekick to listen is only the second step in transforming him into someone with whom you "can do things together." The first step is changing yourself into someone worth listening to. Whining and nagging will not work, nor will giving orders like Armand. Carmen has one major advantage over Armand in this regard, besides having a partner who loves and respects her. She knows how to change herself. Armand does not: he needs Richie to tell him who he is. Carmen's advantage is evident in her and Armand's contrasting attitudes toward "signs," of which they are both close readers. Armand's attitude is passive, Carmen's active.

When the Blackbird, for instance, receives the phone call in his hotel room setting up the hit in Detroit, he picks up the receiver "wanting it to be a sign. He liked signs." The call comes just as he concludes that other signs are leading him to self-destruction. "Try to come along Spadina Avenue," he thinks to himself, "see that goddamn Silver Dollar sign [. . .] and not be drawn in there." Signs tell Armand what to do—or at least, he can make them do so if he tries. Thus, it's the Silver Dollar "sign" that draws the Blackbird in, not his own craving for booze (7). For the alcoholic, there's always an excuse, and always a corresponding sign to match. "He believed it was time to get away from here [. . .] and he wouldn't drink so much" (7). But in order to leave, Armand needs a countersign. He finds one in the "ceiling that looked like a road map, all the cracks in it." "Follow one of those cracks in the ceiling," Armand tells himself (7). As soon as he hangs up the phone, he's "picking out a crack that could be the Detroit River among stains he narrowed his eyes to see as the Great Lakes" (9). Even his request to be paid in "wampum"—the son-in-law's sky-blue Cadillac—is an expression of Armand's semiotic desire: it's the color of his grandmother's house, which he suddenly longs to see, and of his totemic element.

Carmen's attitude toward signs is announced in her decision to learn handwriting analysis. In contrast to Armand, Carmen is active, deliberate, and self-aware, curious not only about who she is emotionally—as shown by where she stands on the "Emotional Expression Chart"—but also about how to become someone new, the person she really wants to be. After her hysterectomy, when the corporeal foundation of her identity as mother and homemaker was destroyed, this is how Carmen began to bring "herself back to life":

> She remembered her book on handwriting analysis saying that if you weren't happy or lacked confidence in yourself you should examine your handwriting. [. . .] That became the starting point, changing her capital I to a printed letter with no frills, like an l; that showed insight, an ability to analyze her own feelings. She devised a clear, straight, up-and-down script, one that said she lived in the present, was self-reliant, somewhat reserved, a person whose intellect and reasoning power influenced emotions. [. . .] [F]inally she had the confidence to write in her new script, "What are you moping around for? Get up off your butt and do something." (40)

Carmen's initiative in transforming herself by manipulating the signs of her identity already shows that her "intellect and reasoning power" can influence her "emotions" without denying their legitimacy. Hers is a traditional story of American self-invention with a quite untraditional protagonist: "the wife."

By transforming herself from a "moping" depressive into someone engaged in "doing something," Carmen gets Wayne to listen, not to what she wants *him* to do, but to what *she is doing*. He quits "stopping off" and spends his evenings with her, expresses support for her ambitions, and sympathizes with her excitement after her first real estate sale. Encouraged by his attention, Carmen sets about changing her husband into someone worth dancing with. His violent confrontation with Richie and Armand, however, causes Wayne to revert to his frontier American prototype—the wronged homesteader reduced to unthinking rage against his Indian and outlaw nemeses—and to bitter sarcasm against the impotent functionaries of official law enforcement. Swinging his sleeve bar with intent to maim, if not to kill, Wayne becomes a version of Richie Nix, violent when "pissed off" to the point of being unrecognizable even to his wife. (Nix is eventually killed wearing one of Wayne's "Ironworkers Build America" jackets.) "It amazed her, she had never seen that cold, intent look on her husband's face before" (61). "You're a completely different person," she later tells him (121). Distracted by his plans for revenge, he's even oblivious to Carmen's attempts to seduce him: "You want to go to bed?" she finally asks point blank. "It's early," he replies, but she can tell "he [is] thinking of something else," Richie Nix (118).

Wayne's focus on his male opponents to the exclusion of Carmen as a person continues in Cape Girardeau, where in belated response to the sexual threat posed by WitSec Deputy Marshal Ferris Britton, who treats the Colsons' bungalow as a private *pied-à-terre,* Wayne finally promises to "wrap a sleeve bar around his head." Carmen replies, "That's what you'll do for him. What will you do for me?" (183). What distresses Carmen is that, even after the move to Missouri, Wayne remains less interested in her emotional state of mind, in "what I felt, was I afraid?" (181), "in how scared I must've been" (182), than in how to respond, physically, to his male antagonist. Carmen often knows things before Wayne does, because she can "feel as well as think." "Feel what?" asks Wayne. "She'd say, Just *feel,* that's all" (147). When Wayne is finally roused to feel something about Ferris's threat, his first thought is about Ferris, not about Carmen. In the honor game, even when women are the *casus belli,* men think about other men first, women second.

The same is true in the conventionally masculine world of *techne.* After the move to Cape Girardeau, Carmen has trouble even "getting through" (181) to her husband, because when he's not talking nonstop about his new job as a welder in a dry dock on the Big Muddy—"the river gets to you"; "it's a life, not just the river"; "big stuff" (222)—he's too drunk, after stopping off with his new workmates, to listen. Wayne's Huck Finn fantasy is about to disintegrate in the face of reality. Just a few hours into his first trip upriver, he finds starting over again as a "punk" in a new profession so demoralizing, and the profession itself so boring, that he decides to go back to Detroit (235). In fact, Wayne has shown decreasing command of *techne* after his run-in with Armand and Richie. He is free to leave for Missouri and try out this "new life" on the river only because his obsession with revenge has distracted him in his old job to the point of getting him laid off for jeopardizing the life of a co-worker. Leonard devotes an entire chapter to this series of events, beginning with Wayne sitting immobilized, on a girder high above the ground, imagining clever scenes of ambush and rehearsing laconic repartee straight out of a spaghetti Western.

> Okay, he sees them in the woods and runs out to the chickenhouse, yeah, and is waiting for them inside as they come past it, heading for the house. [. . .] They go by, he lets them get about ten yards [. . .] that's it, and goes, "You boys looking for somebody?"
>
> "You boys looking for me?"
>
> "You guys looking for me?"
>
> "Can I help you?"
>
> Something like that. (133–34)

Wayne's cinematic wish list spans three pages of free indirect discourse. He sounds like a schoolboy daydreaming about playing cowboys and Indians at recess.

We've overheard these elaborate mental rehearsals before, in Teddy Magyk's and Dawn Navarro's mirror scenes, and we know what they represent: moments of severe self-alienation. Wayne is so in love with an *image* of being cool that he can't *be* cool, so withdrawn into his private mental theater that his body's been left rudderless. Lost in scenarios of revenge, he unspools fifty feet of hose from his "yo-yo" and inadvertently trips a fellow ironworker, Kenny, who drops his "beater" and nearly kills a man watching from below (129). That afternoon Wayne is told to take some time off. He might as well—nobody will work with him now (137). Wayne's emotions have interfered with his *techne*. He has lost his ironworking cool.

Initially, Carmen imagines hiding out in Missouri as a kind of vacation from being herself—not because she lacks self-esteem, but because she's naturally curious about what it would be like to be someone else. She wants to "see the way [other people] look at things," she tells Wayne, "and what their life is really like" (147). She is, like her creator, deeply empathic in a way that none of the male characters of the book can begin to imagine. The WitSec opportunity, she says, makes her think of Jack Nicholson in Michelangelo Antonioni's *The Passenger*, who "takes on another man's identity who died and then finds out people are after him thinking he's the guy" (147). After a week living in a filthy two-bedroom bungalow prowled by the lecherous Ferris Britton while her husband is at work or stopping off, she recalls how the movie ended, with Nicholson murdered in his sleep, alone in a remote hotel. "Poor guy, a passenger all the way," she thinks. "Not knowing when to get off" (202).

Like Armand, "dumb guy along for the ride" on Richie Nix's extortion tilt-a-whirl, Carmen has reverted to being a "passenger" in Wayne's "new life," and he has become a literal passenger on a barge train heading up the Mississippi, from which he can't "get off" before Carmen gets fed up and flees to Algonac in his truck. The move to Missouri, in fact, has been a regressive one for the Colsons' marriage. They are back to where they started twenty years ago. Carmen is cleaning house, shopping, and cooking, while Wayne, "full of his new job," is again coming home drunk and paying little or no attention to her situation or, more importantly, her feelings about it. It's not until the former tenant of the house, a WitSec fugitive named Mr. Molina, returns for some boxes he left behind and reminds Carmen she's under no obligation to stay there that she gets up the nerve to go home.

Molina is only one of a series of strange men who come into Carmen's residences uninvited and unannounced, or who try to, beginning with Armand attempting to mount her back porch steps with a rifle and ending with Richie and Armand making themselves at home in her kitchen while awaiting her arrival from Missouri. In between she has to cope with most of the Algonac police force tramping through (expecting to be served cookies and hot coffee), Federal marshals, the FBI, Ferris Britton, and Molina. This recurrent event will eventually provide her with the motivation she needs to overcome her fear, panic, and moral scruples and shoot Armand Degas with his own gun, the way Martha Cable, her Western prototype, shot an Apache in defense of home and family thirty years before. "You walked in my house!" she shouts immediately afterward, seconds before Armand dies (286).

Carmen's mounting anger at male insensitivity to her feelings—domestic or otherwise—bursts out at a truck stop on her way home, when a man in a John Deere hat tries to pick her up and won't take no for an answer. He soon finds himself being dragged along by the open door of Wayne's pickup as Carmen throws it into reverse: "The door swung closed as she drove away. Hit them with a truck if you don't have a sleeve bar" (257). This is the first time in the book that Carmen has deliberately endangered another person's life. In her earlier confrontation with Armand, she knew she could not bring herself to kill him, only scare him off. Her encounter with the John Deere man is also the first time she's actively *enjoyed* inflicting violence, associating it with her husband's taking a sleeve bar to Armand and Richie in Nelson Davies's parking lot, and his threat to do the same to Ferris. As she drives away, Carmen imagines telling Wayne the story of her encounter once he arrives home, dwelling on her retort to the John Deere man—"Are you serious?" "Wayne would be grinning by then. 'Are you serious?' He would love it. It was the kind of thing Wayne would say" (257).

As she nears her moment of truth with Richie and Armand, Carmen thus begins a major transformation, her last in the book. Getting in touch with her anger, she has begun thinking and acting and, perhaps most importantly for Leonard, even *speaking* to herself like Wayne. Later, trapped in her own home, distracted by fear of what will happen to her and to her husband once he arrives, she is unable to remember what Wayne did with the shotgun she had used to scare Armand away when he appeared in the backyard. Then anger overcomes her fear and saves her. "Mad. The way she was on the porch the time Armand came and she fired twice. Mad because he was so goddamn sure of himself. [. . .] Now think" (274). Far from being distracted by anger, like her husband, Carmen's memory of the original occasion for her long-suppressed rage enables her to "think," to retrace the events that followed with cool clarity, including what Wayne did with the shotgun. Habitually in touch with her feelings, she can, in contrast to Wayne, both feel and think at the same time. Moments later, however, after she retrieves the weapon from under the bed, Carmen has to find the nerve to go downstairs and "do it," and that, as we know from the *techne* of the killshot, requires *not* thinking. Carmen tells herself, "Don't think," but can't stop: "at the bedroom door [. . .] she started thinking again, she couldn't help it" (280).

As we learned in *Last Stand at Saber River*, thoughts of loved ones and feelings of rage, while useful motivations, distract from the task at hand. Being cool comprises a time for thinking—for planning, deliberating—and then a time for not thinking, for just "doing it." Carmen knows how to use a shotgun because her husband taught her how. What Carmen can do in addition is keep her rage, along with her fear, under control. All she needs is a way to stop thinking, and she finds it by listening to a voice in her head, a voice that she makes her own. As she hesitates at the bedroom door, Carmen hears Wayne's voice: "For Christ sake, if you're gonna do it, do it."

> Wayne took her that far, gave her the loaded gun. *Now she had to hear herself say it, in her own words,* and after that stop thinking.
>
> You have to kill him. (281, emphasis added)

If free indirect discourse is how Leonard depicts the identities that his characters assume in moments of silent reflection, Carmen's second-person self-address represents a discursive appropriation that resembles her earlier manipulation of her own handwriting to make it look like another's—someone strong, determined, confident, and competent—so she can become the person that her new "voice" not only represents but commands: "Get up off your butt and do something" (40). That this self-command—"You have to kill him"—should be "channeled" through the voice of her husband appears to be a loss, not a gain, of agency. But it is important to recognize that Carmen's ability to identify with Wayne when she most needs his expertise and encouragement is an outgrowth of a talent and a *techne* that are uniquely hers. Like the authorial ventriloquist who created her (and who also "speaks" to himself in others' voices by literally handwriting them), she not only was born with this power but has actively cultivated it every day of her life. This is something wholly beyond Wayne's ability, but it is something Elmore Leonard understands and appreciates because it is central to the work of writing.

While Carmen is coaching herself, in Wayne's imaginary voice, how to be cool, Armand is gradually losing his cool downstairs. At first, when Carmen arrived home, he and Richie had things under control. "Don't talk so much, all right?" Armand tells Carmen after she walks in the door. Soon, however, he begins asking her questions and teasing her about their last encounter (268). By 11:30 a.m. Armand is getting thirsty (269). Before we know it he's put away four whiskeys (272) and is trying to involve Carmen in his conversations with Richie, until he realizes his mistake: "Their eyes held for another moment and he was sorry he had spoken to her" (276–77).

"Never talk to them before" is good advice if you don't want to think of your victims as human, or what you do as murder. But Armand soon goes beyond the point of just talking to Carmen. When she asks him why Richie calls him "Bird," he can't resist the invitation: "Armand liked her asking him that. It reminded him of who he was. Or who he had been. He said, 'I'm called the Blackbird,' and almost smiled at her" (277). A moment later, when Richie persists in calling him "Bird," Armand shoots him straight through the giant bubble of gum hiding his face from view. Motivated as it is by impulsive rage, this killshot, Armand's last, is anything but professional.

Things continue in a downhill direction for Armand. Pouring himself another drink, he begins the story of his grandmother's attempt to change him into an owl, the same story he told Papa, then Lionel Adam before ordering Richie to kill him (77), and finally Donna Mulry (96), Richie's fifty-something girlfriend. Armand told Donna his grandmother story as a gesture of intimacy, in order to seduce her. But we are beginning to see that he also tells his story, repeatedly, to get his listeners to recognize and accept him for who he is: the Blackbird, master of the killshot. In Carmen, Armand believes he has found a woman superior to Donna Mulry, and his drunken attempts at conversation are meant to break the ice. "This was the kind of woman to have," he thinks (284). When he tells Carmen the grandmother story, however, it comes out different. This time, the grandmother agrees to turn Armand into a blackbird, but the magic doesn't work. After spending hours in a sweat lodge while the old woman beats a drum and chants in Ojibway, little Armand emerges ready to "fly away." "Nothing happened," he says. "I feel my body; I said to her, 'I'm no blackbird, I'm still me.'" Raising his glass to Carmen, he adds, "That's my life story, whether you understand it or not" (279).

The truth of Armand's life story is that, from the very beginning, it has been a series of failed attempts to "fly away" from who he is. Armand became the Blackbird only because his brothers called him that, and because it corresponded to what he did. Like Elmore Leonard's "Dutch," it became a talismanic nickname signifying his membership in a band of brothers. Now Armand is losing the ability to do what he did, and his telling Carmen, his intended victim, his life story is but one more sign of that encroaching loss. At the same time, his confessing the truth represents something of a breakthrough. No more "Blackbird," no more "Bird," no more "Chief"—but who, then, is "Armand"? Carmen will tell him. She is indeed "the kind of woman to have," the kind who listens and understands, who cares for her man, a woman who will gently remove her husband's ironworker's jacket from the bloody head of Richie Nix, fold it carefully, and lay it on the table—"taking care of it for him" (284). Armand is "amazed" (283), and smitten. "I'm not Richie," he tells Carmen. "I'm not the same as him" (280).

Unfortunately, Armand's breakthrough has come too late. Once she descends the stairs from her bedroom with Wayne's shotgun, Carmen is not in the mood to listen, and she's sure not talking. "He was sorry now he had started talking to her," thinks Armand. "He had never talked to a person he was going to kill before he talked to the old man and now he had talked to this woman Carmen." Hearing her on the stairs, however, he can't resist. No reply. "She was there, but she wasn't talking" (282).

Richie had warned Armand about what happens when a woman gets "pissed off." When Donna would get mad, the punk took it seriously: "First thing, they'll stop talking to you. [. . .] You give them any more cause, then look out" (90–91). Throughout *Killshot*, Carmen has had to shut up and listen to men tell their stories: Wayne's tales of "raising iron" and, later, of barges "splattered" on "the Backbone" (179); her son, the aircraft carrier mechanic, filling his letters home with indecipherable acronyms; Ferris bragging about pumping iron and chasing fugitives; Molina talking about life on the run; and now Armand's sorry-ass story about his grandmother's failed magic. Carmen's not going to listen anymore, and her silence in the minutes leading up to her shooting Armand with his own gun tells us so. It also tells us that, this time, she will shoot to kill.

After she's delivered the killshot, however, Carmen can hold back no longer. On the brink of death, Armand's last thought comes as a revelation, voiced as an invitation.

> She said, "You walked in my house!"
>
> Mad. He thought, Yeah . . . ?
>
> She wanted to hit him because he was dead and wouldn't listen to her. The son of a bitch. (286)

That Carmen's greatest strength, her empathic ability to identify with others, share their feelings, and take an interest in their stories, should turn out to be the greatest weakness she must overcome in transforming herself into the cold-blooded killer she needs to be is but one of the many rich ironies at play in this climactic face-off between the marginalized Red Man and White Woman of the traditional Western. Topping them all is the fact that Carmen has just killed the only man in the book, Red or White, who is finally ready to listen *to her*: "Yeah . . . ?" wonders Armand before he passes out, never to resume the conversation.

Dead Cool: Agency

> He wished he wasn't cold.
>
> —*Last thoughts of Al Rosen,* The Hunted

Bleeding to death from a gunshot wound to the chest, Al Rosen, real name Jimmy Ross, has an epiphany. For several years he's been hiding out in Tel Aviv from the Detroit mobsters he testified against. They beat the rap and eventually tracked him down, and now they are waiting outside a remote house in the Sinai desert to finish what they started. But it doesn't matter. "It had taken him fifty years to learn that *being* was the important thing."

> Not being something. Just being. Looking around you and knowing you were being, not preparing for anything. That was a long time to learn something. He should have known about it when he was seven, but no one had told him. The only thing they'd told him was that he had to be *some*thing. (*Hunted* 244)

Within minutes, Rosen discovers that "being" is harder than he thought. "Just being" requires that you "do nothing" (245), but Rosen can't stop planning, wishing, thinking: "Thinking was doing something. He wished he could stop thinking. He wished it wasn't dark. He wished he [. . .] could move. He wished he could swallow some water. He wished he wasn't cold" (246). In short, Al Rosen suddenly finds himself wishing he weren't *being*. And soon, he isn't: "Shit, Rosen thought. Just when he was getting there" (246).

Al Rosen's death scene in *The Hunted* is Leonard's *homage* to Hemingway. It's modeled on that of Robert Jordan in *For Whom the Bell Tolls* as he sits with a broken leg, machine gun in hand, awaiting the inevitable arrival of the Fascist soldiers who will finish him off. Both scenes comprise "big picture" reflections on the ultimate meaninglessness of life in a universe without gods, commandments, or eternal rewards. But Jordan's confirms the importance of giving life meaning by doing something and sticking to it: the gun he holds shows he will fight to the hopeless end. Rosen's death scene, by contrast, points to the attractiveness of accepting, even enjoying, life's meaninglessness by doing nothing. Jordan's attitude is typical of the Elmore Leonard hero. Rosen's is closer to that of the Dalai Lama.

In Rosen's dying thoughts, Leonard narrows his career focus from the possibility of giving life meaning simply by what you choose to do with it—Rosen's former need to "be *some*thing"—to the possibility, and then the impossibility, of "just being" without "doing," of abandoning control over what you do and how it defines who you are, which is to say, abandoning agency. Much as he'd like to, Rosen cannot stop "doing" because he cannot stop thinking: about where he would rather be: "it would be better to do nothing in the sunlight than in the dark"; about how to relieve his discomfort: "He wished he could swallow some water"; about who to be with: "Tali was nice and it would be nice to tell her things" (245). As Leonard learned from the existentialists he read in college, human being is being-in-the-world, embodied and situated, and cannot help but think itself forward or elsewhere, prompted by its needs and desires. Like Leonard the writer, human being is always anticipating "what happens next." The only time it doesn't is when it's dead. Rosen's chill, like his thirst, tells us he's quickly heading in that direction: the dead cool of inanimation, the absolute zero of agency.

The year Leonard published *The Hunted*, 1977, marked a turning point in his life, as we have seen, when he took his last drink and finalized his divorce. The previous three years were eventful, to say the least: he became severely ill from alcoholism, began going to AA meetings, stopped going to Mass, wrote *Swag*, and met his future wife, Joan Shepard. In 1977 Leonard published two more books and tried to publish a third—a remarkable level of productivity in what is by any standard a prolific career. One of these, *Unknown Man No. 89*, with its prominent theme of alcoholism and recovery, we've already examined and will return to, briefly, in a moment. *Touch*, not published until ten years later, and *The Hunted* introduce something new in Leonard's work: explicitly religious themes. This overt concern with religion surfaced in two more novels: *Bandits*, published in 1987, the same year as *Touch*, and *Pagan Babies*, appearing in 2000 (figure 12). These four books, which I call the Catholic Books (Al Rosen grew up as Jimmy Ross, an Irish Catholic),[4] comprise a small portion of Leonard's total output, but their significance for understanding "being cool" cannot be overstated, since they all raise serious questions about "doing" that *techne* alone is incapable of answering.

What happens, for instance, when you can no longer do what you enjoy doing? Al Rosen's volunteer bodyguard, Marine Sergeant David Davis, doubts he can find a job after his impending discharge. "I don't have a trade," he tells Rosen. "My military occupational specialty is infantry, and I don't think there's much call for infantrymen in civilian life." Rather than suggest occupations that might suit Davis, Rosen says it doesn't matter. "Learning a trade, doing one thing the rest of your life, that's for clucks without imagination." Why confine yourself? You'll only end up working for people who know how to be flexible, how to "fit into a situation" or "bend the situation around" to fit them. It's all in how you talk to people, "your tone," says Rosen. Start right off, sound confident, "compliment them, bullshit them a little, they think [. . .] he must know what he's doing" (199–200). Rosen's wisdom has carried him this far and will survive him in cool bullshitters like Chili Palmer, although Chili has already acquired considerable skill in the art of smooth-talking before arriving in the capital of bullshit, Hollywood.

"Bend[ing] the situation around" to fit the person you're pretending to be, you end up being that person. It can even be fun. Coming to Israel as an Irish Catholic money launderer and pretending to be a secular Jew, "Al Rosen" has fashioned a new life for himself: "He felt good and he looked good, a new person" (5). This is his star turn, and it will end up as his final bow. Meanwhile, it's given him an entirely new perspective on life in general, his "revolutionary Will of God theory." All the bad things that happen to people are "God's will," explains Rosen to Edie Broder, the middle-aged Jewish divorcée he's just picked up in a café. "So I decided, wait a minute, why can't the good things that happen to you also be God's will?" (14–15)—like meeting Edie. Edie's not sure about bringing God into it. "You don't have to," replies Rosen, "you just aim in the direction you want to go. [. . .] You're not out to con anybody; you let things happen and you don't worry about it. [. . .] That's the secret. Accept what comes and don't worry about anything you know you can't change" (15–16).

Rosen could almost be reciting the Serenity Prayer of Alcoholics Anonymous: "God grant me the Serenity to accept the things I cannot change, the Courage to change the things I can, and the Wisdom to know the difference." When Leonard joined AA, he discovered the peace of mind that comes from, as he puts it, "handing yourself over to your higher power and not worrying [. . .], leav[ing] it up to Him, whatever He wants to do" (Rzepka, "Interviews 1"). This is the Twelfth Step of AA's Twelve Step Program and it helped put some distance between Leonard and Catholicism—as did two trips to Israel, in 1974 and 1975, the first to write a screenplay, the second to research *The Hunted*. In Israel, the crossroads of world faiths, a land where, in Rosen's words, "Jewish, Christian, and Moslem religions" are "all jammed together" (14), Leonard "felt freer" ("Interviews 1"). By the time he finished *The Hunted*, he had come to see the pointlessness of liturgies, taboos, and rituals in light of the big questions: "I thought, well, we don't need all the rubrics and all the [. . .] smoke and the goings on. I've always thought it was overdone" ("Interviews 1"). Says Rosen, "I don't buy all the kosher business [. . .]. What does Almighty God care if you eat butter with steak?" (*Hunted* 238). Rosen closely resembles the Leonard of 1975: forty-nine years old, five foot nine, a hundred and fifty pounds and balding, a bit of a poser who "never worried about what people thought" (5), a gun-shy army veteran "Storekeeper 3rd Class" (171), and a man in the midst of a spiritual awakening.

Rosen's "Will of God theory" provides the theology buttressing his practical advice to David Davis: go for it, play along, take what God dishes out and improvise, then see what happens. Davis, however, likes the idea of "sticking to what you know" (202). Spending his last official military leave protecting Rosen from Gene Valenzuela and his goons, for neither love nor money, defies any logic but one: he likes what he does. Assigned for the last several years to the front desk at the U.S. Embassy, Davis hasn't had a chance to use his "military occupational specialty" since his last tour of duty in Vietnam. It's not that he misses the violence, he tells Tali, Rosen's private secretary. It's just that Al "doesn't know how to do it himself," and Davis does (156). Moreover, he enjoys doing it, as we learn the first time he finds himself and Rosen cornered: "Davis realized he was getting excited. It was a good feeling. Not being aware of it as a feeling, but thinking, figuring out a way to gain control and either neutralize the situation or kick ass" (113). Davis's delight in his military *techne* points clearly at a number of civilian "trades" for which he is already overqualified, ranging from bodyguard to corporate spy to mercenary.

Rosen and Davis represent two starkly contrasting sides to Elmore Leonard's thinking about life and what to do with it in the mid-1970s. Unlike Rosen in his dying epiphany, Leonard had never been content with "just being" without "doing"—which for him meant writing—and he wasn't about to stop what he was doing now to watch the grass grow. But his troubles with alcohol and his marriage were apparently leading him to the realization that immersion in *techne* could be an escape from life rather than a way of meeting it head on. We can see signs of this realization in Ernest Stickley, Jr.'s "earnest" self-interrogations in *Swag*, published in 1976, just a year before *The Hunted*. Stick's gig with Frank Ryan can buy him all the booze, clothes, cars, and girls he wants. But he doesn't want them. It's not that he can find anything to complain about: "It sounded good." But it leaves hanging the question "what do you want to do with your *life*?" (45). Stick relieves the urgency of that big question by immersing himself in what he does well: the *techne* of car theft and the new, more challenging profession of armed robbery. It looks as though he will at last find the answer in his budding relationship with Arlene Downey, until Arlene decides she has her own professional path to follow. Rosen's dying answer to Stick's question would be "do nothing." "Just be." But his thoughts indicate that's not so easy—in fact, it's impossible. Human beings can never just "be" without "being-in": a body, relationships, the world. They have needs, and also responsibilities, like the seven-year-old daughter Stick left behind in Pompano Beach after his divorce, whom he can't stop thinking about. You can "bend the situation around" to fit you or bend to "fit into the situation," or, conversely, you can immerse yourself in a performance or the task at hand, but all of that's only an evasion of, not an answer to, the insistent demand that you deliberately choose to do something "with your *life*." In the Catholic Books, Leonard exposes *techne* to the critique of *praxis*, a life lived in accordance with some "higher power" or purpose or principle. Al Rosen's death shows you can't "just be," no matter how hard you try.

Once Rosen is dead, the living do something with him. In a highly improbable climax, Davis defeats Valenzuela and his armed men by getting them to agree to exchange Rosen's life for Tali's and his. Pretending Rosen is still alive, he carries the corpse outside and sets it on the ground. Before any of the gangsters can even think to pull the triggers on their drawn weapons, Davis takes his Colt .38 from beneath the compress bandage on Rosen's chest and shoots them all dead, one after another. In effect, Rosen gets his wish: he ends up "just being" without having to think anymore—which is to say, he ends up dead. As an inanimate decoy, he's surrendered his agency to the technically capable Davis, a "higher power" who is appropriating it to save himself and Tali. Rosen's usefulness in death, however, goes beyond mere appearances. His corpse turns out to be a good hiding place for Davis's weapon. When the marine pulls his gun out from under the bandage covering the hole in Rosen's chest, it's almost like extracting a bodily organ.

Readers and viewers who keep up with Leonard's work (a bit of a challenge, even with the author pushing eighty-seven) might think that the organ extraction plot kicking off his latest book, *Raylan*, and the third season of *Justified*, his tandem TV show, is something new in his career. In fact, it first surfaces overtly in *Unknown Man No. 89*. When Jack Ryan visits the Detroit city morgue to identify Robert Leary, Jr., aka "Bobby Lear," aka "Unknown Man No. 89," this is what he sees: "Ryan was looking at the whole body, cut open from breastbone to groin and seeing the man's insides, his vital organs and a slab of ribs, lying in a pile on the table" (107). Someone with a power saw is cutting into the skull: "The brain was exposed for a few moments before the attendant pulled it out of the skull and placed it on the autopsy table" (108).

This fascination with the corpse and the corporeal, with the body's insistent materiality, its divisibility into parts, its mechanical susceptibility to wearing out or breaking down or being broken or, in *Touch*, breaking out (in bloody wounds)—in short, its inherent resistance to agency—appears in all of Leonard's Catholic books. In *The Hunted*, it takes the form of the dying Rosen's inescapable bodily discomfort as he tries to "just be." In *Bandits*, a funeral home provides an opportunity for heightening the contrast between a mutilated cadaver hooked up to a "Porti-Boy embalming machine" (4) that's filling it with pink Permaglo and the late but very animate Buddy Jeannette, a breaking-and-entering expert who made a difference in the life of Jack Delaney, the parolee and hearse driver staring down at Buddy's remains. In *Touch*, a living body surrenders agency to a "higher power" that is using it to cure the blind, the sick, and the dying, while exhibiting, in its spontaneous wounds, the suffering it relieves in others. In *Pagan Babies*, the Rwandan genocide leaves dozens of dismembered corpses piled up and rotting for months inside a village church, while a fake priest goes through the motions of the sacraments and a Tutsi survivor tries to maintain human contact, literally, using the scarred stump of her amputated arm.

The other bodies that Jack Ryan sees awaiting autopsy when he enters the Detroit morgue shock him at first: they don't seem real, but "like props." "They lay naked on metal tray tables waiting, as though with a purpose, waiting to be put to use" (*Unknown* 103). Without agency, the body is of use to no one, and least of all to anyone who might be lingering "inside" it: "He could look, because what had been a person inside, making the body human, was no longer there" (103). In a moment, the body of "Unknown Man No. 89" will show Jack that there never was anyone "inside" to begin with.

> The open body seemed less human than the ones upstairs. It was a carcass with no face, or a face without features, a store mannequin. Ryan stared at the man's head and realized he was staring at the bare skull. The skin and hair had been peeled, pulled down, and lay inside-up over the man's face. (106)

What is "inside" turns out to be merely guts, brain, and bone, covered by a "Robert Leary mask" (108).

Leonard has always been interested in the person "inside," the potential "me" waiting to get out. Is the person "inside," then, just a mirage? Only as long as it remains inauthentic and specular—which is to say, only as long as it remains self-conscious and distanced from the body that performs or displays it, like a mannequin. To become real, the person "inside" must integrate itself with the body in motion. For *techne* there is no "inside" or "outside," no mind or soul separate from the body, just the disciplined awareness of "doing": deliberate and purposeful, playful and spontaneous, agency incarnate. As early as *Swag*, however, Leonard was beginning to explore an alternative path to authenticity, a path that leads away from the self-absorption of *techne*, the body alone with its task, and toward the reciprocity of fully human relationships and larger ends. That path runs through the sense of touch, and the action of touching.

In *Swag*, for instance, touching ratifies the most important moment in Stick's relationship with Arlene. When he tells her he loves her, "she turned to cling tightly against him and that part was good. He could feel her and knew by the touch who it was" (186). The scene is facetiously anticipated by inversion when, awakening in the bed he shared with Stick after sleeping off their bender, Frank Ryan assures him, "I swear I never touched you" (18). Subsequent novels renew the theme: in *Split Images*, Angela Nolan touches Bryan Hurd's face in a tender moment (214), and Bryan later imagines touching Angela's (237); in *Cat Chaser*, Mary Delaney wants to touch George Moran's face (92), and later George touches hers (202); and in *Stick*, Kyle McLaren and Stick need "to touch each other, renew the familiar feel" (264) after their first night together. Sitting on the sofa during their shared "time out," Karen Sisco feels the need to touch Jack Foley's face before kissing him for the first time in *Out of Sight* (261). *Glitz* tells us what's at stake in touching and being touched. Alone with Linda Moon (not the one in *Be Cool*) for the first time, Vincent Mora responds to her asking whether or not he's married by telling her he's a widower, but reassuring her that "he was here now, right here, nowhere else. Touching her, aware of an intense feeling of tenderness, he believed he was falling in love" (148).

At the most obvious level, touching another person's face is an intimate gesture meant to call attention to the one who touches, and to invite reciprocation, acceptance, and touching back. But it also has the effect of bringing the person "inside" to the surface without the mediation of *techne*. At one point late in *Unknown Man No. 89*, Denise Leary finds she cannot get through to Jack Ryan, who is preoccupied with his plans to outwit Virgil Royal, Raymond Gidre, and Francis X. Perez. "Where are you?" she asks, touching him (294–95). Touch is the one sense that confirms, in the most elementary and immediate way, our own embodiment for one another, making the "absent" mind present, here and now, at the surface of the skin, literally palpable, both in the one who touches and the one who is touched. There's nothing to be afraid of, nothing to make either person awkward and self-conscious, nothing but just being there, embodied, for each other. The reciprocal act of touching is thus unanchored to *techne* or performance, but for that very reason, sheer touch without *techne* sometimes runs the risk of evoking a disturbing sense of helplessness, precipitating a crisis of agency. Maintaining a sense of direction in life requires keeping the gyroscope of know-how in motion. In *Touch*, *techne* starts out as nothing more than a way for scam artists to make money from miracles, but it ends up as one half of its hapless protagonist's salvation.

The hero of *Touch*, a Franciscan seminarian named Juvenal,[5] receives the stigmata, the five wounds of the dying Christ, on his hands, feet, and chest whenever he touches someone that his "higher power" decides needs healing. It's a gift, but also a curse, because he can't control it. He has no agency—no choice as to who will benefit or when—and no *techne* by which to direct it. He is surrounded, however, by dozens of people skilled in the subtle arts of publicity who know exactly how to put his gift to good use, if he doesn't. Faith-healing huckster Bill Hill, former pastor of the Uni-Faith mega-church of Dalton, Georgia (now defunct), wants to rebuild his liturgical fiefdom by nabbing the marketing rights to the miracle worker, and he tries to recruit his former baton-twirling lieutenant, Lynn Faulkner, who's just quit her job as a record promoter, to aid and abet. Juvenal's boyhood friend August Murray, leader of the Gray Army of the Holy Ghost, wants to restore the Latin Mass by recruiting Juvenal as the poster boy for his renegade parish, St. John Bosco, and his new movement,

OUTRAGE (Organization Unifying Traditional Rites as God Expects). Howard Hart, a bullying talk show host who thrives on scandal, is eager to give the new celebrity holy man his patented third-degree studio treatment to boost ratings. Juvenal soon becomes the newest rock star of daytime television. His nearest competitors are Elvis Presley, who dies just before Juvenal's interview with Hart, and Waylon Jennings, who gets busted in Luckenback (Luckenbach), Texas, for drug possession the same day.

In *Touch*, organized religion is a celebrity sideshow that wants to make Juvenal its star freak. The book's nods to *Jesus Christ Superstar*, which debuted on Broadway in 1971, are obvious. Lynn Faulkner, who soon falls in love with Juvenal and turns on Hill, is the repentant Mary Magdalene; Hill and Murray are the Judas figures who want to exploit Juvenal for their own ends, whether monetary or revolutionary; and Hart is the Herod of the piece who mocks and taunts the quiet, impervious Juvenal to entertain his viewers. Leonard had used Christian themes and imagery before, in *Hombre*, where John Russell becomes the outcast who sacrifices himself to save those who despise him, and in a walking "crucifixion" scene in *Valdez Is Coming*, which Burt Lancaster made famous in the movie version. But the "savior" in these novels is not, like Juvenal, *Christus patiens*, the Lamb of God who heals the sick and forgives those who know not what they do. He is the kick-ass avenging Christ of the Last Judgment, giving as good as he gets.

Touch is Leonard's closest brush with magic realism. Is Juvenal an instrument of God? Or is this all just a case of psychosomatic mass hysteria? Even Juvenal has no idea. His healing power is a natural talent that defies *techne*, a gift he can't master but is mastered by, leaving him wide open to exploitation. He is "a gentle person being used, not knowing what to do" (115). When a boy with leukemia rushes up to hug him and is miraculously healed during Murray's highly publicized dedication Mass at St. John Bosco, Juvenal is left stunned and helpless. Lynn reads the tormented look in his eyes: "*Help me. I don't know how to do this.* But in the same expression wonderment. *Do you believe it? Look*" (120). Reaching for his bloody hand, she leads him past the astonished congregants, out the door, and, eventually, into a new life: his own.

Juvenal doesn't have to "do" anything with his peculiar talent or his life. He can "just be" if he wants. But he can't stop thinking. He accepts his gift because "it seems to do some good" (135), but the responsibility is more than he can bear. He'd like to leave the Order and his Franciscan name and go back to being Charlie Lawson, the name he was born with, just a regular guy. In the midst of the media frenzy following his appearance at St. John Bosco, he and Lynn hide out for a week at a motel on Lake Michigan. While there, Juvenal sees a boy with withered legs and is tormented by the desire to heal him. "You're not responsible for everybody," Lynn reminds him. "Tell me what I am responsible for," he replies. It's not like being a house painter, they agree. In Lynn's words, "if I'm a house painter I should paint houses, it's what I'm supposed to do. It isn't like that, is it?" (200–01). Experiencing the stigmata is not a skilled trade or a profession. You can decide when to paint a house, and whose house to paint. Seeing the look of "concealed grief" on Juvenal's face, Lynn embraces him. "I need you," he says (201).

As it turns out, it's Lynn whose touch heals Juvenal. Taking him by the hand and leading him out of St. John Bosco's media glare, she brings him eventually to being-in-the-world. She feels compassion for the person "inside" him—"Looking [. . .] into his eyes, she felt strangely moved and wanted to say, I can see you in there, I know you" (56)—and she wants to bring him out, give him agency again over his own body, his own life. Juvenal needs Lynn for her touch, but also for her know-how: her touch when they make love—"I feel you. There you are, right there," she says (171)—and her know-how as they go on to make a life together: "You know," she tells him, "I think you'd make a really good record promoter" (211). As the book ends, the two of them are heading for LA. Lynn's getting back into the record business—maybe in La-La Land she can find someone to work with who really cares about music rather than scoring dope and getting laid—and Charlie Lawson is going to try his hand at the business. They plan to stop at Graceland and Luckenback, Texas, on the way.

Touch is a parable in which Juvenal's power to repair human bodies stands for something both less sensational and, for Leonard in 1977, even more amazing than miracles: the power to heal the anxious, distracted, and benumbed human spirit. Juvenal's mere presence fills with joy those prepared to receive him, bringing peace to tortured souls and life to the walking dead. The experience of Richie Baker, the boy with leukemia, is exemplary: "He wanted to run up there and laugh with [Juvenal]. [. . .] For no reason he wanted to jump in the air, not even worrying about the people watching, and then run somewhere, run as fast as he could, not to get away but to be running" (119). If we can't guess, Sister Lucy Nichols in *Bandits* will eventually tell us what we are witnessing: "unconditional love, love of God through love of man, love without limits, without the language of theology" (106).

More than any other of the Catholic novels, *Bandits* reflects the impact on Leonard's faith and politics of the Church's Social Gospel Movement and the Liberation Theology of the 1960s (Rzepka, "Interviews 9"). Sister Lucy is describing St. Francis, who, like Juvenal, supposedly received the stigmata and healed the sick. But that's all irrelevant. "We lose sight of the act of love in what he did and get carried away questioning details," says Lucy. "He didn't need his hands to touch people." Lucy herself was "touched" by Francis's example and became a nun. "I got out of myself, the role I was playing as the little rich girl, and found myself" (107). The person "inside" Lucy came out and became real as she began to touch the sick and the needy and be touched by them, completing the circuit of God's love.

Lucy Nichols, a daughter of New Orleans high society with the body of a runway fashion model, could have had any man she wanted, but she became a nun because she was moved by the story of St. Clare, who fell in love with St. Francis and, through Francis, with God. Lucy felt drawn to St. Francis in particular because he came from a wealthy family, like her, and gave it all up for the Lord. "He touched people," Lucy tells Jack Delaney, "he kissed the sores on a leper's face" (106). In *Bandits*, morbidity, leprosy, and filth offer a challenge to tactile miracle working that Juvenal never had to face. Jack, who drives a hearse for his brother-in-law's funeral home, first meets Lucy when he stops by Holy Family parish to take her to Carville, a leper colony outside New Orleans. He finds her in the soup kitchen wearing a "high-styled" double-breasted jacket and "pressed Calvins," and "moving down a line of skid-row derelicts, *touching* them. [. . .] look at that. Touching them, touching their arms beneath layers of clothes they lived in, taking their hands in hers" (22). Touching the untouchable is the ultimate test of love, the true Imitation of Christ.

On the drive to Carville, Jack learns that Lucy has returned to her birthplace because the free clinic where she worked in Nicaragua was destroyed by Contra guerillas on the orders of Colonel Dagoberto Godoy. The patients and the doctors were massacred, but she managed to escape with a lone survivor, Amelita Sosa, in a VW she drove all the way to New Orleans. Sosa, a victim of leprosy and a former mistress of Godoy, has been hiding out at Carville. Jack thinks he is driving Lucy there to pick up her corpse, but the death certificate has been faked: Godoy is in town to raise funds for the Contras, and he wants Amelita dead because he is convinced that she deliberately defiled him with her touch, "trying to make him a leper" (29). Jack is to smuggle her out in his hearse. As they enter the grounds of Carville, Jack realizes something about Lucy's work back in Nicaragua: "You touch them, too, don't you? Not just the drunks in the soup kitchen, I mean lepers, at the hospital where you worked." "That's what you do, Jack," Lucy replies. "You touch them" (33).

In *Touch,* Juvenal wants to stop being used by God. In *Bandits,* Lucy craves it: "I need to be used," she tells Jack. But she's tired of being "used" as a nun, and knew it before she left Nicaragua. "I was burnt out," she says. "I was touching without feeling." That doesn't mean she's about to stop caring. The fashionable clothes she wears are "only a cover," she says, like a cocoon, "while I change into something else" (109)—what, she doesn't yet know, but she's sure it will be someone useful to God's holy work.[6]

While in New Orleans, Lucy hears about Godoy's fund-raising and discovers he is not about to return to Nicaragua with his donors' contributions but planning to divert them to his personal bank account. She enlists former breaking-and-entering pro Jack Delaney and some of his less reputable ex-con pals to help her steal Godoy's money (which is conveniently lying about his hotel room in cash) and deposit it in a bank account to support the work of the nuns of St. Clare, back in Nicaragua. In doing so, Lucy comes face to face with a difficult question, the answer to which will determine just what kind of person she is currently "changing into": Is she willing to kill Godoy to get his money?

It's not as though she doesn't know how. Her dad taught her to shoot, and she's gotten hold of his .38 pistol, but for a long while Lucy seems to think she won't have to use it, that Jack and his gang can quietly steal the money or, at worst, might have to scare Godoy into giving it to them at gunpoint. "We're not bandits," she tells Jack. "Tell me what we are," he asks (144). The fact is, Lucy doesn't know. She believes in "doing something for mankind," even dying for it, but can she kill for it? And if they take the money by force and let Godoy live, won't he immediately report them to the police? And won't that make them "bandits" after all? Moreover, the cops will know who they are: wearing masks is out of the question "because the confrontation was more important than any other part of it" (216) for her. Lucy has made this personal. Like Teddy Magyk getting the drop on Vincent Mora in *Glitz,* she needs Godoy to know that she's the one taking his money, and why. It's for revenge. This will be Lucy's "day of retribution" (216) for what Godoy did to the clinic and her co-workers, and to Amelita.

Like Wayne Colson running imaginary film clips of his ambush of Armand and Richie, Lucy enjoys watching this *High Noon* scenario play out in her mind, right through to its studio punch line: "Tell me who you are—please," begs the terrified Godoy, to which Lucy, removing her sunglasses, quietly replies, "The sister of the lepers" (216). Since even the most highly skilled of Leonard's characters can lose their cool and fuck up when they start taking things personally, it's a good thing that none of what Lucy imagines comes to pass. In the end, Godoy's henchman Franklin de Dios leaves Lucy and her gang their share of the money after keeping half for himself. The only person still standing in her way in the penultimate chapter turns out to be one of Jack Delaney's partners, Roy Hicks, who's decided he'll keep the lion's share of their portion for himself. Lucy draws her gun and, when Roy calls her bluff, she shoots him. Fortunately for Lucy's sense of righteousness, it's just a flesh wound.

There is a distinct progression from *The Hunted* to *Touch* to *Bandits* to *Pagan Babies* regarding the protagonist's surrender of agency to a "higher power." Rosen is happy to take whatever his higher power dishes out without doing anything meaningful. Juvenal lets himself be used by his higher power to heal the sick, but then decides he can't cope. Lucy embraces what Juvenal rejects—she wants to be used by her higher power to do "something for mankind." Terry Dunn (in *Pagan Babies*) doesn't believe in a higher power at all, but will end up finding a "use" for his particular powers, his criminal expertise, that amounts to "doing something for mankind" rather than just for himself. Of the four protagonists, only Terry will find a way to integrate his skill set with the desire to "do something with his life." In the process, he will complete the circuit of divine love through touch—the expression and acceptance of love for and from another—and eventually find his authentic place in a community he cares for.

Despite his resemblance to St. Francis (*Pagan Babies* 106), Dunn has no gift except the grift: far from "needing to be used," Dunn, who is as feckless and undirected in his scamming as the early Jack Ryan, has spent his life "using" everyone around him. Like Al Rosen, he is a fugitive from the law, a fake priest hiding out in a Rwandan village because the Feds are after him for driving a truck full of illegal cigarettes—Eddie Coyle's original sin. Everything about Terry is fake. On leaving high school he was supposed to have trained at a seminary to please his mom and Uncle Tibor, a priest. In fact, he left for Los Angeles to shack up with a would-be Hollywood actress and had fake seminary stationery printed to write letters home. He got a job selling insurance and took bribes (he called them "tips") to help customers file fake claims. When the actress left him for a director, he came home to Detroit on the pretext of taking a break from the seminary and started working for his dad, painting houses—Lynn Faulkner's prosaic example of technical agency in *Touch*, and exactly the kind of dead-end trade Al Rosen despises. When his dad died of a heart attack, Terry became a driver with the Pajonny brothers, bullies he knew from high school, who promptly got busted for cigarette smuggling and flipped on Terry to reduce their sentences. Dunn took the money he got from the Pajonnys' buyer and lit out for Rwanda, where his Uncle Tibor had become a priest in the village of Arisimbi. Terry tells Tibor he's now ready to be ordained, but the elderly Tibor dies before it can be arranged. Terry carries on the charade because he doesn't want to return to the States, where he would be arrested, face retribution from the Pajonnys, and disappoint his mom. His older brother, Fran, is a personal injury lawyer who's been working out a deal with the Feds to let Terry off, because, as Fran still believes, he's become a priest. Fran's wife, Mary Pat, who remains skeptical of Terry's vocation, will prove to be the catalyst of his unique salvation through *techne*.

We learn the truth about Fr. Terry Dunn only gradually, over the first ten chapters of *Pagan Babies*. His lackadaisical performance of his sacramental duties has caught the attention of the local bishop. Terry tells the bishop he has a reason for being a part-time priest (4). That reason turns out to be that he's really no priest at all, but we are led to believe it's because he witnessed a massacre of his parishioners during the Rwandan genocide not long after he arrived. His congregants were shot and hacked to death in the church where he was saying Mass, and the experience left him feeling helpless, like Juvenal. Five years later, the volatile political situation still prevents anyone from burying the dead. The book opens with a graphic description of forty-seven rotting and dismembered Tutsi corpses "turned to leather" on the sanctuary floor, their bones "laid in rows of skulls and spines, femurs, fragments of cloth stuck to mummified remains, many of the adults missing feet" (1) because the Hutus, a shorter race, had tried, literally, to cut them down to size.

Terry is an alcoholic whose favorite drink is Johnnie Walker Red and whose answer to any problem is based on a cynical interpretation of the Serenity Prayer: "If you can handle it, do it. If you can't, fuck it" (42). Since witnessing the massacre he has taken a mistress, Chantelle, a Tutsi survivor who lost her left arm during the genocide. The seriousness of their relationship is conveyed through acts of touching, "the touch of someone close" (17), "the familiar way they touched each other" (19). At his lowest ebb, Dunn touches the stump of Chantelle's extended arm as she lies next to him on her side: "he took the hard, scarred end of what remained of her arm and began to caress it lightly with his fingers" (50).

Chantelle's "scarred" stump, grotesque and repulsive, has become, ironically, Terry Dunn's only anchor to human reciprocity. Her missing limb, the severed body part by which human beings ordinarily connect in the most literal and quotidian way, has left behind it a traumatic site of disconnection, suggesting the threat of her own self-withdrawal from human relationships. However, this is also the site where the real Terry Dunn, the one who touches and is touched by it, is trying to emerge. Eventually, he will succeed. Right now, as Chantelle senses, he's about to leave her.

Unlike Juvenal and Lucy Nichols, Dunn has no faith in God, the saints, or the sacraments. "I go through the motions," he says, "who knows I'm not a priest?" (108). He can "do what priests do" and people can "believe what [they] want to believe" (47). For Terry, the Mass and Confession are techniques devoid of spiritual consequences, useless for achieving eternal life but providing comfort to those who believe in them, and serving as props for the priestly role he must maintain for his mother's sake and to persuade the Federal prosecutor reviewing his case that he's changed his life. Confession also turns out to be a good method for gathering intelligence in a dangerous world. Building to a scene of shocking but viscerally gratifying violence, Leonard lets us listen in on the "confession" of a local Hutu named Bernard who has escaped prosecution for his part in the genocide. Bernard taunts Dunn by telling him he plans to start slaughtering Tutsis again, and he ridicules the priest's ineffectiveness and effeminate garb. He knows that the sanctity of the confessional prohibits Fr. Dunn from reporting him to the authorities. Terry bides his time until he finds a double excuse for not hanging around Rwanda any longer: his mother has died, and his brother has finally arranged a meeting with the Feds to discuss dismissing all charges, on the strength of his ordination. He walks in on Bernard and his friends at the local bar, offers them a chance to repent, and then shoots them all point blank with the Tokarev semiautomatic pistol that Chantelle keeps near her bedside for protection. "Rest in peace, motherfuckers," he intones, making the sign of the cross (59). "Fr. Terry Dunn," we begin to suspect, is not what he seems.

Terry apparently feels none of Lucy Nichols's hesitation about killing "to do something for mankind," that is, saving the Tutsis that Bernard and his friends intend to slaughter. But again, appearances can be deceiving. In fact, Terry sees no sense in taking sides unless you're already "with one or the other" (112). As he later tells Debbie Dewey, his new partner in crime after his return to the States, killing the four young men "didn't seem to have anything to do with what happened in the church," adding, "I knew going in I was gonna kill them" (116). Lucy Nichols would have been satisfied with armed robbery.

Debbie is disturbed by this cold-blooded approach to violence, once she begins to see it's not only part of Terry's skill set but something he takes for granted. When she later expresses her fear that the two of them will be targeted by a mob hit man, he replies, "Now we're getting to what I know something about." "It scared her a little, the way he said it [. . .] in the same quiet way" he had told her "I knew going in I was gonna kill [those four men]" (160, 162). Despite her misgivings, Debbie also sees the advantages of teaming up with someone who understands how to handle violence and how to dish it out. She's just finished a stint in prison for assault with a deadly weapon—namely, the Ford Escort with which she ran over her boyfriend for shafting her out of $50,000. In stir, she learned how to deal with the "chicks who found [her] attractive" (66) and make a place for herself in the inmate "family" structure without getting beaten or raped. Her sense of humor helped. Now she's a stand-up comedian who uses her prison experience as material, and as training.

As Terry immediately recognizes on meeting Debbie at one of her gigs, "She's cool" (71). Watching her buy cigarettes, Terry could tell that the guy behind the counter didn't know "how cool she really was—the way she could zing you when you weren't looking; set you up first" (92) to get information, the way she zinged Terry: "Terry would have to remind himself this nice looking girl was not only an entertainer, she'd done time" (95). Debbie "zings" so well, in fact, that she manages to out-priest "the priest" and get him to confess, for the first time to anyone, his imposture. "Don't you feel better?" she asks (98), and he does, he says, "Because we think alike" (99). Terry doesn't know how right he is, but will find out soon enough when Debbie tries to double-cross him, leaving herself wide open to Terry's counterpunch.

Debbie is an ambitious diva, using the survival skills she acquired in prison—standing up to hostile people, manipulating them with humor—to succeed as a nightclub comic. She's also looking for a dancing partner to help her get her money back from Randy, a familiar case in Leonard's fiction of reapplying old skills to a new, more challenging task. Debbie worked as a paralegal for Terry's brother, Fran, the personal injury lawyer. (Fran is how Terry met her.) Now she plans to fake an injury in Randy's posh new restaurant and sue him for all he's worth. Terry has his own plans. He'd used the Polaroid film his brother sent him every month to take pictures of the orphan children that the village church supports. Now that he's back in the States, he'll use his photos to raise money from local parishes for the "pagan babies" in Africa, then take the money and run. Debbie and Terry join forces: Terry will stage the fake injury and help close the deal by showing Randy how he can write off his loss as a charitable donation to "Fr. Dunn's" African orphans' fund. Then Terry and Debbie will split the money from the settlement. This being an Elmore Leonard book, the money ends up coming from a mob patriarch, Tony Amilia, who sees his donation to the pagan babies fund as good PR, but plans to cut Terry out, send him back to Africa, and use the money to finance Debbie's stand-up comedy career. How Terry puts two and two together and turns the tables on Debbie is not as important as what he decides to do with the money once he gets his hands on it, and that's all Mary Pat's doing.

Terry's sister-in-law, Mary Pat Dunn, is the only person in the world who can make Terry feel as guilty as "a teenage kid" (255), which is how he does feel when she and Fran arrive home from Florida prematurely with their two young daughters, Jane and Katy, and find "Fr. Dunn" cohabiting with Debbie in their house. Fran is gullible enough to believe that Debbie's just visiting. Mary Pat knows better, but plays along in front of the kids. After Debbie leaves, she sits Terry down for a heart-to-heart. Sleeping with Debbie just confirms what she's known all along: "You're not a priest, are you?" Terry says she must have guessed, like Debbie. "Terry," Mary Pat replies, "I didn't guess, I know you" (259). She's the only person, it seems, who does, including Terry himself.

Mary Pat is a Catholic convert and for that reason especially conservative in her views of sin, the sacraments, and salvation, which makes her a particularly formidable "mother" confessor and helps explain why Terry feels compelled, despite his reluctance, to tell her the truth. All the more surprising, then, is Mary Pat's calm appraisal of Terry's sacrilegious impersonation, his carrying on with Debbie in Mary Pat's house, and his lying to his nieces, who will now have to be told that "Fr. Terry" was just kidding about being a priest. In the course of Terry's additional revelations about the pagan babies scam, Mary Pat asks two important questions: "Tell me, if you're not a priest, who are you?" (260) and, regarding Debbie, "Will she stick by you, Terry, if you fuck up?" (263).

Terry will discover the answer to Mary Pat's second question when he finds the cashier's check for a quarter of a million dollars that Debbie says she never received from Tony Amilia, hidden in her purse. He doesn't have a real answer to the first question. "I guess I'm back to whatever I was," he says lamely. It's up to Mary Pat to put it into words: "you're a crook . . . isn't that what you are, Terry, a con man?" And for the first time, "telling his sister-in-law of all people what she wanted to know" Terry is "looking at it himself, hearing himself" (260). Being a crook and knowing you're a crook are, apparently, two different things. "Mary Pat," he tells her, "you could've been a good prosecuting attorney." "I could have been good at a lot of things," she replies. "I chose to marry your brother and have children and be a homemaker and that's what I am. If you want to be a crook, Terry, that's up to you" (263). But first he has to admit it to himself and take responsibility for it. He has to choose, deliberately, to be what he does.

Terry's confession to Mary Pat is, fundamentally, about being "*some*thing," as Al Rosen would put it, and as we've seen, the best way to be something is to find out what you enjoy and learn to do it well. Mary Pat, who is apparently good at several things, including cross-examination, chose marriage, raising kids, and housekeeping, and she does all three supremely well. Terry is a very good crook, but never *chose* to do what he does so well. He's always run away from it, and it's always caught up with him. But Terry also has a lesson to learn about human connections, and an answer he needs to find to Ernest Stickley, Jr.'s question: "What do you want to do with your *life*?" (45). The answer comes in the brief time he spends with his nieces after their arrival from Florida, beginning with the moment he first bends down to hug them. "He gathered them to him, his hands feeling their small bones. The older one, Jane, said, 'We know where you were. You were in Africa' " (253). The bones Terry can feel in the bodies of these living children remind us of the bones of the dead children, martyrs to senseless genocide, lying disassembled in the deserted chapel of Arisimbi. The gospel reference to Jesus's reprimanding his apostles in Mark 10: 14—"Suffer the little children to come to me, and forbid them not: for of such is the kingdom of God"—has been anticipated much earlier in the book, when the local Arisimbi police chief, Laurent, notes that despite his slackening of priestly duties, Fr. Dunn "did play with the children" who had survived, "took pictures of them and read to them from the books of a Dr. Seuss" (14). We've learned since, however, that these orphans, preserved on film, are just part of Terry's cynical plan to con donations from Catholic parishes upon returning to the States.

Leonard goes on to reinforce the subtle connection established between the bones of the African children and those of Terry's two nieces. Six-year-old Katy, says her mother, wants to be a saint and "loves martyrs," something she picked up from her older sister, Jane, who taught her how to troll the internet for the gory details (261–62). After greeting them, Terry gets out his photos, "except a stack bound with green rubber bands he dropped in the bag" (272), presumably containing the most gruesome ones. As he shuffles through the photos and answers Jane's and Katy's innocent questions—"What's an orphan?" "Why don't they have any hair?"—Terry tries to avoid explaining why the children have no parents, occasionally looking over at Mary Pat rinsing lettuce at the sink, until one of the girls says, "Mom said that's why you came home, to get money from people for the little orphans" (274), in response to which Terry, having run out of replies, looks to Mary Pat to change the subject. The poignancy of these juxtapositions between massacred and orphaned Rwandan children and Mary Pat's sheltered daughters, with their naive ideas of martyrdom, is underlined by the eloquent presence, on the butcher-block countertop, of a machete that Terry brought home with him to help cadge donations, and the arrival, just at the girls' bedtime, of a mob hit man named Mutt, hired by Randy to "do" Fr. Dunn. "Shit," thinks Mutt, "now what'm I supposed to do? [. . .] he sure didn't want to shoot the mom and dad and their little girls" (306–07). Fortunately for all of them, Terry manages to talk Mutt out of having to.

The book ends with Chantelle coming out to greet Terry on his return to Arisimbi, holding a tray of glasses and ice with "the bottle of Johnnie Walker pressed beneath the stump of her arm. She believed it was good for the muscle to be used this way, squeezing the bottle, and believed she would be using it again and again and again, the woman knowing things the man didn't seem to know" (331). Chantelle knows it's good to exercise this truncated "muscle," to keep using it to connect with the man she loves, whatever form that connection may take. What Chantelle also knows that Terry admits he didn't know until he arrived was that he would stay (333). As they sit together in the yard, listening to the "insects [. . .] making their noise, looking to attract insects like them to have sex with and make millions of more insects," Terry tells Chantelle he has come back to take care of the children, but not as a priest. And he will try to help the people, too, "Even do it like Confession if they want," although he can no longer forgive sins or give penance (333). Terry now knows what to do with his life, and how to do it—not as a fake priest, but as a genuine crook. That is the vocation he has chosen. After kissing her tenderly, Terry asks Chantelle to predict his future. "You mean, what you'll be when you grow up, or when your money runs out?" To which Terry replies, in the book's last line, "I can always get more" (334). It's something he's good at.

conclusion

what happens next?

Just after Bill Hill closes the deal in *Touch* that will make Juvenal a media star, Leonard offers us a glimpse of the evangelical huckster's thoughts, in free indirect discourse. Hill is glad to be back in the saddle and no longer selling motor homes, as he's had to do ever since Uni-Faith folded: "Work work work. But damn he felt good. Bill Hill was promoting people again and not some dead-ass technical specs, which camper body to put on your GMC pick-up bed" (148). Wherever Leonard finds himself in whichever novel he happens to be writing on any given day, he remains responsive to what matters most to him: the satisfaction of knowing how to do a job and do it well, even if it's turning the gifts of God into fungible commodities. In *Be Cool*, a similar moment occurs when we catch record promoter Nick Car (former mobster Nicky Carcaterra) sitting at his desk at Car-O-Sell Entertainment, wearing headphones and fielding simultaneous calls on three lines with the aplomb of a professional short-stop.

> "Howard, what's up, bro? You guys have a good rap? . . . That's cool. Man, that is so fucking cool. Listen, I want to hear about it but I'll have to call you back. I'm banging the phone like a fucking wild man. Five minutes, bro."
>
> Nick pushed a button on the phone console, looked up to see Raji in the office.
>
> Raji saying, "Chili Palmer—"
>
> Nick held up both hands to stop him, Nick's hands free to gesture, scratch, lock behind his head, while he spoke into the little stainless mike boom that hung in front of his mouth—a mouth he never seemed to shut, always making Raji wait. (81)

Three pages of patter and eight button punches later, Nick gets "throw[n] off [his] rhythm" by someone named "Jer." "I start thinking when I'm talking to him instead of just talking," Nick tells Raji, who takes advantage of Nick's momentary dysrhythmia to ask who they should hire to kill Chili Palmer.

Nick's rat-a-tat recitative is a perfect example of Csikszentmihalyi's "flow" in action: self-immersive, focused on the task at hand, and lost as soon as the promoter "start[s] thinking." Nick plays his phone console the way Horowitz played his Steinway. "I can make more in one day wearing this fucking headset," he later tells Chili, "than I do in months" working with Raji (216). Whatever we may think about Nick Carcaterra personally (he's a tasteless, greedy bastard who would gift-wrap his own mother for a top-ten hit), he's utterly cool when it comes to selling records. And he turns out to be crucial to the success of the book's female protagonist, singer-songwriter Linda Moon.

It's easy to get distracted from Linda's story line by the accumulating perils—physical and technical—facing her new agent, Chili Palmer, not least because, in *Be Cool* as in *Get Shorty*, Leonard is writing a meta-fictional account of his own compositional process. A large part of Chili's motivation for getting close to Linda stems from his desire to write a screenplay about an aspiring Janis Joplin–style singer overcoming abusive managers, corrupt record promoters, grasping studio executives, and sidemen of inferior talents in order to succeed with her artistic integrity intact. Like Leonard himself, Chili never plans how things will go, but waits to see "what happens next" based on what his potential characters (Linda and her associates) choose to do. Sometimes, however, he'll arrange a scene just to see how someone will react, as he does when he schedules Linda for an on-air radio interview where she will hear a remixed version of her signature song, "Odessa," for the first time, with the whole world listening in.

Chili knows that Linda walked out on a previous studio contract when the sound engineers tampered with her lean, lonely sound, and he respects her for it. But after discussing the advertising and promotion campaign for her new release with producer Hy Gordon of NTL (Nothing to Lose) records, Chili realizes that Linda will never succeed unless Gordon's sound engineer, Curtis, gets the green light to remix "Odessa"—to "lay some samples around her, fill in, make it bigger" (150). Chili is pretty sure that, while on tour to promote the new record, Linda has gotten hooked on success to the point of accepting her new sound, if she has to. She's already come down with a bad case of what her drummer, Speedy, calls "LSD"—"Lead Singer Disease" (211)—insisting on her own private suite, renaming the band after herself, and "starting to give orders" (245). She's got that diva itch. This is a good thing. As Chili will later put it, Linda has made the transition from talented "little girl with ideals" to "the tortured artist" (256), distracted from the pure joy of singing by the adrenaline rush of fan acclaim and a growing sense of her own self-importance. Hearing the "Odessa" remix for the first time during a live, on-air interview will test whether or not she is ready for the final step, "to the pro, who knows exactly what she wants and is gonna make it happen" (256). If she isn't, Chili still walks away with a knockout scene for his screenplay: "The Artist Betrayed."

We might think that a book whose motto could be summarized by the repeated phrase "Just be yourself" would end with its outraged heroine punching DJ Ken Calvert in the nose for hyping this studio abortion, complete with bagpipes, especially when Ken tells her, "Well, you have your own style now" (252). If so, we would miss the point of both *Be Cool* and being cool. Just being yourself means not only doing what you do best but letting everyone else do the same. Linda can make music, but it's "a business," Hy Gordon tells Chili. "We don't sell music, we sell records" (195). Which means, of course, you can't take it personally, and that goes for Chili, too. When Hy says he's lined up Nick Car to promote the new album and Chili objects because "the guy's a schmuck"—not to mention trying to kill Chili—Hy replies, "We give Nick Car the record, he'll get it on the air. That's what he does" (195). Doing what you do is something Chili can understand, and because she has taken that final step up to being "a pro," Linda can, too. "I loved it," she says, when asked what she thinks of her new sound. If her fellow band members don't, "it's up to them, get with it or quit, the world's full of musicians" (254). In fact, she's going to have Curtis, the sound engineer, "work right through the CD, remaster the whole thing. Put in bagpipes, zithers, tubas, whatever he wants" (255). And by the way, she's through with Chili and NTL—nothing personal. Days later Linda signs with heavy hitter Maverick Entertainment for a million bucks. "She's got that killer instinct," Chili says (273–74), in case we were still wondering.

Linda has learned how to be cool while remaining a team player. She now knows that a true pro draws a championship team together, and then leaves them alone. The book's scenes with Steven Tyler and Aerosmith may seem like celebrity name-dropping, but as in other Leonard books they are meant to help us distinguish fake from real cool—here, in relation to teamwork. Thus, real cool isn't about "hanging" with celebrities, it's about using your contacts to get things done and improve everyone's game. Edie Athens, head of NTL records after her husband's murder, can't wait to tell Chili how she "just pulled off something that is *so* cool you won't believe it." Hy Gordon steals her thunder: having lunch with her old buddy Steven Tyler, he says, knowing she used to do

Aerosmith's laundry as a roadie. No, says Edie, that's cool, but what is "way cooler" is getting Steven to let Linda Moon open for them at the Forum (196). When Linda and her sidemen get a chance to talk to the Aerosmith band members before going onstage, only Linda and Dale, the lead guitarist, see it as a learning opportunity. Speedy takes Joey Kramer's drumming tips as an insult, and Derek, another of Edie's clients, is so intimidated he acts bored. "Waited for them to talk to him," Chili later tells his movie-producer girlfriend, Elaine. "He could've asked questions, or just listened, like Dale, maybe learn something" (203). An apprentice who's trying to master his craft won't let pride get in the way of seeking advice from the old pros, who know how to "make it happen."

The penultimate scene of *Be Cool* features Elliot Wilhelm, Raji's former bodyguard, singing his own rap version of the book's title song at the Troubadour nightclub, backed by a posse of six enormous Samoans. The lyrics seem pretty conventional—drug deals, drug busts, hiding the stash—until we reach the last verse, when the "Swat man" becomes "that man."

> I ain't takin no more that man's shit,
> thought of a way to make him quit.
> One I dream where I hear him scream
> when I throw his ass from off a high place
> and the man is gone without leavin a trace.
> I know how, I've done it, see.
> Throw him away and set myself free.
>
> Uh-oh, uh-oh.
> I'm gonna do it.
> Uh-oh, uh-oh.
> Leave me to it.
> Uh-oh, uh-oh.
> Hear what I'm saying?
> Be cool. (272)

Elliot's not only "gonna do it." He's done it. Just days before, he saved Chili Palmer's life by tossing Raji, the Samuel L. Jackson wannabe, off the balcony of Chili's hotel suite. Now that he's stopped taking shit from his faux-gangsta boss, he can just be himself: lead rapper of "Elliot Wilhelm and his Royal Samoans" (271)—soon to appear in a theater near you. "The guy saved my life," says Chili. "The least I can do is put him in a movie" (267). At last, Elliot has a chance to find out what he's good at, perhaps even a chance to be cool.

Elliot's freakish size, which belies his true talents, would seem to limit him to a career as bouncer, sumo wrestler, or "before" model for Weight Watchers. Like Zenon La Joie, the redeemed misfit of Leonard's fifth-grade adaptation of *All Quiet on the Western Front,* he's easy to make fun of and, like Zenon, he just needs the right situation to let the person "inside" him come out and show his stuff. Linda Moon, however, is the real star of this showbiz *Bildungsroman.* Since the publication of *Be Cool,* Leonard's women have begun hogging even more of the spotlight. Following closely on *Djibouti,* which recounted Dara Barr's struggle to film, compose, and edit her documentary about Somali pirates, Leonard's latest book, *Raylan,* uses its title character as little more than a point-of-view clothesline on which to hang three successive narratives featuring female protagonists whose technical proficiency—starting with black market kidney extraction in motel bathtubs, then moving on to mining company public relations and high-stakes televised poker—drives the action throughout.

Raylan ends with cowboy atavist Raylan Givens falling in love, this time with a woman who understands him. Jackie Reno is only twenty-three, but already accomplished enough at Texas hold 'em to walk away from a televised no-limit game with a million dollars of the old pros' money. "To win a mil," says Jackie, "tells me I could do it," and that, not the money, is what gets her "high" (256). Raylan knows cool when he sees it. "She could be Miss Nevada," he thinks, "but would rather play poker" (192). Nearly forty years old on his 1993 debut in *Pronto,* Raylan should be pushing sixty by now, although in Elmore Leonard's imagination he never grows old.[1] Givens at least seems aware of how it looks. "She isn't the least interested in an old fart like me," he tells his boss, Art Mullen. "'He said humbly,'" Art replies (261). Jackie already has "a serious crush" on Raylan and is "excited by how cool" he is (256). Raylan returns the compliment by telling Jackie how much she'd enjoy being a U.S. marshal. "If I joined the marshals, could I be your partner?" she asks. "I'd make it happen," he promises her (263).

Now in his eighty-seventh year, and hard at work on his forty-sixth novel, *Blue Dreams,* Leonard seems to be saying that age shouldn't matter to two people who share a love of *techne*: being cool will find a way. The idea received a more severe trial run in *Djibouti,* where *techne* also supplied the premise. There, thirty-something filmmaker Dara Barr eventually succumbed to the charms of her septuagenarian assistant, the well-hung Xavier LeBo, who got some help from his own assistant, an aphrodisiac called Horny Goat Weed. Givens is similarly endowed, to judge from the postcoital allusion that ends the book.

> She said, "Remember *Young Frankenstein*? The monster gets it on with what's her name and she starts singing about finding the sweet mystery of life?"
>
> "What made you think of that?"
>
> "I don't know," Jackie said. (263)

The monster in Mel Brooks's film is prodigiously outsized in every respect, and in the scene that Jackie refers to, Madeleine Kahn lets us know it through a series of orgasmic whoops that glissando into an operatic rendition of the hit song "Ah! Sweet Mystery of Life," from Victor Herbert's *Naughty Marietta*. Thus, *Raylan* ends by returning as farce to the theme with which it began as *noir*: detachable body parts.

What happens next? Given the independent initiative Leonard's characters have shown in the past, that question might be unanswerable. Does Jackie Reno have a future as a U.S. marshal? Law enforcement would, after all, be something that she and Raylan could do together—the realization of Carmen Colson's marital ambitions, only way cooler. Leonard says no. Neither character will appear in *Blue Dreams*, and he cannot imagine Jackie ever coming back.[2] At last report, as the first chapter of *Blue Dreams* comes to a close, a racist ICE (Immigration and Customs Enforcement) officer in a cowboy hat—aka the "Ice Man"—has arrested young bull rider Victorio Colorado on trumped-up charges.[3] We can be pretty sure this arrogant asshole will be sticking around when we reach the penultimate line: "The Ice Man's name was Darryl Harris." Which means, for Elmore Leonard, "Remember this guy."

Whatever happens next, it's likely the Ice Man will provide his creator with some serious fun before the book is finished, and more than a few shots at being cool.

Chapter 1 · Being Cool

1. See also Grella on Leonard's "Dickensian liveliness" (37).

2. Leonard freely admits that his characters are less individuals than types individualized (Rzepka, "Interviews 6"; see also Sutter, "Conversation" xi).

3. Thus, I agree with Hynes that pragmatism is "the inevitable rule" for both writers, but not that Leonard is particularly interested in the "moral code" his protagonist "fashion[s] [as] he proceeds" (184).

4. "I could learn through Hemingway exercises to keep my prose lean, but I didn't share his attitude about heroics," Leonard wrote in an essay on Bissell, whose "easygoing attitude, his eye for absurdity, his acceptance of the way people are, his low-key style," all changed the author's "thinking about writing" ("On Richard" 156, 159).

5. The fundamental corporeality of "cool" performance seems to escape critics of a postmodern bent. Chip Rhodes, for instance, believes that in Hollywood satires like *Get Shorty*, identity as performance has "no mooring in bodies, histories, ontologies" (152).

6. See Csikszentmihalyi's chapter 7, "Work as Flow" (143–63), for a close approximation of Leonard's notion of "cool" as essentially physical.

7. Email from Gregg Sutter, 7 July 2012. Leonard has also used a Montblanc and, for "a bolder look," a Paper Mate Ultra Fine Flair ("Lost" 93).

8. Leonard also has what amounts to a staff: researcher Gregg Sutter and Jane Jones, Leonard's daughter, who has for decades typed his second drafts (telephone conversation with Jane Jones, 12 June 2012).

9. Sutter uses a similar terminology of artisanship to describe his boss "at work—slinging his clay, making it stick and shaping it into something wondrous" ("Getting" 5).

10. See, for instance, Pascal on the "dual voice" of author and character in free indirect discourse (17–18), Cohn on "narrated monologue" (100), Banfield on "represented expression" (138–39), Worthington on the "narrative of self" (13), and Fludernik, who considers her book a "handbook on free indirect discourse" (xii).

11. Although it has attracted some critical notice (see, e.g., Rhodes 145; Devlin 125–28), free indirect discourse in Leonard's work is rarely distinguished from his "voice" in general or his ear for dialogue.

12. So accurate is Leonard's ear that it has enabled linguists to identify a unique group of colloquial constructions, dubbed "Elmore Leonard conditionals" (Liberman).

13. Leonard has never been in a fight, and he has witnessed only two of them, one in high school and the other as a Seabee during the war (Rzepka, "Interviews 6").

14. Mrs. Leonard always made the hobos "a big sandwich," recalls her son. "Then they would sit outside by the door [. . .] and eat the sandwich. I never talked to them though" (Rzepka, "Interviews 6").

15. The younger Leonard inherited this dry sense of humor, according to his children (telephone conversation with Jane Jones, 14 June 2012).

16. On the Book of the Month Club's influence on middle-class literary taste and its effeminate associations, see Radway (208–20). To masculine minds, such "reading and culture clubs" were "associated almost exclusively with women" (215).

17. Leonard himself has gotten accustomed to investing the event with prelusive significance in response to a standard question like Joel Lyczak's "When did you first become interested in writing?" (235). However, even with his gift for hearing other people's voices and imitating them on paper, Leonard can't remember any of the lines he wrote for this play, or even if he wrote any at all (Rzepka, "Interviews 8").

18. School as a locale of siege or captivity surfaced much later, in bedtime stories that the adult Leonard would tell his own children, with titles like "Bobby and Gene Get Locked in the School" (telephone conversation with Jane Jones, 14 June 2012).

19. Milestone's film is even more emphatic, opening with brief scenes of troops marching through village streets before the camera settles on a classroom where the teacher, Kantorek, is exhorting his impressionable charges to fight for the Fatherland.

20. Leonard cast Leo Madison, the only black kid in his class, as one of the Germans. "I didn't know what to do with him because I was just up from Memphis," says Leonard. "I didn't know any black guys" (Rzepka, "Interviews 4").

21. At the Tucson Festival of Books in March 2009, "An audience member asked about redemption and Leonard answered about money" (Seliger).

22. Leonard cannot remember any of his childhood friendships before his family's move to Memphis, where he made "a lot of friends," some of whose names he still recalls (Rzepka, "Interviews 8").

23. Soon after the move, Detroit became known as the "City of Champions" when its hockey, football, and baseball teams all won national championships.

24. Hot cooloo, also called "hot ass," was a game of hide-and-seek in which the seeker tried to "tag" the hiders with a leather belt before they reached "home."

25. In *LaBrava* (1983), Maurice Zola performs a similar feat with the stops along the old Key West railroad of the 1930s.

26. Leonard can recall *Being and Nothingness* from his metaphysics class, and says of Sartre, "I liked him a lot" (Rzepka, "Interviews 2"). He also recalls reading Camus ("Interviews 5").

27. Leonard does not believe he read the *Nicomachean Ethics*, but also admits, "I don't remember anything" about Aristotle today (Rzepka, "Interviews 1").

28. For the bases of these distinctions, and their considerable overlap in Aquinas, see Hibbs (22, 78).

29. The literary announcement of this first "step back" among white writers of the 1950s was Norman Mailer's "The White Negro." See also MacAdams (20–21).

30. In contrast to Marcus, Lewis MacAdams believes that "cool" did not begin to whiten up and go mainstream until the late 1950s (27). Blue Note's waiting until then to issue the album *The Birth of the Cool* supports this view.

31. They had spent a few months sharing an apartment after Mr. and Mrs. Leonard returned to Detroit, between their son's high school graduation and his enlistment that summer.

32. Elmore Jr. was even preparing to go to GM's Dealer's Son's School after earning his BA (Rzepka, "Interviews 8").

33. Telephone conversation, Gregg Sutter, 6 June 2012.

34. "Do you think that if you had gone out to join your dad with the dealership," I asked Leonard, "that you would have ended up becoming a writer?" "I don't know. I really don't know," he replied. "It's possible" ("Interviews 8").

Chapter 2 · Being Other(s)

1. Erikson offers the classic developmental account of the father's role in helping the male child master the challenges of identity facing him in both infancy and adolescence.

2. See Devlin on Leonard's sources (38).

3. Challen tells the story of Leonard's nearly coming back to Campbell Ewald for a trial rehire within a year of his departure, only to decide against it (54–55).

4. This scenario is reprised in *Cat Chaser*, in George Moran's obsessive memories of guerilla Luci Palma bounding over rooftops during Moran's tour of duty in the Dominican Republic.

5. He was to publish one of his most popular Westerns, *Valdez Is Coming*, the year after *The Big Bounce* and "touch base" with the Western, as Devlin puts it (14), twice more, in 1972 and 1979.

6. The rejections continued well into 1967, until Greenway Productions picked up the book in September (email from Gregg Sutter, 9 July 2012).

7. The MacGuffin is "the pretext for the plot," "the device, the gimmick," Hitchcock told French director François Truffaut: "The logicians are wrong in trying to figure out the truth of a MacGuffin, since it's beside the point" (Truffaut 138).

Chapter 3 · Plays Well with Others

1. "One must not put a loaded rifle on the stage if no one is thinking of firing it," wrote the Russian playwright to Aleksandr Semenovitch Lazarev on 1 November 1889 (Chekhov 273).

2. "The best crime book there is," Leonard told Lawrence Grobel as late as 1998 (284). It was recommended to Leonard by his agent, H. N. "Swanie" Swanson. For details, see Challen (76).

3. The graphic details of this struggle can be found in "Quitting"—"One day I came back from California throwing up blood" (95)—and in *Unknown Man No. 89*, where the pain of withdrawal is "like a sunburned nervous system" (151). Leonard told me recently that he has resumed drinking occasionally, for example, a glass of wine at dinner.

4. Email from Gregg Sutter, 7 July 2012.

5. Second wave feminism's ordinal designation presumes a first wave that extended from the Seneca Falls Convention for women's rights in 1848 to 1920, the year the

Nineteenth Amendment to the Constitution was ratified, granting women's suffrage. The second wave has been followed by a "third wave," less restricted to the values and viewpoints of middle-class white women (Tong 284–85, 289).

6. This investigator was probably Dixie Davies, the only one with a mustache (like Raymond Cruz). See his photograph in "Impressions" (12).

7. During a discussion of the relationship between Cruz and Hurd, I told Leonard that Hurd struck me "as much more professional, much more a cop, whereas Raymond turns it into this kind of movie scenario." He acknowledged, "That may have been what I was thinking" when writing *Split Images* ("Interviews 3").

Chapter 4 · Choruses

1. "Whenever we sit down in a dark room to watch a movie, a slide show, or television," writes Lee Bailey, "we enter the imaginative world of the *camera obscura*," which has "throughout its history [. . .] functioned as a guiding root metaphor for our modern view of the soul" (63). As a philosophy minor in college, Leonard was likely to have encountered Locke's famous analogy in his introductory course, specifically with reference to "empiricism."

2. Leonard originally conceived the book with this plot in mind, until Carmen started taking over (Rzepka, "Interviews 3").

3. According to Leonard, one major error in the 2008 movie version of *Killshot*, starring Mickey Rourke, was portraying the Colsons' marriage as on the rocks (Rzepka, "Interviews 4").

4. In line with Leonard's ecumenical orientation at this time, Ross/Rosen discovers his immigrant grandfather was in fact Jewish.

5. Juvenal was based on a real Franciscan brother of that name who left a lasting impression on Leonard when he was writing a screenplay for a Franciscan promotional film (Rzepka, "Interviews 1"). The real Juvenal did not experience the stigmata.

6. Nyman says that Leonard's "critique of politics" in *Bandits* "remains loyal to the traditional ideologies" of the Reagan years (14), despite his mainstream liberal sympathies. Be that as it may, Nyman's political focus ignores Leonard's primary interest in faith and its relationship to agency, *techne*, and self-transformation.

Conclusion

1. Telephone conversation with Leonard, 14 July 2012.

2. Telephone conversation with Leonard, 13 July 2012; email from Gregg Sutter, 7 August 2012.

3. Published as the short story "Ice Man," in the July/August 2012 Fiction Issue of the *Atlantic Monthly*.

WORKS CITED

Works by Elmore Leonard

Books

Original publication dates are in brackets.

Bandits. New York: Arbor, 1987 [1987].
Be Cool. New York: Dark Alley, 2005 [1999].
The Big Bounce. New York: Armchair Detective Library, 1989 [1969].
The Bounty Hunters. In *Elmore Leonard's Western Roundup #1*. New York: Delta, 1998 [1953]. 1–172.
Cat Chaser. New York: HarperTorch, 2003 [1982].
City Primeval: High Noon in Detroit. New York: Avon, 1982 [1980].
Comfort to the Enemy. London: Weidenfeld, 2009 [2009].
A Coyote's in the House. New York: Morrow, 2004 [2004].
Djibouti. New York: HarperCollins, 2011 [2010].
Escape from Five Shadows. In *Elmore Leonard's Western Roundup #2*. New York: Delta, 1998 [1956]. 1–162.
52 Pickup. New York: Avon, 1983 [1974].
Forty Lashes Less One. In *Elmore Leonard's Western Roundup #1*. New York: Delta, 1998 [1972]. 173–334.
Freaky Deaky. New York: HarperTorch, 2002 [1988].
Get Shorty. New York: Dell, 1991 [1990].
Glitz. New York: Arbor, 1985 [1985].
Gold Coast. In *Elmore Leonard's Double Dutch Treat*. Introd. Bob Greene. New York: Arbor, 1986 [1980]. 389–594.
Gunsights. In *Elmore Leonard's Western Roundup #1*. New York: Delta, 1998 [1979]. 335–501.
Hombre. New York: HarperTorch, 2002 [1961].
The Hot Kid. New York: Morrow, 2005 [2005].
The Hunted. New York: Dell, 2000 [1977].
Killshot. New York: Quill/Morrow, 1999 [1989].
LaBrava. New York: HarperTorch, 2009 [1983].

Last Stand at Saber River. New York: HarperTorch, 2002 [1959].
The Law at Randado. In *Elmore Leonard's Western Roundup #2.* New York: Delta, 1998 [1954]. 319–485.
Maximum Bob. New York: Delacorte, 1991 [1991].
The Moonshine War. In *Elmore Leonard's Double Dutch Treat.* Introd. Bob Greene. New York: Arbor, 1986 [1969]. 219–388.
Mr. Majestyk. New York: HarperTorch, 2002 [1974].
Mr. Paradise. New York: Morrow, 2004 [2004].
Out of Sight. New York: Dell, 1997 [1996].
Pagan Babies. New York: HarperTorch, 2002 [2000].
Pronto. New York: Delacorte, 1993 [1993].
Raylan. New York: Morrow, 2012 [2012].
Riding the Rap. Rockland, MA: Wheeler, 1995 [1995].
Road Dogs. New York: Morrow, 2009 [2009].
Rum Punch. New York: Delacorte, 1992 [1992].
Split Images. New York: Avon, 1983 [1981].
Stick. New York: Arbor, 1983 [1983].
Swag. New York: Dell, 1988 [1976].
The Switch. New York: Bantam, 1984 [1978].
Tishomingo Blues. New York: HarperTorch, 2003 [2002].
Touch. New York: Arbor, 1987 [1987].
Unknown Man No. 89. New York: HarperTorch, 2002 [1977].
Up in Honey's Room. New York: Morrow, 2007 [2007].
Valdez Is Coming. New York: HarperTorch, 2002 [1970].

Published Short Stories

Many of these stories appear in *The Complete Western Stories of Elmore Leonard.* Ed. Gregg Sutter. New York: Morrow, 2004.

"Apache Medicine." *Complete.* 37–50.
"The Big Hunt." *Complete.* 195–208.
"Blood Money." *Complete.* 263–78.
"The Boy Who Smiled." *Complete.* 223–36.
"The Bull Ring at Blisston." *Short Stories for Men Magazine* 221.4 (Aug. 1959): 48–53, 60.
"Cavalry Boots." *Complete.* 135–48.
"The Captives." *Complete.* 323–56.
"The Colonel's Lady." *Complete.* 89–102.
"The Hard Way." *Complete.* 237–48.
"Ice Man." *Atlantic Monthly* July/Aug. 2012. www.theatlantic.com/magazine/archive/2012/07/ice-man/9005.
"Jugged." *Complete.* 385–98.
"The Last Shot." *Complete.* 249–62.
"Law of the Hunted Ones." *Complete.* 103–34.
"The Longest Day of His Life." *Complete.* 431–58.
"Moment of Vengeance." *Complete.* 399–414.
"The Nagual." *Complete.* 459–72.

"Only Good Ones." *Complete.* 489–502.
"Red Hell Hits Canyon Diablo." *Complete.* 67–88.
"The Rustlers." *Complete.* 163–78.
"Saint with a Six-Gun." *Complete.* 309–22.
"Three-Ten to Yuma." *Complete.* 179–94.
"Trail of the Apache." *Complete.* 1–36.
"When the Women Come Out to Dance." *When the Women Come Out to Dance.* New York: Morrow, 2003. 45–56.
"You Never See Apaches." *Complete.* 51–66.

Unpublished Short Stories

These stories are compiled by Greg Sutter in *The Unpublished Stories of Elmore Leonard.* 2010. Typed by Jane Jones (*née* Leonard). 315 pages. Typescript.

"Arma Virumque Cano." 106–18.
"Charlie Martz." 28–44.
"Evenings Away from Home." 143–62.
"For Something to Do." 163–84.
"A Happy, Light-Hearted People." 87–105.
"The Italian Cut." 185–203.
"One Horizontal." 3–27.
"The Only Good Syrian Footsoldier Is a Dead One." 204–24.
"Rebel on the Run." 289–315.
"Siesta in Paloverde." 45–61.
"Time of Terror." 62–86.
"The Trespassers." 241–66.

Nonfiction

"Easy on the Adverbs, Exclamation Points and Especially Hooptedoodle." *New York Times* 16 July 2001. www.nytimes.com/2001/07/16/arts/.
"Impressions of Murder." *Detroit News Sunday Magazine* 12 Nov. 1978: 12–13, 15, 18, 24, 26, 28, 48, 50, 53.
"Introduction." *The Big Bounce.* New York: Armchair Detective Library, 1989. i–vi.
"The Lost Art of Writing by Hand." In "How to Be a Better Man: The Lost Arts." *Esquire* 137.2 (Feb. 2002): 89–97.
"On Richard Bissell." *Rediscoveries II.* Ed. David Madden and Peggy Bach. New York: Carroll, 1988. 154–59.
"Quitting." *The Courage to Change: Hope and Help for Alcoholics and Their Families.* Ed. Dennis Wholey. New York: Houghton, 1986. 92–99.

Secondary Sources

Amis, Martin. "Martin Amis Interviews Elmore Leonard at the Writers Guild Theatre, Beverly Hills." January 23, 1998. Transcript. www.martinamisweb.com/interviews_files/amis_int_leonard.pdf.

Aristotle. *Nicomachean Ethics*. Trans. W. D. Ross. *The Basic Works of Aristotle*. Ed. Richard McKeon. New York: Random, 1941. 935–1112.

Bailey, Lee W. "Skull's Darkroom: The *Camera Obscura* and Subjectivity." *Philosophy of Technology: Practical, Historical, and Other Dimensions*. Ed. Paul T. Durbin. Boston: Kluwer, 1989. 63–79.

Banfield, Ann. *Unspeakable Sentences: Narration and Representation in the Language of Fiction*. London: Routledge, 1982.

Baulch, Vivian M., and Patricia Zacharias. "The Detroit Race Riots." *Detroit News* 11 Feb. 1999. http://apps.detnews.com/apps/history/index.php?id=185.

Beattie, Ann. "First, Let's Kill the Lawyer." *New York Times Book Review* 1 Feb. 2004. www.nytimes.com/2004/02/01/books/.

Carlson, Stephanie M., and Marjorie Taylor. "Imaginary Companions and Impersonated Characters: Sex Differences in Children's Fantasy Play." *Merrill-Palmer Quarterly* 51.1 (2005): 93–118.

Challen, Paul. *Get Dutch: A Biography of Elmore Leonard*. Toronto: ECW, 2000.

Chekhov, Anton. *Polnoe sobranie sochinenii i pisem v tridsati tomakh, Pis´ma*, vol. 3. Moscow: Nauka, 1976.

Cohn, Dorit. *Transparent Minds: Narrative Modes for Presenting Consciousness in Fiction*. Princeton: Princeton UP, 1978.

Csikszentmihalyi, Mihaly. *Flow: The Psychology of Optimal Experience*. New York: Harper, 2008.

De Quincey, Thomas. "On the Knocking at the Gate in *Macbeth*." *Confessions of an English Opium-Eater and Other Writings*. Ed. Grevel Lindop. Oxford: Oxford UP, 1985. 81–85.

Devlin, James E. *Elmore Leonard*. New York: Twayne, 1999.

Erikson, Erik. *Identity, Youth, and Crisis*. New York: Norton, 1968.

Fludernik, Monika. *The Fictions of Language and the Language of Fiction: The Linguistic Representation of Speech and Consciousness*. London: Routledge, 1997.

Geherin, David. *Elmore Leonard*. New York: Continuum, 1989.

Genette, Gerard. *Narrative Discourse: An Essay in Methodology*. New York: Cornell UP, 1983.

Goodnow, Cecelia. "Researchers Take on Imaginary Playmates—For Real." *Seattle Post-Intelligencer* 6 Dec. 2004. www.seattlepi.com/lifestyle/202632_imaginary07.html.

Grella, George. "Film in Fiction: The Real and the Reel in Elmore Leonard." *The Detective in American Fiction, Film, and Television*. Ed. Jerome H. Delamater and Ruth Prigozy. Westport, CT: Greenwood, 1998. 35–44.

Grobel, Lawrence. *Endangered Species: Writers Talk about Their Craft, Their Visions, Their Lives*. Cambridge, MA: Da Capo, 2001.

Hamilton, Cynthia. *From High Noon to Midnight: Western and Hard-Boiled Detective Fiction in America*. Iowa City: U of Iowa P, 1987.

Hemingway, Ernest. *For Whom the Bell Tolls*. New York: Scribner's, 1940.

Hemingway, Ernest. *Selected Letters*. Ed. Carlos Baker. New York: Scribner, 1981.

Hibbs, Thomas. *Aquinas, Ethics, and Philosophy of Religion: Metaphysics and Practice*. Bloomington: Indiana UP, 2007.

Higgins, George V. *The Friends of Eddie Coyle*. New York: Knopf, 1970.

Hynes, Joseph. "'High Noon in Detroit': Elmore Leonard's Career." *Journal of Popular Culture* 25.3 (1991): 181–87.
Irwin, John. *Unless the Threat of Death Is Behind Them: Hard-Boiled Fiction and Film Noir.* Baltimore: Johns Hopkins UP, 2006.
Lacan, Jacques. *Ecrits: A Selection.* Trans. Alan Sheridan. New York: Norton, 1977.
LaMay, Craig L. "Making a Killing: An Interview with Elmore Leonard." *The Culture of Crime.* Ed. Craig L. LaMay and Everette E. Dennis. New Brunswick, NJ: Transaction, 1995. 145–53.
Lewis, Nathaniel. *Unsettling the Literary West: Authenticity and Authorship.* Lincoln: U of Nebraska P, 1981.
Liberman, Mark. "Baseball Conditionals." Language Log, U of Pennsylvania. 23 May 2007. http://itre.cis.upenn.edu/~myl/languagelog/archives/004521.html.
Lyczak, Joel M. "An Interview with Elmore Leonard." *Armchair Detective* 16.3 (1983): 235–40.
MacAdams, Lewis. *Birth of the Cool: Beat, Bebop, and the American Avant-Garde.* New York: Free, 2001.
Mailer, Norman. "Superman Comes to the Supermarket." *Esquire* Nov. 1960. http://makethemaccountable.com/articles/Superman_Comes_to_the_Supermarket.htm.
Mailer, Norman. "The White Negro." *Dissent* Fall 1957. www.learntoquestion.com/resources/database/archives/003327.html.
Marcus, Greil. "Birth of the Cool." *Speak* Fall 1999: 17–25.
McVeigh, Stephen. *The American Western.* Edinburgh: Edinburgh UP, 2007.
Most, Glenn. "Elmore Leonard: Splitting Images." *The Sleuth and the Scholar: Origins, Evolution, and Current Trends in Detective Fiction.* Ed. Barbara A. Rader and Howard G. Zettler. New York: Greenwood, 1988. 101–10.
Myers, B. R. "The Prisoner of Cool." *Atlantic Monthly* Nov. 2005. www.theatlantic.com/magazine/archive/2005/11/the-prisoner-of-cool/4318.
Nietzsche, Friedrich. "Ecce Homo." *On the Genealogy of Morals and Ecce Homo.* Trans. Walter Kaufmann. New York: Random, 1967. 217–334.
Nyman, Jopi. "The Politics of the Personal: Constructions of Identity in Elmore Leonard's *Bandits.*" *Journal of American Studies of Turkey* 7 (1998): 13–21.
Parker, Dorothy. "Profiles." *New Yorker* 30 Nov. 1929: 28–31.
Pascal, Roy. *The Dual Voice: Free Indirect Speech and Its Functioning in the Nineteenth-Century European Novel.* Manchester, UK: Manchester UP, 1977.
Percy, Walker. "There's a Contra in My Gumbo." *New York Times Book Review* 4 Jan. 1987: 7.
Pinsky, Robert. "Playing Dirty." *New York Times Book Review* 31 May 2009: 10.
Radway, Janice. *A Feeling for Books: The Book of the Month Club, Literary Taste, and Middle Class Desire.* Chapel Hill: U of North Carolina P, 1997.
Reed, J. D. "A Dickens from Detroit." *Time* 28 May 1984: 100–01.
Reisman, David. *The Lonely Crowd.* Rev. ed. New Haven: Yale UP, 2001.
Remarque, Erich Maria. *All Quiet on the Western Front.* Trans. A. W. Wheen. Boston: Little, Brown, 1929.
Rhodes, Chip. *Politics, Desire, and the Hollywood Novel.* Iowa City: U of Iowa P, 2008.
Roberts, Fletcher. "Novels Are Nice, but Oh, to Be a Rock Star." *New York Times* 14 Mar. 1999. www.nytimes.com/1999/03/14/books/.

Rubin, Neal. "Elmore Leonard's Woodward Avenue." *Detroit News* 9 July 2007. www.detroitnews.com/article/20070709/METRO/707090373.

Rzepka, Charles J. "Elmore Leonard (1925–)." *A Companion to Crime Fiction*. Ed. Charles J. Rzepka and Lee Horsley. Chichester, UK: Wiley-Blackwell, 2010. 510–22.

———. "Elmore Leonard Interviews, Part 1." 12 Aug. 2009. *Crimeculture*. www.crimeculture.com/?page_id=3435.

———. "Elmore Leonard Interviews, Part 2." 12 Aug. 2009. *Crimeculture*. www.crimeculture.com/?page_id=3435.

———. "Elmore Leonard Interviews, Part 3." 12 Aug. 2009. *Crimeculture*. www.crimeculture.com/?page_id=3435.

———. "Elmore Leonard Interviews, Part 4." 29 Sept. 2009. *Crimeculture*. www.crimeculture.com/?page_id=3435.

———. "Elmore Leonard Interviews, Part 5." 29 Sept. 2009. *Crimeculture*. www.crimeculture.com/?page_id=3435.

———. "Elmore Leonard Interviews, Part 6." 8 Jan. 2010. *Crimeculture*. www.crimeculture.com/?page_id=3435.

———. "Elmore Leonard Interviews, Part 7." 8 Jan. 2010. *Crimeculture*. www.crimeculture.com/?page_id=3435.

———. "Elmore Leonard Interviews, Part 8." 7 June 2010. *Crimeculture*. www.crimeculture.com/?page_id=3435.

———. "Elmore Leonard Interviews, Part 9." 7 June 2010. *Crimeculture*. www.crimeculture.com/?page_id=3435.

Seliger, Jake. "Billy Collins and Elmore Leonard at the Tucson Festival of Books." *Story's Story* 18 Mar. 2009. http://jseliger.wordpress.com/2009/03/18/billy-collins-and-elmore-leonard-at-the-tucson-festival-of-books.

Skinner, Robert E. "To Write Realistically: An Interview with Elmore Leonard." *Xavier Review* 7.2 (1987): 37–46.

Slotkin, Richard. *Gunfighter Nation: The Myth of the Frontier in Twentieth-Century America*. New York: Atheneum, 1992.

Sutter, Gregg. "A Conversation with Elmore Leonard." *The Complete Western Stories of Elmore Leonard*. Ed. Gregg Sutter. New York: Morrow, 2004. xi–xiii.

Sutter, Gregg. "Getting It Right: Researching Elmore Leonard's Novels." *Armchair Detective* 19.1 (1986): 4–19.

Taylor, M., S. Hodges, and A. Kohányi. "The Illusion of Independent Agency: Do Adult Fiction Writers Experience Their Characters as Having Minds of Their Own?" *Imagination, Cognition, and Personality* 22 (2002–03): 361–80.

Tong, Rosemarie. *Feminist Thought: A More Comprehensive Introduction*. 3rd ed. Boulder, CO: Westview, 2009.

Truffaut, François. *Hitchcock*. Rev. ed. New York: Simon, 1985.

Turner, Frederick Jackson. *The Frontier in American History*. New York: Holt, 1921. http://xroads.virginia.edu/~HYPER/TURNER.

White, William H. *The Organization Man*. Philadelphia: U of Pennsylvania P, 2002.

Worthington, Kim L. *Self as Narrative: Subjectivity and Community in Contemporary Fiction*. Oxford: Clarendon, 1996.

Young, Philip. "The Hero and the Code." *Ernest Hemingway: A Reconsideration*. University Park: Pennsylvania UP, 1966. 56–78.

INDEX